The Death of Danny Daggers

HAYDN WILKS

COVER ART BY JACK SKIVENS

jackskivens@deadbirdpress.com

FURTHER INFORMATION

www.haydnwilks.com

Twitter: @haydnwilks

Email: haydnwilks@deadbirdpress.com

Saturday 1st September

"The date is Saturday the 1st of September," Kelvin Phillips monotonously intoned, keeping steely eyes on the suspect as he spoke. "The time is nine oh four A.M."

The formality of foreplay finished, Kelvin smiled at the suspect, ready to fuck him. He calmly explained the situation. The suspect had been caught red-handed at the scene of the crime. Literally. Literally passed out on the river bank, blood all over his grubby little mitts, as a corpse floated off downstream.

"I don't know why you're giving me all this trouble mun," the tramp snapped, "I've not done fucking nothing mun!"

"Gideon," the weedy little ginger lawyer that had been appointed to the tramp whispered, trying to pull his seething prick of a client back from the brink of premature ejaculation.

"Blood. Hands. Care to explain?" Kelvin Phillips replied.

Excitement bubbled up in Dai Green's cerebral cortex, then travelled down his spine, transferring itself into a tingling sensation in his nether regions. The whole damn constabulary had been gagging on the bit for the preceding five days for a chance to fuck the moronically-monikered hobo, Gideon Wenceslas. None had anticipated the gory glory of a murder charge.

The hobo looked at his hands, still crusted red. "I was... hunting."

"Hunting," Kelvin Phillips repeated, emotionless.

The hobo's eyes fell away from his hands and dropped to the floor, like the eyes of a teenage boy caught mid perverted net perusal by his mum. His eyes then sat there, two big shameful balls, like two big shameful balls beneath the loincloth of a medieval guardsman attempting to ingratiate himself with a sect of treasonous eunuchs.

"You were hunting," Kelvin clarified.

"Yeah," Gideon said, slowly raising his shamefaced bollock eyes to meet Kelvin Phillips' steely testes.

"And what, pray tell, would one be hunting on the River Taff in the small hours?"

"Seagull."

Dai Green laughed. The idiot, the fool, the murderin' hobo Gideon Wenceslas, was making things easy for them. Too easy. He wanted their quarry to put up some resistance, to make some sort of game of it. He wanted to reach across the desk and grasp him by his dirty lapels, then shake him like an unwanted baby, until the idiot saw sense. He wanted to scream at him, "For God's sake man, don't you get it?! Don't you understand the gravity of your situation?!" He wanted to slap him across his face, hard, a regular pimp slap, drop him to the ground with ringing in his ears, kick him in the throat and scream, "And what kind of a name is Gideon fucking Wenceslas for Christ's sake?! Are you a man or a fucking gospel-cum-Christmas Carol?! What are you?! What are you?!", again and again, kicking him hard in the sternum, the ribs, the pelvis, stomping upon his kneecaps, again and again and again, "What are you man?! What the fuck are you?!"

"Objection!" the weedy ginger lawyer suddenly squeaked, snapping Dai Green free of his violent reverie.

Both police officers' great big bollock eyes fell upon the weedy ginger lawyer's shrivelled little Specsavers-protected pair.

"This isn't court mate," Dai Green smiled, pitying the poor cunt, and pitying all the more that poor bastard Gideon Wenceslas, who'd not only been lumbered with a God-awful name and a murder charge, but had also gotten an absolute impotent chode of a lawyer appointed to extricate him from it.

"Timeout I mean," the weedy ginger lawyer said. "I need to converse with my client."

Kelvin Phillips' big meaty sausage of an index finger shot out from under the desk to the tape recorder's pause button: "Interview suspended at nine-oh-six A.M." Then, in the privacy of those four men within those four walls, he added: "The interview will recommence at nine-oh-ten A.M. Four minutes, boys. Three and a half, even."

Kelvin Phillips stood erect and glared down at the two little sad sacks sat at the table – that weedy ginger lawyer, seeming like a work experience kid thrown right in at the deep end, and that viral video star hobo who'd caused them all such bother earlier in the week. Kelvin strolled towards the door as the hobo carried on staring down at the table, hopeless, while his lawyer's glass-shielded eyes fell upon Dai Green, then pulled out immediately and splashed down upon the tabletop.

"Compose yourselves," Dai Green implored, his tone laced with menace, intending to make them do quite the opposite. "Do yourselves a favour, will you?"

Dai Green followed Kelvin Phillips out of the interrogation room and into a narrow grey corridor.

"What do you reckon?" Dai asked.

"Guilty as fucking sin mun. Seagull hunting, have you heard?"

"He'll be in there cooking up a proper defence with him now mind," Dai warned.

"What, with that twat?" Kelvin said, peering into the interrogation room through a little panel of wire-infused glass, glaring at the weedy ginger lawyer who, upon noticing Kelvin's gaze, seemed to panic himself into idiocy all over again. "He couldn't get the telly off."

"Just you watch," Dai warned, "we'll go back in there and there'll be no more of this bloody seagull hunting business, I can tell you."

"Oi!" a voice bellowed out from down the corridor.

Kelvin and Dai turned in the direction of the heavy, authoritative footsteps hammering down on the tiled floor and echoing through the corridor towards them.

"What the fuck are you two idiots doing out here?" Mannoring demanded, whence he was close enough that each of the individual black and grey hairs on the thick slug of a moustache lying across his upper lip were distinguishable. He looked up at Kelvin and Dai, literally speaking, being that the Chief Superintendent was decidedly below average height. Figuratively, Chief Superintendent Mannoring hadn't clawed and scratched his way to the top of the Cardiff Constabulary food chain to look up to anyone.

"The lawyer wanted five with his client Chief," Dai Green explained.

"He wanted five with his client!" Mannoring scoffed. "This is a fucking murder investigation, not an episode of the fucking X-Factor. You," he added, addressing Kelvin, "are not Simon bloody Cowell, and you," meaning Dai, "are certainly no Cheryl cunting Cole. Now get back in there and fucking interrogate him before I have the pair of you struck off and thrown in the nick for wasting your own pissing police fucking time!"

Mannoring turned away from them and stormed back from whence he'd came.

"Fucking imbeciles!" he bellowed as he went.

Kelvin and Dai re-entered the interrogation room with the weedy ginger lawyer in the middle of explaining something to his client. He stopped speaking and stared at them with the panic of a small child laying eyes upon the singer from Lostprophets.

"It's not been two minutes yet!" the lawyer protested, as Kelvin and Dai retook their seats.

"You know what they call that in Norway?" Kelvin answered, his finger hovering like the sword of Damacles above the record button. "Tough fucking titties."

"Interview recommenced at nine-oh-eight A.M."

* * *

Rory Gallagher

Arwyn Davies could scarcely conceal his surprise as he watched Rory Gallagher walk into the office, Caffe Caro coffee cup in hand, on a Saturday morning, at a time that would've been damn near punctual – by Rory's standards, at least – if it were the middle of the week. His eyes didn't have the usual glaze and film of booze abuse. Could it really be that Rory had turned up to work early on a Saturday without any sign of a hangover?

"Rory," Arwyn said, striding across the newsroom, where only about a quarter of the desks were occupied, "to what do we owe this pleasure?"

"Y'll have heard about the body in the Taff?"

"Of course. We are running a newspaper here."

"Then wa's wi' askin' a question like that?"

Rory seated himself at his desk, took a deep swig of coffee, put the cup to one side, and then fired up his computer. Arwyn watched, impressed. On any average day, Rory could charitably be called unreliable; *no*, Arwyn corrected himself, *fuck charity. He's a fucking liability is what he is.* But, give the man a good murder mystery, and the newshound within the boozehound came bounding out for all to see.

"Any thoughts on the case then Rory?"

"Well the cops've go' some hobo in for questionin'. They found him on tha riverbank, behind tha Millennium Stadium, blood on his hands, banged tae fuckin' rights. But I go' a feelin' tha' there's a wee bit o' weirdness wi' this one. Y'know who the victim is, righ'?"

"Yeah. Daniel Covell. Sociology student, Leeds university."

"Better known as Danny Daggers, YouTube celebrity an' general fuckwit who's spent tha last few days runnin' round Cardiff makin' a nuisance o' hi'self. Poor kid's go' hi'self a fair few enemies'd be willing tae fling his corpse intae tha river. Besides, this hobo the cops've go' in, this so-called Gideon Wenceslas, well, I think I might've found tha' wee laddy an alibi; just a bi' along the river bank from where tha cops picked him up, I found a dismembered seagull."

"A seagull?"

"Aye, one of them fuckin' bird things, with wings. White. Vicious fuckers with big beaks on 'em. You only used tae find 'em near the coast, hence the name, like, 'seagull', but o'er the past decade or so tha fuckers've come swarmin' into city centres like they've just joined the E.U. or somethin'."

"I know what a seagull is."

"Well, this one was cut up pretty bad. Looked like a lot o' the meat'd been hacked off. I'm no avian forensics expert, but i' looked tae me as if someone'd been plannin' on eatin' tha fucker."

"And this is relevant because…"

"Because if tha' poor cunt they've go' in fir questioning, who's tha same poor cunt, migh' I add, tha' you and me turned into an internet sensation earlier this week, if he's been huntin' an' eatin' seagull, then there's a perfectly good reason for him tae have blood all o'er his hands. Which'd mean some other fucker tossed Daniel Jim Dylan Covell, A.K.A. Danny Daggers, intae tha River Taff. And as long as tha Ol' Bill're oblivious to all o' tha', we've got ourselves a wee bit o' an advantage over tha hacks at tha nationals who pissed off home after yesterday's excitement. Those fuckers'll be haulin' arse down tha M4 to Cardiff as we speak, probably understaffed and ill-prepared tae boot, wha' wi' i' being a Saturday 'n' all. This wee laddy who's done himself a mischief and wound up face-down in the Taff might be just the boost this dying rag o' a newspaper needs tae survive and thrive through the next century, Arwyn. We do a good job on this one an' we mi' just give this wee paper a bigger shot in tha arm than tha one full o' heroin Kurt Cobain took before he swallowed a mouth full o' buckshot."

Arwyn stared at Rory, the blonde-haired, beer-bellied, knackered-livered, grizzled veteran of the newspaper industry. The editor-in-chief was dumbfounded. "How the hell've you figured all of this out already? The body's not even cold yet."

Rory stared back at his boss with utter disdain. "Because I'm a fuckin' journalist, Arwyn."

Tuesday 28th August

08.54am

Tom

The train rolled through the Valleys in dour silence, save for an occasional cough or muffled buzz from inefficient earphones. Tom watched the dim greenery and grim terraces of the Valleys bleed into the red brick of leafy suburbs and eventual grey matter of Cardiff city centre, watching the weekend ebb away. It'd been a long weekend, and not just in the sense that it'd lasted a day longer than usual. Bank Holiday Monday had been a necessary buffer after the blistering bluster of end of summer madness he'd embroiled himself in. Now, like everyone else in the carriage, he was resigned to returning to the dull autumn of reality. Classical music improbably soundtracked the scene rolling past the window. He wasn't exactly sure how it'd worked its way onto his iPhone, but amongst the four score gigabytes of illegal downloads littering his hard drive back home in Caerphilly, it was a matter of simple mathematical probability that something pre-Beatles would've wound up in his music collection.

The train slowed through Cathays, his destination drawing near. Tom glanced away from a fat block of student housing beyond the sweat-smudged window pane to check his iPhone and put a name to the strings that were rising and falling with conventional form and conservatism. It was a piece by Haydn, something insuccinctly entitled *Symphony no 94 "Surprise": 1st Movement*. He glared at this weird anachronism for a moment, then raised his stoned heavy eyes back to the window as the train rolled into Cardiff Queen Street Station. He rose heavily to his feet and joined the passengers queuing in the aisle, grim-faced, ready for the truncated work-week's imminent beginning.

He glanced up at the scrolling low-tech orange L.E.D. of the station information board as he filed off the train, the strings in his earphones crescendoing and dying away the instant he set foot upon the platform, noting with some small degree of trepidation that the station time correlated perfectly with that on his iPhone, that it was indeed 08:56, 08:56:33 to be exact. He joined the scores of commuters shuffling mirthlessly down stone steps into the bowels of the station.

3 minutes and 27 seconds to get to work – if he wanted to be on time, at least. Probably a good thirty seconds less than that by the time he'd shuffled through the station with all the other grim commuters and made it past the barriers. He readied his ticket as a slow, unfamiliar drumbeat rose up in his ear drums, shortly followed by a layer of punchy but unaggressive guitaring. As his feet did the slow left-right, left-right shuffle of the condemned, he planned his route. Right down Queen Street was the usual option, with a quick cut left through the old St. David's Arcade being the fastest route to the Hayes, though that stint indoors left him with minimal smoking time. The back way, left along the edge of Cardiff's central shopping street, with a quick cut through St. David's 2, was probably a more sensible option.

He slotted his ticket into the automated barrier and emerged out onto the street a few seconds later. The day was a little overcast but warm enough, with a threat of last-burst summer sunshine possibly to come, for what little good it would do him – he'd be locked away from it the whole day, save for during his bi-hourly fag breaks and tortuously brief lunch time. He sparked up a Richmond Superking and strode round to the left, moving quickly, the music in his ears gaining momentum, leaving Tom half-wondering who it was, as tar coated his lungs and nicotine caressed his synapses.

Despite deep drags which, coupled with a fast-paced walk, left him light-headed, Tom had barely smoked half his oversized cigarette by the time he reached the back doors of St. David's 2. He stepped inside and tossed the cigarette out behind him, half-glimpsing some familiar character standing some feet away, smoking a cigarette of his own, besides the grass lawn of the square that lay behind the shopping centre. No time to dwell on that, he thought, pulling the iPhone out of his pocket and quickening his pace upon seeing it was now 9 o'clock exactly, whilst also noting the badly formatted tag identifying the pleasant song soundtracking this last leg of the journey – *126: The Boy With The Perpetual Ner.*

He glanced at the phone as he walked, fast, and was then jolted back into reality by the force of a sudden collision that tore the earphones out of his lugholes.

"Fuckin' hell mun!" an angry lioness roared, staring down at spilled coffee, her enraged face framed with a bobbed mane of bleached blonde hair.

Tom froze, mumbled 'sorry', then stood, statue-like, torn between appeasing the terrifying animal seething and scowling in front of him, or moving on quickly and avoiding the inevitable righteous bollocking he was sure to receive if he were late for work without phoning ahead and letting Matt know yet again.

The shock to the system, the sudden contrast between the mystery song and the seething stranger, was so great that it took Tom a half-second to note the hotness of the girl he'd just stumbled into; the big breasts and sweet curves snugly squeezed into the tight black uniform of one of the shopping centre's many retailers. He was leaning towards formulating a more thorough apology.

"You dull fuckin' cunt, why don't you look where you're fucking walking to? God mun!"

"Sorry," Tom mumbled, the vitriol and violent hatred lurking beneath the pretty face making his decision for him.

Jodie

Jodie stared in disbelief at the idiot who'd just barged into her and bolted off and away, out through the shopping centre's doors, onto the Hayes. For a moment she considered picking the Caffe Carro cup up from the floor and chasing after him, throwing whatever remained of the boiling hot latte over him, before sighing and resigning herself to her four quid loss and a seething anger with only one cure. She stepped over the hot brown puddle and stormed towards the rear exit doors, fiddling in her pockets for her cigarettes as she passed the over-priced food court at the shopping centre's end. She ignored the Yo Sushi! and the Pret-a-Manger, and lifted a Pall Mall to her lips. Outside, her anger billowed out with each exhalation of cigarette smoke, with guilt drifting in to replace it.

What if you really are... ?

She couldn't bring herself to form the word, even internally. The consequences would be too enormous; another mouth to feed, another drain on her salary.

Maybe Joseph'll get the job today...

She thought of Joseph, at the job centre, around the corner from where she stood. *No,* she corrected herself, *he would've been and gone from there by now.* Joseph was great with Daniel. Perhaps it wouldn't be the worst thing in the world, if she really was... But she wasn't anyway, was she? There was surely another explanation for her period's tardiness. She stared down at the cigarette in her hand.

But what if you are... ?

She dropped the cigarette to the floor and stamped it out. She looked up from it and saw a figure standing on the grass lawn, a man, young, blonde, slim, a bright mess of colour adorning his clothing. He was smoking a rollie and staring at her. She turned her back to him and headed inside.

Danny Daggers

Maybe it was time to stop. Slow down, at least. What time even was it? *Must be almost nine by now...* Surely somewhere would be opening up soon. Danny Daggers was not feeling Cardiff, not one bit. He'd caught the red-eyed 5.28am train from Bristol Parkway after a night out on the lash and the 'cotics, and stumbled into the Welsh capital... for what exactly? The night before had been a bit of a washout. This UK tour of his was in danger of turning into a bit of a damp fucking squib... maybe he should've postponed it 'til Fresher's Week. Still, surely it was a good idea to get a bit of promo in... *fuck,* what to do with oneself before the pubs open? At that thought, that moment of total despondency and dawning epiphany, realisation of dependency, he glanced up from the dark grey ovals of chewing gum lining the pavement and looked across the square at some blonde figure stood outside the shopping precinct, smoking and staring at him. Staring. She was most definitely staring. At him. He dropped the rollie and stamped it out, flashing a weak grin from beneath his cheap black aviator sunglasses. She dropped her cigarette to the floor, stamped it out and headed inside. He slumped down onto a curb separating a big patch of grass from the concrete. He took his Nokia Lumia from his pocket and pressed hard on the little rectangle at the top of it. No luck. The battery was dead as the dodo, the dinosaurs, disco and Donna Summer. He'd just have to wait. Wait and watch. He looked around for something to do that to – something to watch. The shopping centre weren't too interesting, just a big concrete block with lots of glass tacked about it. To his left were even drabber concrete structures, one of which was probably a car park; to his right was the dole office, or The Job Centre, as a green-and-yellow hoarding rather optimeuthemistically dubbed it. He saw a mini-crowd outside, three people, two guys and a girl, both falling somewhere in that twenty-to-thirty-something milieu where the age suggested by a person's appearance is far more closely linked to their drug and alcohol intake and the quality of their diet than the number of years they'd spent upon the planet. They depressed him. Danny Daggers removed his backpack, dropped it onto the grass, then lay down upon the earth, resting his head on his bag, to stare up at the dull cloudy-blue of the sky, darkened by his aviators, his Lumia resting on the lawn beside him. He suddenly realised how intensely tired the first night of his tour, that dreadful, messy and eventless first night, had left him. He slowed the pace and increased the intensity of his blinks, and felt himself slowly slip away, away from the blue sky and Cardiff, into soft sleep and the earth…

Joseph

Joseph hated The Job Centre. He hated the passive-aggressive condescension from half the staff. He hated the air of hopelessness that tainted the smiles and good humour of the other half. He hated the stream of tracksuited dolemites that trickled in all around him, swearing loudly and berating staff when they turned up hours, sometimes days, after their scheduled sign-on time. The same tracksuited twats who'd celebrate giro day by blowing their hand-out on drugs and booze. He hated the red tape that he felt form a noose around his neck on any day like today, when circumstances forced him to arrange an alternative sign-on time. That thick red tape that'd grown thicker and darker since the government had turned blue and yellow. Despite this litany of grievances with the place, what Joseph hated most about The Job Centre on this particular morning was that it was fast approaching thirty minutes past the time the government advice line had told him was its scheduled opening time, and the doors were still locked shut.

Joseph reached into the front right pocket of his black suit trousers and pulled out a sky blue Nokia 3310; the time was now 9:00 exactly. He sighed to himself, then looked at and listened to the heated mumbling occurring beside him. Their voices were growing louder; he was beginning to understand little snatches of dialogue, all of it angry. The speakers in question were at that weird drug-induced non-age, the male especially, wearing dirty grey joggers and a black Nike tracksuit top, his eyes sallow and hollow, his hair tussled and greasy, his face unshaven and unwashed. Joseph knew him. Had seen him, at least. And her. Tight blonde hair pulled into a pontytail, pale face with thin lips and lines beneath the eyes that had surely come sooner than nature would've intended. Her clothing was clean and decent, especially compared to the battered old clobber her companion was sporting; a genuinely white white rollneck top, blue denim jeans, black boots. She had her arms folded defensively; his were swinging about, gesticulating, maybe threatening. Joseph caught the odd verb slip from their high-tempo dialogue, without a clue as to the subjects nor objects.

"Just fuck off!" she yelled loudly, finally.

The man's purple-ringed eyes shot straight over at Joseph, a hint of menace simmering beneath scolded-dog shame. Joseph stared back, emotionless, unblinking. The man looked away, then, following his eyes, walked away. Joseph watched him disappear in the direction of Queen's Street. Joseph's eyes returned to the woman. She was watching him. He looked away, back towards the man; he'd gone, disappeared back into the city. Joseph definitely knew him. Well, he'd definitely seen him. Her, too. They were always on Saint Mary's Street. Couple of crackheads. Always bothering people for twenty pences. Fuck knows who would've ever given them one. They'd hang around outside Central Station, trying it on on all sorts. Someone'd be soft enough to give them one, no doubt. His eyes returned to the woman. She was now staring at the door, arms still folded. Joseph hadn't seen the pair around in a long time. Maybe they'd turned their lives around, gotten off the gear. Maybe she had. That's when he noted the bulge beneath her white rollneck top - *pregnant*.

A short and plump middle-aged woman with curly grey hair and glasses suddenly made a noise at the door as she unfastened deadbolts, snapping Joseph's attention back to the task at hand. She was flanked by a thin and unpleasant looking man wearing the shirt-and-tie uniform of a security guard, hat and all. The doors opened and that was that – they were in.

The little woman slowly marched back to one of the countless desks sprawled across the big, bland room as the security guard took up position behind a podium. A couple of others took up position in the queue behind Joseph, but he didn't pay them much attention, his gaze instead being directed at one of the close-up photographs that broke up the bleakness of The Job Centre's white emulsion walls.

The photograph that'd caught Joseph's attention was of a man who looked like a haggard late-thirty-something, his face decorated with a weak smile and the definite air of a heavy skunk smoker. He'd seen it countless times, every time he'd visited the place. The poor fucker's face took up the entire square surface of the wall hanging, a mirthless smile removed from context, taken from above, at an angle that G.C.S.E. Media Studies had taught Joseph placed the viewer in a position of power and was designed to foster a feeling of superiority over the hapless sod in the photograph. 'You're better than this lazy cunt,' the government were surely telling him, 'get a fucking job.' Except the bloke in the photo was an actor being rather nicely remunerated for having his photo taken. Joseph always found himself looking at that photograph whilst waiting around on sign-on day. It quite neatly encapsulated everything he hated about The fucking Job Centre.

"Next," came the dispassionate voice of the security guard.

Joseph saw the pregnant reformed crack-beggar move off to the desks beyond as he approached the podium.

"Name," said security guard.

"Joseph Bradfield."

Security guard's face dropped to watch his finger run along the list of names on the sign-on sheet. "Time?" he queried, his finger finding no name matching Joseph's on the printout.

"It's not normally until ten but I got a job interview this morning," Joseph explained, "I need to do it earlier."

Blank expression. Nothing from security guard.

"Or later, if that's easier."

"Barbara," security guard called, turning away from Joseph and staring off towards the desks, then, again, louder, "Barbara!"

"What?" Barbara shouted back from across the room.

"There's a man here says he's got a job interview. Says he wants to sign-on early."

"Or later, if that's easier," Joseph added.

Barbara thought for a moment, before shouting, "What time's he supposed to be here?"

Security guard turned his head back from Barbara to Joseph: "What time are you supposed to be here?"

"Ten."

"Ten," security guard shouted, turning from Joseph, back to Barbara.

"What?" she shouted back.

"Ten. He says he's supposed to be here at ten."

"Ten?" she shouted back, incredulous.

"Ten," security guard confirmed.

"Ten's only an hour away, can he come back in an hour?"

"I've got a job interview," said Joseph.

"Can you come back at ten?" said security guard.

"I've got a job interview," Joseph reiterated, stressing it, vexed.

"He says he's got a job interview," security guard bellowed back at Barbara.

She thought about it for a moment, then answered, "Well, what time's his interview?"

Security guard turned his head back to Joseph: "What time's your--"

"Ten."

"Ten," security guard shouted back to Barbara.

Joseph turned around quickly and saw the young ginger guy behind him staring up at the ceiling, bored shitless.

"Well can he come here after?"

"Can you come here after?" security guard suggested as Joseph returned him his attention.

"Yeah, sound."

"He says 'sound'," security guard bellowed back to Barbara.

"What?"

"Sound."

"Sound?"

"Sound."

"Yeah, sound, I'll pop back afterwards," said Joseph, turning away and extricating himself from the bureaucratic monotony.

As he reached the door he heard the security guard greet the ginger guy who'd been waiting behind him: "Name?"

Joseph hated The fucking Job Centre.

He checked the time on his 3310; 9.06. He had near enough an hour to kill until his interview. He'd want to get there a little early, but any more than fifteen minutes early would give off an air of desperation. He decided to take a little walk around the city.

There were plenty of paths he could take from outside The Job Centre: he could turn left then make another quick left and walk round to the Hayes, or turn left and go straight past all the gay bars lining Charles Street and wind up at the Burger King on Queen's Street; he could cross the street and pass the car park and keep on walking to Bute and Adamsdown, past the prison and the towering twenty-odd story uni halls; he could turn 180 degrees, walk past some nutbar lying passed out on the grass and head inside the big slick new shopping centre (although this option was probably best avoided, as Jodie had been warned by her bitch of a boss not to entertain visitors when she was supposed to be working); or Joseph could, as he decided on this occasion to do, turn right and skirt around the outside of said shopping centre, winding up a few minutes later in front of Cardiff Central Station.

Joseph slowed down outside the station, looking up at the dual language lettering ('Cardiff Central Station'/'Caerdydd Canolog'). He puffed his cheeks and pursed his lips, exhaling air in a 'what the fuck should I do now' sort of way, before turning to look purposelessly across the rows of bus stops laid out in front of him, and sauntering over to and then sitting upon a big stone block, one of about a dozen, which had presumably been hauled to the outside of the station for the exact purpose of being sat upon. 'A bench would've been cheaper,' Joseph thought, 'and a lot more comfortable.'

He pulled a packet of Windsor Blues from the front left pocket of his black suit trousers, noting with concern that there were just three cigarettes left, two whence he'd lifted the third from the packet and placed it in his mouth. He stuffed the cigs back into his pocket, then pulled out a lighter and sparked up the fag. He stared off across the bus depot with disinterest, focusing on the first few pleasant pricks of nicotine, before turning to stare at the station, trying to find something to focus on. The morning rush had recently subsided and a steady trickle of commuters with relatively late starts were stumbling, morning-eyed, out of the station. He noticed a few taxi drivers at the cab rank, chatting in lieu of custom. He looked up at the big clock face nestled in the big featureless concrete slab of the station exterior. Time weren't doing much of anything. He wondered if he ought to make something of it, something that'd help him out with the interview, then he let that thought taper off into ellipsis as his eyes fell off past the bus depot to the shabby street at the end of it, nestled in the centre of a triangle running between the slick iconic Millennium Stadium, the aforementioned Central station and Saint Mary's Street, the latter being the rowdiest strip of piss-up caterers in Wales. Said shabby street at the end of the bus depot was an antiquated eyesore, a row of shitty shop-fronts and insurance firms that should've been bulldozed a decade ago. Joseph thought back to that rant Cain had gone on about Spiller's Records being bulldozed to make way for Saint David's 2, the slick new shopping centre that Jodie was now working at, going on about how Spiller's was the oldest record shop in the world and had been there for well over a century, and how they'd got planning permission to get rid of it no problem, and how the building had then not even been knocked down, but the record shop had been closed and moved anyway, and its former premises had since become home to an Italian restaurant. Joseph decided a simpler solution would've been to bulldoze that row of shit little buildings in front of him and put the new shopping centre next to the Millennium Stadium.

Joseph wondered who it was making those decisions – what gets knocked down or put up. *Politicians, landlords, the gentried nobles or whatever.* Didn't bear thinking about, really. There weren't much a lowly dole bum like him could do to influence that kind of thing. *No point getting worked up about it,* he supposed.

He turned away from that little eyesore in what he thought should be the city's golden triangle, and instead looked back at the featureless façade of the station. He suddenly noticed someone amongst its exiters, moving quickly, headphones plugged in. A girl of maybe twenty. Maybe older, maybe younger. As she drew closer, he focused on her features; long black hair and grim determination defining a head atop a petite body clothed in short black shorts – nearly fucking hot pants – and a white 'Working Class Hero' T-shirt with a picture of a reclining John Lennon on it. There was something hopelessly alluring about her, something exotic – otherness, Asianess... She was definitely overage, he decided, maybe in her early-twenties. Placing her exact age was almost as difficult as placing her exact nationality. She passed quickly and, after a few seconds of staring off after that arse in those near-hot pants, Joseph's attention fell back to the taxi drivers. He had a sudden urge to get one of them to take him to the airport, take him out to fucking Thailand or something, somewhere far away and foreign, then he took another long drag on the cigarette and found himself wondering what sort of questions they might be likely to ask him at the job interview.

Ji Eun

The Smiths 'Last Night I Dreamt Somebody Loved Me' was playing contrapuntally through Ji Eun's headphones as she passed the bus stands and made the final approach towards the Celtic Media Group building. She was aware of being a few minutes late, on account of getting half way from her home in Cathays to town before realising she'd left her phone behind. Her thoughts fell briefly back to the day before and she wondered if anyone would even notice her tardiness, let alone reprimand her. She'd been stuck at a computer all day doing not a lot of anything, 'soaking up the atmos', as Deputy Head of Content Rhiannon Evans had suggested. She could feel contempt coming from a couple of the journos, one or two seasoned pros who might've been fearing for redundancy and were resentful of her even being there on work experience. Those few resentful souls were most definitely in the minority, however; her existence didn't even register with most of the staff.

A fast-paced few hundred yards and a ride in an elevator later, Ji Eun was facing the violent red walls and open plan frenzy of the Celtic Media Group's newsroom.

"Near enough a dozen regional papers are written here," Rhiannon had explained to her during her on-arrival orientation, which had turned out to be the only remotely meaningful interaction she'd had there, "as well as DragOn-dot-Net, the biggest source of Welsh news for Welsh people on the entire worldwide internet."

Rhiannon Evans had seemed mildly irritated at being handed the chore of orientating a work experience student, and had breathlessly rattled through the history and nature of the Celtic Media Group in a couple of minutes. Ji Eun had struggled to keep up as Rhiannon had galloped from the launch of The South Wales Post in 1869 by the 3rd Marquess of Bute to the modern day, taking in a merger with rival paper The Western Chronicle in the 1920s, and absorption of numerous regional papers as the group expanded throughout the rest of the twentieth century, with the group becoming bloated and porous by the dawn of the internet age. Rhiannon had explained through gritted teeth how the paper had employed over a thousand staff members at the turn of the millennium, a figure that had dwindled to a little over three hundred a little more than a decade later. Rhiannon Evans had quite heavily implied that Ji Eun stood little chance of ever making a living as a journalist.

Ji Eun shuffled over to the coat-stand at the back of the room and hung her bag up, then headed across the newsroom to the swivel chair she'd spent all the previous day sitting upon. She then listened to the ringing phones and loud chatter of a newsroom that sounded like it'd been soundtracked by the BBC Radio sound effects library. She clicked on her computer and looked off across the room for Rhiannon Evans, her would-be mentor, and found her surprisingly quickly, striding towards her office, though her thunder-fucked scowl and fistful of documents belied the insensibility of engaging with her. Ji Eun instead logged into the PC (Username: temp, Password: ********) and fired up Internet Explorer. *Internet Explorer.* She could scarcely believe a serious media enterprise in this day and age still had Internet Explorer installed as the only web browser on their PCs. She was half-tempted to install Mozilla Firefox herself, but instead directed the antiquated net navigator to guardian.co.uk to catch up on the big news of the day. Crazy shit in the Middle East, turgid turmoil in American politics and a celebrity scandal dominated the headlines. She longed to become involved in the breaking of some real news. With Rhiannon's words from the day before echoing through her mind, she doubted that she ever would.

09.16am

Tom was absent-mindedly clicking through Paddy Power's impressive array of in-play bets – impressive for quarter-past nine on a Tuesday morning, at least – and was trying to decide whether to place a punt on the Tropang Talk N Texters or the San Miguel Beermen in the Filipino basketball cup. The Talk N Texters were leading 78 to 55, but Tom couldn't in good conscience back the Talk N Texters over the Beermen, not least of all when he was indirectly employed by Lemon, the UK's fourth largest mobile phone network. It seemed a simple choice between slavery and freedom. Tom placed 50p on the Beermen to overturn the odds.

"Is that work related?" Michael asked, placing a disapproving hand upon Tom's shoulder.

Tom quickly clicked an X and saw the screen return to the dull brown hues of Callex, Mitchell-Loveridge's bespoke database-cum-dialling software.

"Come on Tom, you were late again this morning," Michael reminded him, "try not to make any more trouble for yourself, yeah? How many leads are we on today then lads?" Michael asked, removing his hand from Tom's shoulder and addressing the rest of Team Lemon, who were sitting at a row of PCs lined up back-to-back along one of the dozens of identical desks beneath the fluorescent strip-lighting of Mitchell-Loveridge's ingloriously titled People Outreach Hub (POH).

"I got two," Justin answered with confidence, while a few other colleagues subtlety minimized windows while maintaining vague eye contact with Michael.

Justin was the most natural salesman of the team; a born-and-bred Cardiff boy with total self-belief. He was short and slim, with neatly-gelled black hair, a bum-fluff moustache and baby face, all of which combined to make him look younger than his twenty-something years. He used to deal weed, and claimed to the boys on Team Lemon to have been making three grand a week doing it, until things got sketchy and he decided to get a 9-to-5 job.

"Nice one Justin. What're the rest of you on?"

"I got one," said Sean, resting his heavy bald head upon the palm of his hand, his eyes slightly glazed from his near constant cannabis intake, "and I've got another where I got through to the M.D. and he had a meeting this morning. Asked me to call back in an hour. Think that one's a definite."

Like Justin, Sean was at ease with himself and had no trouble talking, with the sales figures to prove it. But sales figures aside, he was anything but a model employee; he phoned in sick at least once a week, and appeared constantly haggard from heavy skunk intake and playing video games long into the night. But as long as he was getting the sales in, Sean felt confident that Mitchell-Loveridge wouldn't dare let him go.

"Good work Sean. How about you Keith?"

"I am having no luck this morning," Keith emoted with a thick and melodramatic Merthyr Tydfil accent, "half of 'em aren't even answering."

'Confident' and 'natural salesman' were terms that had no relation to Keith, a pudgy, bespectacled, acne-marred mess of nervous tics, anger and awkwardness.

"Keep on trying Keith, you'll get through to someone eventually. Bob?"

Michael stared down at Bob for several seconds as Bob stared blankly at his computer screen. He repeated his name - "Bob?" - and again, louder - "Bob?" - before Bob, the biggest of the all-day immobile lumps on Team Lemon, a fifteen stone mass of lethargy and trans-fats, realised that Michael was talking to him. Bob glanced toward his boss and grunted in incomprehension.

"How many leads have you put through so far this morning Bob?"

"None."

"Brad?" Mike sighed, moving on.

"Nothing," Bradley spat back, fuming. Bradley was a no-nonsense, mind-speaking, sports-playing, beer-drinking Valleys boy who took no shit and gave no fucks. "Nothing at all butt. Not even a sniff. Honestly butt, I'm not being funny like, but this data is fucking shocking. Ninety percent of them we've been calling since Christmas, and they've told us half-a-dozen times they don't want nothing."

"It's a bloody nightmare," Keith said, shaking his head, the plaintive melody of his Merthyr accent giving the situation an air of operatic tragedy. "The one's I've just called now, Hart Family Haulage, I must've called them four times in the last two weeks alone. I speak to them more than I speak to my own bloody mother, mun! I'm not being funny, but it really is taking the piss, like."

"And how's it going to work when the new lot start?" Bradley added, his vexation growing.

"What new lot?" Justin asked, surprised.

"You're hiring a load of new staff for us, 'in'ew?" Bradley said at Michael, showing no regard for Michael's newly-earned promotion to team leader.

"That's the first I've heard of it," Justin said, his surprise having given way to offence.

"Well if you turned up on time, you would've heard me tell everyone about it, wouldn't you?" Michael retorted, squashing that latest little insurrection. "And anyway, we're not 'getting a load of new staff in'. We're hiring a few new staff members--"

"What's the point in that?" Justin smirked back, incredulous. "There's not enough for six of us to be generating leads from, never mind more."

Michael tilted his head to the side and offered up a studied, plaintive half-smile, the kind a commanding officer might've flashed his troops in the trenches whilst telling them that going over the top and into the certain death of German machine gun fire really was in all of their best interests. "I've had a word with Matt and he says they're going through and cleaning the new data up in Leeds at the moment."

"Fucking Leeds," interrupted Bradley. "You know exactly what they'll do. They'll sift through and take all the best shit for themselves and leave us lot with fucking nothing."

"You know, don't you?" Keith agreed.

"Embarrassed," Bradley stated, on its own, rolling the 'r's and adding untold extra syllables, "embarrassed they are, because we are fucking better than them, and Lemon's supposed to be their contract."

"Cut out the language 'en butt," pleaded Sean, "I'm calling someone here."

"Sorry butt," Bradley said earnestly, "it just makes me so fucking angry like. Tom, you won't remember this, but Justin, how many leads more than them were we doing up until a month or two back?"

"He is right Mike," Justin chipped in, "you knows me, I'm always smashing the leads through, but even I'm struggling with this data. The amount of apologising I have to do, we keep getting the same companies over and over, and they keep telling us they don't want it. I've had one on a two year contract, that I put through myself, and they've come back through to me."

"Look," Michael said, exasperated and, in the eyes of 'his' team, out of his depth, "I'll have a word with Matt and see what he says, alright?"

Michael's resolution was met with rolled eyes and sighs.

"Mike!" Matt Davies yelled across the P.O.H.

Michael turned away and walked towards him. Tom watched them disappear out into the corridor together and opened Internet Explorer back up.

"Michael haven't got a fucking clue what he's doing, I swear," Bradley said, picking back up where he'd left off. "There's no way in hell they should've made him team leader."

Tom directed Internet Explorer back to PaddyPower.com. The Tropang Talk N Texters were now walloping his San Miguel Beermen 88-55. No way back for the Beermen now.

"Reckon there'll be any fitties amongst this new lot then?" Justin asked.

Sean glanced around at his slovenly colleagues, ill-fitting supermarket-bought work shirts crumpled over their paunched figures. "I bloody hope so."

09.38am

"Gallagher!"

Ji Eun looked up from her computer screen and saw Editor-in-Chief Arwyn Davies bellowing at a blonde beer-bellied hulk of a man who'd just entered the room. The blonde beast stopped in the centre of the newsroom, all eyes upon him, then slowly turned to greet his accoster.

"What time do you call this?" Arwyn asked, his face crimson with annoyance.

"I reckon i's about half-nine."

"Nine-forty."

"No' far off then."

"And what time are you supposed to arrive?"

"Around nine."

"*At* nine. So what the fuck are you doing coming in at nine-forty? Turning up late in the middle of a fucking recession, during the fall of Rome, with fucking redundancies being forced upon us every other fucking fortnight, in this economic fucking environment of all economic fucking environments, after this very same shit got you kicked the fuck out of Fleet Street, why, Rory Gallagher, Rory fucking Gallagher, why do you think it appropriate to turn up to my fucking newspaper near enough a full half of a fucking football game late?"

"Calm down Arwyn, yiv gon' all red," Rory deadpanned, before reaching into his pocket for his iPhone. "I've bin out reportin'. I bumped intae a wee bi' o' news on tha way intae work an' I figured, ya know, wha' wi' me being a fuckin' journo an' all, tha' i' migh' be worth mae bother tae try an' fuckin' report on i'."

Rory held his thumb on the iPhone's home button to unlock it, then tapped the screen a few times, before handing the device over to Arwyn, who, though still irate, calmed himself enough to take hold of it.

"What's this you're showing me?"

A video was playing of a copper standing outside the back-entrance to the original St. David's shopping precinct.

"Keep wa'chin'," Rory smirked.

A stream of water suddenly hit the copper's head. The phone panned up as the copper turned round. A scruffily-dressed vagabond was stood on a balcony above, cock in his hand, pissing down onto him.

"Oi!" the copper shouted up to him, urine still splashing off his head.

Rory laughed.

"And this is news, is it?"

"Jesus Christ, is tha' fuckin' news?" Rory said, snatching the iPhone back. "Remember tha' fuckin' article Lizzy did about tha' dwarf tha' go' pissed off a' tha council withholding his housing benefit, and he went an' took a shite in tha middle o' their office? What a slow news day tha' were, eh? As absolute a non-entity o' a story as there's ever been, no question, in tha scheme o' things. No' exactly fuckin' Watergate, were it? But how many people wound up sharing tha' on their social networks, eh? 'Dwarf's dirty protest at council offices', 'Wee man lays wee turd on council carpet', or wha'ever tha fuckin' headline o' it were. Ya go' up intae tha millions on the shares o' tha' one, di'n' ya, eh? That's tha fuckin' world we're living in now, man. I've just given you a video of a fuckin' homeless man pissing from a great height onto a copper's fuckin' bonce. That type o' shite's solid gold, man. Stick it on ya fuckin' YouTubes and watch tha ad revenue come pourin' in."

Arwyn stared at Rory, unable to argue with his logic. He sighed and held out his hand.

"Ye can keep hold o' tha' for a bit if ye want," Rory said, handing Arwyn the iPhone, "ge' i' up on tha net nice and early this morn."

His fellow journos stopped gawping at him and returned to their work as Rory gazed smugly around the newsroom. He then took a seat at the desk beside Ji Eun.

"You're a solid gold bullshitter you," Christian Jenkins, a classically handsome thirty-something co-worker sitting at the same desk as Rory and Ji Eun said, shaking his head. "It'll bite you in the arse one day."

"It already has. I'm living in fuckin' Wales, ain't I? A man who fails is a man who winds up in fuckin' Wales, as tha old proverb has it."

"That Burns is it?"

"Prince fuckin' Charlie said tha', night o' tha Queen's fuckin' jublees. Ye broken any stories yet today then Muslim?"

"Nah," Christian replied, "but I got myself a press pass for the Cardiff City game tomorrow."

"Ya got tha', did ya? I thought I was gonna be doing tha fuckin' football matches whilst Jimmy's down wa' tha' fuckin' siphlis or whatever tha fuck he's go'?"

"Yeah, but then you were late, weren't you? Early bird catches the worm and all that."

"Ah, ya wee fuckin' weasel! Would ya jump intae ma fuckin' grave tha' quick? Who's this?" Rory asked, suddenly taking notice of Ji Eun, who'd been staring at him since he'd entered the room, trying to make sense of his accent and soaking up the sheer raucousness of his presence.

"Intern," Christian said, pronouncing it as a near-monosyllabic grunt.

"Intern, eh? Ya got a name there, intern?"

"Ji Eun," she answered, "Kang Ji Eun," then, Westernising, "Ji Eun Kang."

"Korean isit?"

"Yeah."

"How'd you know that?" Christian asked. "I'd had her pegged as a Jap."

"Well some of us know a wee bit more about fuckin' geography than you, don't we, eh? What sort o' twenty-first century news reporter don't know a fuckin' Korean name from a fuckin' Japanese name? I can tell yiv nae ambition o' bein' a foreign correspondent."

"I know Gangnam Style," Christian retorted.

"And I bet yer a right fuckin' riot with ya wee horsey dance down a' Club X on Charlie's Street. Wa' ya make o' this place then Ji Eun?" Rory said, putting his dizzying Scots accent aside to pull off perhaps the best pronunciation of her name's second syllable that Ji Eun had yet heard a Brit produce.

"It's been good," Ji Eun replied, her answer as vapid and empty as it was diplomatic; she found herself immediately wanting to retract it.

"Ye been a' tha' fuckin' desk tha whole time so far, eh?"

Rory read a yes in the dispassionate non-emotion of her face (not the first time he'd done such a thing, though, to be fair, that's another story for another time).

"Tell ya wha' lassy, how'd you fancy joining me on a fuckin' ride-round?"

"Sure."

"Where you off Rory?" Christian enquired.

"None o' yer fuckin' business, lad. Ya can read about i' in tha papers tomorrow." Rory rose to his feet and glared in the direction of the editor's office before bellowing: "Arwyn, are ya done wi' tha' fuckin' iPhone ye'?"

09.42am

Ji Eun quickened her a pace to a half-run to keep up with Rory as he headed down Saint Mary's Street, deftly side-stepping shoppers, clearly with a destination of some importance that he was leading her to. It wasn't without some surprise that she followed him round the corner, onto the street opposite the castle, and then in through the heavy oak doors of a pub with a black-and-white mock-Tudor façade: The Rummer Tavern.

Rory led the way across the wooden flooring – the whole place seemed to be carved from wood – to a table near the back.

"Y'alright there Rory?" said a big bassy voice from behind the bar, full of friendly recognition.

"Alright Munter? Go' 'ny news fir us?"

"Nothin' butt. Weren't a lot 'appenin' last night. Think the long weekend had worn out the worst of them by Monday."

"Nay bother. Tha's always tha way o' it on a bank holiday."

"You want the usual?"

"Aye," and then, directing his attention at Ji Eun, who until this point had felt like an uninvolved spectator, a spectral voyeur, "are ye old enough tae drink there Ji Eun?"

"Yeah," she said, a tremor of uncertainty in her answer, not so much because she was offended by the question, but because she was really hoping to nail her work experience placement well enough to become a real-life salary-earning journalist at the end of it, and getting pissed before ten in the morning didn't seem like the most obvious step to take in pursuit of that goal.

"Wha're ya after?"

"I'll have an orange juice," she said, before quickly adding, not wanting to offend a potential mentor, "with vodka."

"Gi' us a pint o' tha same old shite and a screwdriver," Rory bellowed towards Munter at the bar.

"A what?"

"A screwdriver. A fuckin' vodka-orange, a screwdriver," then, lowering the volume and turning to Ji Eun, "can ye believe this fucker works in a pub and he dinnae know wha' a fuckin' screwdriver is?"

Ji Eun smiled politely. A soft silence hung in the air and she had no idea how to fill it. She guessed Rory wouldn't have such trouble, and sure enough, a moment or two later, he'd ended it.

"So how long ye been in Wales then Ji Eun?"

"Two years. Two and a half. I'm about to start the last year of my uni course."

"What're ye studying?"

"English."

"And ye came over direct from Korea tae study it?"

"Yeah."

"So ye came tae Wales tae study fuckin' English? Christ, ye might as well've gone tae Namibia tae study fuckin' polar bears. Pardon my language, Ji Eun, I really ought tae make an effort tae speak a bit nicer in tha presence o' a young lady like yirself."

The apology was unnecessary: he spoke with such speed, and the difficulty of decoding the thick Scots accent his words were delivered in was so great, that Ji Eun had barely noticed the endless expletives peppering his speech.

"So how'd ya like Cardiff so far?"

"It's great, yeah."

"It's shite. Ye've seen tha' newsroom? Nary a fuckin' story ge's broken in there. Gang o' gobshites, tha lot o' 'em. 'Specially that Christian Jenkins ya were sat near-by earlier. He's a prize prick, him. Then again, all tha best journalists are. Tha difference a' this newspaper is yuv got a room full'f pricks wi' nary a thimble o' journalistic fuckin' nous between them. There's no' a lot you can learn listening to tha' gang o' fuckin' imbeciles."

Rory interrupted his lecture to thank Munter – "Cheers Munter" – as the barman deposited a pint glass filled with thick dark ale and a slimmer glass of fluorescent orange liquid and ice cubes onto the tabletop.

"See, if ye wanna be a journalist, first rule o' tha fuckin' game is ya gotta go where tha stories are. Those twa's sit around in tha' office, waitin' for Idiot-in-Chief Arwyn Davies tae tell them where tae go and what tae do, like a bunch o' fuckin' babies waitin' for their Ma to tell them that their nappy's been shat in. Real journalists – and believe me, Ji Eun, once upon a time, I worked wi' *real* fuckin' journalists – real journalists go where tha story is."

Saturday 1st September

11.09am

"We've got to let him go," Kelvin sighed.

Dai stared at him, clutching the freshly brewed cuppa in his hand: "What do you mean?"

"His story checks out."

"What story?"

"The seagull thing."

"Are you having me on?" Dai grinned. Kelvin didn't reciprocate. Dai's grin evaporated. "Are you serious? He was hunting a seagull?"

"Yeah. They found a dismembered corpse near the river."

"Of... a seagull?"

"Yeah."

"The dismembered corpse of a seagull? By the river?"

Kelvin nodded, struggling to hold back the anger that was brewing within.

"Who found it?"

"Gallagher."

Dai stared at him, eyes widening.

"You mean--?"

"Rory *fucking* Gallagher."

Tuesday 28th August

01.16pm

Danny leapt up from the grass and spun round to look at the patch that he'd been resting upon; nothing. He looked at it, dizzy, his heart thumping through his chest from the fear of it. But there was nothing there. Just grass, green blades folded down in a rough outline of his sleeping place. His heartbeat slowed slightly, beginning its gradual descent back toward an at-rest rhythm. He suddenly became aware of an ache in the lower left side of his back; perhaps he'd pulled a muscle leaping off the ground so quick. But there was nothing there... *must've been a dream*, he told himself. Some dream. An image of a savaged seagull carcass, meat hacked off to the bone, bright red blood staining its pure white feathers...

Where am I? he asked himself, now completely satisfied that the seagull he'd seen had been nothing but a remnant from a dream, a half-remembered dead thing shorn of feathers and context. He glanced at a row of Victorian-looking buildings beyond the edge of the grass lawn, then at a grey multi-storey car park to his right, and then at the glass-and-steel cathedral of consumerism of St. David's 2 behind him. *Cardiff*. How long had he been out? *What time is it now?* He thought to take his Lumia out to check, but then he remembered that the battery was dead. *It's gotta be lunchtime by now*, he reasoned. He supposed that he probably ought to try and eat something, tight and spaceless though his stomach felt. *A beer wouldn't hurt, and all.* He glanced at the red brick buildings across the grass, then at the glass-and-steel of St. David's 2, then decided to wander through it in search of a Wetherspoons and a beer and a burger deal.

* * *

"Have you not got anything a bit less red?" the potential customer said, twirling an orangey-red lamp in his hand. He'd asked specifically for a red lamp, and Gareth had directed him thusly.

"So you want a red lamp," Gareth asked, to clarify, "but not quite as red as this one?"

"Yeah."

"What about that?" he said, pointing to a red-red one.

"Hmm," the bloke in front of him said, pondering its redness. "It's not overly red, but I don't know… do you think maybe this one might not be red enough?"

Gareth did not think thus. He looked up from the potential customer with his potential lamp in his hand and saw Tom staring dumbly at a painting of a Parisian park circa-C19th.

"The walls in me house are all painted terracotta," would-be customer said. "I don't wants to overload them in red when the lamp's on, know what I mean?"

Gareth nodded disingenuously.

"I tell you what, how long have I got to return it if it's not a good match?"

"Twenty-eight days with the receipt, seven without."

"I'd better hang on to that receipt then," he laughed.

Gareth laughed disingenuously.

"I tell you what I'll do, I'll take both of them home with me, then whichever I'm least happy with, I'll bring it back and exchange it for another copy of the victorious lighting fixture."

Gareth glanced up from the customer to see Tom, a few metres behind him. Tom jabbed down towards the ground floor with his left hand, then raised an imaginary cigarette to his lips with the right.

Gareth nodded, satisfying both friend and customer.

* * *

Rory took a swig of thick, creamy Guinness whilst he let his thoughts gather form, in much the same way as the brown foamy sludge that had been pumped into his pint glass had settled into a deep calming black. He let out a satisfied 'aaaahhh' after sipping it, then looked sympathetically at Ji Eun's glass of coke: "Are ya sure ya dinnae wan' some'in' a bi' stronger?"

Ji Eun stared at him, panicked – *what?*

"Ye dinnae fancy another one of 'em screwdrivers? Summin' a wee bit stronger tae drink, naw?"

"I'm fine," she said, smiling sweetly, her head still reeling from all the screwdrivers she'd put away earlier.

"Y'know, there ain't much tae be said fir journalism these days, Ji Eun. I cannae see much'f a future in i', way things are, way they're going. It's all P.R. fluff pieces an' fuckin' studies wiv all tha scientific rigour o' tha Ol' fuckin' Testament, tha's all newspapers're publishing these days. Tha' prick back in tha office, Christian – I cannae stand tha cunt, but he plays tha game a damn sight better than I do. Than I do now, at leas'. See, I wasnae always a two-bi' hack on a rag serving th Valleys and this wee damp squib'f a capital, Ji Eun. Time was I was in London, working on a national fuckin' paper. But then I le'me temper ger tha better o' me." Rory trailed off, ruminating on what was and what might have been.

Ji Eun saw the change that one swig of Guinness had brought to him; the instant philosophical air that it'd injected in him. It had been there before, in the Rummer Tavern, and it had stayed with him as they'd strode back to St. Mary's Street two drinks later, to a Ladbrokes half-way along it. The philosophical air had then slowly wheezed out of him as he lost the last of fifty pounds' worth of bets placed on unsuccessful horses.

Now, with that first sip of Guinness, Rory's philosophical air had come back to him. There was nothing happy in him, but there was at least now an acknowledgement of that on his part. Somehow, he seemed in better touch with the hopelessness of his position, and thus better equipped to make something out of it.

"Actually, I think I will have something stronger."

Rory grinned proudly at Ji Eun: "We'll make a journalist o' ye yet lassy! Wha're ye havin'?"

"A Guinness."

"Good girl. Eh, barkeep!" Rory said, turning around and bellowing across the half-empty Wetherspoons. A surly lad behind the distant bar counter glared at Rory's impertinence, his hands still busy wiping down dishwasher-fresh glasses as he held his face frozen on him. "Gis us another pint o' Guinness, would ya?"

"Coming up," he shot back, in a thick Liverpudlian patois.

"What happened at the national paper?" Ji Eun asked, just the thought of more alcohol going some way towards revitalising her.

"I bit a feller's nose off," Rory answered without hesitating.

Ji Eun stared; for once, she understood every word he'd just said to her, but she couldn't comprehend it in the slightest. Rory watched her cute little eyes narrowing on him, questioning, her thin lips parting gently in bewilderment. He smiled quite involuntarily.

"Well, off is a bi' o' an overstatement," he clarified. "I dinnae come away wi' more than a thimble o' flesh from tha fucker. But, me bosses were none tae happy wi' it, so there I was, out tha door and downgrading tae Cardiff."

Ji Eun paused for some time, making sure she'd understood correctly, before speaking: "You were fired for biting someone?"

"Aye. I prob'ly would-nae'f done it, had I known I'd wind up in fuckin' Wales on account o' i', but tha fucker had it coming tae him, know wha' I mean?"

She quite clearly did not.

"Look, right, I cannae remember all tha ins and outs o' it, I was fairly rat-arsed at tha time, but you dunnae fuck wi' a drunk Scotsman, know wa' I mean? Tha's jus' common sense, tha'. Far as I can recall, tha' cunt was there gi'en it tha big un, and I said 'listen, pal', or words tae tha effect, then he dinnae listen, so I bit a chunk o' his fuckin' nose off. Problem was, he was on staff, weren't he? Pap I think he was. Yeah, right, come t'think o' it, he was definitely a pap. And no-one likes tha fuckin' paps, do they? And he was more o' a cunt than the most of 'em, this feller. Pap," Rory said, repeating the word to try and lead his obviously confused companion to some sort of understanding, "paparazzi. Y'know tha paparazzi?"

"Like... photographers?"

"Yeah, aye. Like photographers, only wi' out a soul and a wi' a sense o' entitlement that wouldnae be out'f place in a Windsor, know wa' I mean? Cunts and charlatans tha fuckin' lo' o' 'em." Rory left the anecdote there, took a big swig of Guinness and stared off at BBC News 24 on a distant television set. A woman in her mid-to-late thirties with neat hair was sat behind the newsdesk, speaking straight down the camera lens, her words a mystery, the volume off.

"Y'know how much one o' them fuckers get paid?" Rory asked.

Ji Eun stared straight at him; *what fuckers?*

"A hundred grand a year, near enough. And all o' it coming from tha taxpayer. Fuckin' travesty. They dunnae do shite but sit behind a desk readin' a fuckin' autocue. If God'd given 'em vocal chords, ya could train a fuckin' chimp tae do tha' jobby."

Ah, Ji Eun understood, *newsreaders.*

"And d'ya know what a real fuckin' journo earns? A damn sight less than tha', I can tell ya. Fuckin' waste o' time, this racket. Sometimes wonder why

I bother. Heck, I'm wonderin' tha' all tha fuckin' time, all tha fuckin' hours God sends. And I dunnae think I've ever come up wi' a decen' answer tae i'. Force o' habit more than anything." Rory trailled off again, feeling a pang of guilt at the gloomy expression with which his young Korean protégée was absorbing all the bile and bitterness of a burnt-out Scottish almost-was.

The silence was broken by the Scouse barman, who arrived suddenly at their table with a Guinness, along with a bowl of noodles for Ji Eun and a bacon-and-onion ring-topped double cheeseburger for Rory.

"Gi' us another pint o' Guinness, would ya pal?" Rory said, having drained almost half his pint in a single gasp upon seeing his lunch. The Scouse barman noted his order with a stern look then walked away from the table.

"So anyway," Rory said, picking up a chip with his hands and smearing it in ketchup, "why'd you want tae be a journo anyway Ji Eun?"

Ji Eun frowned and thought about it, staring at the bubbles racing through the brown sludge in her pint glass.

"I guess I want to help people," she said uncertainly. "Normal people. You know, in Korea, the media's so full of propaganda. They never report anything that really matters. Like last summer, there was a huge scandal where the secret service were accused of rigging elections. It was all over the internet. There were arrests and everything. But the mainstream news, TV and the newspapers, they were just talking about insects."

"Aye?" Rory said, mouth full of cheeseburger, imploring her to continue.

"Aye," she replied instinctively, eyes falling back upon the settling pint glass as her thoughts took shape. "Not even dangerous insects or anything, just some, like, kind of cockroach thing that's numbers had increased. There were big protests outside City Hall. Peaceful protests. The people were just sitting there with candles. And the police were using water cannon to break it up. It was all over the internet. But the mainstream news? Nothing."

Silence. Ji Eun reached out for the pint glass; Rory stuck his own hand out to stop her. "Gi' i' a minute. Let i' settle."

She pulled her hand back, picked up her fork, then twirled some Thai sweet chilli noodles around its tines. She chewed and swallowed before Rory spoke again.

"You're in tha game for all tha right reasons – a lot o' tha same reasons tha' brought me intae it, tae be honest wi' ya. But tha way things are goin', tha way tha world's headin', I cannae be certain there'll be any real field o' journalism left for ya tae work in. I mean, I dunno, maybe I'm just a bitter old sod whose time've past, but I look around and I dunnae see any indication that things'll not keep on declinin'. And no' just for journalism man, fuckin' all o' i'. The whole species is fucked. I mean, Christ, Jesus wept, would you ye look at this fuckin' bell-end?"

Ji Eun turned around and looked across the Wetherspoons at said 'fuckin' bell end', a lad of about twenty or twenty-one, with a big mess of blonde hair, a garish, sequin-adorned T-shirt, and virtually painted-on skinny jeans: "That's Danny Daggers."

"Who?"

"Danny Daggers. He's an internet celebrity."

"Oh aye. W'a's he famous for?"

"I'm not sure exactly. My housemate showed me one of his videos. I think he just, like, drinks. But a lot of drink. Like a bottle of vodka or something."

"Fuckin' hell, is tha' wha' passes for marketable talent nowadays? I think I was born twenty years tae late." Rory polished off his pint and watched Danny approach the bar. "Y'know wha' lassy, this is exactly tha sort'f thing I was tellin' ya 'bout."

Ji Eun stared back at Rory blankly.

"If ya ge' out there on tha streets, out where tha real people are, sooner or later, tha stories will come tae ye."

She still didn't appear to comprehend what it was he was getting at.

"Go over and have a wee word wi' him; find out what he's up tae, tha kind'f thing. I used tae work at a red top, Ji Eun, I know wha' I'm talking about. And I know tha' female journos have a big fuckin' advantage when i' comes tae picking up these kinds'f stories. Go up t'the bar, tell him wha' a fan of his you are, offer to buy him a drink, then sit down wi' him for five and bleed him for anything worth writing about."

Ji Eun looked down at her Guiness. It had settled. She lifted it to her lips and took a big swig.

"Dunnae worry about finishing tha' lassy, get yirself a fresh one. I'll see tae what's left o' it."

Ji Eun looked over her shoulder towards the bar, where Danny was now waiting his turn.

"Go on," Rory implored her.

She turned back around to see Rory handing over a twenty pound note; she took it from him.

"Quick, before he ge's his order in."

* * *

"It's doing my head in though man," Gareth said, leaning against the back wall of the John Morgan's department store, rolling a cigarette. "Almost four years I've been here now. I've had a guts full."

Tom nodded, then took a drag on his Richmond Superking.

"Every day is exactly the same," Gareth continued, "I'm fucking sick of it. As soon as I get my next bonus, I'm out."

Tom could certainly understand his friend's frustration; he'd felt the same stomach-knotting, brain-numbing, soul-devouring sensation in every job that he'd been in since university, the majority of them call centres, none of them lasting more than six months. Four years imprisoned anywhere would be enough to drive anyone to desperate measures, however well-remunerated the prison's inmates were. But that last point was one worth considering; John Morgan's staff were very well remunerated. Despite its prime city centre locations and star-studded TV ads, John Morgan was not the all-devouring capitalist beast it first appeared to be, but was rather a strange bastion of socialism. The staff were not staff, but 'partners'; shareholders in the company, the organisation itself a co-operative. As well as receiving a higher base salary than almost any other retail job, John Morgan's staff were also the recipients of quarterly bonuses, the value of which were tied to the company's performance. They were also granted discount cards, which got them 25% off at about a quarter of the bars, shops and restaurants in the city. Essentially, without ascending to the improbable pipe-dream highs of personal shopper to the rich and famous at a *proper* proper department store, Gareth's current position was as good as retail got. *In the land of the blind, the one-eyed man is king.*

"What will you do then though?" Tom asked, conscious of all the preceding paragraph, but not wanting to spell it out explicitly.

"I don't know man," Gareth admitted, licking the paper and sealing his rollie up. "I want to do something with drawing, man. Art. Make money doing something I actually enjoy doing."

"That's the dream." Tom remembered some quote he'd once heard on the subject: "Find what you enjoy doing and work out how to make money from it."

Gareth nodded; it was sage advice. He lit his rollie.

"That's what I'm thinking man. I look at the paintings they sell in there, this morning I sold one for a hundred and sixty pounds like, and I was looking at it, thinking, 'I could do that.'"

"Why don't you?"

"I don't know man," Gareth said, shaking his head. "I'm gonna have to."

Tom thought back over the succession of calls he'd fielded that morning. Dozens. Had he hit hundreds? He didn't even know – it was all a blur of polite rejection. "I know how you feel," Tom said, taking a drag on his cigarette and mulling it over. "Where I'm working now is better than where I was working before, definitely, but still... when I was working at that last call centre, cold-calling people at home, trying to sell people life insurance, all day long, people would be telling you to fuck off and go kill yourself. At least now, selling business to business, the people I'm talking to are half-way professional about it. They'll turn you down gently, they won't flip out and start screaming abuse at you. But still man, just because it's better than something fucking awful doesn't mean that it's actually anywhere near decent, know what I mean? It's like... getting punched in the face hurts a lot less than getting stabbed in the testicles, but that doesn't mean I enjoy getting punched in the face all day long."

Gareth let out a little laugh, along with a plume of cigarette smoke.

"I don't know man," Tom continued, "it's the repetitiveness that does my head in. It's always the same, call after call, day in, day out, fucking hundreds of them, all following the same script, over and over and over again... and, fuck man, I can't help but think, is this it? Is this what I'm going to be doing for the rest of my life? We'll be twenty-seven next month man, three years from thirty. The age rock stars die at."

"You'd better get working on that album then butt," Gareth jested. "But I know what you mean, man. Twenty-fucking-seven butt. Fuck."

"I know. As if it'll be six years since I graduated from uni, like. Fuck."

"I don't know man, time just seems to be speeding up as we get older."

"It's the repetition butt. When you're a kid, everything's new to you. Time seems to go on forever because you're paying attention constantly, trying to work out what the fuck's going on. But once you start working, you just get into a routine, don't you? Same shit every day. And it's always the same, when you start a new job, for the first week you can remember every little detail, every conversation, it's all sinking in, your brains adjusting to it, sizing it all up, but then after a while, you get used to it and it all becomes normal, then your brain just switches to auto-pilot."

Tom took one last drag, the burning ember at the cigarette's end creeping right up to the ink of the brand name, then dropped it to the floor and stamped it out. He looked at Gareth, with his two-thirds of a rollie of a left; *should I have another one?*

"I know exactly what you mean man," Gareth said, as Tom reached into his pocket for another Richmond Superking. "It feels like the days are flying by, and I'm just drifting through them, directionless. That's why I've got to get from here."

"How's it going with Bethan now?"

"It's good man. Really good." Gareth had been living with his girlfriend for about a month. "She's really laid back man, you know? It's just nice being around her all the time."

"I need to find a girl."

"You will, man."

"I need to find my own place, too. Living at my Mum's house is doing my fucking head in."

Gareth knew Tom's frustration all too well, having lived with his Dad and his new wife before moving in with Bethan: "It sucks man, especially when you're used to being independent."

"Yeah butt," Tom said, sighing out cigarette smoke, "you can't do nothing without being moaned at. I mean, when I was at uni, I lived in a house with six other people, and never mind coming back late, we'd be sat in the living room playing music, drinking and chatting, smoking and whatever, any time of day or night, no worries. Now, I creep in through the front door, and if that fucking dog don't wake up and start barking, then they hear me opening a fucking cupboard in the kitchen, and that wakes them up. What the fuck like? How light of a sleeper can you be, mun? I'm not even allowed to use the fucking microwave now, in case that wakes them. I mean, if I come and meet you or the boys after work, have a few pints like, I don't even get home that late, like, twelve o'clock, or like one, one-thirty at the latest, then I've not had any dinner, I'm gonna have to go into work with a stinking hangover if I don't fucking eat something, and I can't even microwave a Chicago Town fucking pizza, like. Does my head in butt. I just want to get out and rent my own place."

"Then do it then."

"Yeah. I should. I really should."

"Find a house share if you need to. Rent a room with some randomers. That's what I was doing on City Road, and it was sound, man. Much more chilled than living back at home." Gareth paused to smoke. "How are you getting on with Toby now?"

"Alright," Tom lied, not wanting to spend any more time than necessary thinking about his Mum's boyfriend, who'd been living with him for just over a decade. Tom had long given up hope of him ever leaving. "I've got to start doing something with my life though, man. I can't keep on like this, working at fucking call centres, spunking all my wages on getting pissed at the weekend. It's fucking silly mun. We're still young, like, we can still do something with our lives."

"I don't know man," Gareth replied, "are we really that young though? Twenty-six, man, near-enough twenty-seven. I mean, my parents had been married with a mortgage and everything for like five years by the time they were my age."

"But they were completely tied down then, though, as well butt. We've still got the freedom to do anything we want with our lives. Besides, you wouldn't be able to get a mortgage in your early twenties nowadays anyway."

"I don't know butt," Gareth said, taking his lighter from his pocket to reignite his extinguished rollie. "I just kind of feel like my life's fucked already."

02.28pm

"I think people these days, our generation, they don't take no notice of none of it – the old order, the old media, the traditional ways of doing things. It just don't even enter into their heads no more. Think about it, twenty years ago, the only way anyone over here would know there was a famine on in Africa would be if Bob Gedolf and Bono flew over and done a music video. Nowadays, you got people uploading ebola selfies to social media. I mean, in theory, I've not really seen one. But I mean, Saudi Arabia – who knew they were all mentalist drivers, cruising along with the car balanced on two wheels while some mad-head hops outside and changes the tyre, I mean – have you seen that?"

"Uh... I don't think so," Ji Eun said, not quite understanding what 'that' was.

"Here are, I'll show you it now," Danny Daggers said, stuffing his hands into his pockets, trying to find his phone. He gave up quickly. "My phone must be in my bag or something, I'll show you later. But what I'm saying is, these days, anyone anywhere can share anything about themselves, know what I mean? I mean, where are you from?"

"Korea."

"Korea. And I'm from Leeds. And we're sat here in a Wetherspoons in Cardiff chatting away to each other. A hundred year ago, that'd be fucking mental. Well, maybe a bit more than a hundred year ago, I mean you had the British Empire and all that, maybe a couple of hundred year ago, but it really weren't all that long ago that no-one from Leeds had ever seen a Korean, let alone spoken to one. I don't think my Nan even saw a brown feller 'til the seventies. And now you've got 'Gangnam Style' blasting out over here, a billion fucking views on YouTube, know what I mean? We don't need the old media no more. We don't need gatekeepers. If we've got something to say, we can go out and say it to the whole fucking world if we want to. And that's what I do. I mean, it ain't much different than Kurt Cobain doing it through music, or Picasso doing it through painting or whatever. I'm just speaking up for my generation. *Our* generation."

Danny let the claim hang heavy in the air for a moment. To him, Ji Eun looked impressed.

"And... what are you saying?"

"I'm saying get rid of all of it. All of it. Not just the media and all that, but all the traditions." He held out his hand to count them off one-by-one on his fingers. "Marriage. Marriage. What a load of nonsense that is now, eh? How many marriages end in divorce?" He let his hand drop and focused in on a tangent. "And nowadays, you've gays running about, out and proud, and everyone's fine with it. And I mean, brides wearing white, for purity; in this country, if you've bought you first lottery ticket and you're still a virgin then it's a fucking miracle. And the gay thing as well, dividing people up into gay or straight, that's bollocks and all."

"Yeah?"

"Yeah. The idea that you're born gay or straight, it's just plain daft. I mean, I'm not saying it's unnatural or nowt, I mean it is in a way, but so are, like, gyms and the internet, just because it's not natural don't mean there's owt wrong with it, but like, if you stuck a straight man in prison for the rest of his days, it'd be a rare man who don't turn to bumming or being bummed just for the lack of any decent alternatives, know what I mean? If you stuck a guy on a desert island for the rest of his life, sooner or later he's going to be trying to fuck whatever wildlife's on it, or rubbing his nob up against a tree of whatever, know what I'm saying?"

"Yeah..."

"And, like, you see it happening to people, you take two individuals with all the limitless potential people do have, then you put them into a couple together, and they do just kind of melt into some amorphous blob, welded together on the sofa in front of the television every night watching Britain's Got Talent. The birth of a couple is the death of two individuals. And the birth of a baby's the death of them pair done over again."

"So... do you kind of make videos about your philosophies?"

"Sort of. I try and stick a few in where I can. The bread and butter of me view count comes from me pranks and me stunts though."

"What kind of stunts do you do?"

"My biggest one were the piranha," Danny grinned, rocking back and forth in his chair with the passion of his speech, clearly pissed.

"Piranha?" Ji Eun repeated.

"Yeah, you know, them little fish with the teeth on them what bite humans? South American."

"Ah," she said, understanding. "In Korean, we say *pee-rah.*"

"*Pee-rah,*" Danny repeated. "It's more or less the same thing, innit? Well, this thing with the *pee-rah,* pirahanna, potato, po-tat-toe, right, what happened was, my mate, he's fucking minted, right, and he's got this tropical fish tank thing in his home, for like, proper tropical fish, like, and he had some fucking piranhas in there, di'n't he? So we're round his one day, like that, and he says to me, he says, 'Danny, you've drunk some shit in your time lad, but do you know what'll really fucking impress people?', and I'm like, 'no, I don't', and he's like, 'drink a fucking piranha, that'll impress them.'"

"And you did?"

"Yeah, of course I did. Twenty million views on fucking YouTube, that one. Did it in a pint of tequilla, for the South American theme."

"Didn't it bite you?"

"Nah, I think the alcohol probably killed it off first. Calmed him down a bit, at any rate. It was alright mind, we got a bit of footage of the piranha swimming around in it, then immediately cut to me drinking it. You don't even notice it's not moving about when you watch the video of it."

Ji Eun stuck her hands in her pockets and felt a bunch of silver and copper coins remaining from the twenty pound Rory had given her to inebriate Danny with.

"Look, I'd better be going. I'm supposed to be meeting a friend this afternoon."

"Alright, well thanks for all the drinks love, it's been lovely to meet you."

"You too."

"And I'll see you at thingys tonight then, yeah?" he said, referencing his upcoming 'performance' at some student-centric venue somewhere in the city whose name was now escaping him.

"Sure," she smiled, not really meaning it. She'd dug up absolutely nothing of any interest to anyone whilst ploughing the idiot full of free booze, and now had absolutely no intention of going on to watch him make a prat out of himself in front of a paying audience. "I'll look forward to it." Ji Eun saw Danny was a half-second away from rising from his seat to bid her adieu with a hug, or perhaps even a kiss on the cheek; she backed away, waving: "Bye."

"See ya later," he said, head rolling around a little, an expression of hopeless drunkenness falling across his face as he tried to remember what the cute little Asian girl's name was and, in a drunken stupor, tried in vain to comprehend why the fuck she'd just ploughed him full of free drinks and then suddenly decided to leave.

Ji Eun made eye contact with Rory as she walked across the pub; he glanced towards the door, obviously telling her to go through it, then downed what remained of his eighth or ninth pint of Guinness and got up to leave.

02.57pm

"Hello," Joseph said, taking the 3310 from his pocket and pressing it against his ear.

"Hi, this is Gloria from Mitchell-Loveridge. I just wanted to give you some feedback on the interview this afternoon." Joseph zoned out immediately, supposing she'd been charmed enough to call him back, though not enough to actually follow through with a job offer. Her point-by-point appraisal of his performance passed from the phone to his ear without his mind registering it, he instead focusing on what he was to do now, and whether he would ever find work, and how many more lines of text detailing his job search he'd have to produce before leaving the house on the morning of each sign-on day before he could finally break free of the Job Centre. As he walked, his thoughts spiralled so far down into this vortex of hopelessness that Gloria's last few words didn't quite register with him.

"Sorry?" he said, stopping in the middle of the street.

"We'd like you to start at nine tomorrow. Is that a problem?"

"No, no, not at all, not at all. Okay, nine tomorrow. Excellent."

"Okay, well thanks a lot Joseph, we'll see you here tomorrow."

"Yeah, yeah. Thank you. Thank you."

He hung up and put the phone back into his pocket. A stupid grin spread across his face. The sunshine suddenly seemed brighter, the air warmer, the last days of summer all the more beautiful. *Finally*.

He carried on in elated spirits, right up to the door step of Jodie's mother's house. The immense scowl that adorned her face upon answering his knock did little to decrease his joyousness.

"Alright Bev?"

She answered with a glare, still scowling.

"Joe!" little Daniel Brain said, running up to the door to greet him.

"Hey little man," Joseph said, stooping down to lift him up in his arms. "Has he been good today?"

"What's with the suit?" Beverly asked, ignoring Joe's question.

"I had a job interview. I got it and all. Starting tomorrow, I'll be working at a business-to-business sales firm in town."

"Not another court appearance then?"

One court appearance he'd had in the eighteen months that he'd been seeing Jodie. Early on in the relationship it'd been, as well. He'd dropped Daniel off round Bev's house in the morning with the suit on, and as he explained to her that he'd been called as a witness after walking past an armed robbery of a post office on City Road, he could tell by the deep trenches of suspicion that'd wrinkled up over her face that she didn't believe a word of it. She'd greeted him with pure, undisguised distrust from the moment she'd met him, and that incident had seemed to confirm all her worst prejudices. Joseph supposed that with Jodie's ex's track record, her mother was within her rights to be suspicious of any new man that'd entered Jodie's life, but he felt that by this point, a year and a half down the line, he'd done more than enough to convince Beverley that he was a very different man to little Daniel Brain's father.

"I suppose it's time you started doing something with yourself," was the closest thing to praise Beverley could bring herself to bestow upon him.

"So what did you do today then Vader?" Joseph asked Daniel, as the two walked away from Beverly's house. Joseph called Daniel 'Vader' because of the uncanny similarity his small stature and mop-top of mousey brown hair made him bare to the young Anakin Skywalker in 'The Phantom Menace'.

"Me and Nan went down to the indoor market."

"Ah yeah. Did you have fun?"

"Yeah. Nanny bought me a comic book."

"Oh right. What kind of comic did she buy you?"

"Hellboy."

"Okay," Joseph said, a little irritated. The stick Beverley was always giving Joseph because of what a bad influence she thought he might be on little Daniel, then she turns around and buys him a comic book about demons and Nazis. He'd not read any of the Hellboy comics himself, but he'd seen both of the movies, and he was pretty sure it weren't age-appropriate stuff for a six year-old. His irritation was interrupted as an iconic midi approximation of a piano tune rang out from Joseph's pocket. He pressed his 3310 to his ear and spoke. "Hello?"

"S'apnin' bro'seph? It's Cain."

Of course it was – any time Joseph received a call from a withheld number, he knew it had to be either Cain or a telemarketer. "S'apnin' man? You good?"

"Yeah man. What you up to?"

"Just picked Daniel up from his Nan's house. On my way back home now."

"Is it? She still giving you grief?"

"Yeah," Joseph said slowly, determined not to go into further detail on the subject with Daniel within earshot.

"What you up to later?"

"Not a lot man, just chilling at home probably. I'm starting a new job in the morning."

"Yeah? Where's that to?"

"Mitchell-Loveridge's. In town, just off the Hayes."

"I knows it. Round the corner from Metros?"

"That's the one."

"Congratulations, man. Nice one."

"Cheers."

"Well I'm just ringing to see if you wanted a new phone."

"Yeah?"

"Yeah. I've just picked a Nokia Lumia, second-hand. There's a crack on the screen, but it's working fine. Twenty quid if you fancy it."

Joseph though about it; he had a job now. He could afford it.

"That's a smartphone, yeah?"

"Yeah, 'course bro. Wicked camera on a Lumia man, better than an iPhone."

"Alright then bro."

"Sound. When do you want to come and pick it up?"

Saturday 1st September

11.12am

"Well then," Dai Green said, "if Gideon what's-his-face's story checks out, who the fuck killed Daniel Covell?"

"Sometimes," Kelvin Phillips explained, assuming an air of seasoned authority, "the most obvious answer is the correct one."

"And that would be...?"

"Come on, Dai. Who the fuck's been running round town causing all manner of mayhem the past couple of days?"

"You don't think it's connected to them lot do you?" Dai said, realising immediately to whom Kelvin Phillips was referring.

"It's not exactly outside the realm of possibility, is it? If a dead body turns up in the River Taff, and there's been a group of sick psycho fucks running around smashing people's heads in with hammers, stabbing them and all sorts, I'd say said sick psycho fucks'd have to come somewhere pretty close to the top of the list of potential suspects."

"I suppose you're right," Dai agreed. In his experience, Kelvin Phillips usually was.

"Yeah," Kelvin said, staring off across the break room at the notice pinned above the mug-filled sink imploring all officers to wash and put away any items they use.

A few seconds silence followed, during which Dai watched Kelvin and waited.

"You know what Dai, the more I think about it, the more certain I am. Matter of fact, I'd bet my whole bloody career on it; I absolutely guaran-fucking-tee you that those sick psycho fuck Amstell brothers are responsible for that poor dead fucker Daniel Covell."

Wednesday 29th August

02.22am

"Small box of Amber Leaf please butt."

"Do you have any I.D. on you?"

Darren laughed and looked through the glass at him, the clerk; spotty, slender. Young as fuck.

"How old are you butt?" Darren asked.

"Nineteen," the lad responded.

"Well I'm old enough to have gran'kids older than you," Darren exaggerated – even in Wales, having grandkids who were just two years younger than you was unlikely, at best - "go and fetch my baccy butt."

"I'm afraid it's the law. If you haven't got I.D. and I've asked you for it, then I can't serve you."

Darren's smile snapped away; his eyes grew serious.

"What's the matter?" Jonesy said, stepping forward. He was a good few inches taller than Darren, and although his muscles were far more developed, he still came across as marginally less threatening.

"He says I need I.D. to buy baccy butt."

"Come on butt," Jonesy said, grinning at the plasti-glass that separated them from the petrol station's night attendant. "Look at the bloody 'tache on him, how many under-age kids have you seen walking around with one of them on 'em?"

The young clerk looked at the thin line of hair growing across Darren's upper lip; it wasn't exactly the incontrovertible proof Jonesy was making it out to be.

"And ge'me twenty Lambert and all while you're over there," Jonesy ordered.

The young lad behind the plasti-glass gulped before responding: "Do you have any I.D. on you?"

Jonesy grinned. "Seriously?"

Affirmative silence.

Darren drew in breath sharply through his nostrils, curling his face up, regarding the lad behind the plasti-glass with increased hostility.

"Here you go," Jonesy said, pulling his passport out of his back pocket and placing it on the silver shelf running under the plasti-glass divider.

The lad examined its picture intently and tossed the passport back onto the silver tray that connected them: "Twenty Lambert, yeah?"

"And a small box of Amber Leaf," Darren added.

"I'm sorry, if I know it's for you, then I can't sell it to him either."

Darren's hands tightened into a fist. "'uh?"

"I—"

"Come on butt," Jonesy reasoned, "if I'm thirty-fucking-one, as it says on tha' passport I showed you, I'm hardly likely to be knocking about with a moustachioed seven-fucking-teen year-old, am I? Think about it mun, it's fucking nonsense like."

"I'm sorry," the lad said, eyes lowered. "The law says—"

Darren's slammed the plasti-glass with his fist, a beast bashing the side of his cell. "Fucking listen to me, you little prick. Never you mind what the law says. Up until now we've been perfectly fuckin' civil to you. We did what you fucking said and showed you an I.D. and tha', now stop fucking around and sell us some fucking tobacco and fags, how does that sound?"

The lad stared meekly through the plasti-glass; the futility of resistance dawned upon him. The fucked-off slim-built stick of intimidation bellowing at him was clearly old enough to buy tobacco products. "Think 30" be fucked. He nodded acquiescence.

Darren felt emboldened. "I tell you what butt, I think you'd better give me an upgrade on the Amber Leaf box. Ge' me a twenty-five gramme pouch instead. Chuck in a pack of red Rizlas and some Swan filter tips an' all. Extra-slim. Way of saying sorry, like."

Jonesy smirked, turning his face away from the plasti-glass and the conflicted clerk beyond it, not wanting to ruin Daren's ridiculously effective performance by cracking up and corpsing in the middle of it.

"Grab us a can of Coke and all," Jonesy said, turning back to him.

"Can of Coke?" Darren scoffed. "They sell fucking booze in there an' all butt. Give us a crate of Carlsberg and a bottle of vodka. Smirnoff. None of that Glen's shit."

The lad glanced up, terrified. Then he shuffled away from the tobacco counter, out towards the fridges filled with lagers and the shelves of spirits stacked beside them.

"Fucking muppet," Jonesy muttered, turning his back to the plasti-glass, before emitting a low chuckle.

"He's fucking lucky he's got that glass between us, I tell you now," Darren concurred, giggling.

They stared off across the forecourt to the road running past it, and the trees shrouding whatever lay beyond that. A car rumbled down the road and pulled in, the thud of sub-woofer thundering out of it. When it pulled up, the music stopped, and was replaced by the hum of conversation. Darren Amstell tried to hone in on the convo, as he scanned the car and its passengers through its windscreen. A guy got out of the passenger's side, then another guy from the back-right door, leaving a girl in the driver's seat and probably a couple more passengers in the back. Darren looked away as the guy strode toward the cashpoint, about ten metres down along the garage's exterior from the ramp up to the plasti-glass nightwindow on which Darren and Jonesy were standing.

"The fuck's taking so long with them drinks?" Jonesy asked suddenly, turning back to face the night-window.

Darren carried on staring at the trees across the street from the petrol station, trying to train his ears in on the chatter of the two boys at the cashpoint, something familiar in at least one of their voices. One of the boys' phones suddenly went off, and, as Darren's eyes remained averted, he answered it with a flurry of responses: "Yeah… yeah… what, over there by the… yeah… hang on, I'll have a look now."

The boy stepped away from the darkness of the cashpoint and rounded the ramp up to the plasti-glass, passing through the yellow glow of streetlight that illuminated the petrol pumps.

"Oh butt," he said, a slender figure with his hood up, "are you Carl Jones?"

"What's it to you?" Jonesy snapped back.

"What brings you round here butt?" the boy grinned.

Darren and Jonesy weren't grinning.

"You're a chopsy little cunt, ain't you?" Darren said, reversing the flow of questioning.

"Uh?" the boy called back, not quite believing his ears.

"What's it to you what his fucking name is?" Darren said, rephrasing.

"I was just asking him a question like," the boy said, standing his ground but clearly attempting to hide a little bit of Darren Amstell-induced panic.

"What's going on here then boys?" called a gruff, scratched voice, the kind 40 fags and a bottle of spirits a day might leave one croaking out through their throat. He stepped into the light; a bald, mad-eyed roid-head in a Man United shirt, with bulging, chemically-enhanced arms, and slender legs of half his arms' thickness.

"I was just asking them if either of them knew who Carl Jones was, that's all," the boy explained, his eyed locked firmly into contact with Darren's.

"And wha'd'ey tell 'ou?" gruffalo asked.

"They di'n' tell me nothing. They just started kicking off and having a go at me."

Beyond the petrol pumps, another figure stepped out of the backseat of the girl's car, producing a big, bulky silhouette against the lamp light from the street.

"Tha's funny," gruffalo said, sounding as though it were anything but, "'cause he d'look an awful lot like Carl Jones, don't he?"

"Now that you come to mention it…"

"And you look like a soft fucking cunt pumped full of steroids," Darren said, swiftly switching his gaze from the boy to the gruffalo.

"The fuck did you just say?" the gruffalo snarled back, stepping forward.

Darren clenched his fists.

"I said you look like a cunt, butt," Darren summarised.

Gruffalo flared his nostrils and breathed in, deeply and unnaturally, before striding forward, fists at the ready.

"Dar," Jonesy warned, glimpsing something rolling into the petrol station from the road that ran along it.

Darren glanced up as he walked down the ramp, time enough to stop dead in his tracks as he caught sight of the cop car.

Gruffalo strode on, oblivious, until the boy suddenly called out behind him: "Mark!"

Mark the gruffalo glanced back, and he too halted his march toward war as two police officers made their way across the forecourt toward them.

The silhouette that'd appeared besides the girl's car now hung back beside it, frozen in indecision.

"Right then," said the officer leading the way, a woman in her late-30s, "what's the problem here then boys?"

Darren sighed upon seeing her: Bronwyn *fucking* Jones.

"You'd better ask them," Jonesy said, staring daggers at Mark the gruffalo.

PC Bronwyn Jones turned to look at Mark Watts, who was staring daggers straight back through Carl Jones (no relation).

"They've come up to us, kicking off about something," Carl 'Jonesy' Jones explained.

Bronwyn wasn't listening. She looked straight past Darren and Jonesy to the lad, standing sheepishly behind his plasti-glass: "Are you the gentleman who put in the call to us?"

The lad gulped as all eyes fell upon him: "Yeah."

"And who was it that was refusing to pay for their purchases?"

"Them two." Darren and Jonesy.

"Woah, hang on a minute," Darren protested.

"You'll have your chance to speak," Bronwyn interrupted, "now, what exactly is the problem here?"

"These two came here looking to buy tobacco, but only one of them has any I.D. on him, so I said I could only serve cigarettes to the one with I.D."

Darren laughed. "Come on mun Bronwyn, am I eighteen or wha'?"

Bronwyn responded with a look of contempt.

"Then when I refused to serve the one who didn't have I.D.," the lad continued, "they started threatening me and demanding that I give them their tobacco products, as well as several alcoholic drinks, which they heavily implied that they would refuse to pay for."

Bronwyn shook her head at Darren and sighed aggressively: "Did you learn nothing from what happened to your older brother?"

The dumb smirk of incredulity that had thus far adorned Darren's face suddenly slipped away; his face tightened up, his eyes narrowed.

"Have you got any I.D. on you?" Bronwyn snarled.

"No, but, I mean, come on mun, you know I'm over eighteen, dun you?"

"I do," Bronwyn admitted. She knew the Amstell family all too well, "so I suppose the best way for us to rectify this situation would be for you two to pay exactly what you owe for your cigarettes and alcohol and clear off out of here."

"Well, it's getting a bit late now for the alcohol," Jonesy said, rubbing the back of his neck as he did so.

"Pay and get out of here, or hop in the back of my car and we'll have a chat about it back at the station."

Jonesy sighed loudly, muttered 'fucking hell mun' under his breath, then turned back to the lad behind the plasti-glass: "How much is all that then butt?"

The lad glanced down at the box of 12 Carlsbergs, the one litre bottle of Smirnoff vodka, the 25g pouch of Amber Leaf, the packet of Rizla, the box of extra-slim Swan filter tips, and the 20 Lambert & Butler, all laid out in the sliding silver draw beneath the plasti-glass. "That'll be forty-seven pounds and twenty-three pence please."

Jonesy bit his lip and glared with menace through the plasti-glass, then turned his head round to shoot the same angered look at both Darren and PC Bronwyn Jones, before pulling his bank card out of his pocket and sliding it through a little gap in the plasti-glass, just above the sliding silver tray laden with tobacco and alcohol.

"And what's your part in all this?" Bronwyn said, directing her attention to Mark the gruffalo.

"Me?" he croaked. "I've not done nothing mun."

"What's all this about you coming up to these two and kicking off?" the younger male copper, Ivor Evans, asked. Ivor was a lot less experienced than his colleague Bronwyn Jones, but in the two years he'd been serving, he'd already run into the gruff-voiced, slap-headed shit-starter Mark Watts on several occasions, usually bottling someone outside a pub, or glassing someone inside of one. He knew nothing of the Amstells, or the great effort that Bronwyn had expended on putting Darren's elder brother Simon behind bars.

"I just came up, seen these two kicking up a big fuss at the night-window, and all I did is ask them wha' the matter was," Mark Watts told him.

"That's it, aye," the boy to the left of him agreed as PC Ivor Evans's gaze then fell upon him.

"Well the lot of you better finish up your business here quick and get back home to bed," Bronwyn ordered, "and if I hear anything else off of any of you lot tonight, you will be spending the evening round ours, alright?"

The scolded menfolk mumbled acquiescence.

* * *

"What the fuck was all that about butt?" Darren asked from the passenger's seat, as Jonesy drove up the hill leading from The Dip Garage to the roundabout at the start of Trecenydd.

"Nobheads, ain't they?" Jonesy concurred. "Probably got nothing better to do at this time of night, have 'ey?"

It took Darren a moment to realise Jonesy was talking about the coppers: "Not the fuzz now, I mean them boys who come up to us, kicking off. What the fuck was all that about?"

"Oh, *them*," Jonesy said, shaking his head, slowing the car as it approached the top of the hill and the roundabout, "well, you know that bald guy whose voice was all fucked up?"

"Aye."

"Well, I might've sort of slept with his missus once. It was yonks ago, like, before I got back together with Charl, but he's been waiting for a chance to kick my head in ever since."

Darren looked up at the rear-view mirror and saw the police car had pulled out of The Dip Garage and was heading in the opposite direction, towards Penyrheol. "Well, do you want that hanging over you?"

"What do you mean?"

"Do you want that prick wandering around, waiting for a chance to lamp you when you least expect it?" Darren reasoned, the car almost at the roundabout.

"What else can I do like?"

"Turn the car round butt."

"Wha'?"

"Turn the fucking car round butt."

Jonesy glanced at his passenger, whose eyes were locked straight ahead, as he rolled the car round the roundabout. Jonesy looked up as the long, dark, stretch of dual carriageway leading down to Corbett's roundabout, and from there onwards, home, to Llanbradach, loomed into view; he'd be home in less than ten minutes if he took that turning. But, there was a truth to Darren's words, and Jonesy knew he had no option but to obey them.

The car spun back around, 360 degrees, and sped down the hill towards The Dip Garage.

As they zoomed along, St. Cenydd school to the left of them, and a row of terraced houses to the right, they saw a car tearing up the hill in the opposite direction; the girl's car. Darren locked eyes with the boy in the passenger's seat as the two cars passed.

"Fuck, turn around in the garage butt," Darren instructed, "they're heading up that way."

Jonesy did as he was told, roaring into the petrol station forecourt and, with a screech of brakes, back out again. The car tore back up the hill, within seconds getting within view of the girl's car, as it headed straight on at the roundabout, into Trecenydd, bungalows lining the right-hand side of the street, a typical conurbation of terraced housing filling up the left. The girl's car turned left into the mass of terraced housing, streets and streets of it, then rolled through at low speed, Jonesy's car at the back of them, lights on full beam.

"Have you got anything on 'ou?" Darren asked.

"What d'you mean?" Jonesy asked, assuming drugs. He didn't; he'd left them all back at home in the Brad. Not that it mattered either way; he weren't planning on getting arrested.

"Weapons."

"Weapons?" Jonesy repeated, surprised.

"Aye."

"Well," he said, glancing about the car's dark interior, as they followed the girl's car at about 20mph through a maze of terraced housing, "there's that thing by your feet there."

Darren kicked his foot lightly against it, some solid lump, then picked it up; a steel arm with a claw attached to the end of it – a handbrake lock.

"Be careful with that mind," Jonesy warned him. "You might end up killing someone."

"Don't be daft mun butt," Darren laughed. "I'm not gonna aim for their fucking heads with it, am I?"

The girl's car pulled up at an oasis of green, an overgrown area of shrubbery, somewhere deep within Trecenydd's concrete forest. Jonesy stopped his car a few metres behind them, watching the red glow of brake lights on the car in front. After a few moments, a back door opened, and a big, fat, bearded beast of a man got out, the same one who'd been silhouetted against the streetlights back at the Dip. The front passenger door and the back door on the same side then opened up in unison, and the boy and Mark 'the maniacal gruffalo' Watts got out of each respectively.

"Right," Jonesy said, quietly, readying himself, before flinging the door open and joining them in the quiet dimness of the green-ravaged dead-end.

"S'apnin' boys, you alright or wha'?" Jonesy shouted out, mock friendly, as Darren sat in the passenger's seat, watching through the windshield, the handbrake lock perched on his lap like a cat on a Bond villain.

Mark Watts hocked back some phlegm and spat out a big wad of it before answering: "Yeah, I'm alright butt," he said, moving toward Jonesy, arms stretched out at his sides, "how are you?"

They moved to within a foot of each other, then *bam* – as gruffer squared up to him, arms still at his side for show, Jonesy smashed his fist right into his face, knocking him back a few steps. The boy and the bearded beast strode forward, and Darren took his cue to throw the passenger's side door open.

Jonesy flew straight at the bearded beast with a flurry of fists; the boy ran in behind him, throwing a lifted knee into Jonesy's left hip, knocking him off balance. The beast and the gruffalo were too stunned to capitalise, so the boy threw in another two knee strikes, aiming straight for that same spot on Jonesy's hip. After the second blow, Jonesy gathered himself enough to grab hold of the boy's leg, and the boy then desperately fought to maintain his balance, clasping his left arm around Jonesy in a headlock; inevitably, the two quickly tumbled to the floor in an undignified heap.

As they rolled around and clawed at one another on the concrete, the beast and the gruffalo regained enough composure to start stamping and kicking at Jonesy, whilst he lay prone and entangled in front of them.

Darren ran over, wielding the handbrake lock above and behind his shoulder like a broadsword. Gruffalo saw him and instinctively threw a quick defensive punch toward him; Darren swung the handbrake lock forward to meet the fist. Gruffalo spun round with a pained scream, clutching his smashed-in fist in agony.

The beast moved quickly to tackle Darren around the mid-section. His girth being far greater, the beast lifted Darren by the legs with ease, then, as Darren's arms flailed the handbrake lock around in vain, the beast slammed him, hard, into the ground.

Winded, Darren let his guard slip long enough for the beast, sat heavy upon his chest, to slam an almighty right fist straight into his face. Darren felt faint and disconnected, leaving him easy prey to another bash in the face from the beast's heavy fist. Darren felt a kind of airy, floating hopelessness as he blinked up at the beast and saw that boulder-like right fist again smash right down into his noggin.

The beast was then suddenly knocked from view, as Jonesy, having dealt with the boy, at least for the time being, ran over and slammed his knee into the side of the beast's head, knocking him over.

In a haze, Darren rolled himself over, clasped the handbrake lock, pushed himself onto his knees, and then slammed the handbrake lock down onto the outstretched right hand of the fallen beast, eliciting a squeal of pain. Darren slammed the steel lock down on that hand, again and again, each time the squeals growing higher and sharper, blood and bruising appearing and evolving with each successive strike, stopping only when he heard a sharp cry of pain fly out from Jonesy's mouth.

Darren turned round to see Jonesy flailing his arms about hopelessly, the gruffalo behind him, leaning forward like Dracula, his teeth sunk into Jonesy's cheek. Then, before he'd even begun to process what was happening with them two, Darren caught sight of the girl, a slender pretty thing of about 19, creeping nervily from the driver's side door toward Jonesy and the cheek-biting gruffalo, wielding a solid steel handbrake lock of her own in her shaking, skinny arms.

Darren's reaction was instant.

He flew forward, clutching the handbrake lock at his side with both hands, then swung it upwards at the unsuspecting girl, smashing the thick back end of it into her chin at some velocity. She tumbled backwards with the force of it, and Darren's first thought was that he might've killed her.

Shocked, the gruffalo released Jonesy's cheek from his teeth, and as he stared at the fallen female, blood oozing down to his chin, Jonesy swung an elbow into his face. The gruffalo stumbled back, stunned. Jonesy smashed a fist into his face; enough to knock the gruffalo down, if only for a moment.

"We need to get the fuck out of here," Jonesy said, clutching his right hand to his savaged cheek and striding purposefully back towards the car.

Darren looked at the blood-smeared handbrake in his hand and contemplated chucking it, but quickly corrected himself, realising the less evidence he left lying around at the crime scene, the better. The girl had fallen back a fair distance away from him, and all he could make out of her in the early-morning darkness was her feet, which were motionless.

09.03am

"You alright intern?"

Ji Eun looked up for the spot on the computer monitor she'd been vacantly gazing into for the past few minutes to greet Christian's uncharacteristic giving of a fuck. The arsehole beneath the sympathy revealed itself soon enough. "You're looking a bit yellow," he smirked. "More so than usual."

Ji Eun ignored the race-based taunting and returned her attention to the BBC News home page. She was feeling rough, as if her head had been hollowed out and a spikey-shelled parasite was being gestated in her stomach. She stared at the computer screen, eyes unfocused, words and pictures blurred and incomprehensible in front of her. The previous day's alcohol intake had definitely taken its toll upon her; if that was what being a journalist required, she wasn't sure she was cut out for the job.

She brought her eyes into focus upon the main headlines on the computer screen, the blaring light of which was aggravating her queasiness. The headlines told of death and destruction and crisis and horror across the Middle East, in Syria, Iraq, Gaza, in Ukraine, and disease and contagion and death and threat down in Africa, and the whole mess of it was far too depressing and doing nothing but worsening her condition, and she extracted herself from it, and clicked the bar at the top of the page for 'UK News', thinking that would surely be somewhat more subdued in its relentless horrificness, and whence that tab had loaded up, she decided to delve deeper and do something that might be of use in her immediate future, and she clicked to zoom in and focus further, choosing 'Wales' from the four options in front of her. Ji Eun's attention was immediately drawn to the third story down: "Caerphilly Woman in Critical Condition After Assault".

She clicked the link and started to read. The story was short, the kind of bare-bones piece that appears when journalists have first learned of something news worthy, but haven't yet had time to dig and poke and prod and pad and add some meat and colour to the finished product:

A 19 year-old Caerphilly woman is in a critical condition after being assaulted at around 2.30am this morning.

The woman was rushed to hospital with head injuries after being struck with a blunt object during an apparent altercation between two groups in the Trecenydd residential area of Caerphilly.

Police ask that anyone who was in the area this morning please come forward and speak to them.

"Where's Arwyn?"

Ji Eun's attention was snatched away from the computer screen upon hearing that unmistakable Aberdeen accent bellowing out across the newsroom. She wasn't alone in this; all eyes had fallen upon Rory Gallagher.

"Arwyn!" Rory shouted out again. He lowered his voice and mumbled something about a remote control to a journo sat near a row of televisions attached to one of the newsrooms' red walls, each tuned into do a different channel's breakfast news show. A moment later, Rory had what he wanted, and was waiting in front of the television sets in anticipation of something, three remote controls at the ready. "Arwyn!" he shouted again.

Arwyn Davies strolled out of his office without saying a word. Rory fixed him with a big grin. "There ya are! Arwyn, I think we need tae have a wee word about ma salary. Perhaps ye could lemme ge' a bi' o' tha advertising revenue tha' wee video o' mine's been pulling in, eh?"

Before Arwyn could answer, Rory had spotted something on one of the television sets. He fumbled about with the remotes until he managed to crank the volume all the way up on the television set showing ITV's Daybreak.

"And now," Susanna Reid said on-screen, "if you haven't seen it already, a video of a police officer in Cardiff being urinated on has gone viral, notching up more than five million views on YouTube in just under twenty-four hours. We'll be speaking with the officer concerned on the sofa in just a few moments, but first, we'll show you the video. Please be warned, this is footage that some viewers may find difficult to watch. If you're eating breakfast, look away now."

And there it was, up on the big screen; the very same video Rory had recorded the day before.

"Very good, Rory," Editor-in-Chief Arwyn Davies said through gritted teeth.

"Did ya see it, yeah?" Rory grinned, as urine splashed off the copper's head on the television screen. "Everyone ge' a good look a' i', did ya? 'Cause if ya did'nae see it, naw bother, tha other channel's'll all be playing i' again soon enough."

Irritated and embarrassed by the intermittent brilliance of that beer-bellied, bellicose, Scottish thorn-in-his-side Rory Gallagher, Arwyn Davies headed back across the newsroom to his office, slamming the door shut behind him.

Rory handed the remote controls back to the journo he'd picked them up off, jumbling them up and leaving the poor sod to figure out which one he needed to turn the volume back down. Rory then strode over to his desk and took his seat beside Ji Eun and Christian.

"You know, there's a pet shop I walk past on the way in to work in the mornings," Christian said, "and they've got some really cute kittens in the window. You might want to take your camera down there Rory, you might get another scoop."

"A couple'f pussies, eh? Not like you tae notice tha' sort o' thing, Hindi," Rory quipped back. "Ye alright there Ji Eun?"

"Yeah," she said, uncertain, blown away by the tornado of presence that was sat right beside her.

"She's not looking too good," Christian said. "If I didn't know any better, I'd say it looks like Rory Gallagher spent the best part of yesterday plying an under-age girl with alcohol."

"And if I dinnae know no better, I'd say tha' you were a loud-mouthed little prick who could nae get a scoop off'f an ice cream van."

"You've used that one before Rory," Christian warned him. "I think decades of heavy drinking might've taken its toll on that fabled Scottish wit of yours."

"What're ya working on this morn then, Shinto? Reviewing a fuckin' musical again, are ye?"

The stinging reference to one of the less masculine areas of the newspaper on which Christian had previously moonlighted was enough to shut him up, allowing Rory to turn his attention to Ji Eun. He glanced at the headline upon her screen: 'Caerphilly Woman in Critical Condition After Assault'.

"What's tha' yir reading there, lassy?"

Ji Eun opened her mouth to speak, but before she could get her slowed-down, booze-damaged brain into gear, Rory was already back on his feet, reading the short article over her shoulder.

"Is tha' all there is on i'? Jesus Ji Eun, good find! I think we'd best be getting ourselves down tae Caerphilly."

"You interested in that girl who got hit with the steering wheel lock?" Christian said.

"Aye," Rory said, not wanting to let on that Christian had just given him a piece of information that was missing from the BBC News article.

"Maureen and Sanjeev called it already," Christian warned him, "the story's theirs."

"Fair enough, pal."

Rory waved his hand in front of Ji Eun's face as Christian focused on his computer screen; he pointed his thumb at the exit. Ji Eun dutifully got up to follow him.

"That's not your story Rory!" Christian shouted out as they walked away.

Rory ignored him, instead leaning in to give Ji Eun some advice on the matter as they waited for the elevator to arrive in the corridor outside the newsroom: "Lemme tell ya something, lassy; this is nae fuckin' nursery school, and stories are nae fuckin' soft floppy toys tha' us journos are sharing out between us, know wha' I mean? 'That's not your story, Rory!' Did ya hear him?! Soft soppy bastard. Tha news works tha same way as fuckin' antique shops work, Ji Eun; if you break it, ya bought it, understand wha' I'm saying?"

Perhaps becoming more acclimatised to his accent on the second day in his presence, Ji Eun figured she'd just about gotten the gist of it.

09.42am

Tom was staring and scrolling, through statuses, names and faces, sponsored ads, holiday snaps, funny links, trivialities, rants and screeds, making split-second micro-judgments as they passed across the screen in front of him:

Becky Ryan
16 hours ago
Anyone know the rules with fake tan and having a tattoo ?? Lol
18 likes | 24 comments
Kayleigh Davies
Ul b ok luv they wil just wipe the worse of it off, lol xx
16 hours ago | 2 likes

Lisa Evans shared **TheLittleThing**'s photo:
14 hours ago
"Never lie to someone who trusts you, and never trust someone who lies to you."
6 likes | 1 comment
Stephanie Clement
even if the purpatraitor beleaves the lies…
11 hours ago | 1 like

"Hello?" a little voice said to him, no dial tone preceding it.

"Hello," Tom said, surprised. He clicked his way from Facebook to Callex. "I'm looking to speak to a Ms. Maureen Granger please."

"I'm afraid she's not in today."

"Oh. Do you know when she'll be in next?"

"Is there anyone else here who might be able to help you with anything?"

"There might be. I'm calling from Lemon, it's regarding the company's mobile phone contracts."

"Oh right, well, no, it'd be Maureen who deals with all that."

"Alright then."

"Yes. I'm afraid she's not in tomorrow, either. Matter of fact, I don't think she'll be back in this branch before Friday."

"Okay, I'll call back then."

"Perhaps you'd like to try her on her mobile number, if it's urgent?"

"Umm…" Of course it wasn't urgent. For all Tom knew, the company could be locked into the first month of a five year contract with one of Lemon's competitors. "No, no, it's not urgent, I wouldn't want to bother her on her mobile."

"Are you sure? I mean, there's no guarantee she'll be here Friday, either. She keeps very unusual hours see, does our Maureen."

"Yeah… okay… alright then. What's her mobile number?"

"It's 0-7-9-4…"

Tom tapped out the alternative mobile number, thanked the speaker, then ended the call and slipped the record back into the system, to be called back by any agent the following day. He then returned his attention to his Facebook newsfeed as the next dial tone sounded out in his headset.

His aunty, usually prone to posting funny animal pictures or inane truisms, had shared a picture of the White Cliffs of Dover with 'Go Away, We're Full' scribbled messily over the top of them, presumably on MS Paint. He frowned down upon her. Next was a Vice News article about how a condom shortage in Venezuela was altering young people's sex lives. After that, Lisa Evans had shared another quote-containing picture: 'She's broken because she believed'. *Who the fuck is Lisa Evans anyway?*

The dial tone gave way to an answer phone message. Tom hurried to click the call to an end before the beep was reached, then went back to scrolling through Facebook as a new dial tone rang out in his headset. Ryan Taylor had shared a map of countries thus far attacked by ISIS and posed the question: 'Why does 'extreme Muslim' ISIS attack Islamic state after Islamic state, but never fire a shot at Israel?' After a few seconds scrolling through the comments beneath it, Tom saw the general consensus was 'because Israel has lots of weapons'. Beneath that post, Tamara Whitworth had shared a video of Barney the purple dinosaur bopping about, re-cut to N.W.A.'s 'Straight Outta Compton'. Tom watched about half of it, then scrolled straight past the next entry, the video of the hobo pissing onto the police officer outside St. David's, shared by Tom's mother a day after everyone had already seen it, and was suddenly snapped out of his Facebook scroll-trance as a human voice replaced the dial tone in his headset: "Hi, Grand Prix Auto Parts."

"Hi, could I speak to… David Eastman, please?"

"I'm afraid David's out at the moment. I think he'll be back in the office around three, if that's any good for you."

"Sure, yeah."

"Can I just let him know who's calling?"

"Yeah, I'm calling from Lemon, it's about the business's mobile phone contracts."

"Right, well one of your lot called us yesterday, actually, and Dave told me then to let you know that we're actually tied into a contract at the moment."

"Right, okay. And would you happen to know when that contract is next coming up for renewal?"

"I wouldn't, no, but it's certainly not something we'd be looking into at any time in the near future."

"Okay, no problem then, thanks anyway."

"Yeah, cheers."

Tom clicked the 'In Contract' option on Callex, which, in-theory, should've guaranteed the record wouldn't be called again for a year or more, though in the present times of lean data, the record would probably resurface on somebody else's screen in a matter of days.

Tom was back on Facebook, and the dial tone was back in his headset. Terry Ender had shared a Daily Mail article on two Austrian girls who'd been stopped at an airport in Germany, trying to board a plane to Turkey, presumably planning to then travel onward to Syria to go and join ISIS. Terry had added his own comment on the situation: 'Treason is treason. Fucking execute them.' Tom thought such anger was a very strange reaction; he actually kind of envied the girls. Having the courage to give up the comfort of Western capitalism for the brutality and adventure of being a militant embroiled in a far-flung foreign war. It all seemed a lot more romantic than joining the British Army, at least, however brutal some of ISIS' actions might've been. *It's our fault they exist in the first place,* Tom thought. *Us and America.* He wondered what it would take to jolt him out of his dull stasis and send him onto a plane bound for Syria. A few posts down, he found further thoughts on the matter:

Craig Worgan
12 hours ago
Let's just get this straight: Assad is evil, so we need to support the rebels in Syria, but then we find out the rebels are even more evil, so now we need to stop them instead, and so Assad and Iran are helping us out with that... okay? To be honest, if they're the enemies of the American, British, Israeli, Iranian and Syrian governments, don't you reckon that ISIS might actually be... the good guys?
11 likes, followed by a load of vitriolic comments arguing the opposite.

Tom let the cursor hover over 'like' for a second before stopping himself: the post would pop up in the newsfeed of others, announcing to them his approval of it; his cousin in the Armed Forces, his racist aunt, that Australian soldier who'd stayed at the same hostel as Tom in Amsterdam. Perhaps potential future employers would discover it; perhaps he might even be added to some government watchlist. He moved the cursor away and continued scrolling down the page. *Fuck's sake,* he scolded himself, *how are you going to fly out to join ISIS if you're too much of a fucking pussy to even click 'like' on a Facebook post that's mildly supportive of them?*

Cursing his cowardice, Tom scrolled down further, and stopped at a post from Paul Jones:

Paul Jones
4 hours ago
Come on Cardiff, big win tonight!
2 likes

Cardiff are playing. Tom slid his phone from his pocket and swiftly tapped out a WhatsApp message to Steve: *fancy going to the cardiff game tonite?* He then slipped the phone back into his pocket and carried on scrolling through his newsfeed.

"Alright guys, listen up!" Michael shouted.

The whole of Team Lemon looked in the direction of their team leader, standing besides four new faces. "These are the new guys, this is Alison, Harry, Sarah and Joseph."

Tom formed a quick flash of first impressions of the new guys: Alison – *glasses, boring, looks like a maths teacher*; Harry – *abnormally narrow head, too much shit in his hair, smirks like a tosser*; Sarah – words failed him, and he instead greeted a succession of near-perfection (nice hair, pretty face, decent tits, exposed legs) with monosyllabic grunts of approval; Joseph – *looks alright, but wouldn't want to get on the wrong side of him.*

"I'm gonna partner each of you new guys up with one of our 'vets', as it were," explained Michael, "so Joseph, I'd like you to sit here next to Jason, and Alison, I'd like you to go next to Sean. Sarah, could you sit there next to Keith, and Harry, you can sit here beside Bradley. Please guys, I'm relying on you lot to help them settle in, show them the ropes, answer any questions they've got, is everyone alright with that?"

09.50am

"Turn it over to four-three-two would you Chris?"

"Here you are," Christine said, grabbing the Sky remote from behind the bar and handing it over, "you can do it yourself."

Every morning was the same with them lot. Five or six of them would turn up, ages ranging from their mid-twenties to their mid-sixties, all standing outside awaiting opening time. Then they'd spend the day flitting back and forth between the pub and the betting shop, leaving little blue pens and scrunched up betting slips all over the place in the process. Every few minutes they'd be asking for the channel to be changed to catch another race. Christine had long since learned that the best way to make light of the burden they laid upon the bar staff was to hand over the Sky remote and let them get on with it.

"You ought to knock that bloody wall through," she'd said to many a manager in the long years she'd spent in The King's Arms' service. But, licensing laws are licensing laws, and as such, there was probably some prohibition or another about serving pints and taking bets in the same building. So the artifice remained, and the horse racing guys would spend their mornings dashing back-and-forth between the pub and their pints and the bookies and their betting slips.

"Who's this coming up now?" said Ken, sat at the end of the bar, one hand upon a nice early morning pint of ale. With his greasy grey hair slicked back and down almost to the shoulders of his decades-old faded black leather jacket, Ken was the kind of customer for whom the term 'local' was invented. He'd been drinking in the same pub for years, since he was a young rocker hell-raiser with a full set of only slightly-yellowed teeth.

"Who?" Christine shouted back at him.

"This mush by here in the red Volvo," Ken said, looking out the window at the car in question, which had just pulled up outside. "That car's older than this bloody pub mun."

"My Dad used to drive a Volvo," she said, always internalising the external. "Safest cars on the road, they are."

"I doubt that one bloody is," Ken laughed. "Twenty years ago, maybe, but it's not now!"

They watched as Rory emerged from the driver's side door, that middle-aged, beer-bellied, blonde beast of a man being more or less the sort you might expect to be driving around in a haggard old Volvo. Ken and Christine's interest levels rose quickly as they saw a slim young Asian girl get out from the passenger seat.

Ken instinctively looked away as the unlikely duo of Rory Gallagher and Kang Ji Eun entered the pub and approached Christine at the bar.

"I'll take a pint o' Rev. James," Rory said, after scanning the ale pumps, "and..."

Ji Eun glanced at the beer pumps and the bottles of spirits beyond the bar; under pressure, she simply said, "I'll have the same."

"Two Reverend Jameses," Christine said, flying into action with the pint glasses. As she started pouring out the first, she looked upon Ji Eun's youthful features. "I'm sorry love, but do you have any I.D. on you?"

"Sure," Ji Eun said, a little embarrassed, but prepared for this eventuality. She handed over her student card. Christine gave it the once over and handed it back.

"Sorry, we've got to do it, see," Christine said, "'Think Thirty' is the policy now, and if you look under thirty, we've gorra ask you for I.D."

"I notice ye dinnae want tae see mine?" Rory said.

"Well," Christine said, trying to think of something funny to say. 'Well' was enough, and Rory greeted it with a big burst of mirthful laughter.

"I tell ya wha', I could do wi' a pint this morning," Rory said, placing his elbows upon the bar and leaning in towards the barmaid, trying to conjure up an air of closeness. "I was woken up by a load of sirens blaring late last night. I dunnae suppose you'd've heard anything about wha' might'f been tha source o' it?"

"Whereabouts are you living?" Christine asked, placing the first full pint glass upon the bar top and bringing the second one to the pump.

"Trecenydd."

"It'll've been that girl what got assaulted, probably," Christine said, shaking her head at the horror of it. "That was in Treccy, weren't it?"

"Oh aye?" Rory said, feigning ignorance.

"Yeah, someone smacked her in the head with a bloody car steering wheel lock, didn't they?"

"Oh my."

"Yeah, isn't it awful? Poor things in hospital and still not come round, last I heard."

"Would tha' be Caerphilly Miners hospital?"

"No, the Miner's've been closed down ages now. I think it was the Gwent in Newport that they rushed her to."

"God," Rory said, shaking his head and lifting his pint to his lips, "why the hell would someone want tae hit a girl wi' a damn steering wheel loch?"

"Bloody madness," Christine replied, handing the other pint glass over to Ji Eun. "Four pounds thirty-eight for them, please."

Rory handed over a fiver: "D'ya have any idea who she is?"

"Yeah, it was that Matthews girl, weren't it?" Christine answered, popping the till open and getting Rory's change out. "Bloomin' what's-her-name?"

"Vicky Matthews," Ken answered.

"Vicky Matthews, that's the one," Christine said, handing the change over. "Only about nineteen she is."

"Jesus," Rory said, shaking his head at the horrid absurdity of it. "Why tha hell would someone want tae attack a young girl like tha'?"

"It's them dickheads she do hang out with," Ken answered. "That Mark Watts feller, he's a liability, him."

"Mark Watts?" Rory repeated.

"Yeah, he's banned from here, i'n' he?" Christine concurred.

"He's banned from every pub in blooming town," Ken corrected her.

"So do you reckon it's him what done it?" Christine asked.

"It weren't him what done it," answered Ken, "no, but he was with her when it happened. There was a big scrap, weren't there? Two groups of lads going at it. From what I've heard, she got caught up in the middle of it. Probably one of the other lot what done it."

"Who were they then?" Christine asked.

"God knows," answered Ken, "but if you carry on like Mark bloody Watts does, you won't have to look far for a scrap with someone."

Rory sized up the information he'd been given; he'd already known the girl's name, even thought it hadn't been 'officially' released to the press yet, but Mark Watts was a new one. And if he really was banned from every pub in Caerphilly, there weren't much chance of finding him in The King's on a Wednesday morning. Besides, he now knew which hospital's corridors he ought to be skulking around in. It seemed likely that he'd gleaned as much information from the barmaid and the old greasy rocker as he'd be likely to without getting awkward with the questioning. No, the most sensible thing to do now would be to retreat to the beer garden for a cigarette and, after that, head to the hospital, then perhaps on the hunt for this Mark Watts character. "What a world we're living in, eh?"

Christine and Ken watched as Ji Eun trudged along behind Rory, out the back door to the beer garden, waiting for the door to shut behind them before commenting.

"How old was that bloody girl he was with?" Ken asked.

"Twenty," Christine answered.

"Duw."

"And she was a student."

"I figured she must've been a mail order bride."

"Well, it was a student card that she showed me."

"Lucky sod," Ken muttered, quietly enough that Christine wouldn't be able to judge him for it.

11.07am

What the fuck happened last night? The whole scene was a blur. He vaguely remembered the show in Clwb but none of what had followed. Danny Daggers sat up, his body stiff from the cold tiled floor. He was in a corridor, in the clothes he'd been wearing the night before. He felt dizzy and nauseous, a sure sign he'd been on the methadrone – a horrible drug with a horrible comedown. Ages after the once-legal MDMA/cocaine substitute had been outlawed, Cardiff was still flooded with it. He did a quick check of his personal belongings: he still had his wallet – there was no money inside, but he did find a little plastic bag with some white powder in there that he neither remembered picking up nor doing, but which provided an explanation for his enfeebled state; his pockets also contained a squashed and torn cigarette packet, Royals, with two and a half cigarettes inside, one of which was snapped at the base and unusable, the other of which was squashed but fine, along with a stub that ran about a quarter of the length of a cigarette, the rest of which he assumed had been crumbled off into a joint; there was also an equally squashed box of matches. No phone. *Bollocks.* He'd been using his backpack as a pillow. He unzipped it and hurriedly rifled through the mess of clothing inside. Amidst the crumpled T-shirts and boxer shorts were his prized Sennhauser headphones – *much better than Dre Beats*, he smugly reminded himself, *and half the price* – but his Lumia was nowhere to be seen. *Shit.* He'd lost his phone.

He used the matches to light up the remaining good cigarette, then stood scanning the corridor, searching his surroundings for some clue as to his location. The walls, cciling and floor were light and bland. There were a few sand-coloured wooden doors along it. A few notices were affixed to the wall, fire evacuation procedures and other blandly generic information. He guessed it to be a university halls. Where was he? *Cardiff.* He walked slowly to a window at the end of the corridor and stared down onto some railway tracks. Way down. He must've been about twenty storeys above ground level. He could see the buildings of the city surrounding the train station. It looked like a nice day.

11.24am

"Wait here," Rory ordered. Ji Eun stood and watched as he passed through the automatic doors and strode up to the reception desk.

"Hullo there," Rory began, addressing the plump middle-aged lady behind the desk. His thick Aberdeen bellow carried well enough that Ji Eun could make out most of what he said from beyond the sliding doors, though she was still having difficulty working out what the majority of it meant. "I wonder if ye can help me. My daughter was rushed intae here this morning. Some wee fucker brained her wi' a car steering wheel loch. Ye could'nae point me in her direction, could ye?"

"What's your daughter's name?"

"Vicky. Victoria. Victoria Matthews."

"And you are...?"

"Dave Matthews."

"Okay Mr. Matthews," the woman said, tapping away at the computer on the desk in front of her, "just let me check." She frowned as she stared at the screen. "Actually, Mr. Matthews, it appears that your daughter has already been discharged."

"Has she?"

Ji Eun stepped aside to let a family pushing an elderly patriarch in a wheelchair through the sliding doors; when she returned her attention to what was going on inside, Rory was already striding back towards her.

"She's already oot," Rory huffed, annoyed, as he fished in his pocket for his packet of cigarettes. "Fuckin' six-pounds-eighty it cost me tae park in this shitehole. National Health Service ma fuckin' arse." He lit up the cigarette and stood surveying the car park, and the street beyond it. "There's nary a fuckin' story in tha'. 'Girl gets smacked in head, wakes up several hours later and makes full recovery'. What sort'f a fuckin' headline is tha'?" Rory sighed, then spent the next minute smoking in silence. When he spoke again, his anger seemed to have subsided. "Y'know Ji Eun, I think tha' parking ticket I bought's good fir the next couple'f hours."

11.43am

"Ye much of a drinker back at home, Ji Eun?"

"Sometimes," Ji Eun answered, raising a pint glass to her lips.

"What're yir drinkin' over there? Soju, is it?"

"Yeah, soju, makgeolli..."

"Mak-guh-lee?" Rory grunted back, curious.

"It's a kind of milky drink. Alcohol. Made from rice."

"Can't seh I've tried i'. Where were you livin' over there?"

"Seoul."

"Big city girl, eh? Guess humdrum bollocksin' Cardiff must've bin a birruva culture shock tae ye?"

She let the words roll round her mind for a few seconds before attaining something approaching comprehension and offering up a response: "Yeah, it's quite different than Seoul."

"So what d'ye make o' Blighty then?"

She smiled politely and stared at him with wide-eyed bewilderment.

"Great Britian, Ji Eun," Rory clarified. "The UK. Blighty. Britannia. What d'ye think o' it?"

"It's good, yeah," she replied, uncertain, breaking off eye contact.

"Really?" he said, with the disbelief and inquisitive rigour of a hardened journalist.

"Yeah," she said, some tremor in her voice, the mask she'd politely placed upon her true feelings starting to crack.

"Ye dunnae need to be coy wiv me, Ji Eun – I'm a fuckin' Scot, I cannae stand tha Union. About a fortnight from now, we migh' well be shot o' it. And a good fuckin' jobby that'll be an' all."

"I mean, I guess there are some cultural differences, some things I don't quite understand about the place."

"Like wha'? Tha drinkin'?"

"Well, Koreans drink a lot too – the drinking I'm okay with."

"Two nations of alcoholics, eh?" Rory said, raising the Guinness glass to his mouth. He quickly realised he had already drunk the last of it. He tilted the glass to his mouth at an almost 90 degree angle anyway, in a vain attempt to save face by swallowing some of the light-brown foam left stubbornly clinging to the sides of the glass.

"Yeah, you could say that," Ji Eun continued, seemingly oblivious to his error, "the drinking's fine, but the food... not so much."

"Aye. Greasy shite and shitey service."

"Yeah, the service here is so bad," she said, starting to get into it. "I mean, almost everywhere you go, the staff are so cold and unfriendly. In Korea, customers would go crazy if the staff acted the way they do here."

"And I wudnae blame 'em. Take tha surly wee git who's been servin' us in this place. I'm no stranger tae Asia, y'know Ji Eun, and yir right, there's a world of fuckin' difference in tha standard o' service ye get there compared tae here."

"In Korea we have a phrase, 'the customer is king'."

"Aye, we got one o' them an' all – 'the customer's always right' – but these ignorant fuckers I keep runnin' intae at every establishment I frequent've obviously never fuckin' heard it before."

"And teenagers here are really scary."

"Aye, wi'v gorra nation of feral munchkins runnin' riot on our streets, nae question about tha'. I blame Thatcher meself, and all the cunts tha've followed her."

"But there are some things I do like better here. Staff are sometimes rude, but people are polite in a lot of other ways. Like, if you bump into someone on the street, they say sorry to you, even if it was totally your fault. In Korea, someone can walk straight into you and they won't even make eye contact afterwards." She paused for a second, as Rory smiled, silently basking in the unexpected warm flush of national pride. "But actually... that might be true during the daytime. But at night-time... I mean, like I said before, just drinking a lot doesn't bother me. But the way people behave after they've drunk a lot... ohmygod."

Rory nodded; the girl couldn't've been righter.

"I mean... *hol*... Friday, Saturday nights in Cardiff are like stepping into a war zone, or a riot or something... people running around screaming, attacking each other... and the amount of people who come up to me and, like, bow and say *konichiwa* or something... ugh," she concluded, shuddering at the memory of it. "People here are so reserved and kind of... cold and self-interested all the rest of the time, you know what I mean? And then they drink some alcohol and they turn into monsters."

Rory said nothing.

"Sorry," Ji Eun said, blushing, lowering her eyes, Rory's silence and previously-established fondness of alcohol leading her to believe she must've offended him with her critique of British drinking culture.

"Ye dunnae need tae be sorry," he said, smiling. "Everything ye said were spot fuckin' on. A lot o' ignorant fuckers in this country Ji Eun, tha's a given. I mean, '*konichiwa*'? Tha' must rile up a fuckin' Korean some, eh?"

"Yeah," she said, assuming 'rile up' meant irritate.

"I wonder if tha French and tha Germans and tha rest o' 'em ge' annoyed when they go abroad and everyone starts speaking tae 'em in English, eh? I mean, if a Frog or a Kraut walked intae a pub in Seoul, tha barman'd address 'em as if they were Yanks or Englishmen, yeh? 'Hello sir, what can I get for ye?'. All tha' type o' shite."

"I guess," Ji Eun said a few seconds later, just about grasping the gist of it.

"Aye, I cannae imagine they'd be all tha' happy wi' it. Or maybe they're expectin' it? Still, intention's everything, eh? World o' difference in a Korean barman welcoming a Eurotwat intae his establishment wi' a birra tha

Queen's Sassenach, and some pissed-up twat givvin' ye bother on account'f yir ethnicity."

Ji Eun just stared at him; *what is he saying? Something about the Queen?*

"No," Rory said, attempting to allay her bewilderment, "I dunnae imagine ye Koreans are too fond of them there Japanese an' all though, are ye?"

"No," Ji Eun said, laughing at the understatement. "Actually, a lot of Koreans call UK the Japan of Europe."

"Do they now?" Rory said.

Ji Eun could her feel her cheeks turning red from the booze and embarrassment; she was sure that would cause offence to a Briton.

"I did nae know that," Rory said, sounding far more intrigued than offended. "I suppose there are a few similarities, eh? Two island nations, both o' which once commanded large overseas empires."

"The personality is quite similar as well," Ji Eun said, Rory's tone reassuring and encouraging her. "On the surface, both country's are really polite – like I said before, the British are always apologising, and in Japan, the people really go out of their way to appear kind to you – but inside, you know, the mind is different. British people, when they drink, their true character comes out. And like you said, with the empires..."

"I suppose there's naw tae much polite in enslaving as much'f the world as ye can get yir hands on, eh?"

"Yeah. And we say Korea is like the Ireland of Asia."

"Do ye?" he said, smiling.

"Yeah. Divided nations. Both drink a lot. Both conquered by an aggressive neighbour."

"Aye," he said, nodding, "yir right an' all. And wha's China then? France?"

Ji Eun thought about it for a few moments: "I don't know... it's pretty big. I guess you could probably take it to be most of the European Union."

Rory smiled and nodded; the conversation withered. The thought of ordering another pint occurred to him. But then there was the spiralling cost of keeping his Volvo in the hospital car park to consider. No, another pint would be pushing it. Besides, he still had to drive back to Cardiff after they'd finished up in Newport. He took his iPhone from his pocket to check the time; *11.52.* Beneath that, in the centre of the screen, was notification of a tweet from the South Wales police force:

Prisnr absconded from HM Prescoed. V. dangerous. Dn't approach. Call us if u c him plz. #Fugitive #SWPolice #Nowhere2hide #Simon #Amstell

He slid his thumb across the bottom of the screen and then tapped in his passcode: 1985, the year Aberdeen last won the league. An accompanying TwitPic illustrated the @SWPolice announcement. Rory stared into the cold, callous face of a block-headed badass. He looked a right nasty bastard. Rory felt the hairs on the back of his neck stand up; the smell of blood and ink filled his nostrils. Somewhere nearby, news was occurring.

12.46pm

"The fuck are you watching butt?"

Darren Amstell didn't lift his eyes from the television set, though his older brother's booming voice drew his attention away from the high-pitched hysterics being broadcast. Two American women were screaming at one another in a car park. One was white and heavily tattooed; the other was black, with hair twisted into braids. Both were morbidly obese, squeezed into several-sizes too-small jeans and muffin-top revealing vests. Each adopted the same pose as they screamed at one another, arching the top halves of their bodies slightly forward, one hand placed upon a sizeable hip, their free hand wagging back and forth, gesticulating to emphasise the incomprehensible contents of their beep-strewn, heavily-edited, expletive-packed 'speech'.

"Storage Warriors," Darren replied softly.

"Wha'?" Bruce said, standing and staring at the screen from the doorway leading from his filth-smeared kitchen to his cluttered, unclean living room. He was wearing a several-seasons old Cardiff City shirt (blue, obviously) and black boxer shorts, and holding in his hand a butter knife with bits of butter and breadcrumbs plastered to it.

"Storage Warriors," Darren said again, louder and clearer.

"The fuck's wrong with them pair?"

"The white one's accusing the black one of gazumping her."

"Huh?" Bruce said, loud and agitated.

"The point of the show," Darren said, finally turning away from the television and resigning himself to explaining the shows entire premise to his brother, "is that these people go round to these places where they d'have all these storage lock-ups, they're like these garages you can rent out for storing stuff in. And if you rent out one of these lock-ups and you don't pay the money what you're meant to pay for it, eventually they'll give up on you and they'll auction off your stuff to the highest bidder. So these lot on here, these 'Storage Warriors', they do go round to these lock-ups and they do bid on all the stuff inside, sight unseen. The fella what does it all, he d'pop it open, let 'em 'ave a quick look from a distance, and if they like the look of it, they can bid on it, and if they makes the highest bid, then they gets to buy it all. And then these two now," Darren said, turning his head back toward the television screen, pointing at the two women, still screaming at one another, "they're havin' a bit of a tiff due to the white one thinks that the black ones been gazumping her."

"Right," Bruce said, getting the gist of it, "and what the fuck's 'gazumping' mean then?"

"Gazumping's when you're in an auction, and you do bid higher than you plan on paying just to jack the price up for everyone else."

"Why's she been doing that then?"

"Fuck knows, they're all mental on here. They do hate each other. Maybe she's just playing up for the cameras."

"You don't half watch some shit, aye," Bruce said, shaking his head and walking back into the kitchen, where the toaster had just popped.

"It's alright like," Darren said, defending the show, though his brother had given up on listening. "Some of the stuff they d'find's well tidy. We ought to find out if there's anywhere round here with one of them storage lock-ups – we might do alright out of it."

"Fucking 'Storage Warriors'," Bruce said to Kaiser, whilst slathering butter onto the toasted bread. "Have you heard, Kaiser?" Kaiser, Bruce's Doberman, was half-asleep, curled up in his basket beside the stove.

Buttering done, Bruce left the yellow-smeared knife upon the dirt-specked kitchen service and opened the fridge to retrieve a jar of Nutella. Kaiser suddenly leapt up from his sedate position and started barking uncontrollably.

"Shut the fuck up Kaiser!" Bruce snapped at him, to no avail, before turning to see the source of the commotion, a shadowy figure beyond the frosted glass of the back door. Leaving the fridge door ajar, he moved to answer it, then stared in stunned silence at the visitor; the third Amstell brother. Simon.

"S'apnin' bro?" Simon said. Bruce just stared, mouth agape. "You look like you seen a ghost butt." Simon brushed past his brother, making sure to push the door closed behind him. Then he pulled the hood from his head and spotted the toast upon the kitchen surface. "Making breakfast is it bro? Mind if I have a slice? I'm fucking starvin' butt."

Bruce stared in utter disbelief as his brother picked up a piece of toast and bit into it. *You look like you've seen a ghost.* The words echoed in his mind. *A ghost be fucked.* An apparition. *It must be.* He finally formulated some words as his brother munched noisily on his half-inched breakfast.

"When did you get out?"

"This morning," Simon said through a mouth full of breadcrumbs.

Bruce shook his head disbelievingly, then, certain the vision was real, he stepped forward and placed a hand upon his brothers shoulder. "Fuck. Good to see you butt."

"You too butt," Simon replied, shifting the toast to his left hand and tapping his brother on the shoulder with his freed-up right hand.

Bruce mulled the bizarre situation over as Simon tore off another chunk of toast and chewed.

"How the fuck did that happen then?" Bruce asked.

"How the fuck did what happen?"

"How the fuck did you get out this morning?"

"I left."

Bruce nodded falsely; he didn't understand. "What do you mean," he said finally, "you *left*?"

"Well, they let me out on day release, di'n't they? I was meant to go do a shift at Paul's Pies down in Bedwas, but instead of doing that, I hopped on a bus to the Brad to come and see my brawd. Simple as, butt."

"So... you done a runner?"

"That's one way of putting it."

Bruce shook his head again, staring, struck with ketaminesque disassociation from incomprehensible reality.

"What's the matter butt," Simon said, chewing on the last chunk of the first slice of toast, "ain't you happy to see me? It's been a while."

"Yeah... fuck... of course I am, but... fucking hell butt, it's just a bit of a shock, that's all."

Simon bent down to stroke Kaiser, who'd been excitedly sniffing round his legs the whole time he'd been in the kitchen, then strode past his brother, the dog following him, into the living room.

"S'apnin' butt?" Simon said to his youngest brother, while Bruce staggered back into the doorway to survey the scene, shell-shocked.

"S'apnin'," Darren said automatically, eyes still on the television screen, before a flicker of comprehension tore his attention away. "Simon!" He rose to his feet with the same level of excitement Kaiser had shot up with moments earlier. He embraced his eldest brother in a quick hug. "Fuck me butt, what're you doing here?"

"I done a runner." Simon said, smiling knowingly towards Bruce.

"Fuck," Darren replied.

"What the fuck's happened to you?" Simon said, suddenly noticing the heavy bruising around Darren's left eye and on his cheek, along with the skewiff crook of his previously-straight nose.

"Nothing. Just had a bit of a scrap last night, tha's all."

"Yeah? Who was tha' with then?"

"He won't tell me nothing," interrupted Bruce. "I think someone's given him a bit of a hiding and he's afraid of them, he is."

"It's nothing, honestly."

"Fuck tha'," Simon declared. "It don't look like nothing. I'm not having no brother of mine running round being scared of no-one. Whoever done this to you obviously didn't bet on your big brother Simon being around to give 'em a seeing to, did they?"

"Honestly Si, they got the worst of it," Darren said, staring into his brothers eyes with real sincerity. "All I've come away with is a few scrapes and bruises, I put them in fucking hospital."

Simon stared into his youngest brother's eyes for several seconds before nodding. "Fair enough."

Simon stepped forward and sank down into the armchair in which his youngest brother had just been reclining.

"What the fuck are you doing out early then?" asked Darren.

"I've had a fucking guts full butt," Simon said, staring at the television screen, flicking through the channel selector with the remote control. "I done my time. Done more than my time, matter of fact. Much more. Fuck that gash, waiting for them to tell me when I can go. Time to take control, bro. Time to take my life back."

"So," Darren said, slowly. "What's the plan now 'en?"

"Taking my life back, butt," Simon said, looking up at him. "Long story short, I met a feller in clink what's got connections. Said he can sort me out. I'm leaving the country butt, just as soon as I've got my shit sorted. Heading off to Spain, to live the life of Riley, as they d'say. He's got some job for me to do out there. Nice weather, decent paycheck, tidy lifestyle."

"Sound," Darren replied. "So what you doing here then?"

"I came to see my little brothers, obviously. Say my goodbyes and all that. And ask you for a bit of help, truth be told." He stopped with the remote control as he settled on the desired channel - BBC News. A story about a respected elder statesman of the entertainment industry being investigated for decades-old allegations of sexual assault was being broadcast. "I take it from the shock on your faces when you first saw my beautiful mug that you've not heard off the coppers?"

"Nah," Darren said, glancing at Bruce to confirm it; Bruce was still glaring dumbly at Simon from the doorway.

"Well I expect you will, soon enough. They'll probably be tripping over themselves looking for me once they've noticed I've scarpered. That's why we've got to act quick, like. See, there's a couple of things I need sorting before I fuck off out the country. Couple of things I was hoping you two might be able to help me with."

"'Course butt," Darren said, seating himself down upon the sofa. He was quickly joined by Kaiser, who'd until this point been sitting besides the armchair, tongue hanging out, wagging his tail and staring up at Simon. Darren stroked the dog as it rested its head upon his lap. "You name it, we'll do it. Least we can do, all that you've done for us."

"Cheers butt, I appreciate you saying that. You've always had a heart of gold, you Dar. You knows what's important, like. Family. Family means the world to you, and me and all, and I've realised that all the more being banged up, with that fucking tart keeping my own flesh and blood away from me. Fucking wrong of the corrections system that. Big fucking wrong. What fucking right's that bitch got to keep my own fucking seed away from me?"

Darren stared at his brother blankly, not having a clue what he was getting at, but mesmerised by the passion of his speech all the same. For his part, Bruce was still in the doorway, confused as fuck, a million miles from transitioning disbelief into acceptance.

"Fucking women, butt. You got a girlfriend yet, Dar?"

"Nah."

"Good," Simon replied. "Don't bother. They'll all fuck you over in the end. Cunts and whores the fucking lot of them. That fucking slag, word going round is she's got a new man now. Shacked up together. Living with my fucking son, my fucking Daniel. Raising him as his fucking own. Not on, is it?"

"No," Darren said softly, spellbound.

"A son needs his father, know what I mean? I know you was too young when he went to remember our old man Dar, but he thought the fucking world of us, didn't he Bruce?"

"Yeah," Bruce responded, his voice shaking.

"Me and Bruce went through hell when he popped it. Not half as bad as what Mam must've went through, mind. But we did what we could to help, and that's why we've always looked out for you Dar; a kid needs his dad. You didn't have that luxury, so we tried to be as close to a father to you as we possibly could. Didn't we, Bruce?"

"Yeah... yeah."

"But Daniel, well, Daniel ain't got no older brothers to look out for him, have he? And have either of you seen him lately?"

"No," answered Darren.

"Bet you've not seen him once since I've been banged up, have you?"

"Nah," Darren answered again, "we haven't."

"Me neither. Me fucking neither. What sort of life's that for a child? Cut off from your family, while your cunt of a mother shacks up with some prick, some arsehole fucking stepfather? He don't need a fucking stepfather, do he? Not when he's got his uncles around, not when he's got his fucking father around." Simon let silence hang in the air as he focused his eyes upon the television screen, which was now relaying a report on something to do with hospitals and the NHS. "You know, in biblical times, if a man died, it was expected that his brother would marry the widow. Did you ever hear that?"

"Nah," Darren said again.

"Nah. Not a lot of people have. It's true, though. Now, I'm not saying I'd want one of you two to take my place while I was locked up, and shacked yourself up with Jodie. Not at all. I wouldn't wish living with that cunt on my worst fucking enemy. But what I'm saying is, with me out the picture, if Daniel can't be seeing his daddy, then his uncles ought to be the next best thing, know what I mean? It's his uncles who ought've taken my place, not some cunt who's been shipped into the house 'cause that slut wants servicing. Nah, well, anyway, none of that fucking matters now. I'm out now. I'm out and I'm off. Off out the fucking country. And I'm taking my son with me."

Simon looked at each of his brothers in turn, trying to gauge their reaction to that bombshell, the one he'd spent the past few months brooding on. Darren looked game; awe-struck, deferential. He'd always been a good kid. Bruce didn't look like he knew what the fuck was going on. Simon figured he'd get past that sooner or later. Maybe he needed a cuppa. A cup of tea and a joint, that ought to chill him out a bit.

"So, bro," Simon said, addressing Bruce, "the million pound question: have you got any spliff on you?"

01.03pm

Joseph was out of breath by the time he'd dodged passed doddering shoppers and reached the top of the staircase in the strip-lit consumerist mecca of St. David's 2. He'd sprinted near-enough full-pelt from work, and had travelled the short distance across the Hayes from the Mitchell-Loveridge building in thirty seconds or less, severely knackering himself in the process. *Still,* he thought, breathing heavily as he stood static on an escalator ascending to the first floor, a little old lady in front impeding any attempt he might make to walk up, *I shouldn't be this fucked after ninety seconds exercise.* Maybe it was time to quit smoking.

He'd gotten a good percentage of his breath back in about half the time it'd taken him to lose it, but was still a bit gassed as he strode in through the open shopfront of Dezrkr8. He saw Jodie, at the counter, busy with a customer. He watched her until she was done, breathing heavily all the while, then walked across the store towards her. She smiled when she first saw him, green eyes lighting up, before her face darkened and a scowl spread across it.

"Joe," she said as he reached her, "I thought I told you not to come in here when I'm working? You knows what Sandra's like."

"Yeah, I know love, and normally I wouldn't, but I tried phoning you and I couldn't get through."

"Of course you couldn't. I'm working."

"I know, but I gots something important that I need to tell you."

"Yeah? What's up? Nobody's died have they?"

"Nah," Joseph said, a look of supreme seriousness upon his face.

"Oh shit, you've not been fired have you?"

"Nah, nah, of course not. It's... it's Simon."

"Simon?"

"He's done a runner."

"Done a runner? What do you mean, he's done a runner?"

"He's done a runner, Jode. They let him out on day release and he's not gone back in."

Jodie stared off across the store. Sandra emerged from the stock room with an armful of hoodies and, upon seeing Joe at the counter, fixed her with a menacing stare. *Bitch.* Joseph studied Jodie's face; she was betraying little sign of concern. Perhaps she hadn't heard him right, or maybe the news just hadn't sunk in yet.

"The fuzz've put a notice out on Facebook about it," Joseph said, expositioning in an attempt to coax a reaction out of her. "I saw it on one of the lads' computers in work earlier. Apparently, they're out looking for him. Fucking should be, anyway. I don't know," he said, giving up, neither a reaction nor a return to eye contact forthcoming. "What do you reckon we should do about it?"

"What do you mean, 'what should we do about it?'" Jodie asked, finally turning her head back to face him. "It's not our fucking problem. Me and Simon are divorced, Joe."

"Yeah, I knows that, but what about... Daniel?"

He'd hesitated before bringing the name of her son into the equation. He instantly felt he'd been right to be reticent; Jodie again broke off eye contact, staring down at a chip in the wood of the counter that stood between them, ruminating.

"I don't know," she said, looking up with a sudden shudder. "I'm off at three today. I'll go round my mum's house straight after. Maybe we ought to stay there until Simon goes back in.

Joseph nodded; that seemed sensible. "Do you want me to come round after work?"

"Nah, you knows what my mum's like. She don't want me bringing strange men into her house."

Before he could protest the adjective, she'd leant across the counter and kissed him. Out of the corner of her eye, she caught Sandra giving her evils. *Cunt.* "Look Joe, don't worry about it. If he really has done a runner, and the cops don't catch him, chances are it'll be the last we'll ever see of him. Maybe it'll actually be the best thing for us. He'll probably fuck off out the country, go and live in Spain or something. I don't see why he'd suddenly start sniffing round me and Daniel. It's not like he gave much of a shit about us before he was banged up like, know what I mean? Me and Daniel'll stay at my mam's house for the time being, just to be on the safe side, but I really wouldn't worry about it."

"You sure you wouldn't feel safer if I was staying round your mam's house with you?"

"Nah, Joe, you really don't have to. Even if he did try and find us, which he'd never in a million years do anyway, he won't have a clue how to find my mam's place. She's listed under a fake name, i'n'she? After that debt thing a couple of years back. You'd better go anyway Joe, that cunt Sandra's been giving me evils the whole time you've been in here. Thanks for coming to tell me anyway. I'll give you a call later, alright babes?"

"Yeah, alright," Joseph said, glancing over at Sandra and offering up an apologetic smile; it did nothing to change her slapped-arse expression, though his attention was enough to get her to look away from the counter and get back to serious business of replenishing stock on the shop floor.

01.11pm

"This is a nice bit of bud this bro," Simon said, gently rolling the grey accumulation of ash at the end of the spliff into the ashtray. "Who'd you get it off?"

"Hippie Jack," Bruce answered, his voice shaky. He was sat on the edge of his seat upon the sofa opposite, leaning forward, elbows resting on his legs, hands clasped prayer-like in front of him. Simon reached across the living room and held the spliff out to him, hoping it'd calm him down a bit. Bruce took it from him, sat back and inhaled deeply.

"Hippie Jack," Simon said thoughtfully. "He still driving that old camper van about?"

"Nah," Bruce said, exhaling a cloud of smoke as he did so. "I think he sold it."

"I don't suppose you've smoked any of this stuff in ages, have you?" Darren asked, looking far more relaxed than Bruce, sitting at the opposite end of the sofa, Kaiser curled up on the middle seat between them, his head resting in Darren's lap.

Simon smiled at the childlike naiveté of his younger brother's question.

"There's no shortage of dope in clink, bro. The place fucking reeks of the stuff. No shortage of nothing in the nick, like. It's easier to pick up in there than it is outside."

Darren nodded, soaking up his eldest brother's wisdom like a sponge.

"There's more skagheads picked up the habit in clink than anywhere," Simon added. "Who else you still knocking about with these days? Snickers still around?"

"Nah," Bruce said, his voice having become ever-so-slightly calmer. "Snickers's living with his missus now. Not seen head nor tail of him almost the whole time you've been inside."

"Yeah?" Simon said, slightly surprised. "Didn't think he'd ever settle down. Who was that gomping bird he boned outside the rugby club? Suzanna was it?"

"Sophia," Bruce corrected him. "Sophia Grace."

"Sophia Grace," Simon smiled, remembering. "Sophia Disgrace more like. Fuck, she was a wrong 'un. How about you, Bru? You shagging anyone these days?"

"Nah," Bruce said, finally smiling, "no-one serious, anyway. You know what I'm like; treat 'em mean, keep 'em keen."

"Treat 'em to dinner and go home for a wank more like," Simon smiled back at him. The weed was working its magic. "I'm one to talk, anyway. Not had my end away in near enough two fucking years like."

"You been keeping the soap under control in the shower then, have you butt?" Bruce joked.

"No need butt," Simon smiled back. "They know better than to try that shit with me, like. I'd rip their fucking balls off, any cunt tried anything funny."

"So what's it like inside then?" Darren asked, eager, with the wide-eyed wonder of one who'd never been held at Her Majesty's pleasure.

"It's fucking boring, to be honest with you," Simon answered. "You plays some Playstation, do some reading, lift some weights like, sit around talking shit, and that's the end of it."

"What've you been reading?" Bruce smirked. "They've got the Beano in the prison library, do they?"

"I've been reading all sorts bro," Simon smiled back. "I read Howard Marks book, that's a cracker. You know Howard Marks, boys?"

"Nah," Darren said.

"Ain't he that old pot head?" Bruce asked, inhaling smoke.

"Yeah," Simon said. "His life story's mental. Started out just like any other Valleys boy, like, like you or me, but he was smart as fuck, so he got into Oxford, or Cambridge, or one of them, studying astro-physics or some shit. In the sixties, like, so weed was just kicking off. So he got into dealing it. Next thing you know, he's got this multi-million pound drugs empire, importing and exporting globally, running it in and out of America, flying back-and-forth to Pakistan, he's got a holiday home in Spain, the fucking works like."

"Legend," Darren said.

"Yeah," Simon agreed. "It was well informative."

"So they're basically stocking how-to guides for wannabe drug smugglers in the prison library then?" Bruce said, laughing at the thought of it, big cloud of smoke coming out as he did so.

They sat in contemplative silence for the next few moments, the low-volume voice of the BBC newsreader on the TV rattling out a string of vocab relating to the upcoming referendum on Scottish independence. Kaiser, sleeping, moved his mouth with a sloshing of saliva. Darren was the next to speak. "What part of Spain are you planning on fucking off to then?"

"Costa del Somewhere," Simon said. "Porta del Something-or-other. I don't remember exactly."

"And when you going?"

"Soon as bro." Simon said, suddenly becoming serious. "Soon as I get my son back."

Bruce took a final toke on the spliff and handed it over to Darren. Bruce then held the smoke in his lungs, waiting on the eldest Amstell brother to speak. He wasn't waiting long.

"So what you saying then, boys? You gonna help me out?"

Bruce breathed out and stared at the television screen, taking no notice of the small crowd waving saltires outside a pub somewhere in Glasgow. He just wanted to focus his eyes on something other than his eldest brother's expectant stare while he collected his thoughts.

"What exactly do you want from us?" Bruce asked, thoughts collected.

"I want you to help me get my son back."

"And how are we meant to do that then?"

"Well," Simon said, sitting forward, perching his arms on top of his legs prayer-like, mirroring the pose the passing of a spliff had brought his brother out of, "I'm thinking we book a flight to Spain for later on this evening. I'll go wait at the airport. One of you, or both of you, go to Jodie's house, grab Daniel, and bring him to me."

Silence.

"Easy as that, yeah?" said Bruce, several seconds later.

"Why not?" said Simon.

"Well, first thing's first, if you've done a runner, then you book a flight, don't you think there might be something what flags up on the copper's computers? Some sort of warning that a wanted criminal's just booked a flight out of the fucking country? They'll be looking out for your passport number, won't they?"

"Spain's in the E.U. butt," Simon corrected him. "You don't even need a passport to travel there. All you need is some I.D. Anything'll do. A fucking driver's license'll get you through customs bro."

"Customs, maybe, but you need a passport number to book the flight."

"No you don't bro. E.U. I.D.-free travel. Fucking Scheizer zone, or whatever they call it."

"Schengen zone," Bruce corrected him, "and you still need a passport number to book the flight."

"No you don't bro."

"I'm telling you you do," Bruce said, getting irritated. "I went with some of the boys to Majorca last summer. I'm telling you now, when we booked the flight we needed passport numbers. It won't let you go through the thing on the website without one."

"Well..." Simon said slowly, checking his tone to avoid vexing his brother further, "what if I borrowed one of yours?"

Bruce looked at Darren; he was looking at the dog, petting its head, oblivious.

"What happens to us then? After? After you've fled the fucking country with your kid in tow under our passport details? Do you not think we might get in a bit of fucking bother with the five-oh over that one?"

Simon nodded; Bruce was right. They'd be accessories to kidnap, at best. There were probably a fair few other laws that action might fall afoul of.

"Not yours then," Simon agreed. "What about someone else's?"

"Like whose?" Bruce shot back.

"I don't know, anyone. Some fucking skaghead or something. It's not like they'll have any holiday plans we'll be interfering with."

"Yeah, and how many skagheads do you know who've got valid fucking passports?"

"Well get one of 'em to bust in someone's house and nick one or something," Simon suggested. "They'll do anything for a dig, won't they?"

"Alright, let's say we do get hold of a passport from somewhere," Bruce said, conceding that one, "what about Daniel?"

"What about him?"

"Where're you going to get a passport for him from?"

"Just get it when you get him," Simon said, as if it were the most obvious answer in the world. "Take his passport from the house like."

"How fucking old is he butt?" Bruce shot back. "Six? Seven?"

"Six," Simon said, imbuing his words with an entirely false sense of certainty.

"He's six. So he won't have his own fucking passport, will he? He'll be on his mother's, if anything."

Simon nodded; valid point. "Okay then, we'll just have to nick one with a dependant listed on it, won't we?"

"I suppose we will, yeah," Bruce said, looking over at Darren, who was still stroking Kaiser's head like a fucking idiot.

"Look butt," Simon said, suddenly tiring of his brother's nay-saying, "are you gonna help me or am I gonna have to do this all by my fucking self? 'Cause one or way or another, I'm going to Spain, and I am taking my son with me."

"I'm trying to help you," Bruce yelled back. "I'm trying to save you from making some big fucking mistake that'll wind up landing you behind bars for the rest of your natural fucking life!"

Simon smiled. *The rest of your natural life. Fucking drama queen.*

"You can laugh it off all you fucking want," Bruce declared, "but think it through butt. What you're saying we do here is a bit more serious than the twatting of some twat that got you banged up for near-enough two years in the first place." He held his hand out to count off the charges one-by-one on his fat, sausage-like fingers. "Doing a runner from prison – double your original sentence, at the least, I'd imagine. Kidnap – five to ten years, fucking easy. Stealing a passport – what's that? On top of everything else, you're gonna get another six months for that if you're lucky. Very lucky. Then impersonating some cunt to slip through customs. Fucking a year or two extra for that, no doubt. Double, actually; there'll be two charges if you're passing Daniel through as some other cunt's son, won't there? Then what? Let's say you do make it to Spain; that'll bump the charges up, surely. Crossing international borders, yeah? Multiply all the ones I've already told you by about three or four, and what's that?" Bruce broke off his ranting and looked up at the ceiling, turning the numbers over in his mind whilst adding some of them up on his aforementioned fat sausage fingers.

"That's only if we get caught bro," Simon said calmly, finally, smiling. "That's only if I get caught."

Bruce broke off counting to stare at his brother; he was actually serious about going through with this nonsense.

"I'll be waiting at the airport, yeah? We'll put the word out this afternoon, let it be known that I'm looking for a passport with a child dependant on it – one off someone who's at least half as pretty as me, if at all possible. We'll make sure it's nabbed as discreetly as possible, so no-one's likely to notice it missing between now and tomorrow morning. Then we'll get the flights booked. I'll go hang out somewhere near the airport. Far enough away that I'm not exposed and on CCTV the whole time we're waiting for the flight to come in. You go grab Daniel, bring him to me, I'll pop into the airport with him as close to departure time as possible, and there we go: job's a good 'un."

"Job's a fucking good 'un," Bruce muttered dismissively.

"So alls we need this afternoon is that passport," Simon reiterated.

"Do you remember when I had that job in that call centre?" Darren said suddenly.

"What, that job you lasted all of two fucking days in?" Bruce snapped back.

"Yeah, and remember when I got fired? I had to go back like a week later to get my passport, didn't I?"

"You did, yeah," Bruce said slowly, worried; a plan was actually starting to form.

"What's that?" Simon said, interest piqued.

"They took my passport for verifying my details or whatever," Darren explained. "Criminal records check and tha'."

"So..." Simon said, prompting further explanation.

"So what are the fucking odds that a father has, in the past two days, joined the sales force at that same fucking call centre that you got fucking fired from?" Bruce interjected angrily.

"It don't need to be the same place though, do it?" answered Darren. "I mean, all kinds of jobs do that type of thing, don't they? Especially if they're data handling, like. We just need to have a look on the internet, see if there's any places that've had job ads out in the past month or so, and from there we should be able to work out who's likely to have had new staff in."

"Then walk in near the close of business and rob off with one of their fucking passports," Simon said, smiling proudly at his younger brother. "You're a fucking genius, you, Dar."

Bruce's upper body collapsed forward; he sat on the edge of his seat, arms resting upon his leg, holding his head in his hands. It was really fucking happen. *This is really fucking happening.*

"Right then," Simon said, clapping his hands together, "go get your laptop and start looking up some job postings."

He stared at Bruce, who was staring at the television screen, where waving saltires having now given way to slow zooms on photographs of hostages being held by ISIS.

"Bruce?" Simon repeated.

The middle Amstell brother looked up, a dazed look upon his face.

"Go and get your laptop butt."

"I haven't got one," Bruce replied.

"Wha'?"

"I haven't got one."

"You haven't got a laptop?"

"No," Bruce repeated.

"Well then go start up your computer then," Simon re-worded, "you knows what I fucking mean like."

"I've not got a computer butt."

"What do you mean, you haven't got a computer?"

"I mean I haven't got a fucking computer butt," Bruce said again.

"Fucking hell mun butt, it's the twenty-first fucking century like. You got a smartphone?"

Bruce shook his head; no.

"A fucking iPad? Fucking anything what can connect to the internet?"

Bruce shook his head again. Nothing.

"Fuck's sake mun butt," Simon spat. "How the fuck can you live without a fucking computer?"

"What do I need a fucking computer for butt?" asked Bruce.

"Darren?"

He shook his head.

"Fuck's sake mun boys. How the fuck do you two function without fucking internet access?"

"Jonesy've got one," Bruce said. He regretted saying it the second he'd done so; he would've welcomed anything that would've delayed or halted his elder brother's bat-shit crazy plan.

Darren jolted, as if suddenly stung by static electricity, upon hearing Jonesy's name. He quickly glanced at each brother in succession, but saw they were too engrossed in each other to have noticed Darren's involuntary action, though it had woken Kaiser up, the dog struggling to open heavy eyelids as its head remained in Darren's lap.

"Alright then," Simon smiled, crisis averted. "You two go pay Jonesy a visit. Have a gander on the internet, see what jobs are about. Then we'll get ourselves a fucking passport."

02.23pm

The BLTs played through tinny iPhone speakers as the teens sat cross-legged on the long stretch of grass in front of the museum: *"Oil fuel bare oppression, / Oil fuel endless war. / Oil enable government / To feed da rich and starve da poor..."* Taggard lazily rolled his eyes over the other groups dotted about the little island of greenery at the city centre's edge, flanked by a road heaving with traffic filtering in and out of Cardiff. *"...Oil greases da bad man palm, / Oil lubricate de act of rape..."* Taggard closed his eyes and took in a deep toke of marijuana smoke. When he re-opened his eyes, Johnny was staring at him angrily.

"That's four you've had now Tag."

Taggard stared at Johnny for several seconds before realising what the problem was.

"Sorry," he said, spluttering out smoke and awkwardly thrusting his joint-wielding arm in Johnny's direction.

"Do you recognise that guy over there?" Kayleigh asked, directing the gang's attention toward a figure making its way across the grass towards them.

"I think you're getting stoned Kayl," Johnny said.

"Nah, I'm serious," Kayleigh protested. "I swear I recognise him from somewhere."

"Yeah, I think I do and all," Teresa added. "I think he's someone famous."

Johnny passed the spliff to Kayleigh and the teens stared and squinted in silence, their faces scrunched up from the twin efforts of looking and remembering.

"It's that guy off YouTube, innit?" Taggard suggested.

"Yeah!" Teresa said. "Whasisname?"

Danny Daggers' morning had seen him radiate out from the student halls nestled at the side of Cardiff Central station and move through the city centre in ever-expanding circles. He'd stopped and rested quite a few times, first to buy tobacco and skins, then for a fry up and a hangover-busting pint of Kronenbourg at one of the city's countless Wetherspoons, then plenty more times just to roll up and smoke. He had grown bored and tired by the time he reached the grass in front of the museum. He had every intention of lying down upon the grass and passing out for a couple of hours, using his backpack as a pillow. He cursed the loss of his aviators, which could've blocked out the sun and made sleeping easier. This thought reminded him of the far bigger problem of his lost Lumia. The depressing thought of the lost mobile prompted him to ponder getting out of Cardiff. *A few hours kip, get to an internet caff, book the Megabus, fuck off home. Wales is doing my fucking head in.*

He stopped walking upon noticing the group, sat cross-legged on the grass, staring at him. People were usually alright, generally speaking, but he'd had the shit kicked out of him in Newcastle by a group of lads familiar with his work, and had also had a narrow escape on Liverpool's Matthew's Street, which had ended up with him legging it half-way to Lime Street station, which had in itself drawn more unwanted shouts of Scouse attention. Being a quasi-celebrity wasn't always to one's advantage. He scanned the group and made a quick mental judgement. Half of them were girls, which was a double-plus, because it meant he was 50% less likely to get his arse kicked and, well, they were girls. Girls who looked like they'd heard of him. And then there was the cloud of smoke rising slowly up from the group, and the fact that only one member of the group was holding anything that could be responsible for that, which meant a J was far more likely than a cigarette. *Girls and weed.* Danny made up his mind and carried on walking toward them.

01.26pm

"S'apnin' boys?"

"S'apnin' Jonesy! Fuckin' hell butt, what happened to you?"

"You're brother didn't tell you, did he?"

Bruce looked at Darren behind him, then glanced back at Jonesy's face; the large white bandage affixed to his right cheek, and the cuts and bruising around his left eye. "He was a bit fuckin' vague to be honest with you."

Jonesy looked at Darren, who stared him into silence with those sullen, sunken eyes of his.

"The same fucker had the pair of you, did he?"

"Well," Jonesy said, looking back at Bruce, unable to dodge a direct question from the elder brother to appease the death stare of the young 'un, "we got in a bit of a scrap, we did. Others come off worse, mind."

"Where to?"

"Up Treccy way. Ran into a couple of boys at the Dip garage, we did."

"Yeah? What boys were they then?"

"Mark Watts and a few of his mates."

"Mark Watts," Bruce repeated, trying to put a face to the name, "Mark Watts... he's that fucker with the weird voice 'i'n'he? Proper fucking gruff like."

"That's it. The fucking gruffalo, some people do call him."

"What'd he do to your cheek then?"

"He fuckin' bit me, didn' he?"

"Bit you?"

"Yeah."

"Fucking hell mun! You wanna watch out with that butt, fucking biting! You might get fucking tetanus or something."

"I think it's alright."

"Have you been to the doctors?"

"Nah, but it'll be alright."

"Have you had your jabs and that?"

"I think so."

"When?"

"Year Eleven."

"Year Eleven?"

"Yeah."

"Year Eleven at school?"

"Yeah."

"When you were sixteen years-old?"

"Yeah."

"And how old are you now butt?"

"Thirty-two."

"Thirty-two. How long do you think them fucking jabs last butt? Honestly butt, you wanna get to the doctors, get it looked at. Dirty cunt like the fucking gruffalo, fuck knows where his mouth've been."

"Maybe, maybe. What are you two after, anyway?"

"Well, I was wondering if you might do us a favour," Bruce explained. "I needs to get on a computer to do some stuff for my job seeker's I do, and well, mine's on the blink at the moment. Sorry to trouble you and tha', but I was wondering if you wouldn't mind letting us have a go on yours for a bit?"

"Aye, no problem boys," Jonesy said, pushing his ajar front door completely open. "Crack on."

They followed him in through the carpeted hallway to a tastefully decorated crème-walled living room, 40-inch telly in one corner of it, a computer desk in another. A black sofa with purple cushions sat beneath a hodge-podge of picture frames on the wall above.

"Cheers for this butt," Bruce said, following Jonesy to the PC.

"No problem butt. I know what they're like down the Job Centre; absolute wankers, i'n' they?"

"Aye."

Darren stood in the middle of the room, glancing over the picture frames, filled with photos of Jonesy and the family; kissing his wife drunkenly on the cheek as she made a duckface pout in The Railway; holding a young son under one arm and a younger daughter under the other on a beach somewhere; Jonesy giving a thumbs up alongside Jafar, the bad guy off Aladdin, whilst his son stared up at the cartoonishly-proportioned costume in wonder. *Jafar. Aladdin. Disneyland.*

"You working at the moment?" Bruce asked, sitting down on a swivel chair as the machine booted up.

"Not at the moment," Jonesy answered. "I just finished on a site down in Risca, 'bout a week-and-a-half back. Supposed to be hearing about a job down in Pontyclun today or tomorrow. I'm tidy with the foreman, hopefully he'll have something for me, like."

"Good man," Bruce said, double-clicking on the icon for Internet Explorer.

"Do you want a cup of tea or anything boys?" Jonesy asked.

"I'm alright butt," Bruce replied.

"You sure? I was gonna make one anyway."

"Well, if you're making one anyway."

"Two sugars you do have, right?"

"Three."

"Cool. Darren?"

Darren was still staring at the photographs.

"Darren?" Jonesy called again.

"Huh?" Darren said, turning to face him.

"Fancy a cup of tea or anything?"

"Yeah, go on then."

"Milk? Sugar?"

"Yeah."

"Cheers for having us round like butt," Bruce said again, "you know what they're like down that Job Centre. If you don't log on to this Universal Jobmatch, they do stop your payments, like."

"Ah don't mention it butt," Jonesy told him, "I know what they're like."

"Jonesy, can I use your toilet butt?" Darren asked.

"Crack on butt. Just up the stairs, next to the bedroom."

Darren walked back out into the hallway, words repeating in his mind: *Jafar. Aladdin. Disneyland. Paris.*

01.47pm

"Did you get it?"

"Yeah," Darren grinned, slamming the front door shut behind him. He threw the passport to Simon, still sat in the armchair, dog at his feet. Simon turned the burgundy document over and then started flicking through its pages.

"That was quick boys," Simon said. "Nice one."

"Have a look at the name on it," Bruce said, unsmiling.

Simon flicked to the laminated picture page. His grin grew wider.

"Carl fucking Jones. I fucking loves that boy Jonesy, he's a good one him." A thought suddenly occurred to Simon, and his grin evaporated. "So you told Jonesy I'm out, did you?"

"Nah," Darren answered.

"Did he fuck," Bruce spat, sitting down on the sofa and sparking up a Lambert & Butler cigarette. "He fucking robbed it, di'n't he?"

"Chuck us one of them bro," Simon ordered, eyes still fixed on the passport's picture page. Bruce dutifully tossed the cigarette packet across the room, followed by the lighter. Simon sparked one up before looking at his youngest brother Darren, still standing near the doorway. "Good work bro."

"Good work?" Bruce laughed. "Carl Jones is one of your best fucking friends, butt. How long've you known Jonesy? You was at Cwm Glas fucking Infants with him, weren't you? Coed-y-Brain juniors, Saint Ilan's comp. If you hadn't've been banged up, chances are you would've been best man at his fucking wedding. And your younger brother robs off him, and you turn around and say 'good work bro'. Fucking hell mun, butt. Do you not see nothing wrong with that?"

"Not really butt," Simon reasoned. "If Jonesy don't know about it, then he can't get in trouble for it, can he? In the eyes of the law, Jonesy's an innocent victim. If anything, Darren's done him a favour, not telling him what he needed the passport for."

"Done him a favour?" Bruce repeated, an incredulous grin slapped upon his face. "*Pam fi* fucking *duw*, butt."

Satisfied with his eldest brother's approval, Darren stepped across the living room and sat on the end seat of the sofa. But Bruce wasn't finished yet.

"And you butt, you don't have any moral qualms about robbing off of Jonesy? Your brother in fucking arms, who you've been scrapping with? When Bampy come back from World War Two, do you reckon he'd've robbed off any of the soldiers who was fighting along-fucking-side him?"

"Bampy didn't serve in the war," Simon corrected him. "He stayed round here as a fucking coalminer, di'n't he?"

"Yeah, Mam's dad did, but Dad's dad didn't," Bruce replied. "Dad's dad was part of the fucking Normandy landings, butt."

"What do you mean by he's been scrapping with Jonesy, anyway?" Simon said, returning to the point.

"Jonesy told me what happened to him," Bruce said, gesturing towards the swelling, cuts and bruising layered upon Darren's face. "Jonesy's head's in nearly as bad as state as Dar's is."

"What happened?"

"Mark Watts happened."

"The fucking Gruffalo?"

"Aye."

Simon looked at Darren. Darren was ignoring his brothers and staring at the television screen.

"What did Mark Watts wanna do that for?"

"Jonesy fucked his missus," said Darren, eyes fixed on the screen.

"He cheated on Charlene?" Bruce said, shocked.

"It was before they got back together," Darren explained.

"And so Mark Watts fucking done the pair of you, did he?" Simon asked.

"Nah, it weren't like that. Him and his mates got the fucking worst of it."

"They fucking better had." Simon stared at Darren; Darren's eyes didn't move from the television set. It seemed time to bring that strand to a conclusion. "Well, if I ever catch sight of that cunt Mark Watts, I'll give him a fucking good hiding of my own, don't you worry. And I hope you'd do the same, Bru."

"Of course mun."

"Tidy. Well then, we've got our passport, I'd say it looks like we're all sorted."

Bruce reached across the coffee table in the centre of the room to stub his cigarette out in the ashtray. He then reached a little further and took the L&B packet and the lighter from the arm of Simon's chair, then sat back and sparked up another cigarette.

"Everything's sorted then, is it butt?"

"Well, yeah."

"Easy as that, yeah?"

"Yeah. Why? What do you mean butt?"

"Well, like you said, we've got the passport, everything's sorted. Now you can just hop off to Spain, spend the rest of your days living in sunshine and freedom, yeah? Everything's sorted."

"Well, just as soon as I get my son, like."

"Oh sorry butt, I forgot about that part," Bruce snapped. "Yeah, right, apart from that minor detail, everything's sorted. Apart from kidnapping your fucking son, everything's sorted, right? Just a minor little federal fucking offense to commit, but apart from that, everything's sorted."

"A federal fucking offense," Simon grinned. "You're not fucking American, Bru. You've been watching too many movies, butt. You're Welsh. There's no such thing as a federal fucking offense in Britain, you dull fucker."

"It's a phrase of speech, butt. The point's still true. It's not exactly a minor detail, is it? If anything, getting the passport's a minor detail. Kidnapping your son is more likely to be the hard part, innit? I mean, a passport don't fucking scream and shout when you pick it up, does it? And it's the end of August, like. Jonesy probably won't even notice the passport's gone until he fucks off on holiday next summer. But your son, butt… I mean, I know you've been banging on about what a terrible mother Jodie is, but I don't think there's a parent in the world who'd be bad enough not to notice if their child's suddenly disappeared."

"Alright butt, fair dues," Simon conceded, "that'll probably be the tricky part, but I don't reckon it'll be as hard as you're making out. We'll get a flight booked, A.SAP. It's about ten to two now. Daniel'll be leaving school about three-thirty. One of us'll just head there a bit before that, go in and tell his teacher I'm his father, or you're his uncle, and there's been a family emergency or something, his mother's been hit by a car or had a stroke or whatever, and we need to get him out of class immediately. Then bang on over to the airport, and we'll be half way to fucking Espana before Jodie even knows he's missing."

"That's brilliant butt, fairplay. Absolutely brilliant idea, that. Just one minor problem with it, though; what date is it, butt?"

"Wednesday."

"Date, not day."

"I don't know, like August twenty-eighth or something?"

"Yeah, and how many schools do you know that are open in August, butt?"

Bruce had got him. Simon nodded, his plan dashed. He took a final drag on his cigarette, pulling the flame beyond the ink at the nub of it, then reached across the room to stub the cigarette out and grab another from the Lambert & Butler pack. Seeing this, Darren too reached over and picked up a cigarette.

"Fucking hell mun boys, help yourselves like," Bruce protested. Both brothers ignored him, Simon lighting up his cigarette and then tossing the lighter across the room to Darren.

"Alright, alright, fuck the school run then. What about after? What about nighttime?" Simon was thinking out loud. "Wait until everyone's sleeping, then sneak inside and creep back out with him."

"How the fuck are we supposed to do tha'?" was Bruce's answer. "Even if no-one else in the house wakes up, Daniel sure as fuck will. And he'll be screaming his fucking head off, won't he? Seeing us in his fucking room in the dead of night."

"Take some chlorofill or whatever they call it, that knockout stuff."

"Chloroform," Bruce corrected him.

"Yeah, chlorosill, whatever the fuck it's called," Simon continued, "tip a bit of that on a rag and wrap it round his face when you grab hold of him."

"And where the fuck are we supposed to get that from?"

"I don't know. Do you know anyone who we can get any off?"

"No butt," Bruce answered, "I don't know anyone we can get fucking chloroform off."

"Do they not sell it at chemist's?"

"Oh yeah butt, of course they do. They do have it on a shelf right next to the GBH and the fucking horse tranquilizers. Come to think of it, Boots have got a two-for-one offer on date rape essentials at the moment."

"Well fuck it then," Simon said, ignoring his brother's laboured sarcasm, "one of you pair go upstairs and grab him, the other one run around downstairs chucking petrol about the place, then once you're out the door with him, throw a match inside, and burn the fucking house down."

"Jesus Christ," Bruce said, laughing. He took a big drag on his cigarette and leaned forward before he spoke again. "Jesus Christ butt. Are you fucking mental or wha'? You've gone from kidnapping to fucking murder. Double murder, if that feller you were on about is in there with them. And if she's living in a terraced house, which she probably fucking is, the fire'll spread like fuck, won't it? We might wind up killing a dozen people or more if we do that. You fucking bellend. And how big of a manhunt do you think the police will launch for us once the fire's died out? They'll fucking stop the plane mid-flight to bring you back, you try that shit. The shit that you're fucking coming out with butt, honestly, I think prison've fucked your head up good and proper. You've turned into a fucking mongoloid. A fucking mongoloid pyromaniac. That's what you are butt; a fucking mongoloid pyromaniac."

"That's rich butt, coming from you," Simon protested. "What about the old cinema full of skagheads, huh? Who lit the fire that time? When them fuckers weren't paying up, who was the mongoloid pyromaniac then, butt?"

Bruce glanced down the sofa at Darren, who was listening to all intently.

"That was years ago, butt," Bruce said softly.

Simon looked over at Darren and abated, not wanting to expose his youngest brother to any of the wild tales from his and Bruce's crazy teenage years.

"Alright, it was only a suggestion," Simon said. "Forget the petrol then. Just if anyone comes, twat 'em. Knock 'em out. Lock 'em up until morning or something. You don't even need to kill them. Just get them out of action long enough for you to take Daniel to the airport, and for me to be on my merry fucking way, like."

"Jodie'll recognise me though butt," Bruce said. "She'll recognise the both of us. We went to your fucking wedding, didn't we?"

"Wear a fucking mask then butt," replied Simon. "It's not rocket science, is it? That's the plan sorted then, yeah? Sneak in there late tonight, tie her and her cunt boyfriend up, nab Daniel, come meet me at the airport, happy days. That sound alright to you, Darren?"

"Yeah," Darren replied, smiling.

"That sound good to you Bru?"

Bruce sighed loudly. "I suppose it'll have to, won't it?"

"Awesome," Simon said, beaming. He shot to his feet and grabbed Bruce's head with both hands, holding it tightly to his chest. "I fucking love you boys." He bent down to kiss the top of Bruce's head.

"Fuck off me mun butt!" Bruce yelled.

6.13pm

Ji Eun fumbled with the keys a few times before opening the front door of her house and staggering into the hallway. The whole walk home, swaying to and fro on the street, half-cut, she'd been longing to get in, spread out on the sofa and pass out for a bit; the unexpected boom of K-pop from the living room suggested that her longed-for peace would not materialise.

"Hi," Ji Eun blurted out upon entering the living room, doing her best to sound breezy and unintoxicated. She hadn't expected Claire to be back in Cardiff yet.

"Hey," Claire replied, looking up from a thick book that she held in her lap. "How's it going?"

"Good," Ji Eun mumbled.

"*Annyong-haseyo*," Monica said, bowing her head a little and smiling nervously.

"*Annyong-haseyo*," Ji Eun repeated.

Ji Eun sat down on the sofa, at the opposite end of which Monica was sitting cross-legged, staring into a laptop, which was blasting out one of Chocolate Parasol's saccharine K-pop bangers. Claire was sat in the adjacent armchair. Ji Eun's two housemates were diametrically opposed, in terms both of the seating arrangement and their character. Claire was aloof, upper-middle-class and English, with pale white skin and a passion for Japanese fashion - bold, colourful clothing; a day-glo explosion of Harajuku-kawaii overkill. Today, for example, her long legs, stretched out to the coffee table in front of her, were clad in white stockings, running up to a doming pink mini-skirt. On top she wore a white T-shirt adorned with a cutesy pink-cheeked cartoon cheetah. The pale white of Claire's cheeks were similarly powdered pink. Her lips shimmered with salmon pink gloss. Her eyes were accented with enormous fake lashes and copious electric blue eye shadow. Her long bleached blonde hair was adorned with a Hello Kitty-style pink bow spotted with white polka dots.

In contrast, Monica – or Minji, as Ji Eun felt more comfortable in calling her – was short, tanned and, without wanting to be mean, dumpy. Chubby. Plump. Her hair was wild and unkempt, frizzing out to the shoulders of her simple navy blue sweatshirt. Her crossed legs were clad in unremarkable blue denim jeans. Where Claire's appearance screamed like a Japanese visual kei band for everyone to take notice of her, Monica's attire was unconsciously tossed together in a manner that allowed her to recede comfortably into the background. Ji Eun supposed her choice of English name was a reflection of this; after a few weeks of introducing herself to fellow students and eliciting howls of laughter, somewhat-polite suppressed sniggering, or muted shock in response, somebody finally explained to her that her Korean name – Minji – was dangerously close to a vulgar British slang term for a vagina. She'd decided upon introducing herself as Monica in future almost immediately.

Ji Eun rested her back and her head against the cushioned sofa and closed her eyes for a moment, a day spent touring the bars and pubs of Cardiff, Caerphilly and Newport having taken its toll.

"How's your summer been?" Claire asked, causing Ji Eun to open her eyes again.

"Good, yeah," she said, fumbling clumsily to describe it. "I've been doing work experience at the local paper recently."

"Oh yeah, I remember you saying you were going to try and do that. How's it going there?"

"It's going alright, yeah. What are you reading?"

Claire lifted the book from her lap and held it up to her; a serious, stark white cover, with the words 'Ulysses' etched across it in bold regal red.

"Any good?"

"No," Claire said, folding over the page she was reading and placing it down upon a coffee table. "It's a fucking nightmare. I'm about thirty pages in and I've not got a clue what's supposed to be happening. I'm supposed to have read the whole bloody thing before term starts. Are you taking the Irish Literature module as well?"

"No."

"Lucky you. This thing is so bloody hard to comprehend that I'm not entirely convinced it's even been written in English. I should've started reading it weeks ago, but this thing weighs a ton, so I was hardly likely to cart it around with me all summer, was I?"

"How was Vietnam?" Ji Eun asked, having been prompted to mention it.

"Great, yeah. Fantastic. Rode a boat down the river, looking up at the stars. Drank coffee filtered through a rat's arsehole. Amazing. Anyway, what're you guys doing tonight?"

"Nothing," Ji Eun said slowly, glancing again towards Monica, who was completely focused on the laptop and the choosing of the next track, the Chocolate Parasol song having drawn to a close.

"There's a gig on at Welsh Club if you fancy it."

"Who's playing?"

"I don't know, some new NME hype band. Arabian Punk or something."

Ji Eun didn't know what to say, what with the alcohol swirling round inside her, sloshing about in her brain, drowning thought and dampening both inhibition and decision-making skills. She pretty quickly decided to not think about it, not deal with the question directly, just let her mind meld with whatever decision was made through osmosis. "Maybe." *Go out or stay in.* "I don't mind." *Either/or.* "Whatever."

10.02pm

"That was a cracking finish by Whittingham though, weren't it butt?" Steve said, as he and Tom strode along the road back to town from Cardiff City Stadium.

"Yeah," Tom replied, still buzzing from the match, a hard-fought 2-1 win over Preston. He glanced across the street at the profusion of Chinese restaurants and supermarkets that suggested they were almost there, almost back at Cardiff Central. "Do you fancy grabbing a pint at the Prince of Wales?"

"We've got a while until the last train, haven't we?"

"Yeah. Eleven-twenty tonight."

"Class."

10.08pm

"I'm open man, pass it here. Quick, pass it. Fuck, you've lost it now."

"He fucking tackled me, didn't he?"

"You had time man, you should've passed it."

"I was gonna pass it, but he fucking tackled me, di'n't he?" Cain protested. "Quick now, he's up near you, get on 'im."

"I'll close the channel off, mark the runner," Rembrandt ordered.

"I got him."

"Not him... fuck."

A perfectly executed cross. Ball in the back of the net. 1-0.

"I told you to mark the runner," moaned Rembrandt.

"I was marking him."

"It didn't look like it."

"Stop fucking nitpicking bro, we're supposed to be on the same team together."

"Alright, well focus now then."

Joseph was slumped in an armchair at the back of the living room, paying little attention to Rembrandt and Cain as they played FIFA from the room's prime sofa spots. Joseph was staring at the cracked screen of his phone, flicking between news apps and news sites, none of them providing more than the basic outline of the Simon Amstell situation; that he'd done a runner, that he'd been on day release, that he'd been supposed to go and work at the Paul's Pies factory in Bedwas, and other things that Joseph already knew. What Joseph didn't know was what Simon's intentions were. *He'll probably leave the country,* Jodie'd said. *Probably fuck off to Spain or something.* But what if he didn't? What if he... *what?* Joseph didn't even know what he was worried about. He knew he should be happy – he had more than he'd had at the start of the week. He had a job. A smartphone. But what did he really have? *Jodie.* Things were going good. *Great.* But with her husband out... *ex-husband,* he corrected himself. But what would happen there now? She didn't want Joseph staying with her at her Mam's house. She'd gone there seeking safety. *I'm obviously not safety enough.* And as for Daniel... *Simon's his father.* Joseph felt close to him, felt almost as if he was his own, but that would never be more than a feeling, never be real. However long he'd been away, however much damaged he'd caused to his own life and the lives of those around him, Simon Amstell would always have that over Joseph; *he'll always be Daniel's Dad.* And Joseph would always be in the background, a bit-part player, a supporting actor. *Always Joe Pesci, never DeNiro.* In the movie of Danny Brain's life, Joseph would probably get five minutes of screen-time and two or three lines of dialogue.

"Fuck this butt," Cain said.

Joseph looked up from the phone to see Cain drop the Playstation controller in disgust. On screen, Tottenham were celebrating slotting a second goal past Cardiff without reply.

"What are you up to man? It's not even half-time yet."

"And we're getting battered already. I can't hack playing with you man, no offence like, but you're fucking useless."

"Fine, whatever," Rembrandt said, laying his own controller down and taking his phone out of his pocket.

Cain reached out to the coffee table in front of them, picked up a grinder, a pouch of Cutter's Choice tobacco, some Raw papers and a little plastic bag stuffed with bud. He then busied himself with joint construction, the only sound the cheering of the crowd on FIFA and some chilled hip-hop playing out of Cain's laptop speakers.

"What's this playing man?" Joseph said, looking to diffuse the tension.

"Isaiah Rashad," Cain answered, not looking up.

"Who?"

"Isaiah Rashad," Cain repeated.

"Who's that?"

"He's a rapper."

"I know that mun. Where he's from?"

"I don't know, America somewhere. Podge got me on to it."

"Is it? I've not seen Podge in years man."

"Yeah, he's been away, i'n' he? Teaching English. He's back over here for a bit now though."

"Is he?"

"Yeah. We're going out for a couple of pints with him tomorrow if you fancy it."

"Yeah man, definitely. Where's he been?"

"Korea."

"North or South?"

"South, I think."

"Of course the South," Rembrandt added. "The fuck would North Koreans be learning English for?"

"I don't know man," Joseph argued, "it's the global language these days, innit?"

"North Koreans don't go anywhere though, do they?"

"I suppose," Joseph conceded.

"That girl Delveccio was seeing were North Korean though, weren't she?" Cain asked, turning to Rembrandt.

"She was Norwegian."

Laughter.

"Nah, fuck off," Cain grinned, "she was fucking Asian-looking though, weren't she?"

"So's half of fucking Cardiff, ya dull cunt," Rembrandt grinned back.

"Well, you know what I mean, she didn't look the typical Scandinavian, did she? Fuck off."

More laughter. It slowly ebbed away, all focus falling upon the mellow vibe of the music filling the room. Cain finished wrapping the spliff up, lit it, and slowly took his tokes. Joseph focused in on the music, letting Isaiah Rashad's laconic rhymes push the negative thoughts from his mind. He reached out to accept the spliff as Cain handed it over to him.

"This is good smoking music man," Joseph said, sitting back in the armchair and taking a toke.

"Yeah man," Cain agreed. "Weird that it's Podge that recommended, living over there."

"What, they don't have weed in Korea?"

"He said that it's rare, but you can get it. Expensive as fuck, though. Like a hundred quid a gramme or something."

"Shit," Joseph said, recoiling at the ten-fold increase on British prices.

"Cigarettes are a lot cheaper, mind. He said he can get them for about two quid a pack."

"Hope he's bringing a load back with him then."

The conversation slipped away, Joseph concentrating on the weed smoke. A high-pitched squeal of laughter soundly sounded from Rembrandt's end of the sofa. Cain and Joseph stared at Rembrandt as he held his phone up towards the television, frantically tapping on its screen, eliciting little '*pew pew*' laser beam sounds.

"The fuck are you up to man?" Cain asked.

Rembrandt said nothing, focusing on the *pew pew*s and the phone and television screens. Another high-pitched squeal of laughter sounded. Joseph got to his feet and walked over to Rembrandt. He stared down at the screen of Rembrandt's HTC One, on which a cutesy little yellow creature was ducking behind the coffee table, as Rembrandt fired laser beams at him. The little creature suddenly leapt up onto the coffee table, and springboarded off towards the television screen, disappearing into it in a flash.

"That's fucking nuts bro," Joseph said.

"Yeah, this game's awesome man. You have to hunt these little bastards, and if you catch 'em you can use them to battle other people and stuff. They'll pop up randomly all over the place, and they can use flat surfaces as portals, like TV screens or paintings or whatever."

"Woah."

"Yeah man, watch this."

Rembrandt directed the little *pew pew* laser beams at the television screen. After a few seconds of repeated firing, the screen flashed into life, and a stream of furry little blue clawed creatures hopped out of it and started bouncing around the living room, Rembrandt firing laser beams at them wildly. Joseph laughed.

"That's lame man," Cain scoffed. "Childish as fuck. Looks like fucking Pokemon or summin'."

"You can install it on your new phone if you want," Rembrandt told Joseph, ignoring Cain.

"Alright, yeah," Joseph said, taking a final toke and passing the spliff to Rembrandt. He walked back to the armchair and picked the Lumia up.

"The battery's running pretty low actually. You got anywhere I can plug my charger in?"

Cain looked at the overloaded extension lead besides the television set: "There should be a socket free out in the hallway."

10.15pm

The Prince of Wales was packed, as was often the case after a City game. Tom was standing in front of the It Box, playing the Pub Quiz game. Steve was beside him, clutching a pint in one hand and his iPhone in the other.

"Fuck butt," Tom said, the It Box's question stumping him. "Which of these is not a real album by Banarama? A. Deep Sea Skiving, B. Banarama, C. Please Myself, D. Ultra Violet."

"Banarama?" Steve said, looking up from the iPhone screen. "Is that even a real thing?"

"Yeah, it's some eighties pop group. I don't know fuck all about their album titles though."

Steve read through the options again before making a suggestion: "'Deep Sea Skiving' sounds retarded butt, I'd go with that one."

"I don't know man, 'Banarama' is a bit too obvious. Maybe it's that one."

"Nah man, I reckon they probably had a real album called 'Deep Sea Diving', the one on there's a pun on it."

Tom hit the button for 'Deep Sea Skiving' and drew a breaking glass sound effect and a 'game over' screen.

"Maybe not then butt."

Tom fiddled in his pocket for change and pulled out two twenty pences: "Have you got a ten on you?"

"Here you are," Steve said, shoving two fifty pence pieces into the It Box's coin slot. "What time are you in tomorrow?" Steve asked, as Tom brought Pub Quiz back up.

"Nine. You?"

"I've got the morning off. I'm travelling up to Birmingham for a meeting."

"Jammy bastard."

Steve had gone straight into work from school, whilst Tom had spent three years drinking and discovering new drugs and occasionally attending lectures at university. Steve had worked hard and applied himself and clawed his way up from an entry-level call centre position at G&H to a proper job with proper responsibilities, and a proper salary to go with them. Tom envied his drive and the position he'd attained, but didn't think he'd ever be able to overcome the overbearing 9-to-5 boredom of an entry-level call centre job to make the same ascent.

"Why's that butt?"

"Melissa's just messaged me."

"Is that that bird you're shagging?"

"Nah, that was Maria, this is Melissa that I work with. Wouldn't mind giving her a go if I can though. She's just saying that she's over at Clwb and there's some band playing, if you fancy it."

"What band?"

"I don't know, I'd never heard of them." Steve squinted at the cracked screen of the iPhone that he held in his hand. "Iranian Punk Rock."

"I've heard the name."

"Any good?"

"I don't know. I just heard the name." Tom turned his attention to the question on the screen. "Which of these teams did Nicolas Anelka play for first? A. Arsenal, B. Chelsea, C. Paris Saint Germain, D. Liverpool."

"Easy. Arsenal."

"Nah, wait, who did Arsenal sign him from? He's French, i'n' he? I reckon PSG."

"Nah, he was at PSG when Liverpool signed him."

"Nah... really? Who'd Arsenal sign him from then?"

"I don't know, but he definitely went from PSG after them."

"What about Chelsea?"

"Nah, he didn't go to Chelsea until well after."

"You sure he didn't play for them before?"

"Definitely."

"Then what're you saying, Arsenal?"

"Arsenal."

Tom pressed the button and again drew the breaking glass sound and the 'game over' screen.

"What do you reckon about Clwb tonight then, man? Melissa's got a mate with her."

"Yeah?" Tom said, restarting Pub Quiz. "What's she like?"

"I don't know man, she don't work at G&H. Might be worth a shot mind."

"How much is it?

"Five pound in, but then Fosters is only one-fifty."

"Pints or bottles?"

"Bottles. And it's two quid for Jaeger Bombs."

"I don't know butt, Jaeger Bombs on a school night might not be the best idea. How long've we got 'til last train?"

"About forty, fifty, minutes," Steve said, glancing again at the iPhone. "I don't know butt, the train'll only give us about half an hour inside. We're probably best off getting a taxi back if we go."

Tom frowned, thinking of his meagre bank balance.

"But we'll be able to split one with Melissa and her mate. They live in Taff's Well, so we can drop 'em on the way back to Caerphilly. Or we might even wind up stopping round their's."

That last hint of a chance was decisive. "Go on then."

Steve started tapping out a reply on his iPhone as the next question popped up on screen.

"Right, who wrote the classic dystopian sci-fi novel 'Brave New World'?" Tom read. "A. George Orwell, B. Margaret Atwood, C. Anthony Burgess, or D. Aldous Huxley?"

"The fuck's 'dystopian' mean?" Steve asked, still staring at the iPhone screen.

10.41pm

"Did you hear about Pigeon Head?"

Danny Daggers had no idea who Pigeon Head was, or who any of the other people who'd been discussed over the past few hours were. He'd spent his afternoon smoking joints on the fields outside the museum with the teenagers. Johnny, Taggard, Kayleigh and Teresa were all around sixteen years old and enjoying the last few days of their summer holidays. Danny had followed them to a rather grandiosely entitled 'house party', an event consisting of sixteen people in total, nine downstairs in the living room, seven upstairs in the bedroom. Danny was upstairs because that was where the drugs were, and that was also where Teresa was. A week away from her seventeenth birthday, she had a beautiful face, with Mediterranean features and complexion that Danny was having trouble figuring out were of Italian, Spanish or Greek extraction. Perhaps she was even some combination of the three, or maybe her features stemmed from some other race of people that Danny hadn't considered; beyond Great Britain's borders, he really wasn't that well travelled.

"No, what's happened to Pigeon Head?" Teresa asked, sitting on the floor next to Danny.

"He got busted," Yeller explained, sitting on the bed, leaning over to a coffee table where he was using his student card to chop up lines of Mortal Kombat (methadrone and ketamine - MK).

Yeller was a big guy, maybe 6 foot 4, wide too, with short curly hair and a massive chin, or possibly chins – he was a big bloke in every way – though a wispy, unkempt beard obscured any extra chinnage that might have been folded up under his jaw.

"No way," replied Teresa, "what happened?

"He was out in Bristol, at some club, and the dozy pillock asked an undercover police officer if he wanted any pills."

"Fuck," said Teresa, really drawing out the vowel to voice maximum levels of surprise.

"A policeman asked me if I knew where to get pills before," Phil interrupted, "in London it was, in this club they used to have in Central called The End. It's about five o'clock in the morning at this point, the place is closing any minute. I'm fucking half-cut, obviously, so I'm about to tell him who I got mine off, when I think 'hang on a minute, there's something not right about this'. This bloke's about forty-fucking-five years-old, a short little chubby guy with a Mario moustache and a receding hairline."

"What did you say?" Yeller asked, still going about his business with the student card.

"I told him to go fuck himself."

"Did you fuck," Yeller scoffed.

"Nah, well, I told him I didn't have any. Obviously undercover, weren't he? You don't go buying pills at five in the morning when the club's chucking out any second, do you? "

"A fucking narc they call that butt," said a Robinson Crusoe-looking character sat cross-legged on the floor beside Teresa. The guy had black hair almost down to his shoulders and a big bush of a beard that made Yeller's effort look like bumfluff. If Danny had heard the guy's name at any point in the night, it was something that he'd by now forgotten.

"So what happened with Pigeon Head?" Teresa asked, prompting Yeller to return to his story.

"Well, like I say, he's gone up to this copper in this nightclub asking him if he wants to buy any Jack and Jills, next thing you know he's got this copper reading him his Miranda rights, running his fingers through his pockets, trying to find out what else he's got on him, and he finds this little bottle of liquid ketamine."

"Fuck," Teresa intoned again, in a similar fashion to before.

"So the copper goes, 'What's this then?'" Yeller continued. "And Pigeon Head, the dozy prick, he tells this copper that its liquid fucking ketamine."

"No way," laughed Robin Crusoe.

"Fucking idiot," Teresa added.

"So this copper goes, 'What do you do with this then?'" Yeller continued. "And the fucking idiot starts explaining what to do with it! He's like, 'pop it in the microwave, sixty seconds, boom! You've got yourself a few grams of ket."

"What a fucking retard!" Phil said, following his condemnation up with hearty laughter.

"Yeah, fucking bell-end like," Yeller continued, "but anyways, that's not even the worst of it. So they've got him in Bristol with enough on him to get him in a fair bit of bother already, then the coppers over that side of the bridge call up the rozzers down here in Cardiff and ask them to go take a look at his fucking home and all. Now, I don't know if you know this, but Pigeon Head's still living in his mother's house."

"Shit," Teresa said, again drawing out the vowel.

"So the coppers down in Cardiff turn up on her doorstep, explain to her what's happened, next thing you know they're searching her son's room, and d'you know what they find under his bed?"

"I'm scared to think what you'd find under Pigeon Head's bed," Phil opined, "fuck me!"

"Fifty grand in cash," Yeller said, pausing his line-racking to deliver the denouement with maximum gravitas.

"Fuck," Teresa said again, with even greater dramatic emphasis on the vowel.

"No way!" said Robinson Crusoe.

"Now that's a lot of fucking money," Yeller concluded, returning to his task.

"What an idiot," Teresa added, shaking her head in disbelief.

"He'll be going away for a while for all that then," said Phil.

"Tell me about it," said Yeller, then, looking in the direction of the people sat or standing around the computer, controlling the music (some New York-sounding hip hop Danny Daggers wasn't familiar with was currently playing), "oh, Kasey, Gezza, Alice, are you having a line of this?"

"Yeah," Kasey (presumably) shouted back.

"None for me," Gezza (probably) added, "I've got to drive."

"Go on then," said Alice (obviously Alice, as she was the only girl amongst the trio).

"Go on then?" Yeller repeated, "Go on then? I'm not offering you a cup of tea, I'm offering you a line of fucking MK. Fucking 'go on then'." He then turned his attention to splitting the drugs into neat little lines before lifting his eyes to those seated around the table. "I'll take it you're all having some?"

His response was greeted with a general chorus of 'yeah's.

"How about you?" he asked, looking over at Danny. "The madman internet sensation from Leeds? Our special guest of the evening?"

"Yeah, I'll have some," Danny answered, squirming a little beneath the intensity of Yeller's gaze. He was a very big fucker.

"I bet you will," Yeller replied, a little smirk creeping across his face, then, returning to the business of line cutting, "so, tell us, what's it like being semi-famous?"

"It's alright like," Danny answered, all eyes on him.

"I bet it is. You get much in the way of groupies in your line of work Danny?"

"I do alright for myself like."

"I bet you do," Yeller laughed in response. "I bet you fucking do. What do you think of Teresa then?"

"Yeller," Teresa pleaded.

"Yeah, she's alright like."

"She's alright like?" Yeller repeated. "Did you hear that Teresa? He says that you're alright like. What do you reckon of him?"

Teresa left the question unanswered as Yeller rolled up a five pound note lying on the table top, inserted it in his right nostril and hoovered up the largest of the six lines of MK. He sniffed heavily as he reclined back onto the bed, propping himself up on his elbows. Phil took the five pound note from the tabletop, unfurled and then re-rolled it, his eyes fixed on Danny all the while.

"So, Danny Daggers," Phil began, "how the fuck'd you come up with a name like that?"

"I don't know," Danny started, as Phil leaned in to hoover up his line, then, realising something more substantial might be required, "I was just pissing about when I called myself it at first really, then the name just kind of stuck."

"What's your real name then?" Yeller chipped in, lightning fast, as Phil snorted his line.

"Daniel Covell."

"Fuck me, that's strong," Phil said, recoiling, before handing the note to Crusoe.

"Shut up ya fairy," Yeller reprimanded him. "So what gave you the idea to start doing all that bollocks on YouTube then, Daniel Covell?"

"Boredom really."

"Not a lot to do in Leeds then is there?" Yeller asked.

"There's enough like," Danny answered, "but, you know, you can always do with a bit more."

"I don't know," Phil thoughtfully commented, "I've never been to Leeds."

"I've never uploaded nothing to YouTube neither," Yeller added.

"Haven't you fuck," Phil exclaimed. "What about the video you made of Big Chin getting his arse kicked by that Year Seven kid?"

"It weren't me who put that on there," Yeller corrected him, "Yachee uploaded that."

Without Danny having noticed any more lines being done, Teresa was suddenly rubbing her nose and handing the note over to him. He leaned over the table and snorted up the last line quickly, then leant back, note still in his hand, rubbing his nose.

"Were it?" Phil asked, genuinely confused.

Danny sensed he needed to get out of there, fast. Yeller didn't seem like the kind of guy whose drugs he could keep taking without there being some kind of consequences coming along at some point in the evening.

"Can I use your toilet a minute?" Danny asked.

"No," Yeller said, staring at him with dead-eyed intensity. "Nah, fuck it, only messing man, it's out on the landing."

Danny stood up uneasily, then swayed about on ketamine legs. *Fuck me,* Danny thought, *that's fucking rhino K or something that. Thank god for the M-kat to balance it out a bit.* He staggered awkwardly to the door, each lifting and returning to the ground of his feet a chore, as Yeller and Phil fell into some playful nonsense argument behind him. He stepped out onto the landing and closed the door behind himself, then looked down the stairs at the front door. Besides that, in the hallway, the door to the living room was closed. He supposed it might be a good time to get the fuck of there. He clutched the banister as he tackled the stairs as quickly as he could, though, given his state of inebriation, that wasn't very quickly at all. The front door had a Yale lock, thankfully, which meant no faffing about with keys. He opened it, then stepped outside, pulling it closed behind him as quietly as he could. The night and street outside were dark and unfamiliar. He figured he could remember the vague general direction of the city centre and that would probably be the best way to head. He staggered uneasily to the end of the street and to the main road, then onwards past another six or seven parallel streets, before he realised he still had Yeller's fiver in his hand. *Bollocks.* He quickened his pace, no mean feat with the ketamine weighing his limbs down towards the pavement, as he entertained the idea of going back to the house party. *Fuck that,* he thought. The fact he'd disappeared outside with the fiver in the first place would probably be enough to send that big fucking nut into a rage. *What if he comes looking for me?* It'd be a good few minutes before anyone would even notice he was gone, Danny reasoned. With the way the conversation and the drugs were flowing, they might not notice for hours that he'd disappeared. Or at least twenty-odd minutes, when the last lot of M-kat and ketamine had worn off. Yes, Danny reassured himself, he was most certainly taking the absolute best course of action.

10.47pm

"This next song is about Princess Diana," the floppy-fringed Sixth Former fronting the band on stage said, in that soft, Southern English, R.P. accent of his. The band around him started playing the same kind of lo-fi electronica-tinged post-indie they'd be playing since Tom arrived, a lazy, insipid blend of Alt-J, the XX and Radiohcad with the volume turned down. It wasn't exactly the image the band's name – Iranian Punk Rock –

had created in Tom's mind; they were something far worse, far duller, than the firebrand group of Persians in ripped jeans making a three-chord racket he'd envisioned. The floppy-fringed frontman closed his eyes and started producing the same soft, mournful singing that'd been coming out of him all evening.

"Tie a Windsor knot in my tongue,
And serve my body to the masses,
Rip it out and leave me dumb,
Twitching and shuddering, car crashes,
And I feeeeeeeeeel... I'm someone...
And I feeeeeeeeeel... human..."

That was enough for Tom. "I'm going to get a drink," he shouted towards his mate, Steve. Steve was laughing and conversing with Melissa and didn't hear him. Next to them was her mate, the bait with which Tom had been lured into Clwb Ifor Bach to watch the shit-show on stage. Melissa's mate was watching the band, her boyfriend standing behind, arms wrapped around her. Tom reminded himself never to follow Steve along on a potential double-date again, as they inevitably wound up either with Tom forced into polite conversation with Steve's quarry's fat/ugly friend, or left alone as the attractive-enough friend stood firm within her boyfriend's embrace. He thought he should perhaps cut out going to gigs altogether, what with the anaemic electrofied whining that passed for rock music these days. He thought back to all the far superior gigs he'd been to at Clwb Ifor as he approached the bar, teenage years spent with Steve and Gareth and all the rest of them, bouncing up and down the Valleys and back and forth between Cardiff and Newport, seemingly a gig on every night of the week, every fucker but Tom in a band. There were Gareth and Steve's competing outfits, Torn Between Angels and Infix, playing venues that mostly no longer existed with bands who'd long since given up the ghost of a dream and gotten themselves real jobs. Succumbing to drunken revery, Tom zig-zagged back and forth between a list of venues and bands that had long since ceased to be, feeling older as each name cast him back to the happier times of a decade ago – *Siadosa, Opium, Covergirl, Dopamine, Newport T.J.'s, Penallta Rugby Club, the Greenfly, Barfly, Tom's Bar in Trefforest, the Dollhouse in Abertillery,* a forgotten world of almost-was and never-were, unchronicled, unheralded, left to rot in the memory of the half-way drunk on a work night...

"Alright mate, what can I get you?" the bartender asked, snapping Tom free from revery.

"Fosters," he said, wondering whether to follow it up with a Jaegermeister, as he glanced glumly along the bar, and saw her, a pretty young thing, Asian, swaying slightly, all alone...

Ji Eun was deep into drunkenness, an all-day, all-encompassing stupor, intoxication piled upon inebriation, now bobbing up and down upon the surface of the night, unmoored. Claire was somewhere deep within the crowd, her and some big-haired guy in a tight T-shirt smothering each other's faces with their mouths. Minji was at home, eyes most likely fixed upon the screen of her laptop, maybe in Skype conversation with her mother.

"What do you think of the band?"

Ji Eun turned to Tom's question without hearing it, his face a composite of its most apparent parts, slowly ebbing into view, like new polygons loading upon entering a new area of a video game. First came the nose, large and European, perhaps Roman-descended; then the slight-fringed brown hair, green eyes, and then the words repeated themselves: "What do you think of the band?"

"They're okay," she said instinctively, suddenly sobering up to the reality of her surroundings and realising that a tide of sound had been gently washing over her for the better part of however-long without her really being awake to it. Prompted by the question to take note of the sound sloshing all around her, she forced herself into pronouncing some kind of opinion on it: "Kind of boring."

"Yeah," Tom said, glancing back at the stage for something more prosaic to add to what she'd said. Finding nothing, he just nodded again. "Yeah."

"One-fifty," the barman said, placing a bottle of Fosters in front of Tom.

"Do you want a drink?" Tom said, pulling a fiver from his pocket.

"Yeah," she said instinctively, having imbibed too much alcohol already to even contemplate turning down the offer of more. She looked woozily as the posters behind the bar boasting of drinks offers came into partial focus and said the first thing that she saw: "I'll have a Jaeger Bomb."

"Can I get a Jaeger Bomb," Tom repeated to the barman. Then, fumbling quickly through his pocket to count the change that remained, "Actually, could you make that two?"

The barman was quick to oblige, with bottles of Jaegermeister and cans of some cheaper-brand Red Bull knock-off lined up along the bar, ready and waiting. They tapped glasses and cheered and downed them. Tom fumbled into predictable and well-worn questions: "What's your name?", followed by a struggle to pronounce it, aborted after two weak attempts; "Where are you from?"; "What do you do?"; "What do you think of Cardiff?", etc. There was something beneath the bumbling blandness of the chat-up act that Ji Eun found attractive, or maybe she was drunk enough to give herself fully over to chance and the intentions of others, but either way, they were soon both leaning in, eyes closed, tongues lapping over one another's, with a brief respite and smile as the barman interrupted with Tom's change, before returning their tongues to one another's mouths, gaping and ungaping them like two fish lost amidst the ocean.

* * *

With no mobile phone to tell him and ketamine making a complete mess of his time perception, Danny had absolutely no idea how long he'd been walking, but it felt a lot longer than the reverse journey from the city centre to the house had taken earlier. None of the streets or buildings looked remotely familiar, though that was maybe to be expected, as Danny had made the earlier journey in sunlight, without any drugs clouding his mind. Well, any drugs other than weed, which wasn't really a 'drug' drug.

As he moved quickly along the street, worries fumbling for attention in his mind, he saw the trees on the opposite side of the road suddenly drop away to reveal a great hulking 24-hour Tesco. Danny quickly looked both ways for cars – there'd been little more than a trickle of traffic running alongside him the whole journey anyway – then bounded across the road, as fast as his still slightly ketamine-addled limbs would carry him.

Under the punishing glare of Tesco's fluorescent lighting, Danny did his best to avoid the gaze of any staff members as he made his way unsteadily toward the back of the store and the alcohol section, wishing he still had his aviators to both hide and shield his methadrone-enlarged pupils. After selecting a can of Fosters from the fridge, he made his way across the thankfully almost deserted superstore to the checkout and placed it down on the conveyor belt, doing his best to avoid eye contact with the cashier as he searched through his pockets for some cash. She said something to snap him out of his trance, and he handed over the five pound note he'd inadvertently stolen from Yeller.

"I.D. please," the middle-aged women with tight curls of pupley-brown hair repeated.

He stared at her blankly, his big pupils looking like a deer's dilating beneath the menacing glow of car headlights, then, comprehending her, he began fidgeting with his pockets again in search of his wallet. *Bollocks.*

"I've not got any," he said.

"Then I'm afraid I can't serve you."

He ignored her and walked off towards the exit, not so bothered about the beer anymore. His wallet. First his phone and now his wallet. He cursed Cardiff – *fucking shithole of a city* – then realised that as well as his wallet, with his I.D. and his bank card – his *fucking bank card*, lord have mercy, how was he supposed to survive in Cardiff, *how* was he *supposed to fucking get out of Cardiff, without* his *fucking bank card?!?* – and anything else that might've been in there, he'd also left his *fucking backpack* at the house. There was nothing else for it. He'd just have to go back the way he came, shamefaced, return the fiver and collect his belongings. He looked up at the clock hanging over the entrance as he left the store: *twelve minutes past midnight.*

Thursday 30th August

As he walked back towards Yeller's, his legs looser and lighter now, most likely on account of the sobering shock of having discovered he'd lost everything, Danny tried to formulate an explanation, some reason he could give for the hour-plus he'd spent outside Yeller's home. What had he been doing all that time? And why had he taken the fiver with him?

The brilliance of the explanation Danny concocted lay in its simplicity. He'd simply decided, after taking a piss, to get a round of beers in for everyone from the shop, to say thank you to Yeller for being such a great host. Only problem was, when he'd gotten to the shop, he'd realised he'd left his wallet back at the house. What's worse, it was then that he'd noticed he'd accidentally taken Yeller's fiver along with him. This would've been an unfortunate enough little occurrence on its own, but Danny then compounded his first two relatively minor mistakes with a third fatal error; he'd forgotten which house was Yeller's. Worse than that, he'd forgotten what *street* Yeller's house was on. Drugs, eh? He was sure they'd all have a good laugh about it.

Danny thought of adding more detail as he walked. Maybe he got into an argument with someone… maybe someone had attacked him, tried mugging him. Maybe they'd tried mugging him and then he'd told them honestly that he had no wallet, and he'd then held his trouser pockets out by their insides to prove it, drawing a big laugh from the would-be mugger. *Nah,* Danny thought, *a mugger wouldn't laugh about something like that.* Maybe Danny had shown him that he had no wallet, and the mugger had then tried to stab him. Maybe Danny had wrestled the knife off him, lectured him on the error of his ways, confiscated the blade, and told him to run on home. Maybe he'd severed one of the mugger's main arteries in the struggle and left the poor sod bleeding out onto the pavement. Maybe he ought to rough himself up a bit, scrape his elbows, tear his T-shirt, do something to lend the story veracity. *Nah,* Danny thought, Yeller's street surely drawing near, *keep it simple.*

* * *

Danny stood on the street staring up at the old Victorian terraced house that he thought was the one he'd left earlier, but the immense similarity between that one and the ones either side of it led him to question this conclusion. That was before even taking into account the identical houses running the length of the street either side of those houses in front of him, or the row after row of street after street of identical housing running parallel to them for miles on end. There was no real way to be certain – the music outside the house hadn't been particularly loud. He didn't remember being able to hear it from the street whatsoever. Then again, he remembered very little about leaving the house earlier. There was only one thing for it: he'd have to go door-to-door, knocking on every house with both a downstairs and upstairs light on, until he found the correct one. The task sounded monumental, but the late hour made it easier than it at first sounded; in the street he was in, there were only maybe four out of twenty homes meeting this up-and-downstairs-lights-on criterion. If there were maybe fifty streets in the vicinity that looked like that one – and Danny supposed there were a lot less than that, and besides, he remembered the house he'd exited earlier was on a street somewhere towards the middle of the residential conglomeration – then he'd find himself knocking on maybe fifty doors, a hundred tops. Perhaps even less than that – he knew which side of the road it was on, and he knew it was located towards the left-hand end of the street. There were probably little more than twenty houses that could possibly match the description of the one he was looking for.

With this thought in mind, he stepped quietly towards the house in front of him. He balled his left hand into a fist and pressed it gently against the door, summoning up the nerve to knock it. He didn't need to; the door fell open with the slightest touch. It'd been left unlocked. He stared into the hallway. Superficially, it could've been Yeller's, but the sounds of laughter coming from a TV in the living room and a general absence of music or chatter told him that it wasn't. He was about to reach in and quietly pull the door back closed again when, on the floor, he noticed a Nokia Lumia, wired up to a plug socket, on charge. He would've normally put it down to coincidence, but this was starting to feel like a quite extraordinary night, and there was a crack running diagonally across the bottom right-hand corner of the screen, a crack identical to the one on his own missing mobile. He stared down at it for a second. *It couldn't be...* but it was. He was quite certain that that was his Lumia. He stepped inside, quietly as he could, his nerves almost falling to pieces as he heard two male voices rise up in laughter as something particularly funny happened on the television set in the living room. He gently pulled the handset free from the charger, stuffed it into his pocket, pulled the door closed as quietly as possible behind him, then stepped back out onto the street.

He was almost at the end of the street, about to round the corner, when he saw someone walking towards him. Danny almost froze with fear, shoved his hands in his pockets, clutched the phone tightly. He rounded the corner, looked back once behind him, then, certain no-one was watching him, he broke into a sprint, wanting to get as far away from there as possible as quickly as he could.

He carried on running, past rows of repetitive housing, red-brick terraces shaded crimson against the orange glow of streetlight, until a voice screamed out from his pocket: "I AM THE GOD OF HELLFIRE, AND I WANT YOU TO BURN!"

Danny took out his Lumia and began running faster. Somebody called Cain was calling him. He pressed his thumb down hard on the power button, still running, until the synths that followed the demonic intro ceased, and he could see his own terror-struck face reflected, with an orange tint, against the black of the cracked Lumia's screen.

Saturday 1st September

09.31am

"Good mornin' Jenn-eh."

"What do you want, Rory?"

"I just called tae see how ye are. I've not heard from ye in a while."

"Yeah, not since that pensioner dropped dead outside the Asda's in Coryton," Jenny said. "And I take it you're only calling me now on account of that body what's washed up in the Taff."

"No, not all, Jenn-eh," Rory said. In the silence that followed, he quickly realised that total denial of the obvious would only irritate Jenny. "Well, it migh'f bin tha' wha' brought yir name tae mind, but i' is nae the only reason tha' I'm calling."

"Bullshit Rory. And if you want the autopsy report, you're going to have to pay for it this time. I'm not falling for any more of your 'romantic meal' at fucking Nando's shit."

Rory was silent for a time. Jenny could hear the distant buzzing of phone and chatter from the nearby newsroom. He lowered his voice when he next spoke; even though he was alone out in the corridor, you could never be too careful. "Alrigh'. Wha'd'ya wan' fir i'?"

"Five grand."

"Five grand! Jesus Christ Jenn-eh! This is nae fuckin' royalty tha's washed up in tha river. I'm working on a regional fuckin' newspaper here Jenn-eh, we have nae go' the budget tae pay ya five grand even if I thought I' was worth it, which it's fuckin' no'."

"Maybe I'd be better off speaking to someone at one of the nationals instead then."

"Aye, and how tha fuck are ye gonna go about introducing yirself tae them, eh? By calling up their fucking switchboard? That'd be a story in itself tha', tha coroner ringing round tha national papers, trying tae sell an autopsy report. Ye could knock wee Daniel Covell and them Amstell brothers off tha front page yirself wi' tha'."

"I think a national newspaper would be willing to go above and beyond to get an exclusive on this one, Rory."

"Get tae fuck! This laddy wha's died posts fucking vids on YouTube, he is nae fuckin' film star. I tell ya wha', I'll give ya a hundred quid fir i'."

"A hundred quid Rory? Get real. Add a zero and we've got a deal."

"A fucking grand? A fucking grand fir first dibs on tha autopsy report? Jesus Christ, Jenn-eh, it is nae worth half that. If this were one'f One Direction what'd washed up face down in tha river, then mebbe, but this lad were a wee fuckin' nobody 'til his untimely demise, Jenn-eh. It is nae worth five hundred, even; we dunnae even know if tha wee lad's been murdered yet."

"I'd say it's looking pretty likely that he was."

"Why's tha'?"

"Five hundred and you can read all about it."

"I already said, I could'nae pay ye tha' much even if I wanted tae, which I dunnae want tae anyway. One hundred fifty and I'll buy ya dinner. Somewhere nice this time."

"Two-fifty."

"One-fifty-five."

"Two forty-nine."

"Tha's no' gonna work, Jenn-eh. Look, I'm a busy man today. I'm investigatin' a fuckin' murder case, Jenn-eh. I cannae be pissing around, wasting time on these negotiations wiv ya. I'll give ya one hundred and sixty quid, and I'll buy ya a nice bottle of wine when we go fir dinner an' all."

"Two bottles."

"Alrigh', done."

"Okay Rory. They're cutting him up and having a poke around inside at the moment. I can probably get hold of a preliminary report sometime this afternoon."

"Jus' you make sure it's sent tae mah Hushmail account, alrigh'? And don' be doin' anything daft, like sending it from yir work e-mail."

"I won't."

"Thanks Jenn-eh."

Rory ended the call and grinned. Maybe she was bluffing, trying to bump the price up, but he was inclined to believe her when she said the report contained a pretty big clue that Daniel Covell had been murdered. Rory figured the lad's unfortunate end could prove fortuitous to him; perhaps it could even be his ticket back to Fleet Street and a *real fuckin' newspaper.*

Thursday 30th August

03.31am

Strips of duct tape on the window pane glistened silver in the moonlight. The muffled voices of two hooded figures could be heard outside. After rapid half-whispered discussion, the bulkier of the two took a hammer in his hand and slammed it against the window. Spider-web cracks rippled out beneath the duct tape. He gave it another whack, then another, then a fourth knocked the bulk of the glass through. The duct tape softened the sound of it shattering. The bigger, bulkier brother, Bruce, used the hammer to push out the worst of the shards that remained.

"Go on 'en butt," he quietly ordered.

"Why do I have to go first?" Darren asked.

"You're half the fucking size of me butt. Get in and open the door, mun."

Darren sighed and pushed down upon the window frame, then swivelled himself around on the kitchen unit and landed noiselessly inside. He moved quickly to the back door. It needed a key. A scan of the door's surroundings revealed nothing. Darren returned to the shattered window and explained.

Bruce sighed and pushed down upon the window frame, forcing his feet off the ground with great exertion. He clawed at the kitchen unit for greater leverage, rolled himself across the surface of it, and unathletically willed himself inside. Then, in the sudden silence of the kitchen, Bruce brought a shushing finger to his lips and led the way into an empty living room.

They moved on to the hallway, easing the door open, before easing their way upstairs, each gentle creak of staircase jabbing adrenaline into their veins. At the top of the stairs were three doors. Bruce held his hammer out and pointed Darren in the direction of the farthest room, then gently prised open the door to his left. It took a few seconds squinting in the darkness to realise he'd found the bathroom. Bruce returned to the landing and saw Darren reach his door, slam it open, smack his hammer down upon something wooden, quick-flick the lights on and off – "Oh, you fucking twat mun!" – and leave Bruce with no option other than to throw the third door open in similarly reckless fashion, quick-flick the lights on and off, and observe an unmade bed with no-one in it.

"Bru," he heard Darren call out from the end bedroom. "There's no-one in here butt."

08.58am

Danny was sat upstairs in the Burger King at the castle end of Queen Street, staring at the Nokia Lumia in his hand, with the crack on its screen that mostly definitely identified it as *his* Nokia Lumia. He was still terrified of turning it back on, trying to make sense of the bizarre chain of events that'd brought it back into his possession. He'd spent most of the night in the same seat in Burger King, spending his last fiver, that accidentally stolen fiver, on a double-cheeseburger meal. His only remaining money was the grubby penny he'd been given in change. There were a few drunks dotted about the place when he'd come in, with more filtering in and out as the night wore on, but by around 4am they'd all gone away, and he'd been able to get a few hours sleep, resting his head upon the tabletop. The late-shift staff had neither the will nor inclination to wake him up and move him on.

The quiet darkness of the early morning hours had faded into daylight, and there were now a few other customers dotted around the upstairs of the place, all ploughing into their breakfasts. Danny took a cold chip from the few remaining on the tray in front of him and watched one man, a middle-aged balding feller in a suit, bite into a breakfast burger. Chewing the chilled French fry, Danny wondered why anyone would come in to Burger King for breakfast. McDonalds, he could understand. The Sausage & Egg McMuffin had a cheesy deliciousness far superior to any of the meals they sold later on in the day. But Burger King... maybe it was one bad experience that'd put him off, one morning when he wandered in with a hangover and watched some angry-looking blonde girl from Eastern Europe slapping some sub-microwave-burger quality sausage and bacon together on a steel counter in the kitchen. He'd found the scene strangely unappetising. Never again. When it came to the bread-and-butter of the fast food joints, the regular all-day menu itself, BK was superior to Maccy D's in every way, from the fries down to the patty. But breakfast at Burger King? That'd be like going to KFC for Christmas dinner. *Have a word with for yourself.*

Danny's eyes fell instinctively to the screen of the Lumia, wrestled toward it with an urge to tap his observations on breakfast at Burger King into it, post them to Twitter or Facebook, maybe snap a pic of the sad balding feller biting into his breakfast burger to go along with it. But as he stared at his own reflection in the black void of the screen, Danny reflected upon the last sound he'd heard from it, that terrifying devil's proclamation. He shuddered and looked up at a clock on the wall. 9 o'clock. Time to start sorting his life out.

09.02am

Tom stretched out and moaned as he eyes blinked into wakefulness, sunlight streaming in through a window. He felt the kind of fuzzy head-numbed calm that was one of the better potentialities of a night-before spent on the booze – not the feeling of soul-stripped savagery and dehydrated desecration that were waking's first indication of a night of poor decisions and forgotten indiscretions, but the kind of comfortable numbness that followed a night ended in bed beside someone else.

He blinked at his surroundings, little droplets of memory condensing behind his eyes. There were band posters on the walls – The Smiths, Black Rebel Motorcycle Club, Franz Ferdinand. Some clothing and debris dumped in little bundles about the floor. And no other living being. Tom closed his eyes and breathed in the perfumed scent of the bed's owner, her face reappearing to him, her name following, though it came to him in a vague and shapeless form, its spelling a mystery: *Ji Eun.* Ji Eun the Korean. Had he fucked her? *No...* he vaguely recalled heading back to hers, she all fucked up on the liquor, he too, though not beyond reasonable measure of self-control. Then she'd brought him upstairs, to her bedroom, and she'd flopped onto the mattress and passed out, face down. The only clothing she'd removed were her Converse when she'd walked in the front door. And Tom had simply lain down beside her, lying on his side in the slither of space that remained free on her single bed. He'd quickly slipped out of consciousness in a drunken stupor. *Where is she?* Tom sat up and rubbed his eyes. Perhaps she'd gone to the toilet. Maybe she was making breakfast. She might even have left. Maybe gone to work, or uni, or whatever her thing was. *What day is it?* Shit. *What time is it?* Fuck. Tom pulled his iPhone from his pocket. The screen was black. He pressed down hard on the power button. Nothing. Dead. He glanced around the room for some source of time, and found it, a digital alarm clock perched on a desk beyond the end of the bed. He squinted at it, then upon the digits becoming clear, he flung the covers off and sprang to his feet immediately: 09.04.

09.05am

Tom slammed the door behind him and stumbled out onto the street, squinting into the harsh morning sunlight and trying to locate himself. It took a half-second to recognise the street; he was in Cathays, Cardiff's student housing ghetto. He figured it ought to be possible to leg it from there to work within about ten minutes, fifteen tops. He took a few seconds more to connect the scene in front of him to the city's wider mapscape: *Arabella Street, just off Albany Road.* The fact that he'd figured his location out so quickly and so accurately startled him. Cathays was all much of a muchness, street after street of terraced housing. The only markers that could be used to navigate it were pubs, off-licenses, and takeaways, as well as the odd student household who had added some wacky idiosyncrasy to their home, such as a collection of traffic cones in the front garden or a cardboard cut-out of Chewbacca on the windowsill. But Tom knew *exactly* where he was. He turned around to check, and yes, he even knew the house number. 26 Arabella Street. *Fuck...* it couldn't be. He staggered towards Albany Road, a main artery of a road that would guide him back towards the heart of the city centre. *26 Arabella Street.* It had been a long time since he'd been inside that house...

09.06am

Danny was in through the doors of the bank virtually as soon as they'd opened. Although there were a few others milling about outside with the same intention, the moment that the doors had opened at nine, Danny had made sure to be the first one to the counter. He'd actually had to wait a few minutes for the girl behind the counter to sort her money trays out before she could start dealing with his problem. Then, once he'd gotten into it, he wished he hadn't bothered.

"I told you, I've lost my wallet," he pleaded, "my I.D. cards were all inside it."

"Well I'm sorry sir, I can't let you withdraw any money without something to prove your identity."

"Look, I've lost me wallet, me bank card, me student card, me provisional license, everything. What am I supposed to do?"

"You can go and file a report at the police station."

"But I need money now. Listen to me accent, I'm not from round here. I need to get back to Leeds as soon as possible. You must have a photo of me on file you can go and check or summin'? I'm sure you've taken a scan of me passport before now."

"I'm sorry sir," she said, sounding anything but, "there's really nothing we can do to help you."

09.08am

The night before was colouring all Ji Eun's present, the whole world around her murky gloop, she mired in the desiccated embryo of existence, hazy and unfocused, peering into the sneering glow of the computer screen and the unstable jagging lines of newspaper headlines, some words looming larger than others – 'conflict', 'malware', 'warfare', 'cull'. Beneath it, last night was whispering to her, begging her to turn back and watch it played out again, the little jagged chunks of memory that remained within her pulsating and smirking, fiendishly taunting her. That guy she'd woken up next to... had they fucked? *No*. She took solace in reminding herself that she'd woken up fully clothed, he still sleeping beside her. But where had he come from? Why was he there? And what would he do upon waking? Would he walk out the door, leave without being asked, or would she come home tonight to find him, still there, an apparition from a shadowy, murky gloop netherworld night... boozy, barmy Britain. *I want to go home...*

"Mornin'," Rory said, appearing besides the desk, without Ji Eun having noticed him enter.

She looked up at him weakly; he saw her weakness and frowned.

Beside her, Christian was on a phone call, yapping away, words tumbling out of his mouth and into the receiver without Ji Eun's murk-flooded brain having time to process them.

"We're gonna take a wee field trip this mornin', Ji Eun. Remember tha' guy I mentioned tae ye yesterday, tha escaped con wha' did a runner?" He didn't wait for an answer. "We're gonna go pay his family a visit, see if mebbee they've go' 'ny clue where tha fucker's bin hidin' tae. Come on, let's ge' out o' here – the fresh air'll do ye good."

09.42am

Tom stared unhappily into the vast whiteness of the computer screen, the room around him mired in unhappy mid-morning silence. He'd gotten into work a little over twenty minutes late, but his indiscretion had seemingly escaped notice. Now though, he was troubled by something that felt, to him, of far greater importance. He moved the mouse cursor back to the search box at the top of the page and tried again: 'Jee Un'. The search term brought up scores of results, both males and females, a long list of smiling avatars, some with two fingers raised in a peace sign, some with duck face pout, all Asian, none of them the girl he'd met the previous night. He'd exhausted several other potential spellings and gotten nowhere; now he was overwhelmed with possibilities. He scrolled back up to the search box and tried 'Jee Un Cardiff'. No results. The thought occurred to him to check for her on Claire's friend's list, but he'd unfriended Claire long ago, and remembered drunkenly clicking around on Facebook one night and being prompted by curiosity to check up on exes, only to discover that she'd blocked him. Tom sighed. Perhaps he'd never find her. Perhaps the only way of building on last night's beautiful beginning would be to turn up at the house unannounced, which would run the risk of Claire opening the door to him, and what the hell kind of tortuous awkwardness would follow from there...

"Tom, can I see you in my office please?"

Tom turned to see both Matt and Michael staring down at him. He got to his feet and felt a hundred eyes upon him as he followed his superiors out of the People Outreach Hub, into a corridor and in through another door to 'Matt's office', which was more of a meeting room really, with a widescreen TV on the wall and a long table that was used for team meetings. Matt took a seat at the head of the long table. Michael sat down in the swivel chair beside Matt. Tom eyed up the dozen-or-more swivel chairs around the table for a moment, briefly contemplating the ridiculous notion of sitting himself at the very opposite end of it. He instead took the seat beside Michael and braced himself.

"Alright Tom, do you know why we called you in here this morning?" Michael opened, a look of supreme seriousness anointing his face.

"Yeah."

"Why have we called you in here Tom?"

"Because I was late."

"Right. Katrina says she saw you come in at half-nine this morning."

"Uh, I don't know, I think it was about twenty-five past..."

"And what time should you be here?"

"Nine."

"Nine. Not half-nine. Not nine twenty-five. Nine o'clock exactly. And this isn't the first time this week you've been late, is it Tom?"

"No."

"No. And what did we say to you last time?"

"Don't be late," Tom guessed.

"Apart from that."

"Umm..."

"We told that you that if you knew you were running late, you should call ahead and let Matt or myself know."

"Right."

"So did you do that?"

"No."

"Why not?"

"My phone was out of battery."

Michael frowned. The interrogation ceased for a moment, Tom's excuse insurmountable.

"So why were you late Tom?" Michael said, moving on.

"My alarm clock didn't go off."

"And your alarm clock's on your phone is it?"

"Yeah."

Michael frowned again; Tom had defeated him.

"How many leads have you put through this week, Tom?" Matt asked, taking over.

"Two or three," Tom said, guessing.

"Two," confirmed Michael.

"Two. And what's target Tom?"

"Five."

"The basic target is five. And you are on two. And you've been late. Twice. Do you even take this job seriously?"

"Yeah," Tom said, then, realising that was insufficient, "of course I do."

"Well you'd better start bloody acting like it. As you well know, things aren't going too well for your team at the moment. We've got Leeds sniffing round our arseholes looking to shaft us, and we need every man pulling together to stop that from happening. Now, who're you with for this presentation you're giving on Friday?"

What presentation? Tom thought to himself, then, forcing his mind to track back through the previous day to find what they were referring to. He vaguely remembered Michael giving some long-winded speech about new data coming up soon, but them needing to have a plan of attack, or some other war-based metaphor. Team Lemon had been split into small groups, each tasked with producing a presentation on the types of business most commonly found in their designated area of the country. "Sean."

"Sean. Good. Well you and Sean had better bloody well have something half-decent to present to us come Friday, alright?"

"Yeah."

"And I'd better not be needing to have any more little chats with you. You can consider this a verbal warning. Strike two. One more, you're out. Do I make myself clear?"

"Yeah."

"Good. Now get out of my sight and go do the job you were hired to do." Tom got up to leave as Matt added his parting shot. "And no more pissing around on Facebook either."

Tom mumbled agreement, got up, and walked out of the room, back through the corridor, to the People Outreach Hub. His teammates' heads' rose from their computer screens as he returned to his seat. They looked away as Tom put his headset back on and clicked Callex into pumping out a dial tone.

"Whose up for drinks after work?" Justin asked. "Get to know all the noobs a bit better."

"Could do," Sean said.

A few others uttered agreement.

"I can't tonight," Joseph said, "I'm supposed to be meeting some mates. Got a friend whose been away for a while. Not seen him in a couple of years."

"Fair enough," Justin said. "Tom?"

"Alright," Tom said, figuring a few pints would be the best thing to wash away the memory of the last lot.

Joseph looked across the room to check there were no superiors nearby, then slipped his Nokia 3310 out of his pocket; Jodie still hadn't replied. *She's working,* Joseph tried to reassure himself. *Probably not had chance to read it yet.*

"I thought you had a Lumia?" Sean asked, noticing Joseph's downgraded handset.

"Yeah, I did have, 'til last night. Get this, right, I was round my mate's house in Llandaff…"

09.46am

"And what if they do trace it?" Bruce asked.

"Uh?" Darren grunted, still looking at the laptop screen, sitting on the end seat of the sofa, Kaiser passed out by the side of him.

"What if they do trace that bloomin' laptop, mun?"

"What d'you mean, butt?"

Bruce sighed loudly. He couldn't believe that his idiot younger brother could be so naive as to see no problem whatsoever with using the laptop he'd snatched from Jodie's house the night before.

"Flippin' trace it mun! T-R-A-C-E, fuckin' trace it, track it, fuckin' hunt it down and find out we've gotten hold of it."

"How are they gonna do that mun?"

"I don't know, you know what they're like with these computers and tha' today mun. Bleddyn swears down that the reason the five-oh found about that weed grow Pricey had on the go was that they were listening to all his conversations through the mic in his mobile."

"Don't be daft mun," Darren said, looking up at him, "the FBI're hardly gonna be sat around listening in to Pricey's conversations all day on the off chance that he's gonna tell someone he's got a weed grow on the go, are they?"

"Well how did they find it then?"

"They got cameras on their helicopters, mun. Heat-sensitive ones. They'll have seen the warehouse they were doing it in was hotter than the fucking sun and gone to have a look at it."

"The fuck did you nick her laptop for anyway mun?"

"I dunno. Thought there might've been some information on it."

"Information? We're not robbing the fucking Pentagon, butt."

"Well, we needed a laptop anyway. We might as well nick something, seeing as we'd broken into the house already, like. It'd look even more suspicious if the house was broken into and nothing went missing, wouldn't it?"

"Yeah, well, just you be careful you don't get us into trouble, butt," Bruce concluded, looking away from his younger brother to his eldest, Simon, who was slouched in the armchair as he had been for the best part of the last 24 hours, staring at the television screen, as BBC News 24 regurgitated the same few bite-sized chunks of headline news ad infinitum. "More trouble than we're in already, anyway."

Bruce shook his head at his elder brother, thinking of all the expletives he'd like to spout at him, all variations on the theme 'get the fuck out of my house'. He took a cigarette from the packet of Lambert & Butler resting upon the arm of the sofa. *'Course, you can't say that to family, can you? 'Get the fuck out of my house'. 'Get the fuck out of my fucking house'... 'd fucking love to, mind.* Bruce lit up the cigarette. The near-silent living room glowed orange from sunlight beating against drawn curtains. The only sounds were the dog's heavy breathing and occasional sighing, Darren tapping away at the keys on the laptop, and the low-volume news-relaying of the posh-accented BBC newsreader on the television set.

Banging at the door – three quick bangs in succession – changed that. The dog woke up immediately. Kaiser hopped off the sofa and barked loudly in the middle of the room.

"Shut up Kaiser!" Bruce bellowed, getting to his feet and leaving the cigarette to burn out in the ashtray.

His brothers stared towards the door to the hallway as Bruce walked towards it, the dog still barking.

"Shut up mun Kaiser!" Bruce shouted again, stepping into the hallway and pulling the door shut behind him.

Bruce opened the front door to see two police officers standing on his doorstep, smiling at him. PCs Bronwyn Jones and Ivor Evans.

"Good morning Mr. Amstell," Bronwyn smiled. "I'm PC Bronwyn Jones, as I'm sure you know, and this is my colleague, PC Ivor Evans."

Bruce stared sternly at Brownyn. He knew her well. He paid no heed to the youngling at the side of her.

"You are Mr. Bruce Amstell, correct?" she asked.

"You know who I am. Why are you here?"

"Well, Mr. Amstell, we're awfully sorry to disturb you like this, but we were just wondering if you'd heard from your brother lately?"

Bruce stared at her in silence for a few seconds before answering. "Which brother?"

"Simon."

"Simon," Bruce repeated, shifting his gaze around the place, trying to give the impression of thinking about it. "Simon... Last time I heard from him was a couple of months back."

"Is that so?"

"Aye. Maybe in April, or May. March. March or May, I always get them pair mixed up."

"Okay," Bronwyn said, still smiling, "well, would you mind if we came in to talk to you for a minute?"

"I would mind," Bruce said, instinctively reaching out and gripping the handle of the door to the living room.

Ivor Evans glared at him glumly, decidedly not smiling. The tension of eye contact made Bruce feel a more substantial explanation might be required.

"My girlfriend's in there, and she's not decent."

"Well, we can wait out here for a couple of minutes while she sorts herself out," Bronwyn said, still smiling.

"She's bollock naked," Bruce clarified. "We were actually in the middle of something."

"Well, we can call back this afternoon, if that's better for you."

Bruce thought about it for a moment before speaking. "What's this all about, anyway?"

"Your brother seems to have gone missing," Bronwyn explained.

"Missing?!" Bruce repeated, with all the shock and gusto he could muster. "He's in fucking jail, i'n' he?"

"Your brother was on a work release program," Bronwyn told him. "He was supposed to leave the prison and report for work at the local Paul's Pies factory. Somewhere between leaving the prison and reporting for work, your brother appears to have absconded."

"Blimey," Bruce replied. "You don't think nothing's happened to him, do you?"

Bronwyn exchanged a look with Ivor before answering Bruce: "We certainly hope not. Were you close with your brother?"

"Aye. Well, he's my brother like, i'n' he?"

Bronwyn nodded thoughtfully, still smiling. "When was the last time you spoke to your brother?"

"Like I said, I went up the prison to visit him a couple of months back."

"Sometime in April, March, or May," Browyn said, taking a little notepad and a pen from her pocket. "We'll just call it 'spring', shall we?" She jotted the word down. "And how did he seem at the time?"

"He seemed alright like. He's been in clink long enough now, he's used to all the ins and outs of it. Think he's a bit sick of being stuck in there, mind."

"You don't think he might have been planning on absconding at that point, do you?"

"Well... I know he was well past his release date, like. I don't think that was sitting too well with him."

Bronwyn nodded again, a perfect picture of empathy. "I suppose that must be awfully frustrating for him. I suppose that would get to anyone. That'd get to me, definitely. Would it get to you Ivor?"

"Yeah," Ivor said, "it would, aye."

"I suppose it'd get to anyone."

"But, still, let's not jump to any conclusions," Bruce said. "I'm worried for my brother's safety. He's not the type to do things just for the sake of doing them. I'm worried something bad might've happened to him between your prison and the factory."

"What do you think might've happened to him?" Bronwyn asked, frowning.

"Well, anything mun. I mean, he could've been hit by a bus, savaged by an animal, anything."

"So you don't think he's wilfully absconded then?"

Bruce frowned at the artifice of it.

"Done a runner," Bronwyn said, leaning in closer, locking him into a staring contest with those big brown eyes of hers.

Bruce blinked first. "Well... I suppose you can't never say never, like, but I don't know. I just hope nothing's happened to him, really."

"So you would rather he'd done a runner then?" Bronwyn asked, smiling again.

"Well, I'd rather that than have him, like... hit by a bus... or savaged by an animal..."

Bronwyn nodded thoughtfully. "So let's say, for arguments sake, let's say he did do a runner. If he did do a runner, where do you suppose your brother would've gone?"

"Well... I don't know really," Bruce said, racking his brains for something that sounded plausible without being an actual clue as to Simon's true plan. "He might've gone to me Mam's house, up in Crumlin."

"I suppose a lot of people would look for the help of a family member in this type of situation, wouldn't they? What do you think, Ivor?"

"Yeah, I think a lot of them would, Bron," Ivor replied.

Bronwyn nodded thoughtfully. Bruce realised that she was no longer smiling. "Are there any other family members you think Simon might've paid a visit to?"

"Well... there's Uncle Kev and Aunty Brenda."

"Uncle Kev and Aunty Brenda," Bronwyn repeated, writing the names down. "Kev's short for Kevin, is it?"

"Aye."

"Kevin Amstell?"

"Aye."

"Were they particularly close to your brother?"

"Not particularly."

"But you think they still might help your brother out?"

"Not necessarily."

"But you think that he might ask them to?"

"He might do."

"And might he ask that sort of thing of anyone else closer to him?"

"He might do."

"Bruce," Bronwyn said, locking those big bown eyes on his, then rattling off the next few words without blinking, "have you ever heard of aiding and abetting a wanted criminal?"

"I've heard of aiding one. Helping them, like."

"Yeah."

"And what's abetting?"

"Helping them. Like."

Bruce broke away from the stare. He nodded. "Well, I hope none of my family have been daft enough to take him in then. Be a shame for anyone else to get in trouble over this. It's bad enough having a brother inside. I'd hate for anyone else in the family to be behind bars."

"So would I, Bruce. I'd hate for that too. I'm sure your Mam would as well, wouldn't she? Two sons behind bars. One of them there just for doing his brother a good turn. And your brother only got eighteen months initially, didn't he? He might be looking at a bit more now for absconding, but still, aiding and abetting is a much more serious sentence than the one he originally went down for. It really would be a shame if his brother went down for longer than him just for helping out a family member, wouldn't it?"

"It would, aye." Bruce was staring straight at Bronwyn now. A look of grim determination had gripped his chubby face.

"Of course, if his brother were to cooperate fully with the police, if his brother were to offer us any information that led to the recapture of our fugitive, well, that is something that the police would be most grateful for. Wouldn't they, Ivor?"

"They would, aye."

"How long have you and your girlfriend been going out, Bruce?" Bronwyn asked suddenly.

"What?"

"You and your girlfriend."

"I haven't got a... clue actually. We've been kind of off-and-on, like. I suppose it's five years, all told, since we first met each other."

"Aw. That's nice, innit Ivor?"

"It is, aye."

"Ain't that nice?" Bronwyn said, her red lipstick-laden lips curling up into a megawatt smile. "How'd you meet her?"

"We were at school together."

"Oh yeah. Five years ago? How old are you now Bruce?"

"Umm... well, not school like, I do call it school like, but it's more of a college really. I was doing this night course. Car mechanics."

"Mr. Amstell, are you aware that lying to a police officer is an offence punishable by up to five years imprisonment?"

"Yeah," Bruce responded meekly.

"Good. Then maybe you'll stop fucking lying to me." The smile disappeared in a second. "We know he's in your house Bruce."

Bruce stared straight at her. *How the fuck does she know that?* She couldn't. She was bluffing. *She's bluffing. Poker. Poke the bitch.* "I'm not fucking lying," he said calmly, then, raising his voice, "and I don't appreciate the incineration."

"Well," Bronwyn said, suddenly all smiles again. "I suppose we'll just have to take your word for it. I think we're all done here, aren't we Ivor?"

"Yeah, I think we are Bron."

"Alright then Mr. Amstell, we'll leave you and your girlfriend to it. But bear in mind what we've said to you, and if you feel like avoiding a lengthy prison sentence, pay us a visit sometime soon, yeah?"

Bronwyn and Ivor turned to leave. Bruce tensed the muscles in his arm ready to slam the door shut.

"Oh, and Bruce," Bronwyn said, turning back to face him. "Tell your girlfriend we're sorry for disturbing you. What was her name again?"

It took Bruce all of a half-second to think up a pig-based pun. "Babe." He slammed the door shut.

Ivor followed Bronwyn onto the street and into their squad car.

"What do you reckon?" Ivor asked, with the doors closed and them inside.

"Fucking bullshit from the get go," Bronwyn told him, her smile having vanished entirely. "That prick knows exactly where Simon Amstell is. And so do I."

"You don't reckon--"

"Come on rookie, wake the fuck up mun, will you? If Simon Amstell ain't inside that house, I'll leave the force."

"What, do you reckon he was lying about his girlfriend being naked in there?"

Bronwyn stared at her colleague like one would a total moron who'd just said something exceptionally stupid. "Come off it. The last time that fat fuck in there saw a naked woman that wasn't on video was when he came spluttering out of his Mam's birth canal."

Further down the street, Rory Gallagher was parked up in his red Volvo, watching through the windshield as the police car drove away from Bruce Amstell's home.

"Looks like the pigs've go' the same idea we do," Rory said. He took a final drag on a cigarette, then tossed it out the window and rolled the thing closed.

The police car had already been parked up outside when Rory had arrived, and he'd watched them with great interest ever since, going over all he had thus far learned about the Amstell brothers and their storied history of petty misdemeanours, rattling these off to Ji Eun without paying any attention to how she was receiving them. Now, with the cigarette done and the cops gone, he looked across to the passenger seat and saw that was she slouched down low, elbow resting on the window frame, supporting a head in which eyes lay half-open, half-way between the world of the living and the dead. It was a state he knew all too well.

"Y'know, I'd bet good money tha' nae fucker'll be coomin' outta tha house now tha' tha fuzz've been round, not fir a good wee chunk o' time, anyway. Mebbe I'll head back to tha' offy we passed round tha corner, see if we cannae ge' a bite to eat?" No reaction. "It looked like the type o' place that'll do sandwiches, breakfast baps, tha' kind'f thing. Mebbe I'll get us both one?"

"I'm not really hungry," Ji Eun mumbled.

"Ach, it'll do ya good tae ge' a bi' of food intae ye. A breakfast bap, that'll sort ya righ' out. Bacon, sausage, egg, mushroom – all tha' grease an' amino acids is what yir body's cryin' out fir righ' now. And I'll get us some tea tae wash it down wi'. Fuck i', actually, I'll have a tea, I'll get ya a Lucozade Sport. When ye drink tae much, yir body loses tha very same minerals tha' seep out when ye get sweaty playin' sports. Ge' tha' down yir neck and y'u'll feel a world better."

"Okay. Thanks."

"Aye, leave it tae long and y'u'll not be able tae eat all day. If ya don't get some food down yir neck within a few hour o' waking, the hangover'll consume ya, an' tha next twenty-four hours'll be a total fuckin' write off." He removed his seat belt and opened the door. "Right, if ya see anything happenin' at tha hoose, anything a' all, gi' us a call."

09.54am

Danny was sitting on a bench besides an outdoor cafe on the Hayes, staring at a couple of pigeons fighting over half a bacon butty. *What to do, what to do?* As much as he wanted to access his money and get the fuck out of Cardiff, the thing that was bothering him most about his lack of funds was his consequent lack of cigarettes. A joint and a beer would've gone down a treat too – they would've certainly helped wash away the pangs of regret and nausea attacking his brain and his belly respectively – but the thing he longed for most in the world was a fucking cigarette. *What to do...* If he'd been in a real foreign country, instead of a fake foreign country like Wales, he could've simply walked into the British Consulate, told them he'd lost his wallet, and they would be sure to take care of everything. An emergency passport, some backdoor into his bank account. They probably would've even given him tea and biscuits while he'd waited. But no, not in Wales. If he wanted to prove his identity to the idiots at the bank, an emergency passport would require a hundred quid or more in cash. He thought briefly of The Job Centre, of going in and signing on, before realising that even if they did approve his application immediately, and give him his fifty-odd quid of dole money right there and then, which they almost certainly would not, the money would still have to be deposited into his bank account. He took his Nokia Lumia from his pocket and stared at it. Even with the crack on the screen it'd have to be worth at least fifty quid. Maybe he could take it into a Cash Generator. Problem was, he was sure there were some rules that wouldn't allow just anyone to hand in any mobile phone and walk out with some cash-in-hand payment. He'd need some paperwork of some kind, something to prove the mobile was his. And since the SIM card had probably been switched and the phone professionally and illicitly unlocked, proving it was truly his would be all the harder. *What to do, what to do?* His eyes were getting heavy. Behind them, his brain was feeling hollow, its edges frayed. His blinks became heavier, more infrequent... he was losing grip on reality, pigeons still squabbling over the discarded bacon butty on the filthy concrete floor in front of him, lapses into blackness growing ever more prolonged...

Saturday 1st September

12.31pm

"Jesus..." Rory couldn't help letting the mild expletive slip from his mouth, much as he wanted to keep his actions secret. He was at his desk in the newsroom, looking at the iPhone in his hand, reading through the autopsy report Jenny had swiftly supplied him with.

"What's the matter?" Christian said, the name of the Lord arousing his interest. "Got the results back?"

"Huh?" Rory grunted, stunned at the accuracy of it. Christian shifted uneasily; he'd never startled his unflappably pig-headed colleague before. He'd been planning on making some quip, some barb, some reference to a STD check, but the colourless abjection of Rory's face made him reconsider.

Rory looked away from Christian and back at the iPhone screen, taking the strange prescience of his comment to be mere coincidence, and he lost himself again in the black-and-white lines evoking gruesomely colourful images in his mind. Contusions and ruptures, reds and purples on milky white flesh, rendered stark black against a pure white background. Rory thought of the seagull carcass he'd found at the riverside earlier that morning, meat hacked off the bone, its life and body sullied, savaged, desecrated... the seagull's fate and figure meshed in his mind with that of the poor lad on whom the autopsy had been performed... Rory had little doubt from the horrid little details that Daniel Covell, Danny Daggers, had been both raped and murdered.

Thursday 29th August

09.56am

Danny woke up with a start, panic-gripped. Some sound had woken him – a seagull, squawking loudly, snapping its superior beak at the bacon butty-munching pigeons, frightening them off in a flutter of fallen feathers, lashing out and tearing a blood-dipped feather from one as it fled. *Bloodied bird corpse.* What did that mean? The words had been cast adrift into the raging tempest of Danny's consciousness, unmoored of context. The seagull flipped the remnants of the bacon butty up into the air and swallowed it down whole, then flew off, squawking its superiority, alpha male of the inner-city aviary. Danny felt some connection to that bird, something beyond comprehension, some shuddering sense of destiny. *Maybe I envy him his freedom,* Danny thought to himself. *Envy him his freedom,* he repeated to himself. *That's good, that. Sounds poetic. Proper English.* He wondered if he oughtn't get a tattoo of it. On his forearm, maybe; a squawking seagull and the legend underneath, etched with feather-moulded quill pin: 'Envy him his freedom'.

The bird disappeared above the buildings. Danny cast his mind back to the dream, if you could call the disconnected chain of terrifying images that'd danced before his briefly-sleeping mind a dream. Just faces, names, and fear. An overriding sense of impending dread. Suddenly it all became clear to him, in his mind's own drug-ravaged, sleep-deprived way; *Envy him his freedom.* Get the fuck out of Cardiff. *Bloodied bird corpse.* Get the fuck out of Cardiff or die.

10.01am

Barriers. *Bugger.* Barriers and ticket collectors, mundane men in green uniforms, working together to block his only way out. Danny looked at them, those guardians of the station platforms, the barriers to exit. There was no way of sneaking or forcing his way past. The stairs to the platforms stretched out far behind them, back all the way to platform 8 at the station's end, and there were no more than a dozen people walking to or from the platforms at any one moment. The morning rush hour had clearly ceased. Danny stepped back outside the cavernous grey hall of Cardiff Central station and looked up at the giant clock-face embedded in it. It was just after ten, a minute or two past at the most. *Surely ten is the cut-off,* he thought, banking on the barriers disappearing during off-peak times. Of course, there was the very real possibility of the station's platforms being guarded all day, and the ticket collectors and barriers only exiting the scene whence the evening rush hour had concluded, which would leave Danny stranded in Cardiff until maybe six or seven p.m., or later. *Give it 'til half ten,* he thought, looking up once again at the station's clock. It wasn't like he had anything better to do.

His eyes then fell from the clock-face to a guy with a trendily-gelled footballer's haircut, wearing a brown leather jacket over suit pants, a suitcase at the side of him. The guy was smoking a cigarette besides an ashtray affixed to the station's front wall.

"Excuse me mate," Danny said, drawing a look of irritation, "would you mind if I bought a fag off you?"

"Buy?" the guy sneered back.

"Yeah." Danny always said 'buy' rather than 'crash', 'snag', 'pinch', or any other synonyms of 'borrow', 'steal' or 'beg for'. He found people were much more giving, and almost never genuinely expected cash in return. Almost.

"How much were you thinking of paying?"

Danny stuck his hand in his pocket and pulled out the grubby penny Burger King had given him in change. The guy's sneer increased in severity.

"You'll not get much for that these days."

Danny stared at him, unsure if the rebuke was final, or just verbal jousting. The guy answered by hurriedly inhaling and exhaling a few more puffs of the cigarette, before stubbing it out in the ashtray, a good quarter left on it. He then headed off into town, pulling his suitcase behind him. *Wanker.* Danny spotted another smoker, a meek-looking middle aged man, with a horseshoe of hair clinging to an otherwise bald, bulbous skull. "Excuse me mate, would you mind if I borrowed a fag off you?"

10.04am

The cigarette nearly done, Danny noticed some movement around the ticket barriers. He watched through the transparent plastic panels in the station's sliding doors as the mundane men in green started packing their ticket machine away. As they fiddled and faffed around with it, the barriers suddenly sprang open. Danny smiled, his brain basking in the warm glow of addiction satiated. *Problem solved.*

10.18am

"Excuse me, sir."

The voice that called out to him was not of the same scene as Danny. Danny was lying on his back, floating gently down a river, a conduit through his consciousness, on a mellow-white summer's morning. On one riverbank loomed the great steel struts and hulking frame of the Millennium Stadium, one of few Cardiff landmarks that had impressed themselves upon Danny, whilst on the other riverbank a tramp squatted, gnawing at a bloody hunk of prey.

"Sir," the voice called out again.

Danny heard it without waking, or rather, he remained in his dream without sleeping, if the succession of surreal images that his mind had conjured instantly upon his eyes closing could be called a dream. "Sir." The voice was louder now, and more insistent. Danny yielded, and opened his eyes to the purple-lined interior of the First Great Western railways service from Cardiff Central to Manchester Piccadilly, greenery zooming past the window.

"Could I see your ticket please, sir?" asked the inspector, a man with sad droopy jowels and a First Great Western-branded cap covering up his baldness.

"Yeah," Danny mumbled, not at one with the world of the waking.

He made a big show of patting down his jeans, then sticking his hands in his pockets, then leaning back on his seat and thrusting his hips upwards to check his back pockets, before checking the front again, and then, ravaged shell of a thing that Cardiff had left him, he made a pitiful attempt at play-acting. "I've lost my wallet."

The droopy-jowelled employee of First Great Western's face remained unmoved, locked into the perpetual frown of a man who'd let his best years slip away from him without incident. "If you don't have a ticket, or any means of buying one, I'm afraid I'm going to have to ask you to alight at the next station."

"What's the next station?" Danny asked, holding out hope that he'd slept through at least one of them and made it across the border into England.

"Newport."

10.26am

"Bristol."

"That'll be thirty quid mate."

"Can you not do it on the meter?"

"Not for Bristol I can't," the taxi driver told him. "I'll have to pay six-eighty coming back over the bridge, won't I? Sorry butt, cash up-front only for England."

Danny got out of the taxi without saying another word. He'd planned to get off in Bristol, in friendly territory, the country of his birth, do a runner from the taxi, and from there concoct a plan to get the rest of the way back to Leeds, far away in the north-east of England. He didn't have thirty quid to pay for the taxi fare up front; all he had in the world were the clothes on his back and that grubby penny from Burger King. And his Lumia. By no small miracle, he still had his treasured Nokia Lumia. Danny took the phone from his pocket and stared into the cracked obelisk for a few seconds, summoning up the nerve to act. Nerve summoned, he held his thumb down on the power switch. His Lumia beamed back into life. The battery was dwindling, but wasn't yet critical; 64%. The time was 10.27. A few notifications about texts and Facebook messages popped up, all from unfamiliar names, all intended for whoever had stolen the phone from him. Danny didn't feel up to the task of investigating the phone thief's identity. Unsure of how long it would be until he'd be able to charge his phone again, he held down the power button until the screen went black, then slipped his Lumia back into his pocket.

Danny looked down the taxi rank at the other cabs. He considered hopping in the next one, but it seemed pointless. *The definition of madness is doing the same thing over and over again and expecting a different result*, he reminded himself, not entirely sure where he'd picked up that little nugget of wisdom. There was no way Danny was getting in a taxi without thirty quid in cash, and if he had thirty quid in cash, he could've simply plopped that down on a train ticket and probably gotten at least half-way across England. *Half-way home*. So how the fuck could he get hold of thirty quid? Or better yet, the actual cost of a train ticket all the way back to *sodding Leeds*. *And a couple of quid for a can and a sandwich for the journey. And a pack of fags*, the satiation of the one he'd inhaled outside Cardiff Central having long-since passed.

He took a quick look at his surroundings, turning his head at a blur of grey, catching amongst it the yellow sign of a Cash Generator. He'd already ruled out pawning his Lumia, but did he have anything else he might be able to sell? He thought briefly of his Sennheiser headphones, before remembering they were in the bag he'd left back at Yeller's house. There was one other way he could get money – *Mum and Dad*. But he didn't much fancy 'fessing up to having lied about spending a couple of weeks down in Cornwall with Simon Granger. How could he possibly explain his presence in Newport? And how could he actually go about receiving any money they sent? He'd have to get the money wired through Western Union or something – *maybe a Post Office?* He'd never before tried obtaining money without a functioning bank card. It seemed far too desperate a quest... *No,* he was leaving his parents out of it.

He looked at the grey mess of a city slumped around the train station. Perhaps it wasn't so bad. He knew Newport was a big university town, and there were probably tons of bars and clubs that'd be rammed with pissed-up young adults by the time the evening rolled around. Surely a few would recognise his face and help him get some booze down his neck. Apart from that, he knew very little about Wales' third city. Squeezed between Cardiff and Bristol, a few parodic rap songs were the only culture of note Newport had ever produced. *Unchartered lands.* Danny figured he could shape the city's narrative himself, make it his own. Perhaps he'd been brought there by destiny... *destiny...* he saw a seagull walking along the main thoroughfare running past a Yates, fluttering its wings and half-arsedly flying a metre or so forward every couple of seconds, scanning the scummy floor for scraps of food. *Maybe that's the same one as earlier...* perhaps he'd flown from Cardiff to Newport, much as Danny had, and was free to do as he pleased in either city, pushing pigeons around, flying on whenever he felt like it... *Envy him his freedom.* Through the funk of sleep-deprived, drug-worsened hangover, Danny reached an epiphany, a true moment of clarity... this bloody mess of a situation he'd gotten himself into, this forgotten city in which he now found himself, all of it, it was all nothing more than the arduous writing of a story that'd be his forever – the story of a young YouTube sensation, an audio-visual artist, down and out in Cardiff and Newport. What adventures may this new city hold for him? What next in Danny Dagger's wild nationwide tour? It'd make for bloody great memories, and even better anecdotes, just as soon as he'd ceased living the moment and begun refining its details. This charmless, shitty, chavy town was all his for the taking. Danny smiled for the first time in a long time. *Destiny.* He strode away from the station, a new chapter unfolding in front of him.

10.32am

"Any sign of the escapee?"

"No."

"Good. Well, I've let Cardiff know about his ex-wife, they'll send someone round to call at her address later on today. I guess that's all we can do at the moment."

"Actually Sarge," Bronwyn replied, "I think Simon Amstell's brother might've been lying."

"Really?" Sergeant Glyn Thomas said, seeming utterly surprised and perhaps even a tad amused at the idea. "Whatever gave you that impression?"

"The excuse he gave us for not letting us come in was, pardon my language Sarge, piss-poor. It sounded exactly like something dreamt up on the spot to fob us off."

"Really? Why, what did he say?"

"He said we couldn't come inside the house because his girlfriend was naked in the living room."

"Gosh," Sergeant Glyn Thomas said, smiling softly, a little red blush touching his grey-bearded cheeks. "Well I'd say that were a reasonable enough reason not to let us in Brownyn, wouldn't you?"

"No I wouldn't Sarge."

"Why not?"

"For one, Mr. Amstell himself was fully clothed. For another, he's not exactly Cassanova, Sarge."

"Well, it's not for us to judge what others find attractive, Bronwyn. We're not the thought police, are we?" he reasoned, cracking a smile. "No, we're the actual police. And without any evidence to the contrary, I don't see why we shouldn't take this fellow's word at face value. I've been in the force forty-six years, and you'd be amazed at the amount of dreadfully ugly couples I've come across in that time. In fact, many of the ugliest men and women I dealt with as a young officer forty-six years back have long-since produced equally aesthetically-offensive offspring, and a good deal of them have gone on to produce grandchildren who are even viler in appearance."

"It's not just that, Sarge. The way he was speaking, he seemed to be hiding something. Didn't he, Ivor?"

"Yeah," Ivor said, speaking for the first time since their conversation had begun. He was standing beside Bronwyn in the Sergeant's grey-walled office at Ystrad Mynach police station. The Sergeant himself was sat behind a cheap and drably-efficient desk, reclining in a similarly perfunctory grey-clothed chair, master of his meagre domain.

"And the whole family've got form," Brownyn continued. "The Amstell brothers have got more previous than the Kray twins. I mean, it was just the day before yesterday that I'm convinced Darren Amstell smashed that poor girl in the head with his car's steering wheel lock."

Sergeant Glyn Thomas sighed; he'd heard more than enough about that girl and that pissing car steering wheel lock. "Come on Bron, we've already been over that one ad nauseam. If the girl doesn't want to press charges, it's a waste of time and effort pursuing anyone in connection with it. We'll never get a conviction."

"Regardless Sarge, it shows exactly what kind of people we're dealing with with these Amstell brothers. I know Bruce Amstell is hiding Simon Amstell in that house, Sarge, and that's all there is to it."

"Alright then, Bron, let's suppose you're right, and he is in there, what do you propose that we do about it? I don't know how you're expecting to cobble together a search warrant based on nothing more than a hunch."

"Just put the place under surveillance, Sarge. Watch who goes in, who comes out. Hell, get Caerphilly to lend us one of them thermal imaging cameras they stick in their helicopters to find weed grows. Point that at the house and we'll know within ten seconds if Bruce Amstell's hiding anyone in there or not."

"Come on Bronwyn, that's not realistic, is it? Forget the thermal imaging camera, you know how protective Caerphilly are over their toys. And as for round-the-clock surveillance, well, we just don't have the man-power."

"I'll do it. Me and Ivor. Just stick us outside their gaffe."

"I'm afraid I can't do that, Bron."

"Why?"

"You two have other important matters to attend to."

"Like what?"

"Like that lunchtime meeting at Bedwellty showground, for one."

"Bedwellty showground?" Bronwyn scoffed. "I'm sorry Sarge, but do you not think tracking an escaped con is a bit more important that attending a meeting for a pissing horse show?"

"It's not a 'pissing' horse show," Sergeant Glyn Thomas shot back, his cheeks flushing crimson with rage. "It's one of South Wales' longest-running agricultural shows. My great-grandfather was one of the members of the organising committee of the first Bedwellty show back in 1864, and the show has been a cornerstone of this area's summer entertainment calendar ever since. This year is the show's 150th anniversary. That might not mean nothing to you, a bloody Cwmarthen girl, but to me, a Blackwood boy, born-and-raised, that show is to us what the F.A. Cup final is to Wembley, what the Olympics were to the bloody Athenians. That show is the very essence of who we are as people and as an area. It is a bit more than 'a pissing horse show'."

"Fair enough, Sarge, but--"

"But nothing. This is not *CSI Miami*. This is not *The Wire*. This is Ystrad Mynach police station, and we have been providing policing for Bedwellty show since the year dot. As a senior officer here, you, Bronwyn Jones, have been chosen as our representative to the show committee. You have been charged with the prestigious task of overseeing the policing of this area's flagship event. That is a position of some privilege and respect."

"I know that, Sarge, but--"

"But nothing! Twelve o'clock, Bedwellty showground. Now get the fuck out of my office."

Rage bubbling up beneath the surface, Brownyn turned her back to Sergeant Glyn Thomas and led Ivor out into the corridor.

"You were a great fucking in help in there," she snapped at her one-word spouting colleague.

"I'm sorry Bron," Ivor said, as the pair of them walked slowly away from the Sergeant's office. "Maybe we can keep an eye on the house on our own time."

"I suppose so," Bronwyn sighed. "It's not like either of us have got anything worth going home to, is it?"

"Besides XBox and Netflix, you mean? No, I don't mind putting some extra hours in keeping an eye on Bruce Amstell's place."

"Cheers Ivor."

"What did Simon Amstell even go down for?"

"GBH. He was in a pub, the Courthouse in Caerphilly, on a Friday night. The place was packed. His missus, Jodie, was in there with him. Some guy started chatting to her, so he smashed him in the head with a bottle. The glass didn't break, but the poor guy's skull did."

"Jesus."

"And it came out after that the guy weren't even hitting on her. Just an old school friend of hers. She filed for divorce pretty sharpish after Simon went down for it."

"So you don't reckon he'll be heading to her place?"

"No, no way. He's at Bruce Amstell's place, Ivor. I'm sure of it."

12.12pm

"Mebbe we oughtae ge' some lunch in, Ji Eun, wha' d'ya reckon?"

The sudden sound of Rory's voice jolted Ji Eun from half-sleep; she looked at him in panic, then remembered where they were and what their purpose was, and a second or two later, she understood what Rory had just asked her: "I'm okay."

"Did I wake ya?"

"Yeah. Sorry."

"Heavy couple'f days we've had, eh?" Rory rolled down the window. He picked a pack of Benson & Hedges up from the dashboard, pulled one out, and lit it. He rested his cigarette-wielding arm on the window, trying to avoid blowing smoke over Ji Eun's side of the car. "I cannae blame ya for feeling rough from i'. Shite, yiv been unlucky gettin' stuck alongside a haggard old pisshead like meself on your work experience, Ji Eun. But I guess tha's wha' happens when a boozehound newshound winds up in a town where this is nae news o' note tae report on; tha booze ge's ahead o' him a bit. I mean, I did nae go easy on tha stuff when I was working on Fleet Street, but Christ, seems all I do in Wales is piss about pub-tae-pub waiting on a story tha's never comin'. It's a bi' sad really, ya know, 'how tha mighty have fallen' and all tha' shite, but wi' any luck, we'll catch summin o' interest from tha' Simon Amstell feller. Break a story. That'd be somethin', Ji Eun, I' really would. Christ, I'm hungry. Ye sure ye dunnae wan' anything else tae eat?"

"No," Ji Eun said instinctively, before noticing a heavy appetite had settled in atop the earlier hangover-absorbing breakfast roll. "Actually, yeah, maybe I could eat."

"I have nae noticed nothing else round here, other than where I went this morn' for tha breakfast rolls. I could pop back there, I s'pose. I think i' said tha' they do sandwiches in there."

"Sandwiches are fine."

"You eat a lot of sandwiches over there in Korea, Ji Eun?"

"Not really."

"Nah, I don't s'pose ya would really, would ya? Stupid question. So what, are ye starting your last year of uni next month, righ'?"

"Yeah, I go back next week."

"Righ'. So what are ya then, twent-eh? Twent-eh one?"

"Twenty," Ji Eun said, being sure to quote her age in the British rather than Korean age-counting system.

"And wha' year did yous lo' host tha World Cup? Were it Two-Thousand? Two-Thousand and Two?"

"Two-Thousand and Two."

"So you'd've been, wha', eight years old a' tha time?"

"Yeah, something like that."

"Can ye remember i'?"

"Yeah, a little bit. I remember us beating Italy."

"Did ye go tae any o' tha games?"

"No. I just watched on TV."

"I went over there, y'know."

"To Korea?"

"Aye."

"To support Scotland?"

"Ah, fuck no, we did nae qualify. We have nae qualified for a World Cup ye' this century."

"England?"

"Support England? Fuck naw! Christ. Absolutely no', no. Naw, I was supporting France, oddly enough. I was seeing this French girl at tha time, Clementine. Clemmy. She had high hopes, y'know, with them havin' won tha last one. But our relationship did nae survive the trip."

"No?"

"Naw. France were a shower o' shite. We stayed in Seoul, got tickets tae a game there, and one in… wha's the name o' the city where tha big airport is?"

"Incheon."

"Incheon, aye, tha's the one. Well, we saw them ge' beat one-nil in Seoul by one of tha African teams, then I think it were Sweden or Norway or some other shite Scanadavian team wha' beat 'em in Incheon. So she flew back home when they left. I stayed on 'til tha end o' it, cheering on your lo'. Then a couple'f weeks in Thailand. Heck o' a summer."

"How was Thailand?"

"Thailand... well, we were s'posed tae be going there together, me an' ol' Clemmy. But... shite happens. It's not tha worst place on Earth tae be a man by hi'self, mind." Rory cracked a little laugh that hung awkwardly in the silence that followed. He held a smile on his face as he cringed inside, thinking of the thoughts that comment had probably conjured up in young Ji Eun's mind; all the imagined attendant filth and disgust of a middle-aged man's solo trip to Thailand. *And she would nae be far wrong.* He dropped his cigarette out the window. "I'll ge' us some sandwiches," he said, letting himself out of the car and leaving Ji Eun alone with the middle-aged natterings of the DJ on the radio.

Rory felt some horrid, sinking feeling as he walked from the car through the housing estate. He knew his best years were long behind him, and that was of minor concern to him at this point, but the filtering of those 'best years' of his through the imagined lens of Ji Eun's eyes was the first time he'd seen them reduced to something less than the thrilling moments he'd lived through. Some melancholia, some sadness, washed over him as he walked. He wasn't quite sure why his instinct was to place so much stock in this paranoia that'd come to him through silence, and why it had settled in now, when for the last two days he'd felt a real kinship with her, as if he'd truly become a mentor, even a role model. After about two minutes walking, he entered the shop and found his answer, the reason for the sudden departure of meaning and certainty and confidence from his character. He looked at it for a moment, before reaching out and grasping liquid solution – a can of Kronenbourg – and heading to the counter to peruse the list of sandwiches on offer.

01.34pm

"Then when I woke up, she was gone," Tom said, taking a drag and bringing both his story and his cigarette to their conclusions. He dropped the fag butt on the floor behind John Morgan's, then stamped on it and tore it apart with his shoe.

"That sucks butt," Gareth said, still a good half of his rollie remaining. "But I don't know man, if you're that intent on seeing her again, you know where she lives. I mean, you don't want to come across as a stalker or a psycho, but maybe you could drop a card through her door or something? I mean, she must have had some interest if she brought you back there in the first place."

"Maybe."

"Or maybe she was just pissed out of her mind. She might've panicked when she woke up, wondered who this strange guy lying next to her was, and got out of the house as fast as possible."

"Maybe." Tom pulled a ten pack of Richmond Superkings from his pocket, pulled off the plastic wrapping and inner foil, then lit one up.

"You might as well go for it, butt. You'll never know otherwise."

"Yeah, there's another problem though."

"What?"

"I don't think I can go and stuff a letter through the door."

"Why?"

"Remember that girl I was seeing for a while, Claire?"

"Claire?"

"I don't know if you met her actually. She's from Shropshire or Shrewsbury or something. Weird fashion sense. Lots of pink shit. Really annoying."

"Oh, her? Yeah, I remember her butt." Gareth remembered one night at least, when Tom had brought her to their local pub in Caerphilly and tried to ingratiate her into their group, but a chasm of cultural difference and social ineptitude had been widened, rather than bridged, by pouring alcohol into it. He'd never heard Tom mention her since.

"I left the house this morning, went outside, and realised it's the exact same house Claire was living at."

"Shit man," Gareth laughed. He took a final drag on his rollie and dropped it to the ground. "That's fucking hilarious butt. Does Claire still live there?"

"No. Yeah. I mean, I don't know, maybe. I didn't see her there."

"Fucking hell man. So the love of your life is your jilted ex-lover's housemate?"

"Maybe, yeah."

Gareth laughed to himself as he padded his pocket, checking for his tobacco. His laughing ceased upon realising he'd left it inside.

"Sorry butt, could I crash a fag off you? I've left my stuff in the staff room."

Tom handed over the Superkings.

"Cheers butt. Maybe it's alright anyway," Gareth mumbled, holding a cigarette in his mouth and pulling a lighter from his pocket. Job done, he exhaled and handed the box back. "It was ages ago you were seeing that Claire girl, and you can't have been with her more than a month or two. I think she'll've gotten over you by now butt. She probably don't even remember what you look like."

"I don't know butt, we didn't have the best of break-ups."

"Come on butt, how bad could it be? You weren't with her no time."

"I don't know butt, I think she'll remember it."

"Why?"

"Well, remember she was really annoying, right? Like *really* annoying. But she looked alright, and she was always up for it, and I was happy just to be getting some off of anyone at the time, you know, but at the same time, I was trying to break it off before it went on too long with her, and one day... an opportunity presented itself."

"Yeah?"

"Yeah. We were out in town one night, and we stayed at hers after, and in the morning, she realised that she'd lost her phone. It was a weekday, and I was working at that life insurance place in Atlantic Wharf at the time, so I had to go to work, like, so she told me to write down my number for her. So I did, except I changed a couple of digits on it."

Gareth laughed. "Ah, you fucking prick, butt."

"Yeah, I know."

"But, well," Gareth began, about to console Tom, before being overcome by laughter. "You fucking pussy butt. But, I mean, maybe she doesn't even know that you did it on purpose? Maybe she thought it was an accident?"

"What, and I'd been sat around ever since wondering why she hasn't phoned me? And never thought to send her a message on Facebook or pop round her house or something? No butt."

"So what happened then? You gave her the wrong number and you never heard off her ever again?"

"No." Tom paused to take a drag on his cigarette. "It's worse than that butt." He sighed before continuing, the story being one of such excruciating embarrassment that he'd never before told it to anyone. "I think it was autumn when this happened, maybe September or October, so most days it weren't that cold, but it was a bit chilly at night, right, so if I weren't planning on going out or anything after work, I didn't bother taking a coat with me. So one day, I was supposed to meet you or Steve or someone after work, so I wore a coat. I don't know if you can remember it, but I still had that black coat, the one with the couple of gold buttons on it."

"Yeah."

"I'd had it for ages by this point, so it was pretty beat up, and there was a hole in the pocket that went straight through to the coat's lining. And I was walking back from work, on my way into town to meet whoever I was meeting, and I suddenly felt the coat, like, vibrating."

Gareth smirked, knowing exactly what was coming next.

"So I stuck my hand inside, and do you know what I found in the coat's lining?"

Gareth couldn't say a word in response; it was all he could to stifle complete hysterics.

"Her fucking phone."

Gareth burst out laughing. Tom shook his head, remembering the stupidity of it all.

"So what did you do butt?"

"I answered it."

Gareth laughed even harder.

"Yeah, I explained what'd happened, and she sounded pissed off as fuck, obviously, because I'd had her phone this whole time, and we were meeting like every other day up until this point, so she must've tried ringing me loads of times, and released that I'd given her a fake number."

"Fuck butt," Gareth said, in a short gap between laughing fits. "Did you give the phone back to her?"

"Yeah. She came straight into town to get it. Was cold as fuck butt. She came up to me scowling like fuck. I handed the phone over, then she walked off, and that's the last I seen of her."

"You fucking tit butt," Gareth laughed. "Fucking hell, that's ridiculous."

"So, yeah, maybe I'm best off not posting a card through the door telling that Korean girl to get in touch with me."

"Well if you do, just make sure you write the right number down."

Tom sighed and took a drag on his cigarette as Gareth carried on laughing.

02.18pm

"Is there any weed left Bru?"

"Nuh."

"Have you got any fags left?"

"Nuh."

"Darren?"

"Sorry."

Simon sighed. The living room was static purgatory, bathed in stale smoke and humidity. Simon rubbed at his face. "Fuck boys, I'm starting to think clink weren't as bad as this," he said, rising to his feet. "Do you mind if I crack a window or something?"

"Up to you butt," Bruce said.

Simon moved towards the curtain-veiled living room window.

"But it's only you who'll suffer if someone outside overhears us speaking."

Simon stopped and sighed. Options and tempers were wearing thin. They'd spent hours trying to track down Jodie's mother's address via a tenuous internet connection made on the stolen laptop via their neighbour's wifi. The search had come to a halt when Simon had mentioned the vast debts her mother had accumulated and the fact that she'd already lived under two different false names in an attempt to avoid them. Guess-working their way to false name number three had quickly proved impossible. Attention had then turned to Jodie's new partner, Joseph Bradfield. An agonisingly slow internet search for 'Joseph Bradfield Cardiff' had turned up dozens of pages related to the Manic Street Preacher's frontman James Dean Bradfield, before they'd eventually discovered a slew of addresses across the city registered under the surname Bradfield. Bruce had shot down the idea of going door-to-door in hopes of stumbling across the right guy. Simon stared at the curtains, which glowed orange with the force of the sunlight behind them. This wasn't what he'd escaped prison for.

He turned around and scanned the room. He quickly found what he was looking for; a Kung Fu Panda DVD case with torn up bits of cigarette and weed debris scattered over it. Simon sat on the arm of the chair he'd just risen from and reached over to the pile of debris, picking up a red Rizla and carefully tipping the discarded green and brown flakes onto it. He then ripped a small rectangle off the Rizla packet, rolled it into roach, rolled the Rizla into a slightly-weed-infused rollie, and sparked it up. He looked at the television set for a moment. BBC News was still cycling through the same summaries of the same stories that had seemed stuck on a loop since Simon had arrived; ISIS, Ebola, Ukraine, Scots independence. Simon looked at Darren, passed out on the sofa, laptop on his lap, Kaiser asleep at the side of him. He reached over and gently took the laptop, then sat back down in his armchair. His younger brother had left Facebook logged in. He thought for a moment of Fraping him, sticking on a funny status update, but it didn't really seem an appropriate action given the circumstances. Then he wondered if his brother might not have comprised himself in anyway by logging into Facebook from a stolen laptop. Simon logged out for him and closed the window for Internet Explorer. He took a drag from his weed-infused rollie, then looked over at Bruce and held it out to him. Bruce took the rollie and sank back into his seat.

"What are you doing butt?" Bruce asked.

"I dunno man, just having a mess about on it," Simon said.

"Nah, not with the laptop butt, in general, like."

"What d'you mean?"

"What do I mean?" Bruce laughed to himself. He took a drag on the shitty pseudo-spliff and stared at the television. "How long have you been watching BBC News for now, butt? I mean, I do feel like I'm one of ISIS's hostages myself, the amount of times I've seen 'em waving guns about. What are you expecting, butt? That they're gonna add you to the news loop once you've been on the run long enough? 'Today's main headlines: war, terrorism, and some cunt in the South Wales valleys didn't show up for his shift at Paul's Pies down in Bedwas'? You're not fucking Raoul Moat, butt." He took another drag. "But just 'cos it's not on telly dun mean it's not 'appening. The police've been round once looking for you already. The same police officer what put you away last time. And I know she knows you're in here. Well, she might not know for certain, but she seem certainly seemed suspicious." He took another drag, still staring at the television, his elder brother still staring into the laptop. "They're probably down that station now, putting together a search warrant. Any minute now, they'll be banging tha' door down, looking for you. And when they find you, they'll take me and Darren away with you. 'Aiding and abetting a criminal'. Then you'll be back in prison, where you started, and what'll happen to me and Darren then, butt? Huh? Have that entered your thinking at all, what'll happen to your brothers?" He took another drag, bringing the flaming end on the ultra-slim combustible almost to the roach. He took another quick toke and then dropped it into the ashtray. "So what's the plan, butt? We're gonna sit here watching BBC News until the police come bang that fucking door down, is it?"

Simon barely looked up from the laptop screen as he took the Sky remote from the arm of his chair and tossed it across the room to Bruce. "Change it if you want."

"I'm serious though," Bruce said, tapping out 3-8-3 on the Sky remote. BBC News was replaced with Clubland TV. High-frequency sped-up vocals squealed over bouncy happy hardcore beats, as scantily-clad ladies bopped about inside nightclubs "This whole plan of yours, it's fucking stupid, butt. How long d'you reckon you can spend sat on your fat fucking arse in my living room before the police d'find you?"

"We'll make a move tonight."

"Right, yeah, course we will," Bruce said, grinning. "Yeah, we can't find where the fuck your ex is hiding your son to, but maybe me and Darren can just go bang on the door of every house in Cardiff 'til we find him. And even if we do find him, what happens then, butt?" Bruce looked away from the television, at Simon, who was still staring into the laptop. Bruce had had enough. He pressed the button on the remote to switch the Sky box off. "Fucking look at me when I'm talking to you, would you?"

Simon looked up from the laptop.

Bruce repeated his question. "Even if we do find your son, what happens then?"

"Then I fuck off to Spain with him."

"Right. And the fuck are me and Darren supposed to do after that? You can't lose either way – best case scenario, you're sat on a beach in fucking Spain for the rest of your life with your son by the side of you, worst case, you'll be back in prison, where you started from. Me and Darren are free fucking men butt. We've got a lot more to lose than you. And once you've fucked off out the country, who do you think the police'll be sweating to try and work out where you and your son have disappeared to?"

"Come with me then, butt."

"Come with you?" Bruce scoffed.

"Yeah."

He looked his brother straight in the eye; he was actually serious. "To Spain?"

"Yeah. Why not, butt? There's fuck all keeping you two round here. Neither of you've got a missus, or a little one, or a job, or any other fucking reason to stay. I mean, what's here for you, really? This house ain't really yours, it's rented."

"What about Mam?"

"James'll look after her. What do you reckon, butt?"

"What do I reckon?" Bruce asked himself, breaking eye contact and mulling it over. "Well, what I do reckon don't matter anyway, do it? Because we're still no closer to finding out where your son is."

"We'll find him. And if we find him, are you up for it?"

Bruce stared at the blue television screen and sighed. "Fuck it. Go on 'en."

"Simon smiled. "You'll see Bru, a few days from now you'll be sat on a beach in Espana sipping cerveza and munching paella, watching the sexy senoritas walking round topless, and you'll be glad you went along with this."

"We'll see, butt. And 'if's a big fucking word, mind."

Simon nodded. The point was a fair one. He looked back at the laptop screen. He noticed an icon on the desktop labelled 'Find My Nokia'. He double-clicked it.

"I've found 'im Bru."

"Who?"

"Joseph Bradfield." Simon looked up from the laptop screen, beaming. "It says by here he's in Newport."

02.24pm

"Oh butt, are you alright?"

Danny looked up at him, blinking. From the tone of his voice, it obviously wasn't the first time he'd asked the question. The guy in front of him was about sixteen, wearing an up-turned oversized baseball cap, a gold sticker still stuck to the underside of it. He was wearing a black tracksuit zipped up to 11, despite the sunshine. Two similarly attired teenagers stood either side of him. *Chavs.* Danny sat upright and looked at them. *Newport chavs. Shit.* He must've fallen asleep, passed out, on the bench the chavs had now surrounded, besides the river flowing through the city's centre. He looked around – there was no-one else in sight.

"Oh butt, he said 'are you alright?'" the smaller one to the left of the head chav asked.

"Yeah," Danny mumbled, noticing the head chav's fists were clenched.

"Where you from butt?" the bum-fluff sporting chav to the right of the head chav asked.

Don't say England, Danny's instincts told him.

"Oh butt, he asked where you're from," the head chav said.

"Cardiff."

"Cardiff," the head chav laughed. The other two laughed. They were now clenching their fists as well.

"What you doing in Newport?" the head chav asked.

"Meeting a friend."

"What's your friends name?"

"Gregory."

"Gregory," the head chav laughed. "Gregory sounds like a poof's name."

"He's big," Danny said, desperate for any advantage.

"He's big," the head chav laughed, turning to each of his laughing henchmen in turn. "Gregory the big poofter."

"He's a drug dealer," Danny added.

"Is he, yeah?" the head chav said, obviously a little unsettled by that.

"What's he deal?" asked bum-fluff.

"Coke." Coke dealers were usually the henchest.

"Coke," the head chav said, turning to each of his henchmen, not laughing now. "You was gonna pick up some coke off him, was you?"

"Yeah." *Oh fuck.*

"That's expensive, innit?" the head chav said, smiling. He clearly thought he'd hit the jackpot. "How much is a gram of coke nowadays boys?"

"About forty quid," the little chav said.

"Forty quid be fucked," remarked bum-fluff. "Double that. Eighty."

"Eighty quid," the head chav smiled.

Oh fuck.

"I tell you what butt," the head chav continued, "hows about you give us whatever money you was gonna give to Gregory the big poof drug dealer, and we'll sort you out with a gram off someone we know?"

"I don't know," Danny said, wondering if he may have unwittingly found a way to escape without getting the shit kicked out of him. "Gregory's stuff's good."

"Our stuff's good. Are you calling me a fucking bullshitter? Boys, is he calling me a bullshitter?"

"I think he is, yeah," snarled bum-fluff.

"No, no," Danny backtracked, "I wasn't, honestly."

"Then why don't you want to buy no coke off of us?"

"I don't have the money on me," Danny explained.

"Well, we'd best get ourselves to a cashpoint then, hadn't we?"

So off to a cashpoint they went.

The head chav walked alongside Danny at the front of the pack, with bum-fluff and the little one following close behind. They walked from the riverbank to a subway passage running beneath a thick road that led to the city centre.

"You wanna be careful picking up by yourself butt," the head chav said. "You never know what might happen."

Behind them, the smaller chavs started laughing. Danny made out some familiar sound through the laughter, refracted through tinny phone speakers; his own voice.

"Oh Daz, have a look at this," bum-fluff called out.

The head chav, Daz, stepped back a second.

"That's him, innit?" bum-fluff said.

"It is and all," Daz the head chav said.

Fuck. YouTube.

Danny started running.

"Oh!" Daz called out behind him.

Danny ran through the subway passage, hearing the three chavs pounding along the tiled floor behind him. He rounded a corner and flew up a flight of stairs two at a time, emerging onto a street lined with bars. He ran forward and spotted a taxi rank. He pulled the door of one open and jumped inside.

"Drive, drive!" he ordered the driver.

"Not this one butt, you have to take the one in front."

Danny looked out the window. The three chavs were standing at the end of the street he'd just emerged from, waving their hands in the air and making the wanker symbol. Danny got out and walked round to the taxi at the head of the cab rank, the chavs yelling out 'poofter', 'faggot', and other homophobic slurs behind him.

"Friends of yours?" the driver asked as Danny got in.

"Take me to Cardiff."

Danny took his Lumia from his pocket and held down the power button.

02.38pm

"I was in mah early twenties and I'd just go' my first job in tha industry, working a' tha Aberdeen Herald. In them days, regional newspapers were in rude health compared tae where thir at naw, and another thing that these days is a shadow o' wha' i' were back then is football hooliganism. There was this trend tha' had started off in England wi' Liverpool, but i' were Aberdeen tha' first introduced i' tae Sco'land, where fans would nae wear the typical team colours and all tha' guff nae more, naw, they'd kit themselves out in smart, kind'f modish clobber, y'know, parkas and polo shirts and all tha' shite. Well, a lo' o' young lads go' back intae i', y'know, i' looked a lo' cooler than tha old fuckers ya'd ge' a' games, football shirts pulled down tight o'er their beer bellies, know wha' I mean? Casuals, they called 'em, this new breed o' football fashionistas. A lot o' tha older element did nae like 'em, mind. Thought they were a bit soft, y'know? Caring about haircuts and brand-name clothing, load o' ol' poofter shite in tha minds o' tha old guard, eh? Matter of fact, once tha Aberdeen Soccer Casuals started tae make a wee bit'f a name fir themselves, a lot o' tha other teams in Sco'land tried tae follow suit, but quite a few did nae get nowhere for tha' very reason. Take Celtic – actually, I mebbe overwhelming you a wee bi' wi' all the places names and tha', do ye kno' much o' anything 'bout Scottish football Ji Eun?"

"Not really," she admitted. She'd felt enthralled by the passion with which Rory was setting the scene for this latest anecdote and didn't feel good about making an admission that might cause him to hold back on it.

"Well, yiv go' tha two biggest clubs in Glasgow, and two biggest teams in Sco'land, Celtic an' Rangers. An' they fuckin' hate each other. The long an' tha short o' i' is yiv go' tha Catholic side, Celtic, an' tha Protestant side, Rangers. A fuckin' religious sectarian war wi' football as tha battleground, righ'? And a bunch o' young Celtic lads seen wha' tha Aberdeen lo' were gettin' up tae with this new soccer casuals fad, righ', and they decide tae hop on tha bandwagon. So, tha ways I heard i', a load o' them turn up tae meet with all tha ol' Celtic fans before tha Old Firm derb-eh, their big showdown with Rangers, righ', and tha auld Celtic lads are so incensed by wha' they perceive tae be this gang o' ponces associatin' themselves wi' their team, tha' they dunnae give a fuck about tooling up together to go fight the Rangers lo', naw, instead, they turn on their own and give the Celtic casuals a bloody good hiding."

"Wow." Ji Eun wasn't sure what Rory had just described to her, but it sounded violent.

"I dunno Ji Eun, the whole concept mebbe a bit odd fir ya, I dunnae expect you'd ge' much in tha way of soccer violence in Korea, would ye?"

"No," she said, laughing at the prospect. "The Korean league isn't really that popular. Most people just watch EPL or 'A' games."

"Eh gems?" Rory repeated, having never heard the term before.

"Yeah, 'A' games. When the national team plays."

"Korean call them eh gems, eh?" Rory laughed. "It would nae be anything above a D game when tha Scots team plays."

" Baseball's probably the biggest sport people would actually go watch."

"Righ'. And ye dunnae see many fans crackin' each other wi' baseball bats or anythin', do ye?"

"No, no. You know, it's been quite surprising to see Cardiff on a matchday, how passionate people get about it. It's different when you have the rugby games, and everyone's in the Welsh shirts, but the Cardiff football fans seem a lot crazier than Korean baseball fans."

"Fuck aye, I'd imagine so. Cardiff Cit-eh fans are nae softies."

"I think people feel more connected to the team here than Koreans do. I mean, I heard a lot of people complaining about, you know, changing the shirt colour..."

"Aye, tha' crazy Malaysian fucker and all tha'."

"...yeah, in Korea, I don't think people would really care if that type of thing happened. Most of the teams are just named after companies."

"Yeah?"

"Yeah. SK Wyverns, LG Twins, Samsung Lions..."

"Shite. I could nae imagine tha' going over well in this country."

"Yeah. The fans chant the company's name at the games. *Sam-sung, Sam-sung*..."

"Christ. Well. I did nae know tha'."

Conversation fell away as Rory tried to picture it, a crowd of South Korean baseball fans, chanting 'Samsung' in unison. Or British football crowds chanting the names of their shirt sponsors. Betting websites and pay-day loan lenders. *Won-ga! Won-ga!* If anyone could actually make it happen, there'd be a fortune to be made – the legitimacy of a crowd of thousands singing your company's praises, to a global television audience of millions...

They were still in the red Volvo, still parked in the street outside the Amstell's house, still no sign of activity from anyone inside, the radio still tuned to Radio 2. Some God-awful jaunty old novelty hit was currently playing, its singer 'ooh'ing and 'aah'ing in a thick West Country accent. Listening to it, Rory thought perhaps the past wasn't as great as people were always making it out to be. His mind then wandered away from the vehicle, back along the street to the corner shop, and their fridge stocked full of cold beers. He thought about shot-gunning another can, out of sight of Ji Eun, but quickly corrected himself – *that'll be six y'll have sunk then pal, ya cannae be drivin' back tae Cardiff with tha' much inside ya.*

"Wha' were we jus' talkin' abou'?"

"You were talking about Scottish football hooligans."

"Oh righ', I was, yeah. Well, as I were saying, back in tha mid-eighties, I was nae much older than you are now, working a' tha Aberdeen Herald, and our soccer team's casuals were making a hell'f a name for themselves. Y'know, back then, we had Alex Ferguson managing us, y'know, tha old fucker who was in charge o' Man United 'til they turned tae dogshite?"

"Yeah. Manchester are really popular in Korea."

"Aye, o' course they are. They're the most popular team everywhere outside o' Manchester. But we had a hell of run wi' Fergie in charge, y'know, Sco'ish cups, European cups, plus our soccer casuals were blazing a bloody trail all aroun' Sco'land. O' course, if ye yerself cannae innovate, than all you can do is imitate, so we go' a couple o' copy-cat soccer casual groups establishing themselves wi' other clubs, and as I said, they did nae go over too well a' a lot o' clubs, bu' one club tha' managed to ge' 'emselves a big casuals following were Hibs, Hibernian, this team out o' tha capital city, Edinburgh."

"I've been to Edinburgh."

"Aye?"

"Aye... yeah..."

"How were it?"

"It was nice. I liked the castle."

"Aye, the castle's alrigh'. Bi' of a smarmy posh cunts place, mind. No' quite as bad as London in tha' regard, but still, a lot o' Edinburgh folk are pretty fuckin' self-regarding. And none more so than their fuckin' soccer casuals. So as I say, I'm working on tha paper a' this time, righ', and Aberdeen are travelling down tae Edinburgh tae face off agains' Hibs in tha league. And when they ge' there, tha Hibs fans just ambush 'em, I mean, there's shite flying off o' buildings, bricks raining down, fuckers runnin' a' us from all sides, fuckin' deadly shite. And I mean, tha's all par for the course, righ'? Ye dunnae sign up fir being a fuckin' soccer casual if you cannae handle a wee bi' o' tha old ultraviolence. But there's somethin' about tha way it goes down, righ', I just think i's all a wee bit tae perfect, know wha' I mean? So I says tae myself, 'Rory, there's somethin' going on here.' And I remember, on tha way down, a lot o' the lads on tha train are reading a paper. But not ma paper. Not tha Aberdeen Herald. Naw. They're reading The Scots Post. And ye may then be wonderin', Ji Eun, why would a bunch o' no-good niks off tae brawl before a soccer match be reading a newspaper? To brush up on current affairs? Keep abreas' o' tha latest comings and goings down in Westminster? Fuck naw. The Scots Post has this wee pull-out section in i', a weekend guide tae Edinburgh for away fans. Now, tha Scots Post is a national paper, and as wi' most of tha world, national newspapers are based in tha capital city. And wha's tha capital o' Sco'land?"

"Edinburgh?" Ji Eun said, the suddenness of the question making her unsure of herself.

"Righ'. Fuckin' Edinburgh. So, on tha ways back, I pick up a discarded copy o' i' on tha train, righ', and I start reading through tha' wee pull-out section for all tha soccer fans, and y'know wha' I come tae realise? It's telling them exactly where tae go tae get their fuckin' heads caved in. It's positioning them exactly righ' for tha Hibs casuals tae come in and brain tha fuckin' lo' of them. Now, obviously, if tha Aberdeen lo' know about this section in tha newspaper, tha fuckin' Hibs lo' 'll kno', righ'? The paper's printed in their fuckin' city, for Christ's sake. And I dunnae think it's naw concidence. So, tha next weekend, Hibs are playing Motherwell, so I travel down tae Edinburgh, grab a copy o' tha Scots Post, and wha' do I find? Tha exact same fuckin' thing goes down, tha paper tells them where tae go, an' tha Motherwell lo' ge' their fuckin' arses handed tae 'em. So I check tha name in tha byline, righ', and it's a Mr. Shawn Mooney whose been writing this shite each time, and there's a picture o' tha wee pug-nosed fucker right there in tha paper. So, two weeks later's tha next Hibs home game, they've go' Kilmarknock, and I head down tae our wee capital tha night before, tae check up on this Shawn Mooney fucker. I go' special dispensation tae ge' out'f tha office early on tha Friday, y'know, I tell the editor, I says, 'trust me, I've got a big fuckin' scoop, and if I dunnae turn up wi' tha goods on Monday, yous can fire me for i". So I get tae tha Scots Post offices around three, three-thirty, and I sit on a bench across tha street from 'em for tha next few hours, just watchin' and waitin', with my wee camera, well, they were naw wee in them days, i' were a big clunky fucker, but I've go' my camera, and I'm waiting for him, and sure enough, Shawn Mooney comes ou' tha office, righ', and I start snapping, and I follow tha' fucker round all Friday night, see him boozing it up wi' his workmates, tryin' it on wi' tha local lassies, tae nae avail I migh' add, and a' the end o' tha nigh', I follow him home. So now I've go' tha cunts address, righ'? And I dunnae have a great deal o' money, junior reporter like, and I cannae be arsed with tha rigmarole o' checkin' in tae a hotel anyways, righ', I'm planning on gettin' up real early, so tha' night I sleep rough, just me and a couple o' tinnies on a park bench, and thank fuck naw fucker came across us an' started anythin' durin' the nigh', but first thing in tha mornin' I'm round his, waitin' for i', an' around twelve he finally emerges from his fuckin' hovel, tha' wee fuckin' troll, Shawn Mooney, and ambles he's little arse intae town, naw fuckin' idea o' me followin' him, righ', and then he ge's there, and ya know wha' he does?"

Ji Eun stared blankly at Rory for a few seconds before hazarding an answer: "No."

"He meets up wi' tha fuckin' Hibs Casuals. So I ge' plenty o' fuckin' footage o' this wee snake in tha grass doin' his fuckin' thing with them lo', an' I head back tae tha paper in Aberdeen wi' it tha' day. Sunday morning it's fuckin' front page news, tha scandal o' one o' tha national papers supporting tha' Hibernian soccer casuals, channelin' away fans right fuckin' intae them. I win a fuckin' journo of the year award off tha back o' it, and a short time later I'm in London, twenty-four year old, workin' at a national fuckin' paper, and I dunnae mean naw fuckin' Sco'ish national paper, I mean a fuckin' British national paper. And tha' wee cunt Shawn Mooney's down tha fuckin' dole office."

Ji Eun sat and sifted through the nuggets of Rory's narrative that she'd been able to understand, trying to piece them together into some coherent whole. Rory rolled down the window and took a cigarette from the B&H packet on the dashboard.

"I migh' go run tae tha shop again, Ji Eun. Grab a pack o' gum or somethin'. Do ye want anything?"

"I'm okay."

Rory looked at Ji Eun; she didn't look okay. She looked better than she had done at the start of the day, but still a long way from 'okay'.

"This takes a lot outta yeah, staking a hoose out," Rory said. He lit the cigarette. "'Course, wi' modern technology, we should nae have tae fuck around like this nae more. All we'd need's one o' them heat-sensitive camera thingies and we'd be able to look straight in there, find out whether Simon Amstell's hiding out with his brothers or no'. A thermal imaging camera, tha's the jobbie. Ye can ge' an attachment tha' clips ontae ye phone, y'know, i' cannae be more than a couple'f hundred quid. But I asked Arwyn about tha paper buying one or two for tha use of us journos, and he wasnae havin' any o' i'. Said if I wanted one, I should buy i' myself. Can ya believe tha'? Buying my own damn investigative equipment, on my fuckin' salary." Rory took a drag on his cigarette. "Y'know, back when I were in London, ten, twenty year ago, we had technology straight out'f a James Bond fillum. I used tae use this directional microphone thingy, y'could hear a pin drop through a twelve-inch thick wall from a hundred metres away. We could be sat here righ' now, listening tae every word tha' them there Amstell brothers are saying tae one another. But this rag I'm working on now, they dunnae even have a colour printer tha staff can use. Can ya believe tha'? A fuckin' newspaper, and they'll only let tha journos print out in black and fuckin' white?" Rory took another drag. "Cost saving measure, apparently. They cannae afford fuckin' coloured ink cartridges. Tha only colour printer we go's in Arwyn's office, so if ye wan' tae print out in colour, you'll have to argue yir case tae him, and then e-mail tha thing you want printed across. Fuckin' dog shite." Rory trailled off, ruminating on his fall and the media gutter in which he now found himself. He took another drag on his cigarette. "Aye, I think I'll head over tae tha' shop again Ji Eun, are ye sure I cannae get ye anything?"

03.16pm

Danny stared at the Lumia as the taxi took him along an unfamiliar stretch of the M4, from Newport to Cardiff. The deeper Danny looked into the Lumia, the more certain he was that it was his. The background image was generic; no passcode had been set. The only customisation was the demonic ringtone hollering something about hellfire that'd startled Danny the night before. The only photos were of three guys in a living room, perhaps the living room of the house Danny had found the phone at. *Testing the camera out.* The only window into the phone thief's life was the logged-in Facebook app.

"Where to in Cardiff butt?" the driver asked.

Danny looked up from the Lumia and saw they were approaching a multi-laned roundabout, a flyover ferrying traffic above it.

"Can you drop me by the twenty-four hour Tescos?"

"Which Tescos butt – Culver House Cross or Gabalfa?"

"Gabalfa," Danny guessed. He remembered there being a small forest at the side of the Teso Extra had been refused alcohol in the night before; perfect for doing a runner. Danny saw the mtere had already hit £16.80. The taxi roared straight on at the roundabout. Danny looked at the Lumia, at Joseph Bradfield's Facebook account, at the built and bad-tempered looking guy with a pint in his hand in the profile pic. Danny thought about delving deeper, reading through Joseph Bradield's messages, looking through his photographs, getting some idea of who he was. Then he thought of taking revenge, of sending mean – no, *vindictive* – messages to friends and acquaintances, of updating Joseph Bradfield's status with a declaration of homosexuality, or a socially-corrosive racist rant, but then Danny looked again at the thick head in the profile pic. He decided not to provoke him. Danny logged out, then logged back in as himself. He ruminated on what to write as the taxi rolled past familiar red-brick terraced housing. He gave up summarising the madness of the past few days as Tesco Extra loomed into view, opting instead to pose a question: *'Whose in Cardiff tonite?'*

The taxi pulled up outside Tesco's entrance.

"I just need to run in and get some cash out."

"I'll come in with you," the taxi driver said, unbuckling his seatbelt.

Shit.

Danny got out of the car and walked in through the automatic doors, the taxi driver at the side of him, and turned right, towards the tobacco counter.

"Twenty Marlboro light please."

"Have you gor any I.D. on you?" the woman at the counter said.

Danny made a big show of patting down his pockets. He turned to the taxi driver. "I think I left my wallet in your car."

The driver sighed and led the way back out to the car park. He walked ahead, rounding the vehicle to open up the driver's side door. As the driver fumbled around for his keys, Danny took his chance.

"Oi!" the driver yelled.

Danny sprinted off towards the trees at the car park's edge, the driver giving chase.

04.32pm

"Time's ge'in' on a bit," Rory said, looking at the clock on the Volvo's dashboard. "Maybe I ought tae run ya home."

"No, it's fine," Ji Eun said. She'd been enjoying it, eyes focused on the house, mind lost in a meditation soundtracked by Radio 2's M.O.R. soft-rock, and punctuated whenever a question or an anecdote popped into Rory's brain and tumbled out from his mouth. She wanted to see the thing through to its completion.

"Naw, ye kno', it could be all nigh' I'm sat ou' here, watchin' an' waitin' on 'em." He turned his key in the ignition. "Come on, I'll drive ya home."

"No, really. What if they come out while you're away?"

"I'd say there isnae much chance o' tha'."

"But you can't be sure."

"No, bu'--"

"And we've waited so long already. All this time would be wasted."

"Aye, I suppose, bu'--"

"Really, it's okay. I can wait until they come out."

"Naw, really, I could nae do tha' tae ya. We might be sat ou' here 'til tha wee hours. Hell, I migh' still be sat ou' here this time tomorr'. I'll tell ya wha', hows abou' a compromise? I'll run ye up tae tha train station. Remember tha one we passed on tha way over here?"

"The one just up the hill?"

"Aye."

"It's not far. I can walk."

"Yir righ', it's no' tha far. I'll be back in a jiffy."

"But what if they leave the house while you're driving me there?"

"Come on, if they did nae show themselves since nine this morning, they're hardly likely tae pop ou' now, are they?"

"Murphy's law."

"Murphy's law," Rory smiled, repeating it. "Sod's fuckin' law. Aye, I guess if them fuckers're gonna show themselves, that'd be the time they'd choose tae do it. In the five fuckin' minutes wiv taken us eyes off tha prize. One more wee kick in tha balls from tha good lord on high."

"Yeah. I can just walk there. It can't be more than ten minutes away."

"Alrigh'. Well, be careful mind. You're in tha Valleys now. Folks round here can be pretty fuckin' feral at times. Gimme a call if anything happens. Anything a' all."

"Okay."

"And gimme a text when you ge' tae tha station, let me know ya made it fine."

"I will."

"Alrigh' then. Well, thanks fir your company today, Ji Eun. It's been a pleasure."

"Thank you. It's been really educational."

"Aye, well, guess I'll see ya tomorrow a' tha office then, just s'long as I'm not still sat ou' fuckin' here."

"Okay. Thank you."

"And don't forge' tae send tha' tex'."

"I won't," she said, opening the door and stepping out onto the street.

Rory watched her disappear round the corner, then turned his attention back to the house. *Bollocks,* he admonished himself, *I shoulda given tha poor lass a few bob fir train fare.* He thought about getting out and running after her, but making a big commotion in the street seemed to be the exact opposite of what he ought to be doing on a stake out. *Naw,* he told himself, *I'll reimburse her fir it tomorr'.* He wondered how long he might be sat outside the house. He looked down at the empty wrappers and discarded packets of sandwiches and chocolate bars he'd picked up at lunch time. He was starting to feel a wee bit peckish. *And a couple more tinnies could nae hurt, no' if I'm no' driving nowhere.*

03.28pm

The forest opened up to a river. Danny Daggers followed the river as quickly and as quietly as he could, twigs cracking and dirt crunching beneath the taxi driver's feet behind him. The river was wide and fast moving, but seemed shallow. Danny hesitated for a second, then stepped into it. He bounded across to the other bank and pulled himself out of the water. He carried on running through the trees on the opposite side, the only sound now the gushing of the water behind him and the beating of his own heart. *I should've taken me shoes off,* Danny thought, taking note of his sodden Vans.

The forest soon opened up to the wide grass fields of a park. Danny slowed his pace to a walk, not wanting to appear strange to the groups of people lounging around sun-bathing or playing football. His heart was still thumping in his chest, invigorated. Beyond the park, Danny saw familiar rows of red-brick terraced housing. He moved towards them and smiled.

Find Yeller's house. Apologise. Make up some excuses. Get the back bag. Hope he's not a dick about the fiver. Maybe he didn't even notice it. Get to a cashpoint. Get some smokes. Get to the train station. Get the fuck out of Wales.

He tried to picture the house, and he pictured Yeller inside it, and a hopeful flutter in his fast-beating heart gathered momentum, and threatened to take control of him, to take him down, to take him out. He pressed his hand against his chest to feel the tempo of it. He could feel the beating, but was unsure if it was normal. He thought a heart attack was a possibility, with the amount of chemicals he'd put into his system, and the lack of sleep he'd inflicted upon himself. *You're alright*, he told himself. *It's all in your mind.* It wasn't an attack of the heart he was experiencing; it was an attack of anxiety. He tried to breathe slowly, deeply, but that only exacerbated things. Holding air in his lungs, his chest unmoving, the beating of his heart became all the more noticeable.

He'd experienced several panic attacks over the years; the first had been the worst. After smoking his way through the best part of an eighth of skunk back in his first year at uni, he'd lain in bed at night, his thoughts flitting fearfully to the grandfather he'd never met, who'd died of a heart attack in his early twenties. His family had never explained why that heart attack had happened, so there was a possibility that whatever took out Danny's granddad was hereditary. Danny had lain there in bed, gripped with icy, stinging anxiety, certain of impending doom, for an hour or more, before realising urgent action was necessary, and heading to the nearest hospital's A&E department. They'd given him an ECG and the all clear. The nurse had asked if he'd taken any drugs. "No... well, only cannabis." That'd been a panic attack then, and this was most certainly a panic attack now. That time, weed had been the cause of it; this time, it was Wales. *Calm down*, he told himself. *Calm down. Just ignore it.* He moved forward, through the park, trying to concentrate on the end goal; the house, his wallet, a train ticket, home.

Determination fuelled him through the first few streets of terraced housing, repeating his goals in his mind, his hand held against the left side of his chest as he walked. On the fourth street, determination left him. He'd completely failed to locate Yeller's house the night before, a mere hour after stumbling out of it. In the harsh light of day, almost twenty-four hours removed from the MK madness of the night before, his task had become impossible. The idea occurred to him that he could make the hunt easier by skulking and loitering around until nightfall, however many hours away that may have been. *But there's no guarantee you'll find it then.* And there was no guarantee that, if he were to find Yeller's house, the drug-hoovering behemoth inside would do anything other than smash his face in for fucking off his with fiver. Doom and dread gathered pace in Danny's chest. Perhaps Yeller had already pawned off all the possessions he'd left behind. *And the phone.* The Lumia. Somewhere within the maze of terraced housing was the house he'd taken the phone from. Perhaps someone had noticed him. Perhaps they'd be waiting for him.

Joseph Bradfield. Danny pictured the stern face, the square jaw, the thick arms. He shuddered, and the shudder prompted tingling in his arms, followed by sharp stabbing anxiety, piercing his thoughts and his chest, tricking him into intuiting another heart attack. He clutched his right hand tight to the left side of his chest, the beating inside it offering no confirmation of whether what he was feeling was real. *Just because you're paranoid, don't mean they're not after you.* And the thought occurred that maybe nothing was real, nothing that he was experiencing; not just his impending death, but the life that had preceded it.

He remembered a night he'd stayed up late with Jay back at halls, caning ket, with nothing much happening to them, beyond an unusually in-depth conversation on the artistic merit of producing one's own YouTube videos, but the next day they'd gone to a park, and they'd smoked a joint, and they'd tripped out, and it had seemed as if the ket had lain dormant inside of them and been somehow triggered by the weed smoke... *Maybe that's what's happening now...* Maybe he was hallucinating everything, all of it... And he stood there on the street, clutching his chest, wondering if he was dying or living or dreaming, and having no way to be sure of any of it, and the answer came to him... *Wales...* Wales was the source of all trouble, Cardiff was the source of all trouble... *This fucking street is the source of it...* And he knew that he had to get away from it, get away from the area where dread and fear and paranoia hung all about him, lingering in the air like a fart at a funeral, morose and unsettling... *Get back to town,* he told himself. *Get on Facebook. Get on Twitter. Get the word out.* 'Danny Daggers is in Cardiff! Who the fuck fancies a drink?' *A drink.* That'd been the cure any time after that first panic attack that the skunk had gotten the better of him; a couple of tinnies to chase the spliffs down with. They'd taken the edge off and gilded the paranoia into a confident, perfect, blissed-out, pissed-up high. Alcohol was the cure for anxiety. Danny removed his hand from his chest and took his phone from his pocket, then walked back towards town, tapping out a Tweet as he went.

04.40pm

As she traversed the unfamiliar landscape of green hill-bordered terraced housing, Ji Eun waded back through the ocean of anecdotes and advice that'd spilled out of Rory during their epic car-sitting session: the football hooligans in Scotland; the record company execs in London plying starry-eyed girls with drugs and unfulfilled promises; the bankers he'd stalked through shady deal;, the footballers in night club fracases… the man had lived quite a life. His rise and bitter fall from and to a regional paper, the wild and glorious years on Fleet Street – if Ji Eun could stake out a career in the newspaper industry a tenth as eventful as Rory Gallagher's, she would surely die happy.

She was shaken from these thoughts by the vibration of the iPhone in the front pocket of her shorts. She took it out and saw a WhatsApp message from Marianne: *'Hey Ji, how are you? I'm back in Cardiff! Are you in town? Want to meet up for some drinks tonight?'* Ji Eun's first reaction was to recoil from it; the day had been a long struggle back to emerge from a hangover and feel half-way human again. Now, still feeling fragile, she thought another night of drinks would be a dreadful idea. But then she thought back to Rory, his wild abandon, his oft-repeated creed: *'Real journos go where tha fuckin' story is'*. And where was 'the story' likely to be found? Chilling out at home, watching TV? *No*. What would Rory do?

Ji Eun tapped out a reply to Marianne, glancing up from the iPhone as she walked, catching sight of an old man leaning on the gate of his garden, fixing her with a look of friendly curiosity. She wondered how many Koreans had walked this street. Perhaps she was the first. She had that same impulse toward discovery, that same journalistic impulse that'd propelled Rory through his own colourful escapades. She marvelled at her surroundings as she walked and typed, the squat terraced housing, such stark contrast to the towering grey high-rises of South Korea, six thousand-odd miles away. Rory had explained to her that these houses had all been built for coalminers, 'way back when this place were tha engine room o' a global fuckin' empire, if ye can believe tha' now'. She sent the message and put the phone away, then looked both ways before crossing a road to a petrol station, then up a hill, on which was sat a Chinese takeaway. A half-thought about the interconnectedness of the modern world came to her, a Korean, sending a message to her French friend, passing a Chinese takeaway in the South Wales valleys. A steel shutter covered one window of the takeaway. A swastika had been crudely scratched onto it. The other window was unblocked, and she peered inside, at a middle-aged Chinese woman behind the counter watching a small television set, a nodding good-luck cat sat beside it. The swastika… it was a common enough symbol in Seoul, with entirely different connotations, always affixed to the front of Buddhist buildings. Here, it was surely linked to the Nazis and pre-1945 Germany, and thus facism and racism, and the whole mess of connections and –isms and –ologies that'd led someone to crudely carve it onto the steel-shuttered façade of a Chinese takeaway made her more curious than anything; hungry for understanding, and maybe some Chinese food…

She heard mumbling and guffawing from across the street, and glanced at a group of tracksuited teenage boys, one with a bike, the rest on foot. As she rose further up a terraced-housing clad hill, nearing the train station, the boys called out some garbled imitation of what Chinese sounded like to Welsh valleys teenagers, followed by hearty, mean-spirited laughter. She felt it should intimidate or shame or otherwise attack her, but somehow she felt immune to it, simply wondering, wondering who those boys were, who that old man was, what their lives were, who these people were... and she suddenly remembered the guy she'd woken up next to, the guy she'd met at the gig the night before, the one who'd filled her with such fear and shame in hungover-morning, who know seemed so much more in bright summer's afternoon reflection. *What was his name?* She wondered if she'd ever see him again...

05:02pm

"What else've changed?" Podge asked.

"I think that's about it, innit?" Cain answered/asked, turning to Rembrandt.

"Yeah, I think that's all," Rembrandt confirmed. "Not much've changed really."

Podge raised the cool glass of lager to his lips and swigged; his two companions did the same.

"So what's it been like living over there?" Cain asked, picking the conversation back up.

"Mad, man," Podge replied, looking away, shaking his head and searching for a succinct description.

"What sort of food do they eat out there?" Rembrandt asked.

"Spicy foods mostly. Lots of barbecue. You have, like, a barbeque grill in the middle of the table and cook pork on it. It's class. My favourite's dakgalbi though, it's like spicy chicken with vegetables and noodles and stuff, all fried up in this pan in the middle of the table. Well nice."

"*Dakgalbi*," Rembrandt repeated softly.

"You got out of there at the right time though, bro," Cain remarked.

"Yeah..." Podge began, having fielded a dozen questions on the matter from all manner of family and friends, each hungering for a little insider info, having watched the whole thing unfold through the flare of a media lens. "I don't reckon anything's going to happen, really. I think that little fucker up North's just sort of slapping his dick about."

"Slapping his dick about?" Cain laughed.

"Yeah," Podge smiled. "Y'know, trying to show off about it like."

"How old is he anyway?" Cain asked.

"I think he's about twenty-nine."

"Fuck, are you kidding me?" said Rembrandt. "He looks about fucking twelve."

"I know, he is a baby-faced little bollocks i'n' he? But what I reckon, or, well, one theory that I've heard, is that he's a new, unproven leader, and there might be a bit of a power struggle going on inside the country, and to stop that, and to show what a fucking badass of a leader he is, he's doing what he's doing now, which is basically just slapping his dick about."

"Bit scary if it does all kick off though, yeah?" said Cain. "You'll be glad you got the fuck out of there if it does."

"Well, I'm going back there, ain't I?"

"Really?" Rembrandt interjected, shocked. "Are you being serious?"

"Deadly man. It's awesome out there."

"You ain't worried about getting nuked?" Rembrandt asked.

"Well," Podge answered, "if worst comes to worst and that does happen, well, the rest of the world's fucking fucked anyway, innit? If it's World War Three, you're either getting nuked to bits, or you're getting drafted in to be Chinese cannon fodder, so you're fucked wherever you are. Not really worth worrying about. You're more likely to die being thrown through the windscreen of Mikey's fucking Vauxhall Corsa, with the seat-belt jammed in the door, when he's bombing down the M4 to Swansea, chunging on a spliff."

"What happened to Mikey's Corsa?" Cain enquired.

"Ross slammed the door on the fucking seatbelt and now it's fucking stuck inside of it," Podge explained. "You can't open the passenger's side door, nor use the seatbelt."

"Shit," Rembrandt remarked.

"Dozy prick," Cain grinned in response.

They all took pause to take big swigs of lager. Podge stared out of the window of the Owain Glyndwr pub to the people flowing through the street outside. The time meant shoppers and suit-wearing workers were largely headed to the right of the little old stone church, off across the Hayes towards Cardiff Central station. The steady trickle of night-lifers hadn't really begun as of yet. Podge stared at the church, and did the same as he'd already done with scores of other buildings he'd previously seen often enough for them to completely blur into the background of the everyday, but, having now not seen them for two years, had suddenly become briefly new again. He began to bring to mind a few random recollections of experiences and significances that that particular church on the edge of the Hayes had had in his life. He remembered being a child, walking alongside his mother and grandmother, towards the older part of the St. David's shopping centre, asking what all the numbers on the wide path between the church and the little park en route were. His mum had told him they were graves. He'd felt a strange sense of fear and superiority, passing over the dead to go ogle toys in The Entertainer. He also remembered another occasion, many moons after that, when Rembrandt had drunkenly lobbed a bin over the church wall. His girlfriend at the time had gone mental at him, screaming about how disrespectful it was, how her nan went to church, asking him how the old folks would feel to go to church in the morning and see all that crap littering the graveyard.

"Gutted I was away for the Olympics," Podge said, turning his attention back to his companions. "Did either of you get down to London for it?"

"Nah," Rembrandt answered.

"Yeah man, I was selling flags," Cain replied. "I gots a mate down in London who offered me a place to crash for the weekend whilst it was on, so I was like 'alright, sweet', then while we're there he's got this racket going on, standing out near the Olympic venues selling flags at a fiver a piece. Hell of a profit margin on that, man. So we was doing really good out of it, raking the money in, then after maybe like five or six times of doing it successfully, this one time this guy comes up to us and he's like, 'are these flags for sale?'. So, obviously, I'm like, 'yeah bro, five pounds a pop, what country're you after?' Then the handcuffs come out and he's like, 'you're nicked'."

"Shit," Podge smiled.

"Yeah, he was an undercover copper like," Cain said, smiling wistfully and shaking his head. He took a swig of lager, then continued. "I had to go to court and everything."

"Shit," Podge said, smiling no more, "what happened?"

"Well, basically, I got an official police caution and had to pay five hundred pounds court costs."

"Shit."

"Yeah, but the guy I was with, the guy who's racket it was with the flags, he paid the whole thing."

"Sound man," Podge remarked, genuinely impressed.

"Yeah, good guy, like. Andy Palmer. Have you met him before?"

"I don't think I have, no."

"You've met Andy, haven't you?" Cain asked, turning to Rembrandt.

"Maybe…" Rembrant replied, trying to picture him.

"Well, anyway, he's a top guy. You'll have to get down to London with me while you're back and pay him a visit."

"Definitely," Podge replied. He took a big swig of lager, then continued the conversation with another question. "Were you in London when Thatcher died?"

"Nah bro, we was in Liverpool for that."

"Fuck!" Podge exclaimed. "That must've been amazing."

"Yeah, it was fucking crazy, weren't it?" Cain confirmed, seeking further confirmation from Rembrandt.

"Yeah man, the bars were rowdy as hell that night. The Scousers were going mad for it."

"I bet."

"A friend of mine came up with a good joke about Thatcher," said Cain, "he wrote this one on his Facebook status update; he goes, 'First Jimmy Saville, now Margaret Thatcher… it's been a good couple of years for minors.'"

Podge and Rembrandt both laughed heartily: "That's classic, man."

Their laughter suddenly faded away and Podge rose to his feet, calling off across the bar: "AY-OH!"

"S'apnin' bro!" Joseph yelled back at him, moving quickly from the front entrance to the table, greeting Podge with a slap of the hand and a quick embrace. "How are you boys doing?" Joseph continued, taking a seat beside Podge, across the table from Rembrandt.

"All good man," Cain answered, "how's work?"

"It's a job like, know what I mean?"

"Fair enough. You gonna get a pint in?"

"Yeah man, what are you guys drinking?"

"Anything wet and cold."

"And cheap," Rembrandt added.

"How much are beers over there?" Cain asked Podge, as Joseph got up and headed to the bar.

"Cheap as for Korean beer, but it's awful shite. You pay a bit more for imported stuff, though probably a bit cheaper than over here, maybe, in most places. They have these bars with fridges along the wall with all kinds of different beers from around the world. You have a basket at your table and at the end you just take the empty bottles up to the counter and pay."

"That's cool," Cain said.

"It'd never work over here though," Podge added. "Can you imagine? Everyone'd be shoving the empty bottles in their bags, trying to hide them and shit."

"Yeah man, at the end of the night the fridge's empty and they're like, 'What the fuck? All we've sold is a can of Fosters.'"

Cain's comment drew laughter from the group. Rembrandt was next to speak: "It was a bit like that in Germany, weren't it?"

"Yeah man," Cain said, suddenly struck by the memory of it. "It's mad, there's no barriers or ticket inspectors anywhere on the public transport there. They just expect people to pay, like an honour system. Never fucking work over here."

"When I was in Italy it was the same," Podge added, "nobody pays for shit there. They don't give a fuck about any kind of rules in Italy. I was walking through Milan train station and there's literally 'No Smoking' signs plastered about the place every couple of inches, but everyone's walking through with cigarettes sparked."

"Can you smoke inside in Korea?" Cain asked.

"Yeah," Podge replied, "well, they have sort of introduced a kind of smoking ban, but it's only like big chain pubs it applies to I think, but to be honest with you, apart from in Gangnam, which is, like, the rich people's district--"

"I've heard of Gangnam," Rembrandt grinned.

"--yeah, of course, well, apart from there and a few other places, everyone just ignores it. Even in Gangnam, a lot of places ignore it. They just give you paper cups with a bit of water in it now instead of ashtrays."

"It was a bit like that in Germany and all," Cain responded.

"Nah man, we could smoke everywhere over there," Rembrandt replied.

"In Berlin, yeah, but I've been Frankfurt and Munich as well, and there it's a bit more like fifty-fifty smoking and non-smoking, or even less smoking," said Cain. "See, the E.U. rules means there's supposed to be a smoking ban in every part of Europe, but in Germany, they get around it by calling some of the places smoking members' clubs. But you don't need a membership or nothing, it's just a fucking bar or a pub like, the only difference is you can smoke inside."

"How was Berlin anyway?" Podge asked, as Joseph returned to the table and plonked down a tray carrying four pints of lager.

Cain, Rembrandt and Joseph exchanged knowing glances, then smirked and swigged their lagers.

"Insane," Joseph finally answered.

"Fucking mental bro," Cain said, shaking his head, "this guy here was knocking out bad guys left, right and centre."

"We said if we ever go back there we're buying him a Batman costume," Rembrandt grinned.

"Why's that?" Podge asked, turning to the man himself, Joseph Bradfield.

"I don't know man," Joseph said, "shit got out of hand."

"Shit got fucking out of hand man," Cain laughed. "We were there four nights and you brawled on all of the first three. By the fourth we were too knackered out to do anything."

"Who were you fighting with?" Podge asked Joseph.

"Well," Cain explained for him, "on the first night it was a neo-Nazi, second night some guy with a truncheon, and on the third night he went after a wife-beater."

"Wow," Podge responded, eager for greater detail, adding, when none was forthcoming, "so how did that happen?"

"Well there was like eight of us went all together," Cain explained, "us three, Delveccio, Gordon, Porridge, Shrimpy and Lionsgate, and, as you know, it was Gordon's stag, so, night number one we decide we're gonna go out into the city and find a stripclub, proper stag it up like, so we're walking along and dickhead by here," he said, indicating Rembrandt, "went up to these guys and asked if they knew where to find one."

"I didn't know like," Rembrandt protested, "and they was quite friendly at first."

"So he goes up to these guys," Cain continued, "three big fuckers, all in army jackets with big black fucking boots on, all skinheads, and he asks them if they know where the stripclub is--"

"And they were telling us, to be fair," Rembrandt pleaded.

"Well, they might've been to start with," Cain conceded, "but then they took one look at Lionsgate and they goes, 'we're romper stompers'--"

"Romper stompers?" Podge enquired.

"Skinheads," Rembrandt explained, "BNP like, neo-Nazis."

"--yeah, so these three guys go, 'we're romper stompers', pointing at Lionsgate, and Joseph goes, like, 'are you, yeah?' and fucking leathers one of them."

"Shit," laughed Podge.

"He batters him a couple of times and the other two just watch, then this dickhead," Cain continued, indicating Rembrandt, "tries to break it up, he gets in the middle of them, pushes them apart, like, 'calm down guys, chill', and the fucking neo-Nazi leathers him in the face four fucking times."

Podge erupted with laughter at this point, while Joseph flashed an embarrassed smile and then took a big swig of his pint.

"So Rem stumbles away, punch-drunk, then Joseph steps in and fucking cracks the romper stomper a few times in the face, then the three of them fuck off into the night from whence they came."

"That's fucking funny man," said Podge.

"They were British as well, weren't they?" asked Rembrandt.

"Yeah man," Cain confirmed, "English boys."

"Fucking up British Nazis in Berlin," Podge summarised, smiling. "Awesome. So what happened with the other fight?"

"The other fights, plural," Cain corrected him. "I might as well go through them one-by-one. So that shit with the neo-Nazis was on the Thursday, which was the first night, the night after that we were in a bar near the hostel, all getting pissed up and rowdy, giving Gord hell like, him being the stag and all, when shit starts getting a little bit silly, everyone winding each other up like--"

"We'd drunk about ten shots of Jaeger by this point," Rembrandt interjected, clearly attempting to cover his back and absolve himself of responsibility for the events that were about to be retold.

"And the rest. Well, we're all acting like a gang of dickheads, as you do, and Rembrandt suddenly gets the idea to tip a fucking ashtray over Delveccio's head."

"Fuck," Podge laughed.

"Wait, he tipped a beer on me first," Rembrandt protested.

"Did he?" Cain asked, genuinely forgetting that fact.

"Yeah, he tipped a beer over my head, so I retaliated, like--"

"Actually," Joseph interrupted, "do you remember what you said to me just before you did it? Funny as fuck."

"No?"

"You turns to me and you go, 'oh, do you wanna see what Delveccio's gonna like when he's fifty years-old?' Then you went and tipped the ashtray on his bonce."

Everyone at the table erupted with laughter.

"Fucking classic," Podge remarked.

"Then Delveccio starts going mental," Rembrandt continued.

"Obviously," Joseph added.

"So someone, I think it's Lionsgate, he's like, come outside, quick, so I goes outside for a cigarette, and next thing I see, is Delveccio comes stumbling backwards out the door, screaming at the bar staff."

"Then what happened?" Cain enquired, prompting a few moments silence as the three involved parties tried to recollect the exact chain of events.

"I think Delveccio was just going mad at everyone," Rembrandt said, definitively and concludingly.

"Yeah, well, Delveccio is outside fucking going nuts, as is his wont, then this fucker at the table next to us cracks a fucking kosh out," Cain continued.

"A kosh?" Podge asked, clueless as to the word's meaning.

"Yeah man, a kosh, you know, one of them fucking batons the fucking riot police carry round with them, and he just sits there at the table with this fucking nightstick, this fucking kosh, staring at us, and we stare at him for a few seconds like, 'seriously?', then me, him," Cain said, indicating Joseph, "and Delveccio all run at the fucker, and he sprints off over the road to the fucking train station."

"I watched the whole thing from the street outside," Rembrandt added, "it was hilarious. All we saw from outside was the silhouettes of them all head up the stairs, confront the guy, then fucking mayhem. We saw the guy with the kosh and Deleveccio tumble down the fucking stairs, it was well funny."

"Yeah, Delveccio fucked his knee up pretty bad from that," Cain smiled.

"That and kneeing the fucker in the head," Rembrandt grinned.

"And what was that big fucking rasta's problem?" Cain remarked, suddenly turning serious.

"Who?" Rembrandt asked.

"Do you remember us saying about some guy with dreads who suddenly got involved and started swinging for us?"

"Oh yeah," Rembrandt remembered, "he must've just seen three guys beating the fuck out of one guy and thought he'd help him out a bit."

"Yeah, that cunt deserved what he got though," said Cain, "anyone who bops about with a fucking baton in their pocket is obviously going out to cause shit."

"Yeah, you don't do that, do you?" Rembrandt agreed. "Think of how many randomers he's probably hit with that thing who'd done nothing to deserve it."

"Totally," Cain agreed.

"You boys are fucking psychopaths," Podge said, smiling and shaking his head in disbelief.

"That weren't even the end of it," Cain continued.

"Next thing I saw was you two bopping down the stairs," Rembrandt added, indicating Cain and Joseph, "and I can still see Delveccio's silhouette through the station window, with people crowding all around him. You two get to the bottom of the steps, realise he's not with you, then run back up and it all fucking kicks off again!"

"Shit," laughed Podge, "what happened to the guy?"

"He hopped on the next train and got the fuck out of there," Cain smiled. "He won't be doing that again, that's for sure."

"You boys fucked him up pretty good then?" Podge asked Joseph, who looked a little less comfortable revelling in the relived carnage than the others.

"I guess we did, yeah," Joseph reluctantly confirmed.

"The best was when you first went up to him in the station, you was like, 'put the baton away, we want to have a word with you,'" Cain said to Joseph, "then as soon as it's in his pocket you fucking smash him one, bam."

Everyone smiled and took swigs of lager – everyone except Joseph, who swigged without smiling.

"So this all happened right outside the hostel, yeah?" Cain said, suddenly returning to the story. "So afterwards, we're heading back there--"

"Yeah, basically, like I said, I was watching all this unfold from outside the bar across the street, and it's been going on a bit long at this point, so me and Shrimpy decide to cross the street and find out what's happening," explained Rembrandt.

"Where did the others go?" asked Cain.

"They stayed with them girls we were chatting up in the bar before the shit kicked off."

"Really?"

"Yeah, they went to a fucking Korean restaurant with them, funnily enough, Angry Chicken."

"Shrimpy weren't there when the police showed up though?" said Cain.

"Nah, fuck knows where he disappeared to, but anyway," Rembrandt said, turning his attention to Podge and the remainder of the story, "we fucking sprint across the street to the hostel, furiously pressing the buzzer for them to let us in, then all of a sudden these eight police officers run down the fucking alleyway with flashlights, screaming, 'Get against the wall! Get against the wall!'"

"Fuck," remarked Podge, impressed.

"So we're all there with our hands against the wall--" Rembrant continued.

"You're all there going fucking mental," Cain interrupted, "I'm there trying to talk calm to them. You were jabbering like an idiot about what you saw from across the street," he continued, indicating Rembrandt, "Delveccio's screaming like a madman, telling the police to go fuck themselves and fuck knows what else, Joseph's just... fuck, what were you doing?"

"Can't remember," Joseph answered.

"Well, anyway, I'm the only one lucid enough to give them a rundown of what's just happened, like, then once Rembrandt gets wind of what I'm trying to do with them, he starts screaming that the guy had a knife."

Podge and Joseph laughed as Rembrandt quickly stepped up to defend himself: "He was carrying a weapon on him though."

"Yeah, but it weren't a fucking knife though, was it? It was a fucking kosh."

"So were there any consequences, like, from the coppers or anything?" asked Podge.

"Nah man, we explained what'd happened - well, *I* explained what'd happened – and the police said they'd go looking for this guy we was on about."

"Did they find him?" Podge asked.

"Did they fuck. Probably didn't even bother looking. But at the end of the day, only Delveccio got his details taken, and then that was just for mouthing off like a spaz at the coppers anyway I think."

"What did they take?"

"Passport number, phone number maybe, that kind of thing. Weren't that big of a deal in the end, really," Cain said, bringing the story to a close.

"There was blood all over the steps in the train station when we went back there the next day," Rembrandt added gleefully.

"Fuck," remarked Podge. "Maybe I'm glad I missed out on Gordon's stag then boys!"

"It was a bit fucking manic, weren't it?" Cain rhetorically asked Rembrandt and Joseph. "When people ask me, 'Did you have a good time in Berlin?', I'm like, 'well, I think it was fun, maybe...', you know what I mean?"

"'A good time' isn't the first phrase that springs to mind when I think of it," Rembrandt added.

"And what happened with Gord?" asked Podge. "Did you stag him?"

"Stagged the fuck out of him," Cain laughed. "Poor boy."

"What did you do?"

Jaunty midi music interrupted the conversation and Joseph pulled a sky blue Nokia 3310 from his pocket: "Hello? Woah, slow down, hang on." He got to his feet and headed out the door, clutching the phone tight to his ear, the boys watching him through the window.

"I'm listening, yeah... look... alright... calm down... just, calm down..."

"I can't fucking calm down," Jodie screamed over the phone at him. "Someone's broken into our fucking house, Joe."

"Did they take anything?"

"Fuck... I don't know..." she started crying. "I don't know Joe... but someone's broken into the house Joe, and you know, he's done a runner, haven't he? What if it's him, Joe? What if Simon's broken into our house looking for us? Looking for Daniel?"

"Look, look, I knows it's bad... just calm down a minute... where are you now? Your mam's house? Yeah? Yeah? Look, don't worry, I'll be over now... I'll be over now... I'm just in town, I'll be there in a couple of minutes... honestly, I'll come there as fast as I can... don't worry, I'll be over now..."

The boys looked on in silence as Joseph strode back into the bar, still clutching the 3310 tight in his hand, a look of extreme seriousness on his face. "Sorry boys, I'm going to have to shoot off."

"No way," Rembrandt said, "Podge's just got back."

"It's alright man," Podge intervened, "I'm back for at least month, maybe two."

"That's cool man," replied Joseph, "I'll try and link up with you a few times while you're back then."

"Why've you got to rush off now?" asked Rembrandt. "You've got more than a half a pint still sat on the table."

"Yeah, I gots to get home," Joseph explained, "Jodie's not feeling well."

Rembrandt lifted his right hand in a fist then brought it down quickly over the table, making a whip-crack sound as he did so, before singing a little burst of Rolling Stones lyrics: "*Under my thumb...*"

"Fuck up Rem," Cain ordered.

"The fuck's wrong with you?" Rembrandt protested. "He knows I'm only messing mun."

"If he says he's gotta leave he's gotta leave," Cain explained, "leave it at that. Say your goodbyes. Drink your pint and leave him the fuck to it."

"Alright. Fucking hell like."

"Anyway," Podge interjected, "really good to see you man."

Joseph accepted his held out hand, slapped it, then transitioned smoothly into a fistbump: "Likewise man, I'll give you a buzz soon. Laters boys."

"Catch you soon bro."

They watched Joseph walk to the door, then watched through the window as he headed off towards Queen Street. It was a few moments before the tension that'd flared up between Cain and Rembrandt dissipated - the source of said tension an utter mystery to Rembrandt – and Podge stepped in to get the conversation going again: "So what happened with this other fight then?"

"What other fight?" answered Cain.

"When you were in Berlin for Gord's stag do," Podge explained, "you said that you got into fights the first three nights running. You told me about the neo-Nazi and the guy with the kosh, you've not told me nothing about the third night."

"Well…" Cain began cautiously.

"I can fill you in on that one," said Rembrandt. "We were all walking through Berlin, I'm not sure where we were exactly, it might've been in Kreuzberg, near our hostel--"

"I think it was, yeah," Cain confirmed.

"--so we were walking along, the others were a bit up ahead, some of them might've been in the pub already, but I'm walking along the street with Gord, who we've plied with so much Jaeger by this point that he can barely stand, let alone converse with me, so I'm walking along with him, and up ahead I see this guy pushing this girl about, and I'm thinking to myself, 'that's not right,' but I don't know, I was pretty pissed like, so I didn't think too much of it, then as we're going past, this guy just spits in this girl's face."

"Shit," Podge remarked.

"Yeah man, full on gobs in her chops like, fucking disgusting. So obviously I'm none too happy with this but, like, given the shit that's unfolded the previous two nights, I'm not exactly too keen on letting the boys get wind of it, know what I mean, least of all Joseph fucking 'Batman' Bradfield. I've spent the last few days bopping round Kreuzberg looking over my shoulder, expecting a revenge attack from a bunch of neo-Nazis or baton-wielding maniacs at any given moment, know what I mean, but all the same, it's not every day you see someone full on gob a wad in a bird's face, so I'm standing there, staring, and I ask Gord what to do, does he reckon I should tell the boys or not, and he's fucking gone, man, no help at all, he's standing there like a fucking lemon, I've seen fucking deep-south Americans more aware of the world around them than Gordon was at this point, but eventually Delveccio comes over and he's asking what's happened, and at first I'm like, 'I don't want to tell you man', but eventually I can't help but let him know, so obviously, everyone goes steaming after him, Joseph in the lead, they chase him down some little alleyway in between some houses, Joseph starts fucking pounding on him, this bitch we was trying to help screaming at him the whole time, she goes fucking mental, starts scratching him with her fucking nails like--"

"Fucking hell," Podge remarked.

"Looked like he'd been in a fight with a cat the next day, I'm telling you bro," Cain added.

"Yeah, so it's all going fucking mental like," Rembrandt continued, "all kicking off, then all of a sudden these two big fuckers push past me, and I mean *big* big fat fuckers, big fucking dudes, like, and I start trying to explain to them what's been happening, that we're doing a good deed, that this prick's been pushing this girl about and spitting in her face and whatnot, and I'm like, 'who the fuck are you guys? Are you friends of his?', and they go, 'We're the police.'"

Cain laughed and then took a big swig of his lager.

"Shit man," Podge said, before taking a swig of his own, "were they actually?"

"Nah, were they fuck," Rembrandt smiled in response, "they fucking were like Turkish fucking mafia or something. So one of these big fuckers swings for Joseph, I see him reeling back, proper fucking punch-drunk like, and at that point we decide 'fuck this', grab hold of Joseph, and leg it the fuck out of there."

Podge took a pause to laugh, added another 'shit', then took a swig of his pint, before adding: "What about the last night?"

"What about it?" asked Rembrandt.

"Did you do any brawling on the last night?" Podge clarified.

"Nah man," Rembrandt replied, "we spent the last night searching for a brothel."

05.32pm

"Where's he too now 'en?"

"He's back in Cardiff now boys," Simon said, looking at the little green blip on the laptop screen.

"So let's head to fucking Cardiff 'en," Darren said, straight to his feet, ready for action.

"Woah now, hold your horses butt," Bruce ordered, "let's see if he's stopping in fucking Cardiff before we go charging in there."

"Of course he's fucking stopping, that's where he lives mun."

"There's no rush butt," Simon told him. His eldest brother's words had an instant calming effect upon the youngest of the Amstell brethren. "The plan's exactly the same as it was before. Slip in there late at night, cause as little ruckus as possible, nab Danny, and I'll meet you both at the airport."

"How are you getting to the airport?" Bruce asked.

"Taxi."

"Have you got enough money for that?"

"Come on butt."

"It's a serious question butt. It'll cost you a small fortune to take a taxi from here to the fucking airport."

"Butt, I've not had fuck all to spend on for the past few years, have I?"

"Yeah, aye, well, you might have money in your bank account, but you'll need it in cash for a taxi, won't you?" Bruce retorted.

"I can lend you the cash," Darren said.

"Cheers bro," replied Simon.

"How the fuck can you lend him the fucking money?" asked Bruce.

"I gots it butt."

"How much have you fucking got?"

"Enough."

Bruce shook his head. The whole dumb enterprise was just a few short hours away from becoming a reality. *Fine fucking family I wound up being born into. Cheers for that Mam, Dad, God, whoever the fuck...* "We've not got fucking chloroform mind. We still not managed to sort that fucking shite out, have we?"

"Don't worry butt," Darren said calmly. "We'll be alright with a couple of hammers."

A car pulled up at the end of the street, far enough away from the Amstell's home that they weren't aware, but near enough to be seen by Rory Gallagher, still parked up in his red Volvo at the other end of the road, nursing the third can from a six pack of Fosters.

"What do we do now then Bron?" Ivor Evans asked.

"Wait," Bronwyn Jones replied.

05.39pm

Jodie was sitting in the kitchen, dabbing at her eyes with a tissue, her mother sitting opposite, regarding her daughter with a mixture of sympathy and 'I told you so' admonishment. They both looked up as the door to the living room opened and Joseph appeared in front of them.

"Alright Jode? Bev?"

"Alright Joe," Beverley replied, regarding him with contempt. *They're all the bloody same.*

Jodie sniffled a couple of times and composed herself before speaking. "Someone's broken into the house."

"Did they take anything?"

"No. I don't think so."

Joseph was unsure if that was a good or a bad thing. Probably the latter.

"Maybe someone scared them off," Joseph suggested, trying to reassure her. It didn't seem to work. "You should probably keep that front door locked Bev, if it is... you know..."

Beverley stared straight at him. *They think they know it bloody all. Always got an answer for everything.* "They won't find me here. Vera Lynn I registered this place under."

"Still, best not to take any chances." Joseph saw the contempt burning in Beverley Brain's eyes and moved his focus back to Jodie. "Have you spoken to the police about it?"

"Yeah," Jodie told him. "A woman come round the house earlier. Had to wait in there by myself. Bricking it, I was. I told them that I thought it might've been Simon."

"And what did they say?"

"They just told me not to worry about it."

"Bloody useless, them police are," Beverley commented. "They're happy enough with our taxes paying their wages, but as soon as you want something in return, they don't want nothing to do with you."

"Where's Daniel?" Joseph asked.

"Upstairs."

Joseph nodded, then walked back into the living room, pulling the door closed behind him. He walked up the stairs and opened the door to the guest bedroom. Daniel was sat on the bed, flicking through a comic book.

"What are you reading, Vader?"

"Hellboy," Danny said, without looking up from it.

Joseph sat down on the bed beside him.

"What does 'adjure' mean?" Danny said, now looking up at Joseph.

Joseph looked down at the comic book. A priest was holding out a crucifix at some crazed girl in Victorian dress, saying, "I adjure thee, evil spirit."

Joseph tutted. *Exorcisms, mun. What's Beverley playing at, buying this for him?* Then he thought about the word, 'adjure'. "I don't know, to be honest with you. I think maybe it's just some old-time word. I don't think people really use it now."

"When are we going back to our house Joe?"

"I don't know Dan. Maybe in a couple of days."

"Why are we all staying round Nan's house?"

"There's been a problem at our house," he said. Danny's eyes looked up at him, full of wonder. Joseph glanced at the comic book before speaking again. "There's some sort of evil spirit. But don't worry about it; we've got people there, getting rid of it. It'll be fine by the time we go back."

"Is that why Mum's so upset?"

"Yeah. Yeah."

"Do you think the evil spirit wants to hurt us, Joe?"

"No, no, you don't have to worry about that, Dan. The spirit might be evil, but it's weak." Joseph got up from the bed and lifted Danny up in his arms. "And Joe's strong."

He spun around and placed Danny back down on the bed. Danny laughed.

07.36pm

The little green rectangle at the top right hand corner of the screen had dwindled to the point that only an ominous red rump remained. *Problems, problems. Endless fucking problems.* Danny Daggers swiped and clicked across to 'Settings' and turned the brightness down. He contemplated turning off his 3G service – it was a battery devourer, no doubt about that, but turning it off meant sequestering himself away from the universe, isolating himself in Cardiff, and also had the added practical disadvantage of leaving him no longer immediately alerted to any replies to his Tweet or status update asking if anyone was up for partying in Cardiff.

What now? He slid the Lumia back into his pocket, and looked up and down the closed shops that lined Queen Street. A steady trickle of early-evening pissheads passed by. Cigarettes were a priority. So was alcohol, albeit less so. *Fags and booze don't rustle themselves up,* he mumbled internally, nicotine craving blurring his thoughts, tiredness impeding their progress. He rose from the bench, got to his feet, and set off in search of a cigarette. He walked a now well-trodden path along Cardiff's central pedestrianised shopping street, away from the castle and towards the station end, eyeing all that passed by for any sign of a spark.

"Excuse me mate," Danny blurted out, as a cigarette-wielding lad in a business suit walked by him. The man continued on his way, puffing a big cloud of smoke up in the air as he steamed right passed without so much as a glance of acknowledgement. *Maybe I'm dead already,* Danny thought to himself. *Maybe I died and became a ghost, and no-one can see me, and I'm doomed to wander Queen Street, craving an unattainable cigarette, for all eternity.* Half-believing his own bullshit, Danny continued on down Queen Street, passed Thorton's and Lush at near-enough the arse end of it, when he saw a brown-skinned feller in a pink cowboy hat puffing a biff a few metres away from the entrance to the two-storey, brown-brick, car-park-eqsue Capitol shopping centre.

"Excuse me mate," Danny began, drawing a big smile from the fag-wielding feller in the pink cowboy hat, "could I by any chance buy a cigarette off you?"

07.56pm

"Honestly, I don't see the point in them things at all," Myrig squealed in that theatrically camp way of his. "If you're gonna smoke, smoke."

"It's better for you mun, innit?" Frank answered, exhaling a thin cloud of nictoine vapour that dissipated within seconds.

"You say that, but they've not done proper tests and that on 'em yet," Miranda, the sole girl at the table, reasoned.

"Yeah, but they must be better for you than proper cigs," Frank replied.

"Why?"

"Well you're not smoking smoke, are you? It's water vapour. Nicotine liquid."

"Frank," Myrig interjected, "speaking frankly, I never thought I'd see the day where you were fretting about putting a fag in your mouth."

Danny sat and stared at the half-drained pint of lager on the table in front of him, as Myrig howled with laughter at his own double-entendre. Danny was mesmerised by the song playing in the bar. It was an old '80s tune. Talking Heads. The mostly spoken word one. The lyrics struck a chord.

How the fuck'd I wind up here? A gay bar in Cardiff. *How the fuck'd I wind up here?* Amongst this unlikely foursome, a mutual love of cock the only bond between them.

It occurred to Danny that Myrig was the kind of homosexual that, were he a television character being played by a straight actor, would draw scores of complaints from viewers for inaccurate stereotyping. Übercamp. The kind of person who jazz-handed his way out of the womb gay, making an over-sexed quip to the doctor after being welcomed into the world with the customary arse slap. Myrig had glasses and short curly hair; he wore a black T-shirt that was a little too tight and thus unflatteringly drew attention to his man-boobs.

Frank was an utterly average bloke. He wore a plain black hoodie and kept his brown hair at a sensible length, opting to eschew any unnecessary styling or sculpting in favour of practical functionality.

Miranda was the token female. *Fat and gobby*, Danny summarised. *Typical Welsh girl*. Myrig's B.F.F.. Danny knew she weren't a lesbian, as one might've expected in the type of establishment Danny now found himself in, due to the comments she made about the arse on every guy that walked passed their table.

Then there was Mandeep, the brown-skinned feller in the pink cowboy hat whose cigarettes had lured Danny into this environment in the first place. He was spaced-out and drippy. *A brown bimbo*, Danny thought to himself, before wondering whether or not such a description might be considered racist.

How the four of them had come to know each other was a mystery. And how Danny would fit into their evening was an even greater one. *Never mind,* he thought to himself, reaching across the table for his pint glass, *free drinks and cigarettes are free drinks and cigarettes.*

"I'm gonna go outside for a smoke," said Mandeep, all the talk about Frank's e-cigarette having brought forth the urge.

"I'll join you," replied Miranda.

"You're not gonna leave me in here with him, are you?" Myrig asked, indicating Frank. Then he glanced over at Danny and suddenly remembered that they had a stranger in their midst. "You're awfully quiet love. Everything alright?"

"Yeah," Danny said, tensing up.

"I think your friend's a bit shy," Myrig smiled at Mandeep. "I hope we're not scaring you."

"No, it's fine," Danny said.

Mandeep grabbed his pack of Marlboro Lights from the table and stood up; Danny did the same, hoping to pinch another one off him.

"Nobody's got anything stronger, have they?" Myrig asked, his acute lack of an attention span prompting him to dread spending up to ten minutes without a group of people to play around with.

"I've got a bit of bud on me," Frank answered.

"I thought you weren't smoking?" said Myrig.

"I'm not smoking cigarettes," Frank explained. "I've not given up the weed like."

"Sit down while he skins up then boys," Myrig ordered Danny and Mandeep. "We'll all go out in a minute now."

08.02pm

"Fucking well tasty like," Podge beamed. "Best thing about the place. Legs like you wouldn't believe. Mini-skirts, short shorts, all the rage out there boys. Fucking brilliant. Honestly, walking down the street in summer, you don't know where to look."

"They easy like?" Rembrandt asked, enthralled.

Podge drew a big swig of mojito up through his straw as he pondered the question.

"Not compared to Welsh girls like, but I do alright for myself."

"Fucking primary school maths isn't as easy as Welsh girls," Rembrandt concurred, grinning.

"How come I never see you with anyone if they're so fucking easy like?" Cain scoffed. "Then again, you've always been shit at maths and all."

Rembrandt scowled at Cain, well and truly burnt.

"Most Korean girls don't tend to shag about the way Welsh girls do," Podge expounded, eager to embellish upon his favourite topic. "You've got to date them and shit first like. Worth it though. Fucking amazing bods on them. Nothing like the fat slags you get over here."

"The fat slags *you* get," Cain said, feeling strangely patriotic about the matter.

"Actually," Podge continued, ignoring Cain, lowering his voice, "I think that girl on that table over there's Korean."

Rembrandt rotated himself around in his chair to look across the street-front bar area to four girls sat a few tables away from them.

"Don't make it obvious, you tit," Podge scolded him. "You look like a fucking owl mun."

"She's butters, man," Rembrandt said, turning back to face Podge. "I thought you said you don't get fat slags out in Korea?"

Podge stared at the table for a few seconds before realising that Rembrandt had clocked the wrong girl. "Not her, you dull twat. The other one."

Rembrandt spun back around like a fucking owl and spotted her. "Oh yeah. She's alright, yeah."

"How do you know she's Korean?" Cain asked.

"'Cause she looks Korean," Podge smirked, thinking the question a stupid one.

"How do you know she's not Chinese or something?"

"I can tell."

"How?"

"I don't know. They look different."

Cain stared at the two girls on the other table, trying to see what it was that distinguished them from the populace of their neighbouring countries.

"I suppose you get used to it after a while," Rembrandt reasoned. "You've been living out there two years like. You ought to know what a fucking Korean looks like by now."

"Do you reckon you could tell the difference between us lot just by looking at us?" Cain asked. "Like, could you spot the difference between a Welshman and an Englishman just by looking at them? Or a Frenchman and a German?"

"Yeah," Podge replied instantly, "course you can. Frenchman do wear fucking berets and strings of garlic round their neck, Germans do wear lederhosen. An Englishman'll have an air of arrogance and sense of entitlement about him, while a Welshman'll be salt-of-the-earth and ruggedly good looking."

"Is it true they don't shave like?" Rembrandt asked, returning to the main theme of their conversation.

"What, Germans?" Podge said, thinking of armpits.

"Nah, Koreans," Rembrandt clarified, "well, Asian girls in general."

"What, down there?"

Rembrandt greeted Podge's down-pointed finger with a nod.

"Yeah," Podge replied with absolute certainty. "I think shaving's just a western thing like."

"Have you picked up much Korean over there?" Cain asked.

"A little like," Podge answered. "Enough to order in a restaurant without making a tit of myself. The alphabet's easy, like, there's only twenty characters. The vocabulary's fucking rock hard to remember though. There's nothing to tie it to in English, like if you were learning a European language, like French or Spanish or something, there's a lot of overlap with English words, and it makes things easier. There's no relation to English at all in Korean vocabulary. And the sentence structure's totally backwards. It's almost the same sentence structure as Welsh."

"*Mewn gwirionedd?*" Rembrandt said, smirking.

"*Chin-cha,*" Podge replied, seeing Rembrandt's Welsh and raising him badly-pronounced Korean.

"Go over and talk to them then," Cain dared. He had no interest in taking the dumpy little grenade sitting beside the slender young thing that had piqued Podge's interest, but the two blondes sat opposite them, their backs turned to the lads, were intriguing.

"Nah, I don't know," Podge said, tensing up a little bit.

"Pussy-o," branded Rembrandt.

"It's a bit weird like, innit? What am I going to say them? 'Hey, you look Korean. I live in Korea.'"

"Speak some Korean to them," Cain said. "They'll love it. They won't be expecting some white Welsh boy in Cardiff to start gabbing at them in their mother tongue, will they?"

"I don't know," Podge squirmed, suddenly wishing he'd put a bit more effort into learning the language while he'd been over there. *Shillae ham nida,* he rehearsed in his mind, *cho-nun Liam.* Then what? *Yo buddah. Tang shi nul won haeyo.*

"You should mun," Rembrandt goaded him, feeling the same desire as Cain to get a better look at those two blonde pieces, chunky fourth wheel be damned.

Podge pulled hard on his straw, finishing off the first of his two-for-one-before-eight mojitos, running through his limited stock of Korean phrases in his mind, wondering what might be an appropriate way to get a conversation started. *Shillae ham nida, hajang shil odi-soyo?** (* *Excuse me, where is the toilet?*) No, too weird to say that to a table full of girls, whatever language you say it in. Besides, Cthulhu weren't exactly fucking cavernous; the answer would be pretty bleeding obvious to anyone with half a brain and a single functioning eyeball in their head. *How about 'where do you come from'?* Better. But how the fuck do you say it? He'd been asked the question by Koreans more than enough times to be familiar with it. At first, he'd insisted on 'Wales-uh', but soon realised this just caused unnecessary complications if the asker didn't have a decent grasp of English. Eventually, he settled on '*Yonguk*', England, for sake of convenience. If the person he was talking to had a decent grasp of the Queen's, he might explain to them that he came from a rump of land that was connected to England but not technically part of it. His difficulty in explaining this had lessened somewhat when Swansea won promotion to the Premier League, though he then had to deal with the indignity of his country's name drawing an immediate reference to the Jack bastards in that pretty shitty city to the west of his hometown. Thankfully, the references to Swansea stopped once Cardiff gained their first ill-fated season of Premier League football, with Kim Bo-Kyung's presence in the team ensuring the majority of their games were broadcast on Korean television. Still, none of this tangential revery of remembrance brought him any closer to the answer: *how the fuck do you ask 'where are you from in Korean'? "?...? odi-soyo?'*

In the end, the situation resolved itself without Podge finding the words for it; one of the blonde girls rose from the seats opposite and turned towards the bar, presumably in search of the *hajangshil* herself, with Cain eyeballing her, at first with interest, then with a sudden sense of recognition.

"Cain!" she exclaimed, catching sight of him.

"Marianne!" he beamed, jumping up to greet her.

08.32pm

"...and then I hopped in a taxi and came back to Cardiff," Danny concluded.

"Why?" Frank asked.

"I dunno," Danny admitted."Better the devil you know, I suppose."

"How did you pay for the taxi then?" asked Miranda.

"I didn't." Puzzled looks. "I did a runner." Laughter.

"You're mental, you!" Frank cackled. "I tell you what, I'll get another round in. On me buddy. You're quality."

"Get some shots in!" Myrig shouted, as Frank headed off across the bar.

"What kind?"

"I dunno, anything mun. Aftershocks or tequilas or sambucas or Jaegers or something like."

"So what are you gonna do now then?" asked Miranda.

"I don't know," Danny said, feeling pissed and stoned and perfectly comfortable in the here and now, the future a foreign land, like a war-stricken or disaster-ravaged country viewed on a 42 inch plasma screen TV from the comfort of one's living room.

"You can't call your family or something?" Mandeep suggested.

"I don't know," Danny said again. "I suppose I could, if I get desperate. It's just a bit... embarrassing really, like; having to explain to my parents how I've ended up stranded in Cardiff without any money or anything."

"You'll be alright mun," Myrig reassured him. "We'll take care of you tonight."

Danny wasn't sure whether Myrig had winked at him when he'd said it or if it'd just been an illusion caused by the low lights of the bar being refracted in the thick glass of his spectacles. Either way, he felt a wave of weed-induced paranoia roll right the way through him. *Alcohol*, he told himself. *Alcohol'll kill the para off.*

09.02pm

"You're not getting back in here mate."

"What?" Tom gasped, incredulous.

"You're too pissed," the bouncer elaborated.

"But I just came out for a cigarette, all my friends are still inside."

"I don't care mate. You're too pissed. You'll have to hang out with them another time."

"Fucking hell mun," Tom spat, "I only came out for a fucking cigarette like. If it weren't for the fucking smoking ban then I'd still be inside there fucking hanging out with them."

"Well then write a strongly worded letter about it to your local MP. Far as I'm concerned, you're too fucking pissed for my bar. There's a million other bars in Cardiff, give one of these mates of yours a call and get them to trot along somewhere else with you."

"Can I go inside for a second and speak to them?"

"Can you fuck. If I've told you once then I've told you twice, you are not getting back in here tonight mate, you're too pissed for it."

"Fucking bollocks like," Tom muttered.

He turned his back to the bouncer and stumbled away from Varsity, heading uneasily along Greyfriar's Road. The street was teeming with bars geared to the after-work drinks crowd. With some difficulty, he staggered as far as Lloyd's Bar, all of five metres away. He reached into his pocket for his cigarettes and sparked one up as he stared in through the window at a heaving red-lit human meat market, with will.i.am playing far too loudly.

The state he was in, he'd have no luck inside; no, if he were to stand any chance of salvaging a sinking vessel of a night, if he were to sail back to port with a lover, mate, or a semen receptacle on board, feigning comfort as he flailed his limbs to the limp beats and meaningless words of a poverty-stricken, mentally-deficient man's Kanye West was not the way to do it. Tom really did hate that cunt will.i.am. *No*, no Lloyd's Bar tonight; *Live Lounge?* No sooner had the words occurred to him than he was walking in that direction, away from the dull beats resonating out through the window of Lloyd's Bar, off to the end of Greyfrair's Road, past Tiger Tiger, and left towards the wide alleyway that led back to Queen Street.

The crash of hi-hat and muffled, wailed vocals coming from the venue told Tom that he'd made the right choice. *Bon Jovi.* There is a time and a place for everything, and the time and place for Jon Bon Jovi is most definitely a bar full of pissed-up students on a Thursday night. The cordoned-off smoking area out in front was teeming with life. The night would be a good one yet. Tom halted as he moved towards it, to check his remaining fag count. *Two.* He frowned at this. *Best make preparations.* He turned away from the scene and headed off towards the Spar at the end of Queen Street to stock up.

Two women were ahead of him when he got to the Spar's night window, mini-skirts concealing nothing of their cellulite-scarred tree trunk legs, tops misshapen and stretched over rolls and bulges of fat, barking orders at the staff as they argued with each other about what kind of ice-cream they wanted.

Tom kept his distance, finishing off his cigarette some feet away from the garbled drunken instructions and bickering. It was then, mildly irritated and inconvenienced, swaying from all the alcohol, that he looked up and saw a vision that illuminated the dimming early-evening light; rounding the corner that led passed the Spar towards the Hayes, leaning in to talk to a friend, it was *her*, the girl whose house he'd woken up at, the girl he'd tried and failed to track down on Facebook. Lo, truly, she had appeared unto him; *Ji Eun.*

Tom let the cigarette drop from between his fingers to the floor as he stared, steadying his swaying frame to behold her, the warm rush of serendipity melting his inebriated irritation away; Ji Eun, moving towards him, leaning in to talk to her friend, another Asian girl, then besides them... some white guy. A plump stubbled ape in a polo shirt.

Instinctively, Tom turned his back to them and let them pass without incident, then watched the trio head off down Queen Street, followed by two guys and two girls, two couples, in close enough succession and proximity to suggest the whole lot of them were out together as a unit. He focused on the last of the girls, the blonde hair... it was she. *Claire.* Tom felt the world slip away as they walked, growing smaller, until they reached the point in the street opposite the main glass-fronted entrance to the St. David's Shopping Arcade, at the end of the alleyway that ran back towards Greyfriar's Road. The alleyway on which Live Lounge was located. They stood there in semi-circular discussion for a few moments, clearly talking about heading into the very same place he'd intended going.

* * *

"I think we're going to head home," Ji Eun announced.

Podge frowned; he'd expected the worst when she'd broken away from his small talk to conference with the little fat one in Korean. Claire scrunched up her face in disapproval, making sure Ji Eun noticed her flick irritated eyes towards Marianne.

"Come on girls, the night's young!" Rembrandt said, trying to salvage things.

"Yeah," Claire added, "why do you have to leave anyway?"

Ji Eun looked at Monica, who was shaking a little as she stared at Claire; she was far too afraid of the angry look with which Claire was now regarding her to say anything.

"We're feeling tired," Ji Eun said.

"Have a Jaeger bomb," Claire suggested.

There was no arguing with that. Ji Eun looked at Monica, who was still trembling beneath Claire's stare.

"Didn't you say you have to Skype your Mum?" Ji Eun asked.

Monica nodded, not taking her eyes off Claire: "Yeah."

"Well you don't both need to go home for that, do you?" Claire said.

"Yeah," Monica said, acceding, "you can stay out. I'll see you later."

Ji Eun looked at Podge; she supposed he seemed harmless enough. Friendly, if a little dull. And then she looked at Cain and Marianne, and Claire and Rembrandt; the numbers were against her.

* * *

Ji Eun's attention broke off from the group for a few seconds, and she stared back down Queen Street, seemingly straight at Tom, but this brief hopeful interlude soon passed without incident, and her attention was back on the boys she was standing closest to. Crestfallen, Tom turned away and headed to the Spar's night window, away from which the two fat birds had now flown.

"Can I help you?" one of the young brown guys inside asked.

"Yeah, can I get ten Richmond Superkings," Tom began, and then, wanting something to wash the pain away before the now-inevitable journey home, "and a bottle of Stella please. A big one."

09.12pm

Stumbling down Queen Street, a dulling grey fog of booze hanging over his head and blotting out the memories of that which had occurred no more than ten minutes prior, Danny suddenly farted through enough of the mental fog to slow his pace and consider that perhaps there was something irrational in all this. He'd done *something* stupid, of that much he was fairly certain, but quite what was lost to the mists of wretched luminous Aftershocks, overcast with sharply inhaled plumes of marijuana smoke.

He stopped and thought, trying to force his mind back to the dancefloor, that strobe-lit, man-heavy dancefloor; that girl with the nose ring and the haircut like Skrillex he'd tried it on with, the girl who'd sneered and turned away – an obvious lesbian. That crew that he'd been with, the three gays and the cock-hungry straight girl – was it something they'd done? Was it something that he'd done to them? Had he tried it on with Mandeep? A 'thank you' for all the cigarettes? Or Myrig? Mincing man-mountain Myrig? Or worse, that fat lass that'd been with them, the gobby cock-thirster, what's-her-name? *Why is that worse? What the...?*

Danny realised that he was swirling, circling the drain, standing there on Queen Street in the evening air, unfocused and sombre, far from home, far from sobriety. Another cigarette might've helped alleviate the crushing confusion and depression of it all. The overwhelming sense of regret and purposelessness he was feeling didn't usually hit until the morning after. What the hell kind of a drunk was it that summoned forth those kinds of phantoms to torment and tease their vessel? *Must be the weed,* he told himself, though he knew it not to be true. The ghosts that haunted him, those ghosts of ten minutes ago, were no more composed of chemicals than he; a reductionist way to view a man, indeed – a bundle of bumbling chemicals, blundering through a field of consciousness, trying to reflect and refract and to somehow shed light upon itself. *No,* he said, he told himself, lost in swirling whirlpools of words and meaninglessness, *this means something. I mean something.* Why the fuck had he fled Mandeep and his cigarettes?

Then he saw him, coming toward him, in a tracksuit and a low-maintenance haircut; a smoker. He stared at him, lips parting slightly, salivating, wanting. He waited until he was almost upon him before he spoke: "Excuse me..."

The chav stopped and stared at him, cigarette in the hand dangling at his side.

"...could I borrow a cigarette off you?"

The chav sneered, not having none of it. "There's a fucking Spar down there, buy your own."

IF only life were that simple... he took his phone from his pocket and dumbly pressed at the blank black slab of a screen for a few moments, before navigating his way to Facebook to check up on his status update: *'Whose out in Cardiff tonite?'* No replies. *Nobody.* He was alone.

09.16pm

Tom stepped into the quiet of Queen Street station. It was empty, a world away from the rush hour bustle he mirthlessly shuffled through each morning. Steel shutters had long since come down over the newsagent's kiosk and the manned ticket windows. Alone in the station, Tom looked up at the orange L.E.D. on the black screen of the digital timetable, mounted high up on the filth-smeared wall. *Pontypridd – 21.18 – Platform 2; Coryton – 21.20 – Platform 3; Rhymney – 21.29 – Please use replacement bus service.* Replacement bus service. *Replacement bus service.* Tom repeated the words to himself, in silence, in the isolation of the empty station. He swigged back a bit more lager from his big bottle of Stella, swaying a little. *Replacement bus service.* Right there, in immutable orange-and-black; *replacement* fucking *bus service.* He stared at the letters, willing their form to shift and reshape and spell out something other than *replacement* fucking *bus service.* Replacement bus service. *How the fuck long's that meant to take?* He knew the answer, or a rough approximation of it anyway, having been stung by this type of bait-and-switch more times than he cared to count. *Replacement fucking bus service,* his internal monologue repeated again, as he took another swig of Stella. His eyes made a quick dart to the entrance as a couple walked in, talking lowly; a suit-wearing blonde feller with his arm draped over a demure young lady's shoulder. Tom stared back up at the train times board until they'd passed, then glanced back at them, at the round cheeks of her arse beneath a floral print dress, wondering if they'd get to the platform only to discover, to their great disappointment, that, after wining and dining the evening away in town, the passionate lovemaking they'd been planning on capping it off with would be curtailed by a more-than doubling of the journey time and the indignity of being charged the same price as a train ticket to judder home upon a replacement *fucking* bus service.

09.22pm

"I dunno really," Ivor said, having spent some time mulling Bronwyn's question over. "I was thinking of moving out to Australia. My cousin went over there as a carpenter, said he could sort me out with a job. But I didn't get round to sorting out the visa in time, so, I dunno, I was looking for something to do, and the police force were hiring."

"Is that it?"

"Yeah."

"That's the reason you became a police officer? Because you were too lazy to get your visa documents sorted to be a carpenter in Australia?"

"Yeah. Yeah, I suppose it was, really. Why? Why'd you become a police officer, Bron?"

Bronwyn sighed. "I wanted a life with a bit of excitement in it. I wanted to do something meaningful with my life. Help people."

"Yeah?" Ivor said, sounding disinterested.

"Yeah." *And what a great fucking decision that had turned out to be.* "Fuck," Bronwyn said, snapped from her disillusionment by the opening of Bruce Amstell's front door. "They're coming out."

"Is that him?"

"That's Bruce," Bronwyn said, watching the stocky silhouette move from the house to the street.

"Is that Simon behind him?"

"No," Bronwyn said, squinting through the dimming evening light. "That's Darren."

They watched as the Amstell brothers glanced up and down the street, clearly up to no good, before getting into their car, Bruce in the driver's seat.

"What should we do?"

"I don't know," Bronwyn answered. "Simon's not with them."

"Maybe he's in the car already."

"We'd've seen him come out, wouldn't we?"

"Maybe he was hiding in the car."

"What? For the past four hours odd we've been sat here?"

"Yeah," Ivor said, "maybe he was hiding in the boot or something."

Bronwyn sighed.

Further down the street, Rory was half-asleep, his half-full last can of Fosters half-balanced in his lap, leaking down onto his jeans. "Fuck," he said, hearing the engine rev up in the Amstell's car. He let the car roll out of the street before turning the ignition and releasing the clutch awkwardly, stalling with a big clunking of misaligned engine parts.

Bronwyn watched Rory's Volvo roar off a moment later. "Who's that?" Whoever it was, it was clear that something was happening. "I'm going to follow them. You wait here, see if Simon Amstell pops his head out."

"What? Wait by myself?"

"Hurry up and get the fuck out the car."

09.28pm

Tom tipped the last few drops of lager from the big green bottle into his mouth, then laid the bottle gently to rest on the pavement. He stepped toward the big burly bald man guarding the rickety, battered old bus Arriva Trains Wales kept on hand for the endless 'planned engineering works' that necessitated replacement bus services. Why they couldn't plan engineering works for the long stretch of night during which no trains were running was a mystery which Tom wanted answers to.

Tom made his way to the back of the bus and sat and stared across the road at Queen Street station, trying to figure out how much longer it'd take to get home than usual. Cardiff Queen Street to Caerphilly by train generally took no longer than fifteen minutes. At night, with limited traffic on the road, driving should've taken twenty minutes tops. But that was going direct, either via the winding ascent up Caerphilly mountain, or zooming down the A470. The replacement bus service would duck and weave between all the stations from A to B.

Tom fiddled with his earphones, untangling them and popping them into the headphone jack of his iPhone, as the last of the passengers clambered onto the worn and tattered seats of the sparsely-populated bus. The engine chugged and sputtered into consciousness. In the absence of much of anything else to do, Tom ran through the stations between Queen Street and Caerphilly: *Heath High Level; Lisvane & Thornhill; Llanishen*. It'd probably take forty-five minutes, minimum. Maybe as much as an hour. Earphones connected, Tom clicked on the music icon on the iPhone screen, then clicked shuffle. He wondered if he ought to alight at Caerphilly station itself or the nearby Aber. A crash of drum and a throaty bellow, underpinned with jagged riffs, suddenly hit Tom's eardrums as the bus started moving. He turned quickly to the screen. From Autumn to Ashes, 'The After Dinner Payback'. He pressed the forward-pointing arrow to skip it – it was a bit much for the present moment. A reminder of very different times – his teenage self would've listened to almost nothing that wasn't similar.

Caerphilly or Aber... a vague memory suggested that, as Aber wasn't considered a 'main' station, being less than ten minutes walk from the larger station at the top of Caerphilly's town centre, the replacement bus service might omit it from its route. And seeing as Tom would be plugged into his iPhone, he might miss any announcement on the matter that was made by the driver. Besides, the slow-chundering bus wouldn't take him from Caerphilly to Aber station much faster than his trained-to-avoid-excessive-unpunctuality legs would. All things considered, he'd be best off walking home from Caerphilly. So if it took him about forty minutes to get from there to his house in Caledfryn, he'd be home by *what... 11? 11.30?*

Slow, melancholic synths rose up in his earbuds: The Streets, 'Blinded by the Lights'. A song about taking ecstasy alone at a club and not being able to get hold of your mates. It cast his mind's eye back across his mess of an evening and into a staring match with the grim memory of the night that he'd first met Claire.

He'd been in training for the swine flu advice call centre at the time, training for a job that'd obviously never fully materialised on account of the devastating pandemic petering out long before it could decimate the world's population and segue into another World War in the manner of the Spanish flu before it. After a month of training on the taxpayer's coin, the staff had been informed the whole thing had been scrapped, and Tom was swiftly back in the dole office, withdrawing a reduced stipend from the treasury's coffers.

He'd been training alongside a Japanese girl, Miki. It'd been the first time he'd ever really met one, and he'd of course been instantly rather keen on her. After a couple of weeks anxiously looking out for an unawkward in, Miki mentioned something about going to a dubstep night at the students' union. Tom had been big into dubstep when he was at uni, being introduced to it by Max in first year, long before it had been transported out of the grimy basement clubs of East London and appropriated by the likes of KoRn and Taylor fucking Swift. Trouble was, none of his Caerphilly friends were particularly keen on the genre. But, an opportunity to hang out with Miki outside of work might not have presented itself again, so, having failed to convince anyone to come along with him, he'd at least managed to source some drugs in 'Philly whilst having a few pints with the boys. He'd left the pub and spent about twenty minutes waiting at the bus stop opposite the Tesco by the castle before his drugs source arrived in a Golf gti; Kev Jenkins, a shaven-headed, twitchy, intensely quiet teenager, who struggled with stringing together cognisant sentences due to the inadvisable quantities of chemicals he'd been ingesting since before he was old enough to buy a pint in a pub. Kev was himself heading to the very same dubstep night Tom was following Miki to, and half-heartedly told Tom to give him 'a text or something' later on.

As the Golf gti disappeared into the night – Tom neither being offered nor really wanting a lift into Cardiff with awkward Kev the teenage drug dealer – Tom nipped into Tesco to grab a couple of cans for the journey. He ploughed through one Stella on the platform and another on the train. Dubstep blared through his earphones as he rolled through the night, blocking out the noise of rowdy Valleys revellers making the pissed-up Saturday night journey into the capital. Tom had livened the fifteen minute train ride up further by popping into the toilets to try out some of Kev's M-kat. It seemed decent enough; the night was shaping up nicely.

Tom had grabbed a big bottle of Tiger from the Spar opposite Queen Street Station and necked it during the walk to the student's union, taking every precaution to ensure he'd arrive in a suitable state for dubstep, and that all hints of awkwardness or underconfidence would be eliminated from his interactions with Miki. With the drugs stuffed in his socks, he breezed through the checks of the zealous door staff, and came to what he figured would be the most difficult phase of the night; finding Miki amongst the mass of drugged up, fucked up uni students.

The task proved surprisingly easy – he'd been wandering around the main hall of the multi-roomed dubstep-fest for all of five minutes before stumbling upon her, slim Japanese body swaying to the sub-bass, sunglasses on, at night and inside. She greeted him warmly, before introducing him to her dancing partner, some white guy in a checked shirt who eyeballed Tom suspiciously. That was it; the gig was up. All the prep and pre-drinks and procurement of drugs had been for nowt, and the night was destined for disaster. Remembering it now, from the warmth and comfort of his seat at the back of the replacement bus service, Tom supposed he should've turned around and gone home, right there and then. But hindsight being what it is, and trying to stop a speeding train being what that was, Tom had instead taken leave of Miki and white boy and headed to the toilets for another dose of M-kat.

The night there after was a blur of toilet trips and dancing solo, until he and another unmoored soul had locked eyes upon each other at the edge of the dancefloor. "Hi," Tom recalled having said to her, before bumbling through some bullshit like, "what university do you go to?" "I'm a slut," she'd told him bluntly. They'd kissed aggressively, tongues probing each other's mouths hungrily, and after that she'd walked away, leaving Tom alone again, though now with a dangerous sense of possibility to underpin his increasingly wanton inebriation.

It may have been around this point in the night that it dawned on Tom that everyone in the student's union was on M-kat. Everyone. This wasn't remarkable due to anything as silly as Tom expecting to find a student union dubstep night anything other than awash with drugs; rather, it was remarkable that everyone inside had settled upon getting fucked up on the exact same substance. The reason for this was obvious; M-kat – or methadrone, as Tom suddenly remembered he'd clumsily and narcishly referred to it in his initial conversation with Kev the teenage drug dealer – was, through some fluke of laws and loopholes, completely legal in the United Kingdom at the time. Despite a high that felt somewhere between coke and ecstasy, without 100% of the bite nor beauty of either, and a comedown that could drive the Samaritans to group suicide, M-kat was labelled as plant food, with a sarcastic red square on the packaging warning against human consumption. It was available to anyone and everyone, completely legally, regardless of age. Its legality had given it ubiquity no drug had enjoyed since LSD in the 1967 summer of love, or ecstasy in the second summer of love in '89. Tom supposed that would have to make 2010 the summer of M-kat, though 'third summer of love' would be a gross misnomer; 'the summer of despair and insomnia' would be a more accurate description.

Back in the now, at the back of the bus, Tom zoned out on music for a while, burying prickly memories underneath it. An Arctic Monkeys song, followed by Foals, Tom looking out the window all the while. A melancholy violin was the thing to zone him in again as the bus rolled through red-brick leafy suburbs toward the first stop, Heath High Level. He stared straight ahead as rich basslines stuttered out beneath the oriental-sounding string instrument. 'Cockney Violin'. What a track that was. Dubstep and orientalism, all rolled into one. How could it not prompt Tom to trawl back through the narrative that unrelated music had distracted from?

Where had he gotten to... a stolen kiss with a self-proclaimed slut. Had he texted Kev the teenage drug dealer *before or after that?* Tom shuddered with embarrassment as he tried to recall the content of the message; something about the night being banging, something about Kev oughting to hurry up and get there. Had he seen him during his time there? *No...* Kev had text back at some point, saying something as perfunctory and unindulgently not-unfriendly as the relationship between dealer and fucked-up customer warranted. He'd not seen him until he'd gone outside, *after...* Had Tom gone out for a cigarette at any point in the night? Perhaps there was an inside smoking area, or maybe people were lunging fags in the toilet or something, or were they just smoking on the dancefloor, the methed-up masses blocking them from bouncers' view? *No...* he'd smoked quite freely, he was certain of it. With the state most of the punters were in, then-recently-enacted puritanical anti-smoking laws were the least of the venue's worries. *Anyway*, details, *details...* unimportant shit. The crux of the night, and the reason for Tom to now be sifting uncomfortably through the dregs and the lumps of it that were still clogging up the back-passages of his consciousness, was Claire.

He couldn't remember when he'd first seen her, or what he'd first said to her, or why he'd spoken to her, or anything else like that. She was with two friends, he remembered that much. Had he kissed her? *Yeah... definitely.* Quite soon after meeting. Then he'd gotten her phone number and, with the worst part of a gram inside him, he'd decided to extricate himself from the situation, before he made a tit out of himself. But he'd kept running back into her. *By chance!* Purely by chance. The first time had been okay, the second a little... y'know... but the third time, in one of the smaller rooms, perhaps the smallest, she'd rolled her eyes and turned to her friends, and he'd realised that a prospect to salvage anything of any worth from the night had been put into serious and unnecessary jeopardy. He'd immediately turned around and headed back to the toilets, and that was when the next thing had happened... he walked into the toilets, and some proper fucking dickhead Cardiff chav was standing there, and he asked him if he had any M-kat. Moments later, with Tom sequestered in a toilet cubicle shovelling a key full of the stuff up one of his nostrils, the dickhead chav – he had buzz-cut black hair and a blue dickhead-chav jacket zipped half-way up his chin – stuck his dickhead-chav buzz-cut head over the gap above the cubicle door, to peer down and say something along the lines of, "Yeah you fucking have!", in reference to Tom's earlier denial of having any drugs on him. Then he'd snatched the drugs – whether he'd swiped an arm down from above the door and grabbed them, or dropped back to the floor, opened the door and snatched them, Tom couldn't remember now (though he supposed the first scenario was physically impossible, and hence unlikely). But he'd snatched the drugs. Then he'd stood in the doorway, flanked by two – *or three? Four?* - dickhead Cardiff chav mates, all grinning and gloating and daring him to do something about it. What was he supposed to do, *fight them?* Get his head kicked in over barely a quarter of a gram of fucking M-kat? What else was there to do – tell the fucking bouncers? *No* – Tom had shuffled off, back into the night, dejected, drugs confiscated by the bigger boys, bad going to worse, shame and anger replacing whatever positive effects the sticky white stuff had bestowed upon him.

Then... *fuck*... he supposed something else must've happened in the mean time... he recalled at some point bumping into Elmore, a pudgy twerp who'd worked alongside him at the Sky call centre down in Cardiff Gate. Tom had barely said two words to him when they worked together. Now, drugged up and alone, he'd figured he'd introduce himself.

"Hey," he'd said (or something like it), "you used to work at Sky, yeah?"

Elmore had stared at him, with disdain and disinterest, and said absolutely nothing. Malice flushed hot in Tom's face as he remembered it, more anger than the incident with the chavs in the toilet had induced in him. The chavs were just being chavs. Dickhead Cardiff chavs. Their actions served a purpose; they'd wanted drugs, so, chavs being chavs, they'd gone and nabbed them off of Tom. Fair dues, all told. But Elmore blanking him, to his face, in response to a direct fucking question... really, *what a nob head.*

And Tom now supposed it was with a similar sort of reductivism, a similar viewing of the dickhead chavs' actions as a by-product of their shitty single-parent upbringings and a society made cold by Thatcherism, that Tom had approached the ringleader, the cunt with the jacket zipped up over his chin, and attempted to appeal to his better nature. Tom had found him at the edge of the dancefloor and had proceeded to ramble on at him with some impassioned plea about the inherent unfairness of what he'd done in the toilets. The chav had listened to him, intently it had seemed – perhaps he was getting through to him – before summarising the situation: Tom's points were fair and logical, but if he wanted whatever M-kat remained smeared on the inside of the baggy, he was going to have to fight him for it. Defeated, Tom had returned to the dub and din of the dancefloor, upon which nothing else of note happened until closing time.

Tom spaced out on this final point, the dubstep in his earphones transporting him back to the darkness of the union's dancefloor as the bus pulled up beside the steps leading up to the platform of Heath High Level station. The doors opened to the sound of a gush of compressed air being released. Nobody got on or off. The bus waited there for several seconds before the engine roared back into life, and the handsome houses of middle-class Cardiffian suburbia then began flickering past the window at ever-increasing speed.

The low-tempo dubstep suddenly gave way to quick-stabbing staccato synthesised drumbeats. Tom hurried to take his iPhone from his pocket and skip the track, surprised and embarrassed that at some point he must've downloaded 'Poker Face' by Lady Gaga. As he dragged his thumb across the screen and prepared to tap in his passcode, the music suddenly cut out and the screen was reduced to black, save for a wheel of white dots rotating in the centre of it. *Bollocks.* The phone's battery had been being a bit temperamental over the preceding few weeks. Tom remembered it being on something like 54% when he'd plugged the earphones in back at Queen Street station; now it'd tumbled all the way to zero, without any form of prior warning. Perhaps it was time to shell out on an upgrade. Tom tried to remember what it was he'd heard manufacturers called that thing; making devices shittily so that they fucked up at the end of a predetermined product life-cycle, forcing consumers to plump for the latest model... *planned obsolescence*. That was it. *Planned obsolescence*. The built-in betrayal of intelligent design.

09.49pm

The fuck are they up tae in there? Rory's Volvo was parked up at the edge of a flat concrete oasis of free parking, behind the museum. Across a darkness barely troubled by streetlights, Rory could see the Amstell brothers parked up in their lime green Renault Clio. The bigger one in the driver's seat was Bruce, he'd established that much, but he was still unsure if the character sat beside him was Simon. He was smaller than Bruce, which wasn't how Rory had pictured things, though Rory had yet to see him clear and close enough to be certain. And then one other question remained: *Wha' tha fuck are them pair up tae in there?* They'd driven from Llanbradach to Cardiff at some speed, bombing down the A470, only just remembering to slow down enough to avoid the speed camera in Nant Garw. Then they'd simply parked up and, guessing from the weak light shining up onto the face of the Amstell brother in the passenger seat, they looked to have been staring at a laptop ever since. Beyond them, at the farthest end of the car park from

Rory, was the same midnight blue Vauxhall Astra that Rory had seen outside the brother's house back in Llanbradach. He was certain he'd seen two passengers inside previously, a man and a woman, but now it seemed to contain the woman alone. As Rory stared across, far along the darkness, her features slowly came into focus; a pretty face, from what he could make out of it, his vision obscured by both the dark of night and the funk that had followed polishing ten cans of lager off. *Christ, I'm thirsty*, Rory thought. He looked around at the floor of the car for a forgotten water bottle, finding only crushed cans and empty crisp packets. He popped open the glove compartment, and found nothing but a mess of papers and empty cigarette boxes. He looked up and his thirst was forgotten in an instant; the brothers had gotten out of their car.

09.37pm

The woman on stage, a thirty-something brunette in a little black dress, with a big voice built for this exact environment, crooned the opening lines of 'Don't Stop Believing'. The mass of people packed onto the dancefloor in front of her joined in, belting out the words.

"Fucking tune!" Rembrandt said, getting to his feet. "Come on, let's go have a boogie!"

He held out his hand to Claire, who leapt to her feet. Then he looked at Cain and Marianne, seated at the edge of the group's sofa, upstairs on a balcony overlooking a dancefloor jam-packed with pissed-up students.

"Nah mate," Cain said, smirking at the very idea of him getting up to have a boogie to fucking Journey. "Actually man, I think me and Marianne are gonna head off now."

"Come on mun, the night's young!" Rembrandt pleaded. He looked over the hot French blonde piece Cain was heading home with. *Jammy bastard. How the fuck does he do it?* Then Rembrandt looked at Podge and Ji Eun.

"No," Ji Eun said, smiling, leaning forward to take a sip of her Jack and Coke. She could feel the night disintegrating all around her, with no energy or impulse propelling her downstairs towards that dancefloor.

"Come on mun!"

"No, I'm fine, really."

"It's alright butt," Podge said, sensing a good chance to get closer to the girl through small-talk, "you crack on, we'll wait here for you."

Claire pulled Rembrandt away before he could pester the others any longer. Cain and Marianne then rose to their feet and said their goodbyes and disappeared down the staircase into the swarming, singing mass.

"So how long have you been in Cardiff?" Podge asked.

"Two years. I'm just starting my third one now."

"Are you at uni here?"

"Yeah."

"What are you studying?"

"English."

"You came to Wales to study English?" Podge smirked.

"Yeah. What do you do in Korea?"

"I'm an English teacher."

Of course he was. Every white guy in Seoul was either an English teacher or U.S. military.

"What age do you teach?"

"Kindergarten."

"How is it?"

"It's alright. They're really cute. Sometimes they're annoying. I love Korea though."

"Yeah? What do you love about it?"

"I don't know," Podge said, glancing down at the heaving dancefloor. "The atmosphere. It's exciting. Nothing ever closes there. Here, you can't find a shop open past six. And pubs are usually chucking out by eleven. In Seoul, they stay open all night. I don't think I've ever seen the city quiet. What do you think of Wales?"

"I like it."

"Yeah? What do you like about it?"

"The atmosphere. The castles and stuff. All the old buildings."

"Yeah? I guess you get used to the castles and stuff, growing up here. Korea's probably the same for you."

"Yeah."

Downstairs, Danny entered the establishment and did a quick scan of his surroundings; the misfits on stage, the brunette in the little black dress, the tattooed and bearded hodge-podge of sub-cultural appropriation playing instruments behind her; the long bar, running almost the entire length of the left-hand side of the place, with people queued up two-deep in front of it; the mess of bright young things bouncing up and down en masse across the dancefloor, jabbing their hands towards the ceiling as they bellowed along with the brunette in the little black dress, half of them splashing and spilling drinks as they did so; the other groups seated at tables all throughout the rest of the place; the table full of drinks beside Danny, next to the door, where people left their beverages whilst heading outside for a cigarette. The table was the perfect place for a man with Danny's lack of funds to stock up on liquor, but a bouncer was inconveniently stood right beside it, a bouncer who'd unfortunately beckoned Danny into Live Lounge just seconds earlier. But surely there was more than one way to minesweep. *Minesweeping.* The phrase alone excited him, bringing back memories of countless nights getting pissed up for free, taking unguarded drinks, so often unsure of their contents. One time he had hit the proverbial mine: back in Leeds, he'd chugged down a drink in the student union, then sat down with his mates for a bit. When he got up to do another quick sweep about the place, everything went dark and, next thing he knew, he was on the floor. It was half an hour before his vision had come back, and when it had, it had been blocky, like a low-resolution video clip. Nevertheless, more often than not, the potential haul far outweighed the potential risks.

Danny saw what would likely be his greatest opportunity, an area at the end of the bar closest to the stage, currently propping up a number of unattended drinks, most likely belonging to a group of guys skanking away directly in front of the band. He pushed his way through the dancefloor and grabbed a pint.

09.58pm

"That's what it says butt," Darren argued.

"He's not gonna be staying in the fucking Hilton is he?" Bruce spat back.

"That's what it says on here."

Darren was sitting on the stone steps outside the hotel in question, with Bruce standing in front of him, at the bottom of the steps, smoking.

"We went to their house, di'n't we? And there weren't no-one in there, were there? So chances are, there'll be staying at fucking hotel, won't they?" Darren reasoned.

"This is Simon's fucking ex-missus we're talking about. I can imagine her and her new feller hiding out at a fucking Travelodge or something, but she's hardly gonna have shacked up with Bill fucking Gates, is she? There is no fucking way they are staying in the Hilton."

"See for yourself butt."

"Fine."

Bruce took a final drag on his cigarette, threw it onto the road behind him, then sat down besides his brother to have a look at the map on the laptop screen. He could see the outline of the Hilton, and the alleyway running behind it, with a green blip indicating the phone of their quarry was located somewhere in between the two. Bruce got back to his feet and walked around the corner. He reappeared in front of his brother a few seconds later. "Let's have another look."

Darren turned the laptop screen around to face his brother. Bruce studied the map one more time, focusing on the position of the green blip relative to the Hilton's entrance and the alleyway, then went back around the corner. Bruce stared down the alleyway at a number of people standing behind steel railings, smoking cigarettes. A few feet away from them, three boys were screaming at each other, bouncers standing between them barking orders, the lads paying no attention to them. After a few moments, one of the parties involved, a muscle-bound blonde guy in a tight pink T-shirt, acquiesced to the bouncers orders and started walking away from the scene, towards Bruce, while the other two stayed behind, arguing their case. Bruce headed back round the corner to his brother and pointed at the laptop screen. "I reckon that thing's saying he's in that bar round by there butt."

"You reckon?"

"I'm fucking positive, butt."

"What do we do 'en?"

"We wait out by here until he comes out."

09.52pm

Rembrandt and Claire removed their mouths from one another as crunching nu metal riffage kicked in on stage, her arms still crossed around his neck, his hands still clasped tight to her hips. As they gazed dumbly and drunkenly into one another's eyes, Podge seized his chance: "Fancy a drink?" They followed Podge and Ji Eun to the bar, where Podge set to ordering beers for the boys and cocktails for the ladies, before asking: "Should we get some shots in?"

"I don't know," Ji Eun said, "I should probably head home soon. I've got work experience again tomorrow."

"We can head back together," Claire said, Rembrandt stood behind her, hands still stuck to her hips. Claire turned her head to Rembrandt. "All of us."

Ji Eun looked at Podge as he moved her Jack and Coke towards her. He smiled. She forced a smile back. He was nice enough... but... but... *what would Rory do?*

The brunette in the little black dress start shouting out the words to Papa Roach 'Last Resort' on stage, as awkward and unnatural at rapping as she was perfectly suited to belting out the chorus of boisterous rock anthems. "Don't even fuck if I cummiah bleeding!" Danny bellowed back to the stage, pumping his fist in the air. A girl standing near him flinched at his fist-pumping. He locked his eyes on hers. "Do you even wear when I die screaming?" he yelled. She turned away. Danny was too caught up into the buzz of booze and half-remembered song lyrics from his childhood to care. "Would I be wrong, would I be right!?" he shouted, fist still pumping, turning to his left and catching another girl eyeing him with disgust and then quickly looking away. He let the fist drop to his side and let the on-stage brunette in the little black dress deliver the next line herself, his euphoria suddenly overtaken by an urge to drink more alcohol. He looked back at the edge of the bar nearest the stage that he'd pilfered a pint from earlier.

Rembrandt, Claire, Ji Eun and Podge knocked back their tequillas in a blur of salt-licking and lemon-biting, then slammed the shot glasses back down on the bar, faces scrunched up from the taste of it. Rembrandt finally removed his left hand from Claire's hip and grabbed a pint from the bar and took a swig of it.

"Oh mate, that's my pint you're drinking," said a burly blonde guy with gym-pumped muscles in a tight pink T-shirt.

Rembrandt looked at the area of the bar he'd just taken it from; the pint he'd taken had been the only one there. "This is mine mate."

"Is it fuck, I just put mine there."

"I just bought this."

"Are you calling me a fucking liar butt?"

Danny backed away into the crowd, keen to avoid any involvement in the fracas his pint swiping had provoked. Rembrandt and the blonde quickly fell into a mess of pushing and shoving. The bouncers swooped within seconds, grabbing the two of them by the arms and escorting them outside.

"Shit," Claire said, watching the boys disappear out the front door with the bouncers. "Shall we go out after them?"

Ji Eun didn't say anything for a few seconds. The pushing and shoving had all happened too quickly for her to have any real grasp on what had happened, but she sensed an opportunity to avoid Claire's intended bringing of the two boys home with them, and any awkwardness that may have later led to when it became clear to Podge that Ji Eun had no intention of shagging him. Then Ji Eun found just what she was looking for: "Isn't that Danny Daggers over there?"

"Who?"

"You know, the YouTube guy?"

"Oh yeah," Claire said, locking eyes on him, him staring straight back.

"I met him the other day actually."

"Really?"

"Yeah. Shall we go and say 'hi' to him?"

10.11pm

Rory sat and watched from a bench in the dark of a park opposite the Hilton as she walked towards him, definitely her, definitely Ji Eun. He wanted to call out to her, but he couldn't risk alarming the brothers, who were still sat on the steps of the Hilton with their laptop. *Ach, she's go' her own life tae live,* Rory told himself, *you cannae expect tae be privy tae every fuckin' detail o' it, just 'cause you're mentoring tha wee lassy at work.* He saw her pass along the paved square beside the park, taking no notice of him, nor of the plain-clothed police officer skulking in the shadows at the edge of the lamp-lit square. He knew exactly what she was up to, the police officer, and it was the exact same thing that he was doing; trying to work out what the hell the pair of Amstell brothers were playing at, sitting on the steps of the Hilton, peering into the laptop screen. As for Ji Eun... *she'll've just been fir a few drinks in town wi' her friends,* Rory told himself. But he felt a real fear for her safety as he watched her disappear into an underground passage beneath the main road running into town, still staring over a minute later as she re-emerged on the opposite side, walking towards City Hall and the museum. The farther away she got, the smaller she appeared, and the more fear Rory felt. He tried telling himself to forgot about it, that she surely knew what she was doing, that she must've walked the same walk home a hundred times before, but he could nae help himself...

Ji Eun was herself thinking about Rory, wondering how many nights he'd had like the one that was now winding down for her, how many scores of characters had crossed his path and disappeared again, sent out packing into the night by bouncers, or simply walking away to carry on ploughing through the narratives of their own lives. The whole thing was thrillingly, mundanely transitive, the whole mess of drunken nights and short-lived loves, a microcosm of life... and she thought again of the guy who'd stayed with her the previous night, wondering if she'd see him again, and if there was any greater meaning to any of these brief encounters, or if it was just a bunch of interconnected but independent stuff that overlapped, and then she felt a drop of water hit her head, and she quickened her pace, and then another one, and within a minute she was running, and the rain was hammering down hard.

11.09pm

"It's fucking moving butt."

"Huh?"

"The green blip," Bruce said. "He's leaving."

"What way's he going?"

Bruce stared at the laptop screen, rain hammering down hard in front of them, the Hilton's overhang keeping them dry. "I think he's coming this way."

Bruce's eyes flitted back and forth between the green blip on the screen and the rain hammering the whole world around them. The blip drew parallel to them, and Bruce looked through the rain at a couple huddled beneath the awnings of a closed pub a little ways down the street from them.

"Is that them?" Darren asked.

"Yeah," Bruce said, glancing down at the laptop, then back at the huddled couple.

"Who's that he's with?"

"Must be Jodie."

"Nah."

"It's gorra be," Bruce said, squinting through the rain at the blurry outline of a blonde.

"It's not."

"Who else would it be, mun?"

"I dunno, but it's not Jodie."

"Shut up mun," Bruce scoffed.

"I'm fucking telling you butt, that's not her."

Bruce sighed and looked at the laptop screen for some solution. He found it quickly, and moved the cursor to a button that said 'Emit Sound'.

"Let's ring for one," Claire told Danny, huddled beneath the awning of a closed pub a little ways down the street from the Hilton.

"Do you know any numbers?" Danny said, taking his Lumia from his pocket.

"Yeah, Dragon Taxis - oh-two-nine-two-oh, treble-three, treble-three."

Danny tapped the number out and then held his Nokia Lumia up to his ear, awaiting a dial tone. Instead, his Lumia emitted a high-pitched electric scream, straight into his ear drum, the whole handset shaking. The shock caused the phone to fall from his hand and bounce hard in a pool of water on the pavement.

11.17pm

Rory sat on his bench in the park, soaked, rain still hammering down all around him, without so much as a hood to protect himself from it, his mind a meditative blankness, the unrelenting bleakness of it all ignorable, until everything suddenly happened at once; a taxi pulled up, outside a closed pub a little ways down the road from the Hilton, and the brothers shot up immediately, the one whose identity remained a mystery to Rory running out into the street, as Bruce fumbled to stuff the laptop into a backpack before joining him, the two shouting at each other, frantic, in the rain, until a taxi came along a few seconds later, the brothers flagging it down furiously, hopping into the back of it, and Rory was off, on his feet, running to the road through the rainstorm, scanning both directions for any signs of a taxi, none forthcoming, until seconds became tens of seconds became a minute, and the moment had passed, and the chase had been lost, and he turned back to where the police officer had been stood earlier, and saw she was stood there no more, and in an instant the hours of waiting and waiting and waiting and waiting had culminated in a quick flash of action, and now it was over, and the only option that remained to him was to drudge back through the rain to the car park behind the museum and go home and sleep and wake up the next day, praying it'd be a better day than *this fuckin' mess o' one.*

11.25pm

"That's them," Darren said, pointing out the window at a side-street, as the taxi ploughed through City Road in the rain.

"Stop here drive," Bruce ordered.

Bruce ran his hands through his pockets as the taxi pulled up at the side of the road. He turned to his brother: "Have you got any money on you?"

"Nah, I left it all with Simon, di'n't I?"

Bruce sighed. "Sorry drive, I'll just have to run across the road to that cashpoint outside the Tesco's over there, I've not got no money on me."

"Just so long as your mate waits in by here with me while you do so. I've had someone do a runner on me once already today."

Bruce got out of the taxi and stepped into the road, and watched as the taxi they'd been following drove away, leaving a couple fumbling for keys outside a house. He stepped forward and squinted, counting the houses down, trying to work out the number of the one they were outside of.

"Oi!" the taxi driver shouted out through the window. "The fuck are you playing at, standing in the middle of the road in the pissing down rain, mun? Hurry up and get that money out!"

Bruce held up his finger to finish off counting the houses, then jogged the rest of the ways across the road to the cashpoint.

11.37pm

Ivor watched Bronwyn's midnight-blue Astra pull up in the driving rain. He was stood with his back pressed flat against a garage across the street from Bruce Amstell's home, the slight overhang from the roof of it failing miserably to keep the rain off him. As the car crept closer, her face became clear through the windshield. She was smiling.

"What's so funny?" he snapped, opening the door and jumping in out of the wet.

"Look at the state of you," she said, still smiling. "I bet you wouldn't get rain like this in Australia."

"Ugh?"

"At least it's not cold out. Anything much happening while I was gone?"

"Well, there's definitely someone in there."

"Yeah?"

"Yeah, definitely. I saw the light in the hallway switch on and off a couple'f times, and the living room light's been on constantly. What happened with you? I've been standing out in this pissing-down rain for hours."

"I don't know. The brothers... I don't know what they were doing. They were sat on the steps of the Hilton in Cardiff for ages, playing with a laptop. Then all of a sudden, they got up and flagged down a taxi. Seemed like they were in a rush. I couldn't make head nor tail of it."

"What about that other car we seen drive off after them?"

"He followed them all the way to town, keeping his distance from them. He clocked me following but he didn't seem too bothered about it. He was just standing out watching them, same as I was."

"That's weird."

"My guess is he's a journalist, looking for a lead on Simon Amstell's whereabouts, same as us."

"Well I'd say there's a bloody good chance Simon Amstell's sat inside that house."

"And I'd have to agree with you."

"So what do we do now then?"

"We wait."

"By ourselves? Do you not reckon we ought to put a call into the station or something?"

"Glyn was more concerned about that pissing horse show on Saturday than catching Simon Amstell. Nah, I reckon we handle this one ourselves. It'll be us who's covered in glory when they find out we've been working round the clock to collar him."

11.41pm

Ji Eun couldn't take it anymore – the dull repetitive thud of electro house beats, the occasional flare up of giggling and pre-sex conversation filtering through the wall from Claire's bedroom, while Ji Eun lay in bed, the room not quite spinning, but swaying slightly to-and-fro. Ji Eun sat up and reached for her laptop. No sooner had she opened it and awoken it from sleep mode than a Skype call was coming in from her Mum. She froze for a moment, unsure of whether to click the green or red button as her Mum's smiling avatar flashed up on the screen in front of her. She really just wanted to drown out the sound from next door and slip away from consciousness, and there was the risk of her mother noticing and remarking upon her drunkenness, but it'd been more than a week since she'd spoken to her, and she knew how funny her mother would get about it if she rejected the call... She clicked green.

"*Annyong, Ji Eun-i!*"

"*Noona! Annyong!*"

It was Ji Eun's elder sister, Ji Hye.

"How's it going in Cardiff?" Ji Hye asked (in Korean, obviously).

"It's good! I've been doing work experience at a newspaper here."

"Yeah, Mum told me you were doing that, how is it?"

"It's cool. A guy I'm working with is kind of mentoring me. He's teaching me so much about journalism."

"You seem kind of drunk."

"Yeah... maybe."

"Did you hear Su Min's getting married?"

"No! I didn't even know she had a boyfriend!"

"Yeah, they've only been dating for like a month or two."

"And he's proposed already?"

11.48pm

"So wha'd'you reckon 'en butt?" Darren said, watching his brother's chubby fingers shove a sauce-loaded kebab into his mouth, smearing burgundy flecks of barbeque and chilli sauce and white garlic mayonnaise over his stubbled cheeks. "Time wise?"

"Give it a couple'f hours," Bruce said, open-mouthed chewing over a wad of pitta bread and doner meat. "Let 'em get to sleep an' tha'."

Darren nodded. He picked up a chicken wing and nibbled at its fried coating. He'd barely touched his food, too eager, too excited, his body buzzing with anticipation and adrenaline. He still had four of his six chicken wings remaining, excluding the one he was now nibbling, whilst his brother had ploughed through all but three of his cheese-covered chips and two-thirds of a doner kebab heavily laden with sauce, sans salad. The kebab shop they were in was doing a brisk trade, with plenty of drunks wandering in, looking for somewhere to dry off from the rain, and something to soak up some of the alcohol.

"What do you reckon 'en?" Darren said, finishing the chicken wing off and returning the bone to the box. "About two?"

"Somethin' like tha', aye," Bruce said, gob full of meat, bread and sauce. "Two-thirty, three. Maybe later. Four. Some time when there's no other fucker around to see us."

"Right." It seemed sensible. "Wha' are we supposed to do 'til then though?"

Bruce looked about the place as he swallowed. He supposed it would look rather odd if they sat in the same kebab shop for the next four hours.

"Le's get back and grab the car after this. We can chill out in there for a bit, listen to the radio or something."

"Alright, but we're listening to proper radio mind. None of that weird shit you like to put on."

"What weird shit?"

"That fucking positivity bollocks. 'Find your fucking destiny', 'envision your dream', all that fucking bollocks."

"'Fucking bollocks?' How is tha' fucking bollocks? Les Brown, butt. You should try listening to him. You wouldn't believe how much he's changed my life, mun."

"You're life's changed fuck all, butt. Months you been play that shit for now, and wha's different butt? You're the same fat fucker you were when you first started listening to it."

"Oi, watch your fucking language, you," Bruce said, taking another big bite of doner. "And I mean my inner life, butt. My self-image, my hopes, my dreams."

"Fucking hell butt. It's you're outer-life you wanna be worrying about."

"Fuck up mun butt! Le's not fall out before we get started, yeah?"

"Alright. Just so long as we're listening to proper fucking radio, music an' tha', none of this self-help 'sieze the fucking moment' bollocks."

"Alright mun butt, stop fucking going about it."

Friday 31st August

04.24am

Ji Eun lay in bed, staring up at the ceiling, streetlight filtering in through the curtains. She lay in a confused funk for several moments, half-way between sleep and waking, before she heard it again; three quick taps in succession. She blinked and adjusted her eyes and mind to reality and waking. She lay there a while longer, until she heard the taps again, slightly louder this time. She rolled over and pulled back the curtains slightly, then looked down at two figures standing outside the front door. *Tap, tap, tap*, again, louder this time. She sat up and reached for her phone. *04.25am.* She remembered a quote she'd once read in a Vice magazine article about all-night partying: *nothing good ever happens after 4am.*

She got out of bed, wearing an oversized sweatshirt branded with the name of some generic American college. She picked up some jeans from the floor and pulled them on, then walked into the hallway. She saw Danny freeze at the top of the stairs, Claire standing in the doorway behind him, bedsheet wrapped around her naked body. She'd clearly sent Danny down to investigate the sound, and he'd pulled his jeans and T-shirt on for the occasion. Claire pushed the door closed upon seeing Ji Eun. Beyond her room, at the back of the house, Minji was probably still sleeping.

Ji Eun walked along the landing, the *tap, tap, tap* echoing up from the front door again, her iPhone held tight in her fist. Danny crept down the stairs. Ji Eun reached the top of the stairs, then loosened her grip on the phone, ready to dial 999 at a moment's notice. Danny looked back up at her, fearful, then stepped towards the door, as Ji Eun moved a few steps down.

"Keep the chain on," she called down to him, in an impulse torn between whispering and shouting, wanting to be certain that he'd heard her, but not wanting her words to be heard by the two figures outside.

Danny did as she said. He shook as another *tap, tap, tap* rattled out from the door, then he slid the chain into action, and carefully pulled the door open.

Bang.

Danny stepped back from the door as the noise echoed up the stairs to Ji Eun.

Bang again, harder this time, then one more time, *bang,* and the chain had snapped from the frame, and the figures were inside, the bigger one in front, ramming his knee into Danny's gut, then wrapping a thick arm around him and grabbing him in a headlock.

"Fucking get her mun butt!" Bruce yelled at his brother.

Darren darted up the stairs as Ji Eun instinctively slid the phone back into her pocket. He grabbed her by the hair, slammed her head against the wall, then dragged her, stumbling, down the stairs.

With a quick slamming and opening of doors, they were all in the living room. Bruce and Darren threw Danny and Ji Eun down onto the sofa. Bruce walked away for a moment as Darren stood in the darkness staring at Ji Eun, eyes aglow with menace. Bruce found the light-switch and returned to them. The first thing Ji Eun noticed about the black-clad intruders was the hammers they held in their hands, gripping the steel heads of them with their fists, arms otherwise relaxed and stretched out at their sides.

Bruce let a fearsome silence fill the room, undercut only by the bigger brother's heavy breathing. It was maybe thirty seconds or less until he spoke, but for Danny and Ji Eun, it felt far longer. "Where's Daniel?"

No answer.

"Where's Danny?" Bruce shouted, slamming the hammer down on the centre-of-the-room coffee table.

Danny flinched. "I don't know."

"Who are you?" Bruce asked.

Silence.

Bruce smiled. "You don't even need to bother answering tha', actually, butt. We know exactly who you fucking are. Joseph Bradfield."

Joseph Bradfield. Danny stared at Bruce. *The Lumia. But they want me.* Confusion. Panic.

"And who's this fucking tart you're with?" Bruce said, holding up the hammer and pointing it at Ji Eun, who Darren had yet to take his eyes off. "My brother's missus not enough for you, is it? You gotta go fucking some Chinese bit on the side, have you? Fuck, I feel sorry for Jodie. And not just 'cause you're cheating on her. No, I feel sorry for her 'cause she went from being married to my brother to fucking you in the first place. Fucking hell." Bruce broke off, laughing. "Look at the fucking size on you. Look at the fucking state of you." Bruce could see the absolute terror that his speech had instilled in Danny, who was sitting on the couch, shaking, blinking three times a second. "But you know what? Maybe it's not such a bad thing, you playing away with Qui-Gon Jinn by here. I'm sure you wouldn't want us to hurt her. Or you." Danny closed his eyes for several seconds, his whole body trembling. When he opened his eyes again, Bruce was smiling at him. "And we don't wanna hurt no-one neither. All we want is for our brother to have his son back. Now, since I take it he's not in this house with you, I think the best thing for you to do would be to tell us where he and his mam are hiding." Bruce sat himself down on the coffee table before continuing. "I gather she's at her mam's house. Right?" Danny said nothing. "Right?"

"Y-y-yes," Danny stuttered.

"Good. Well where does her mam live?" Nothing. Bruce slammed the hammer down on the coffee table again. "Where does her fucking mam live?"

Danny closed his eyes. *What's happening? What's happening?*

Ji Eun screamed. Danny felt his head pushed to the left, fast, then an explosion of pain pulsating out from his jaw. He opened his eyes to Bruce, teeth gritted, standing over him, hammer in hand. Danny held his shaking left hand up to the spot on his jaw where the hammer had hit him.

"Where the fuck does her fucking mam live?" Bruce growled.

"20 Llid yr Amrannau," Darren stuttered. He'd seen the address on the Lumia, in the 'recently visited places' section of its location settings. He assumed it was the address he'd found the phone at.

Bruce looked at his brother. Darren was still staring at Ji Eun, unblinking. Bruce looked back at Danny. He passed the hammer from his right hand to his left, then used his freed-up hand to closed-fist jab the same spot on Danny's jaw he'd thwacked with the hammer.

Danny screamed in pain.

"You'd best not be fucking around with us, butt. 20 Llid yr Amrannau, right?"

"Yeah."

"Definitely?"

"Definitely," Danny said, his head dropping, delicately lifting his left hand to his hurting jaw. The pain he was feeling intensified the moment his finger brushed against it. Danny started to cry.

"Fucking hell mun butt," Bruce said, shaking his head. "Pull yourself together mun, will you? I'll never know what the fuck Jodie seen in you. Nor you, neither," he said, looking at Ji Eun.

As the scene had unfolded around her, Ji Eun had been taking mental note of all the names and details, trying to piece them together, to work out what was happening, why the names matched up so perfectly with the details Rory had fed her about the escaped con Simon Amstell. It had become pretty clear pretty quickly that the fat one doing all the talking was Bruce Amstell, the same guy she'd watched from afar dealing with police the previous morning, while the younger one, the creep who kept staring with those dark, soulless eyes, looked similar enough to Bruce that Ji Eun assumed he was an Amstell brother, regardless of the duo's massively contrasting body shapes. They were clearly trying to track down Simon Amstell's ex-wife, and the Danny to which they were referring was obviously Simon's son, but why they'd turned up at her house looking for him, and whether it had anything to do with Danny Daggers sharing the same first name as him, was all of a mystery.

"Why'd you hesitate before you said the address to us?" Darren said, finally moving his eyes off Ji Eun.

Danny looked at him, confused.

Darren snapped. In a half-second he'd stepped forward, swung his hammer-wielding right hand back behind him, then slammed it into the side of Danny's face, shattering his jaw and a couple of teeth in an explosion of pain and screaming agony.

Ji Eun saw even Bruce was regarding his brother with terror after that, as Danny folded over, instinctively holding a hand up to his face, drawing it away the second it brushed against his smashed-up nerve endings, sobbing into his lap.

"Don't play silly buggers with us butt," Darren warned him. "We'll fucking end you if we have to."

Bruce looked up at his brother, at the rage and carnage writ large on his face. He held his hand out and touched it gently against his brother's arm, looking to calm him.

"Alright, alright," Bruce said, slowly, softly, "this is what we're gonna do now, anyway." Darren's eyes were still fixed on Danny, who was still hunched over and sobbing, holding his left hand up near the hammer impact point, terrified of touching it. "We're gonna wait 'til Jodie goes to work. It's the summer holidays now, innit? So we're gonna head round her mam's house once it's just her and Daniel in the house, and you," pointing the hammer at Danny, "are going to tell her to hand the boy over, say you wanna go fucking play with him in the park or something, and you," pointing the hammer at Ji Eun, "are gonna come along as collateral, to make sure he don't do nothing fucking stupid, then we're gonna piss off and you'll never have to fucking see us ever again, alright?" Silence. Bruce slammed the hammer down on the table once more. "Alright?"

Danny stuttered through the tears. "Y-y-yeah."

"Good. Right then, since we're settled in here for the next few hours, why don't one of you go and get a brew on the go?"

Still shaking, Danny leant forward on the sofa.

"Not you. Qui-Gon."

Ji Eun got to her feet.

"Darren, you go on through and keep an eye on her."

Darren looked away from the quivering wreck he'd turned Danny Daggers into. He looked at Ji Eun. He smiled.

"How do you like your tea butt?" Bruce asked Danny.

No answer. Just sobbing.

Darren stepped forward, turned the hammer upside down, stuck the claws of it in Danny's nostrils, then pulled his trembling head up to look at him. "Oh butt, my brother asked you a fucking question."

"How do you take your tea butt?" Bruce said, cracking a smile at the ridiculous image of the hammer pulling Danny's nostrils up, making his nose look like a pig's.

"M-m-milk and t-t-two sugars," Danny said.

Darren slipped the hammer out of from Danny's nostrils and his head dropped down, back to the near-foetal position he'd been in before, hunched over, shaking.

"What about you butt?" Darren asked Bruce.

"Are you serious?" Bruce laughed. "How fucking long have you known me, butt? We've fucking lived together since the day you were born mun. And you don't know how many fucking sugars I do have in my tea! Can you fucking believe that?" Bruce said, turning to Ji Eun. She forced a nervous smile. "Can you fucking believe that?" Bruce said again, this time to Danny.

Danny didn't answer. Darren stepped forward, upturned hammer at the ready, but Bruce held a hand up to his brother's stomach to stop him. "Three sugars I do have butt. I suppose I'd better send our other brother a text now, let him know wha's'appenin'." Bruce took an old LG flip-phone from his pocket. He started tapping out a message to Simon as Ji Eun and Darren disappeared into the kitchen. *found joe fukin sum chinky bird,'* Bruce wrote, *'hes guna take us to jodies mams house 2 get danny once jodies fuked off to work.'*

Darren reappeared in the living room doorway. "There's no milk butt."

"Huh?" Bruce grunted, looking up at him, message sent.

"There's no milk here. They're out."

"Fuck," Bruce muttered.

"You can have it black."

"Black?" Bruce scoffed. "Fucking black tea? What the fuck do you think I am butt?"

"Well there's no fucking milk here."

"There's a Spar just around the corner," Ji Eun said, reappearing behind Darren. "I could run out and get some."

Bruce laughed. "Could you fuck! You've not got no powdered milk or nothing?"

Silence.

"Alright, well what about coffee?"

"I think there's some here," Ji Eun answered.

"Right 'en. Make us all a cup of coffee instead."

"Black coffee?" Darren said, scrunching his face up at the thought of it.

"Well it's better than black fucking tea, innit?"

Darren followed Ji Eun as she walked back into the kitchen. She opened up a cupboard and pulled out a sachet of coffee Claire had brought back from Vietnam, the stuff that'd been filtered through a rat's arsehole. "There's this stuff."

"The fuck's that?" Darren said, snatching the foreign-lettering clad packet from her.

"It's Vietnamese."

Darren stared at her, looking as if he'd never heard the word 'Vietnamese' before. He handed the packet over. "It'll do."

Darren watched her with great interest as she pulled a special metal coffee-brewing pot out of a cupboard, filled it with water at the sink, then placed it down upon the stove. Darren looked her up and down, the slim legs wrapped in tight black jeans, the hips and upper body beneath the brown sweatshirt, elongated in comparison to the European equivalent. He moved behind her, pressed his hands on those slim hips. Ji Eun shuddered at his touch, sliding a draw open to retrieve a tea spoon. She tore the packet open and carefully spooned the brown powder inside into the coffee pot, as Darren leaned in and breathed heavily against her neck. The proximity made her nauseous. She shifted away from it awkwardly, placing the coffee packet back down upon the counter. His grip on her hips stiffened. She turned the stove up to 6. The gas rose up into flaming life as she pressed the ignite switch. She felt the rough hairs of Darren's stubble brush against her bare neck. His lips pressed into a moist kiss as she held the spoon over the flame. She kept it there as his hands rose at the hips, pushing her sweatshirt up above her midriff. She felt something rise in his jeans and press against the back of hers. She held the spoon as his breath sounded heavily in her ear. He leaned his head down, lower on her neck, as she steeled herself for action. In one swift move, she touched the heated spoon to his cheek. "Argh!" he yelled, recoiling from the burn. In a flash, Ji Eun pulled a short sharp chopping knife from inside the still-open drawer, gripped the handle tightly, and plunged the blade into his crotch. He grabbed at her, hands around her neck, choking her, screaming in agony, as a great load of sound from the living room suggested Bruce's impending arrival. Darren's eyes glowed with menace as he tightened his grip on Ji Eun's throat. Her hands flailed about upon the counter, time running out. Her fingers fumbled upon a fork in the drawer, which she swung up and shoved in his eye. Ji Eun snapped it out of the socket quickly, shocking Darren's grip off her neck, he screaming and clutching at his oozing eye socket, as Ji Eun placed the fork, with the eyeball skewered on the end of it, atop the flames of the lit stove. She ran to the back door and turned the key as Bruce appeared at the kitchen doorway: "What the fuck's going on in here?"

Bruce looked at his brother, one hand clutched to his oozing eye socket, the other clasped tight to his crotch. Then he looked at the open door, and Ji Eun running through the garden beyond. He ran out after her, she throwing the gate open and sprinting off into the lane behind the house, he giving chase.

In the living room, hearing the commotion, Danny seized his chance, getting to his feet and running to the hallway, Darren shouting after him. Danny threw the front door open and ran out into the street. Darren staggered after him, waves of fury washing over the intense pain coursing through his body. He staggered through the door to the street, watching Danny run away to the end of it, and realised chasing was futile. He pulled his phone from his pocket, a basic Samsung handset, brought up the contacts list, blood pissing out from his balls and his empty eye socket. With his remaining eye, he directed his fingers to the name 'Simon', and called.

"Everything's fucked," he yelled down the phone, "get the fuck out the house now butt."

"Where's Danny?"

"20 Llid yr Armannau."

"Where?"

"20 Llid yr Armannau," Darren screamed back, the pain taking over. "Cardiff."

Bruce ran through the lane behind the house, Ji Eun sprinting off ahead of him, nimbler and more agile. He stopped, panting, knowing it was all over. *Survive.* That was the only thing there was to do now. *Survive.* He pulled his phone from his pocket and flipped it open.

9-9-9.

"Hello, which service do you require?"

"Police! Quick! My brother's've gone fucking psycho!"

04.47am

Simon listened to the rain hammering down on the street outside, striking the living room window with a hundred dull little thuds every minute. It had been clear from the tone of Darren's voice that 'now' meant 'now'. Not in ten minutes time, not after waiting for a taxi to turn up, *now*. Simon got to his feet. The television was again tuned to BBC News 24, which was still regurgitating the same stories that'd been playing on a loop since he'd gotten there – Ebola, ISIS, Syria, Ukraine. No mention of his own abscondence. He picked the remote control up from the arm of the chair he'd been sitting in and turned it off. On the sofa, Kaiser lifted his head and wheezed softly.

"Alright then Kai," Simon said, "I'll see you when I see you."

Kaiser got up and stretched his legs out, then hopped down onto the floor and wandered off into the kitchen. Simon listened to the rain hammering down and bothering the windowpane. He walked out of the living room and headed upstairs, to Bruce's bedroom, where he fumbled through foul smelling clothing strewn about the floor until he found a zip-up Nike jacket, hooded and waterproof, silver with blue trim. He zipped it over himself and headed back downstairs, where Kaiser was waiting by the front door, holding the brown handle of a silver chain lead in his mouth.

"Cheers butt," Simon said, crouching down to take the lead from him. He stuffed it into his pocket and then pushed the confused dog back into the living room, pulling the door shut behind him. Then he lifted the hood up over his head, opened the front door, and stepped outside into the rainstorm.

"There he is," Bronwyn said, scarcely believing the climax had been reached.

"Huh?" Ivor grunted, half-asleep. He saw Bronwyn throw the car door open and step out into the rain. He fumbled through his drowsiness and pushed his own door open.

The sky was faint blue and sunless, the streets empty, the rain incessant.

04.58am

Time. The word came clear and alone. *Time.* Simon looked around the narrow alleyway, flanked by the concrete breezeblock walls of the Cwm Glas estate's back gardens. He looked at the floor, avoiding his fallen foes, scanning the pools of blood and rainwater. *The rain'll wash the worst of the blood away.* His eyes wandered across the floor to the main street he'd just come into the alleyway from; there, at the edge of it, was a squat yellow box. A grit salt bin. *Time.* He strode to it, fast, and threw the lid off. The thing was barely half-full with grit salt, along with a few plastic bags and empty cans of Coke. *Time. Fast.* He headed back to the alleyway for the bodies. *How did they get here?* He shoved his hands inside the woman's pockets and found it – a car key. *Perfect.* He grabbed her under the arms and dragged her towards the grit salt bin.

04.52am

Ivor wanted to shout to her, tell her to call for back-up, but they were already outside, already pursuing him, and he was all of ten metres away, and even in the hammering early-morning rain, he surely would've heard him, and that would be certain to compromise everything. He followed instead, their hooded quarry ahead, setting a brisk pace through the rain, Bronwyn keeping her distance but keeping up with him.

Simon could sense it; something not right, something uncalm in the rain-hammered early-morning emptiness. He listened as he strode through the rain, hands in pockets, right hand feeling the steel chain of Kaiser's dog leash, wrapping it around itself, palm to knuckles, palm to knuckles. And he heard it: breaks in the rainfall; footsteps.

05.37am

Cain looked at her, lying beside him. Beautiful, blonde Marianne. He'd met her in May, just a week and a half before she'd headed home for the summer. Back to Brittany. He'd wondered then if he'd ever see her again. They'd spoken of meeting in the summer, about him visiting France, but it hadn't happened, and she'd receded to memory. Memory of the four times they'd met, the four times they'd... *the four times three... or four...* well, the four occasions on which they'd... and then, last night, there she was, at a table a few feet away from him, and they'd had their fifth liaison... he wondered if he should wake her, if she'd be ready for more, more multiplications upon the fifth meeting... *What time is it?* The bedroom glowed with curtain-filtered light from outside. He reached over to the bedside chest of drawers, to his phone on top of it, his Samsung Galaxy. 05.38. *Why the fuck am I even awake?* He put the phone back and returned his head to the pillow, staring up at the ceiling, listening to the rain hammering down outside. He decided something must've woken him. *Thunder?* He listened for further evidence of it as his blinks quickened, his brain slowed, returning to rest... then he heard it... downstairs; a door creaking open.

04.54am

Simon Amstell's back was pressed flat to the wet of the concrete-breezeblock back-garden wall, the chain of the dog leash wrapped around the fist of his right hand. He struck the second she appeared, slamming his fist into the side of her head, metal crunching bone. She hit the puddled floor and he swung a trainer-clad foot at her, hitting the same spot on the same side of the head he'd just struck with a chain-loaded fist. He lifted his foot up, over her, then held it for a second, hearing running through the rainfall. He stamped the foot down, her head feeling solid and unbroken, though he didn't waste time looking down at the consequences; he turned and saw the second one was upon him, the second obvious plain-clothed police officer. Simon struck, smashing the chain-wrapped fist straight into Ivor Evans's nose, causing him to stagger back against the concrete-breezeblock back-garden wall. Simon hit him with another chain-enhanced punch, then another, then another, Ivor reeling, dazed, eyes unfocused, his nose a flattened mess of flesh, spluttering out blood. Simon pulled the chain loose from his fist and held it hard against Ivor's neck, pushing him into the concrete-breezeblock wall, eyes still moving, hands grabbing faintly at it, veins and Adam's apple resisting hard as Simon pushed skin down with the chain, a strange gargling sound welling up in Ivor's throat, something akin to the sound of flushing a blocked toilet. When the sound ceased and the eyes were fixed upwards, motionless, Simon pulled back with the chain, and turned to see Bronwyn behind him, clawing her way back to her feet, fingers pulling at the thin lines of cement between the breezeblocks. *Time,* Simon told himself, the word the first to enter his consciousness since he'd entered the narrow breezeblock-walled alleyway. Then more words came: *Get this over as quickly as possible.* He saw a slab of rock at the edge of a puddle on the ground, a smooth grey piece that appeared to have been snapped off somebody's wall. Simon shoved the dog lead back into his pocket and picked the slab up with his right hand, lifted it high above him, then slammed it down on top of Bronwyn's skull. She slumped to the floor, hands falling free of the cement lines between the breezeblocks on the wall, but he hadn't felt the skull break. Simon crouched and lifted his right hand up, then slammed the slab down once more on top of her head, this time with a satisfying crack. He lifted the thing up, its smooth grey angles now smeared with something deep crimson and viscous. He dropped the broken slab of wall to the ground and stood himself upright, rain hammering down all around him. *Time.*

05.41am

Simon froze. Footsteps. On the stairs. Getting closer. He stood in the middle of the living room, clutching the handle of the carving knife he'd picked up in the kitchen tight, ready to defend himself. The door opened. "Hello Joe. I take it you know who I am?"

Cain recognised him instantly; Simon Amstell. Joe's missus's ex. *Hello Joe?* Cain repeated the words to himself. *Why's he think I'm Joseph?*

"Where's Danny?"

The gears of Cain's mind whirred, trying to think of a diversionary tactic, a way out, of saving himself, of protecting Marianne. "He's not here mate. I'm not Joseph."

Simon smiled. Cain noticed the knife.

"I'm not Joseph," he said again. "Joe stayed here once or twice, maybe that's why you've gotten confused about it."

"Cut the shit Joe. I knows it's you. I'll ask you again. Where's Danny?"

07.26am

"I'm phoning in sick."

Jodie looked at her mother, sat beside her in the kitchen. Beverley silently passed judgment as she stared through the open door to the living room and the television set, ignoring Joseph's presence in the doorway.

"The police'll be round soon," said Jodie. "You've only been in the job two minutes, you can't go phoning in sick already."

"We've been waiting hours on them police Jode. God knows what might happen by the time they get here."

Jodie sighed and took a sip of her luke-warm tea. Maybe Joseph was right.

"I can't support you mind, if you get yourself fired," Beverly warned, eyes fixed on the television set and BBC Breakfast News.

"No-one's asking you to support us Mam," Jodie snapped back.

Joseph moved out of the doorway and filled the kettle up in the sink. "Anyone fancy a cuppa?"

"I'm alright," Jodie said.

"Bev?"

Beverley ignored him. He returned the kettle to its stand and sat down next to Jodie, watching the news, which had moved on from the wild events in Cathays and was now focusing on an interview with the all-female members of some pop group Joseph had never heard of. Daniel was sat in the middle of the living room, oblivious, playing with his Avengers figures.

Joseph kept his mind free from thought as the girls from the girl group smiled at the questions of the tidily-dressed BBC Breakfast presenters, the volume turned down too low for Joseph to hear what they were saying. Then the guy looked serious, and turned away from the pop stars, and said something directly into the camera, then the TV cut away to Sian whatshername in the far smaller BBC Cardiff news studio, sitting at a cramped desk with images of Cardiff Bay superimposed onto the green-screen behind her. Nobody moved to turn the volume up; Joseph, Jodie and Beverley each sat there, straining their ears to hear Sian thingy's gentle, flattened, TV-sheened tones, saying something about another attack in Cardiff, and then BBC Breakfast cut away from her to show the outside of a house, somewhere in town – *Llandaff* – a Victorian terrace – *Cain's*. Those words stuck out, alone, in Joseph's mind, as a thicker-accented male voice took up the narrative, little pieces of it snagging upon those jagged little words – *Llandaff, Cain*… "…two… inside the house at the time… broke in… stabbed…" Then the exterior shot of the Victorian terraced house in Llandaff was cut away from, to a still image, unsmiling, staring: *Simon*. Simon Amstell's mugshot.

"Danny," Jodie called, on her feet and moving towards him.

Danny looked up from Thor and Iron Man, not noticing his daddy's face frowning out of the television set behind him. As Jodie reached her son in the middle of the room, someone banged three times on the front door. Nobody moved or said anything for several seconds.

Beverley rose to her feet and broke the silence: "That'll be the police now."

Joseph held up a flattened palm, telling her to stop; he got to his feet and stepped slowly into the living room, towards Danny and Jodie. The television had cut back to the London studio, to the BBC Breakfast presenters apologising to the girls from the girl group for the interruption. Someone banged on the front door again.

"Take Danny upstairs," Joseph said.

Before Jodie could act on his words, they heard banging again, this time followed by smashing glass. They heard the front door open, then saw the living room door do the same. Simon walked in, smiling.

"Hello Jode," he said. "Danny." He pulled the hood off his head and stared at Joseph. Joseph stared back. "I've come to pick up my son."

Joseph thought of the kettle; the water inside it would be near boiling. Then he thought of the other weapons to be found in the kitchen; knives, glasses, pots and pans he might be able to bludgeon him to death with…

then Simon looked away from Joseph, and down at Daniel. "Hello Danny." Simon stepped forward and crouched in front of his son, Jodie holding a protective hand to his head. Danny looked at his father in quiet confusion. "How'd you like to go on a trip with your old man?"

"Simon..." Jodie said, her voice trembling.

"Let's get out of here, yeah? Go somewhere nice, where it's not raining all the time."

"Simon... what are you doing?"

Simon stood up and looked at Jodie. He smiled as he spoke: "I've not seen my son in years, Jode. I just think I'm due a bit of time with him, that's all."

"We've seen the news, Sime."

Simon stopped smiling. "Yeah? They say anything about me on it?"

"Yeah. They said... they said they think you killed two people... and... they said, your brother... your brother's dead, Sime."

Simon looked at her, the malice draining from his face. Then he looked at Danny.

"What are you doing mun, Sime?" Jodie said softly, a tear streaming silently from each eye. "You'd been moved to an open prison mun. You'd've been out in a year, tops. Now what's gonna happen?"

"Which brother?" Simon said quietly.

"What?"

"Which brother." He snapped at the words, his face again flush with malice.

"Darren."

Simon's head dropped. He held a closed fist to his forehead for a moment, composing himself, suppressing, then dropped back into a crouched position in front of Daniel. "Come on Dan, we're leaving."

"You're not taking him," Jodie said.

Simon looked at her, then looked at Joseph, then looked at her again. "Wha'd you say?"

"You're not taking him."

"Yeah? Why, what're you gonna do about it?"

"What're you gonna do about it, Sime? Are you going to fucking kill us, too? Is that it? And what then, Sime? The cops'll be out looking for you everywhere, and even if you do sneak passed them, if you do manage to avoid the whole fucking police force, what then? Huh? What's Daniel's relationship with you going to be like after you've killed his own fucking mother in front of him?"

The malice again receded. Simon looked up into Jodie's teared-up eyes, saw that she meant what she was saying. It was real. Too real. *Darren*. Simon stood up and took two steps back, towards the television set, and perched himself on the edge of the wooden cabinet supporting it. He hunched himself over, pressing closed fists to his temples, staring at the ground, getting his thoughts in order, before sitting up and looking at Jodie, eyes wet, trying to speak: *Is Darren really dead?* He could think the words, but couldn't say them; he looked at her, eyes welling up, his lip quivering.

"I'm sorry Jode."

Simon let his head drop forward again, almost between his legs; he held flattened palms to his temples and started to sob.

Joseph stood and watched the strange spectacle; a man who'd smashed his way in through their front door, a man who'd in all likelihood just stabbed his best friend to death, along with some girl who'd been in the house with him, a man who'd come in likely intending to kill Joseph and Jodie, and perhaps even Jodie's mother too, a man who was now crying his eyes out in front of them.

As he cried, Jodie stepped toward him. She placed her hands at the side of Simon's head, then spoke to him in a hushed, calming tone: "It's alright bae. It's alright."

"It's not, bae. He's fucking dead, bae."

That last line was too much for him, and he was full on blubbering now. Jodie sniffled, looked down at the devastated, reduced creature in front of her, tears rolling down her own cheeks.

Joseph gritted his teeth and looked at Danny, in the middle of the room, looking up at them; his parents. Joseph wanted to grab a blunt object and bludgeon the pair of them to death.

"What were you thinking mun Sime?" Jodie said, voice shaking. "Another year, and that would've been it. There's no way back now, bae; they'll lock you up for good, won't they?"

"I know bae, I fucking knows it."

"What were you thinking?"

"I don't know, bae. I weren't fucking thinking."

"You're a fucking idiot Sime."

"I know, bae. I know. But I fucking love you Jode."

Jodie blubbered and burst into full-blown tears: "I fucking love you too."

Joseph clenched his fists. He half felt like vomiting, half felt like doing something to make them notice him, to end their sickening display. The thought of all the times he'd fucked Jodie now disgusted him. *Never again.*

Then he heard it: outside – sirens. Jodie bent forward, her head level with Simon, and the two kissed, tears streaming into their mouths and onto their tonuges. *You'll fucking rot in prison now, you fucking cunt,* Joseph thought, with some satisfaction, wishing there were something he could do to make the fuzz put his ex-wife away with him. But there wasn't, and as the sirens drew nearer, Joseph knew that he was watching the end of it; standing there, inert, as the woman he'd been so close to until a minute before kissed and consoled the guy who'd just brought his best friend's life to an end. A memory came to mind, back when he was a teenager, when he'd been jumped by a couple of pricks, Ginger John amongst them. As soon as Cain had heard about it, he and his two older brothers had gone and found Ginger John and his mates and kicked the shit out of them. *Now's your chance to do something to pay him back for it.* Joseph urged himself to do something, anything, to make them pay for what they'd done, but instead he just stood there, the sirens getting louder, he inert, irrelevant, obsolete. Then he noticed, on the hand Simon held against Jodie's head, blood tipping the fingernails. Joseph scanned Simon for more, and saw little dots of red decorating the silver and blue of his Nike jacket. He had no doubt who the blood belonged to. *Cain.* As Jodie and Simon kissed, and the sirens grew louder, a thought entered Joseph's mind; *kill Daniel.* Right there in front of the pair of them. He was small enough that Joseph could probably snap his neck with his bare hands. He looked at the dots of red on the silver and blue Nike jacket. *Just do it.* But he didn't; he did nothing. The sirens grew louder, then reached a constant level as the police car pulled up outside. Jodie and Simon kissed and smooched and Joseph just stood there, any chance of revenge ebbing away.

Saturday 1st September

11.09am

"We've got to let him go," Kelvin sighed.

Dai stared at him, clutching the freshly brewed cuppa in his hand: "What do you mean?"

"His story checks out."

"What story?"

"The seagull thing."

"Are you having me on?" Dai grinned. Kelvin didn't return the gesture. Dai's grin evaporated. "Are you serious? He was hunting a seagull?"

"Yeah. They found a dismembered corpse near the river."

"Of... a seagull?"

"Yeah."

"The dismembered corpse of a seagull? By the river?"

Kelvin nodded, struggling to hold back the anger that was brewing within.

"Who found it?"

"Gallagher."

Dai stared at him, eyes widening.

"You mean--?"

"Rory *fucking* Gallagher."

"That prick," Dai Green sighed. The same prick whose viral video earlier in the week had turned a damn good officer into a laughing stock. "Well if Gideon what's-his-face's story checks out, who the fuck killed Daniel Covell?"

"Sometimes," Kelvin Phillips explained, assuming an air of seasoned authority, "the most obvious answer is the correct one."

"And that would be...?"

"Come on, Dai. Who the fuck's been running round town causing all manner of mayhem the past couple of days?"

"You don't think it's connected to them lot do you?" Dai said, realising immediately to whom Kelvin Phillips was referring.

"It's not exactly outside the realm of possibility, is it? If a dead body turns up in the river Taff, and there's been a group of sick psycho fucks running around smashing people's heads in with hammers, I'd say said sick psycho fucks'd have to come somewhere pretty close to the top of the list of potential suspects."

"I suppose you're right," Dai agreed. In his experience, Kelvin Phillips usually was.

"Yeah," Kelvin said, staring off across the break room at the notice pinned above the mug-filled sink imploring all officers to wash and put away any items they use.

A few seconds silence followed. Dai stared at Kelvin, waiting for him to speak again.

"You know what Dai, the more I think about it, the more certain I am. Matter of fact, I'd bet my whole bloody career on it; I absolutely guaran-fucking-tee you that those sick psycho fuck Amstell brothers are responsible for that poor dead fucker Daniel Covell."

Dai nodded. It made all the sense in the world. They were responsible for all the other bodies that'd turned up in and around Cardiff over the past day and a bit. But then something occurred to him. "I don't know though. The times don't match up, do they? I mean, the Amstells were all dead or in custody by the time Daniel Covell died."

"Yeah," Kelvin sighed.

Dai fell quite. It upset him to contradict Kelvin, and to see that hero of the constabulary become chastened, unemboldened.

Kelvin stared at the sign above the sink for a long moment before speaking again. "I don't know then, Dai. If that tramp we brought in really was hunting seagulls, and if it weren't them Amstell brothers what done it, then who the fuck did kill Daniel Covell?"

Friday 31st August

10.34am

Sean trudged through the People Outreach Hub, red-faced, red-eyed, and glum. He avoided the stares of his teammates as he sat down and put his headset back on.

"Wha'd they say to you?" Bradley asked.

"The usual," Sean replied.

"Don't be late again," Bradley said, doing his best to impersonate a harsh reprimand delivered in Matt's lilting North Welsh accent. "I'm surprised near-enough everyone've turned up today, the state we were all in last night. It's only Sarah and Joseph who are missing."

"And Joseph weren't even out last night," Keith added.

"He weren't out with us," Justin said, "but he said he was meeting some mates in town."

"He'll be hungover an' all then," Bradley concluded.

"I know the feeling," Keith moaned, red-faced and ravaged, the image of the morning after.

"Maybe he's been stabbed," Harry smirked.

"That's not funny man," Alison said, grimacing at the flippant reference to the bloodbaths in Llandaff and Cathays that had dominated the morning's chatter.

"Well I hope he comes in eventually," Justin said. "Joe were meant to be my partner, weren't he?"

"Your partner?" Sean enquired.

"Yeah, for that presentation."

"What presentation?" Then Sean remembered. "Shit, is that today?"

"Yeah. After lunch. Who're you working with?"

"Tom."

Tom looked up from his computer screen, the sound of his own name drawing him out of the self-imposed seclusion he'd been skulking in, silent, hungover, tormented by anxiety and paranoia about what he might've said or done the night before.

"You done anything for that presentation, butt?" Sean asked.

It took Tom a few seconds to realise what presentation Sean was referring to. "No."

"Well you'd better get something done," Justin warned them. "Matt and Mike seem to be making a pretty big deal out of it."

"It'll be alright mun," Sean scoffed. "What're they gonna do, fire us?"

"Well, I doubt they'd go that far, but I'd imagine they'd be pretty vexed if you've not done nothing for it."

Sean nodded, then removed his headset, got to his feet, and walked over to the command desk at the head of the People Outreach Hub to ask for a pen and some paper.

"What happened to you last night anyway, Tom?" Justin asked. "At some point you just disappeared."

"The bouncer wouldn't let me back in," Tom admitted. "After I'd been for a smoke. Said I looked too pissed."

"What, at Varisty?" Justin laughed. "Shit man, I think we'd all had a few too many by that point!"

"Here you are," Sean said, placing the pen and paper on the desk in front of Tom. "See what you can come up with."

Tom stared at the blank piece of paper as Sean retook his seat, thoughts coming...

"Fucking hell," Bradley exclaimed. "Have you seen this? They've found two more bodies. Coppers. Stuffed into a fucking grit salt bin."

"Jesus," Alison said, horrified.

"In Cardiff?" Keith asked.

"Llanbradach," Bradley said, checking the article on the computer screen. "Where's that?"

"Dunno. Says here it's in Caerphilly County Borough."

"Is it connected with them stabbings?" Justin asked.

"Dunno. Maybe. But they found two dead coppers in a fucking grit salt bin, like. That's mental."

"That's how you make ham, right?" Harry said, smirking. "Store dead pigs in salt."

Bradley and Justin raised wry smiles; Sean laughed out loud.

"That's really not funny," Alison said, disgusted.

"That's a serious crime, that is," Sean quipped, "assaulting a police officer."

Harry, Justin and Bradley laughed; Keith smiled despite himself; Alison looked horrified.

"They'll probably make a TV series about it," Harry smirked, "a gritty police drama."

More smiles and laughter, except from Alison, and Tom, who was engrossed in writing.

"It might not be true, mind," Justin added. "You've gotta take anything you read on the internet with a grain of salt."

A few smiles followed; the law of diminishing returns was in effect. A silence fell over the team, their thoughts focused on turning phrases like 'salt of the earth' or 'grit your teeth' into serviceable one-liners, until too much time had passed, and they mostly fell back into doing the job they were being paid for.

Tom lay his pen down on the desk and read back through what he'd just written:

All that's in Wales is call centres. Back in the day, there used to be coalmines, but these have all closed down now. Now, the only businesses that exist in Wales are call centres. As call centres businesses are centred on telecommunication, they're likely to have already sorted out their own phone contracts. Therefore, I don't think we should bother calling any Welsh businesses.

"Sean," he said, "I've finished our presentation."

Tom handed the piece of paper over the desk. He watched Sean reading, smiling, as he finished up his call.

"No problem, I'll call back another time. That's brilliant, that is," Sean said, his call finished.

"What's that?" Justin asked

Sean handed the piece of paper to him. Justin smirked as he read. Tom smiled, his joke having gone over well.

"Matt, come and have a look at this," Sean shouted.

"What's that?" Matt said, approaching the desk.

Shit. Tom cringed as Justin held the piece of paper up to him.

"That's awesome," Justin laughed.

Matt read it without smiling. "What's this?"

"Our presentation," Sean said. "Tom's just written it up now."

"Very funny," Matt said, his expression suggesting it was anything but. He handed the paper to Tom. "I hope you'll have something a bit better than this for us by this afternoon."

Saturday 1st September

12.53am

Rory and Ji Eun walked from the police station to the car without saying anything, neither of them trusting the boys in blue not to eavesdrop. Once they'd gotten into Rory's Volvo and slammed its doors shut, Rory made a tentative effort to break the silence.

"How were it?"

The silence resumed.

"Ah shite Ji Eun, tha' were a stupid fuckin' thing tae ask. I mean--"

"No, it's fine, I was just... trying... to find the right words... to describe it."

More silence. Rory turned the key in the ignition. As he started to reverse out of his parking space, Ji Eun spoke again.

"They asked me questions. About what had happened. Four or five times, the same questions."

"They'll've bin makin' sure ya story checks oot. Naw inconsistencies."

"Yeah… that's what the lawyer said."

"I'd say they're satisfied ye were nae lying. They would nae of le' ye go elsewise."

"I suppose."

"Y'must be exhausted."

"Yeah. I couldn't really sleep after… what happened…"

"Fuck, o' course no'. Where'd'ya wanna head now? I can take ya back tae yir own house if ya want, but I mean, there'll probably be press pissing around outside, i' mae even've bin cordoned off for forensics tae have a look a' i'. Ya can ge' some kip round mine if you'd rather. Or I can take you tae a friend's place, it's up tae you."

"What are you doing now?"

"Me, well, I mean, y'll have heard wha' happened tae tha' Danny Daggers feller, I take i'?"

"Yeah."

"Aye, well, I've jus' bin havin' a wee look intae tha' this morning."

Rory put the Volvo in gear and drove out of the police station car park.

"What did you find out?"

"No' much. I found tha guy tha cops'd collared did nae do it. Homeless feller, tha same fucker I filmed Tuesday pissing ontae a cop's head, funnily enough. Mad bastard'd bin chopping up a fuckin' seagull, believe i' or no'. Go' blood all over his hands on account o' i', an' tha police'd pu' two an' two taegether an' go' five."

"What are you going to do now?"

"I guess once you're safe an' sound, I'll head over tae tha spo' behind tha stadium were tha poor lad copped it, see if there's any more clues lyin' aroun'."

"Let me come with you."

"Ack, I dunnae think ya should be doin' tha', after tha night yiv jus' had. Ya must be fuckin' knackered."

"I don't feel like sleeping."

"Y'll feel a world better fir i'."

"And by then, the story'll be over. The national newspapers in London will have sent their journalists down and they'll have gotten everything covered."

Rory looked at Ji Eun with suspicion. She had a look of grim determination on her tired face. Her face was puffy, bags swollen up beneath her eyes, but pure life and hunger twinked in her pupils. His pupil.

"Are ye sure?"

"Positive." She wanted to sleep, she felt her brain and body crying out to her for rest, but there was something else coursing her through her, perhaps adrenaline, keeping her alert, pushing her forward. She'd somehow found herself in the eye of the storm, chaos all about her. She figured that such a perfect storm of happenstance would probably never again encircle her; it was far too great of an opportunity to sleep away.

"I dunno if I should really be tellin' ya this, after all yiv been through, bu'... well... I go' tha autopsy report on Danny Daggers, and well... he was nae just murdered..."

Friday 31st August

02.06pm

"Guys, can you come through to the meeting room please?" Michael said, appearing at the head of the desk in the P.O.H. as Team Lemon returned to their seats, booze-weary, a few minutes late back from a liquid lunch.

Oh fuck. Tom had forgotten all about it. *The presentation.*

The team walked single-file through the People Outreach Hub, then through the hallway, and into the meeting room. Matt was sat at the head of the long desk inside, eyes stern beneath his glasses.

"Right then," Matt said, the team taking their seats. "Who's first?"

Tom was hanging back, waiting for the others to file past and take the seats in front of him, hoping to seat himself as far from the head of the table as possible.

"Tom, Sean, why don't you get us started?"

Tom looked at Sean, standing beside him at the back of the room. Sean was staring down at the table, red-faced, red-eyed, stoned as well as pissed. Everyone else in the room was looking at the pair of them. Tom coughed, then began to improvise.

"Our area was..." Tom began, trailing off, trying to remember what their area was, "Wales?" All eyes on him, except Sean's red eyes, which were still focused on some spot, some grain on the room's long table. "There's a lot of businesses in Wales that need mobiles. Shops... companies... that kind of thing. Factories. Umm..."

"Is that it?" Matt said.

"Yeah, umm, to be honest, we didn't really..."

"Get out."

Tom stood still.

"Get out. Now."

"Seriously?" Sean asked.

Matt nodded, then said it again. "Get out."

Sean headed straight for the door. Tom stared out into the corridor, then looked back at Matt, who stared straight back, eyes unblinking beneath his spectacles. The rest of Team Lemon looked away, directing their eyes to the table, to the wall, or to the ceiling. Tom shuffled awkwardly towards the door.

"And don't bother coming in on Monday."

Tom stepped out into the corridor. Sean had already hit the button to call the lift up.

02.34pm

Shoppers moving around him, staring at him, hour after hour, alternating between walking and sitting, drifting out of consciousness when sitting, brief seconds filled with disconnected images of death and fear and... as Danny now walked, one dream, or nightmare, or daymare, or string of images, haunted him in particular; he'd been back at home, with parents, friends... and all had been bald... shaven-headed... cancer-stricken... he'd woken with a start, saw he was still upon the bench, at that point in a narrow strip of retail that connected the shiny new St. David's 2 with its grubbier, elder forefather, the original St. David's Shopping Centre. He'd then allowed himself to slip back, through quickening blinks, to unconsciousness, and found the faces of his baldened social network reaching arms up at him, grabbing at him, and he'd awoken again, and risen to his feet immediately, and began walking, and had walked until this point, at which he now stood at something of a crossroads somewhere within the city within a city of chain-store sprawl... he slowly turned around, 360°, taking in the swirl of people, the coffee shop, the jeweller's, the perfume shop, another jeweller's, a cards shop, Boots, Greggs, then back round again, some of the shoppers stealing glances at him, not – he had to remind himself – because they recognised him, but more likely because of the mess of bruising and congealed blood getting thwacked with a hammer had left on his face... then he caught sight of it, and ceased rotating: a payphone. He staggered towards, a little dizzy, nauseous, and a dozen other negativities, as hunger rumbled in his guts, and pain throbbed unmercifully from his jaw.

He reached the phone and dialled 1-0-0. A woman's voice answered. He barely heard her speak beneath the din of shoppers' footsteps and conversations echoing all about him in the capitalist purgatory in which he'd secluded himself.

"Idliketomakeareversechargescall," Danny said, the words running together, he slurring, every syllable causing a thousand nerve endings inside of him to recoil from volts of electric agony spraying forth from his wounded jaw.

"I'm sorry sir, could you repeat that?" the woman said.

He closed his eyes, tried to focus, then spoke slowly and deliberately, clutching the receiver tightly with both hands, trying to channel the electric pain coursing through his body into the telecommunications network: "I'd... like... to... make... a... reverse... charges... call...".

He gasped at the end of it, she understanding him, and offering a follow-up question: "Okay, and to what number would you like to make this call?"

Danny recited his home telephone number, his *real* home, not the house he shared with the lads at uni, but his parent's home – the tour was over.

There was a few moments pause before the woman spoke again: "I'm sorry, but nobody answered."

Danny hung up the receiver, rather than force his jaw through the agony of conversing with her further. He knew his father was likely at home, his mother's reasonably-sized furniture business being the family's sole source of income. But he knew his father never answered the house phone; 'it's always damned sales calls,' his dad had told him once, when Danny had sat at home with him, the phone bleating out endlessly. Yet he didn't disconnect the phone; he just left it there, a ghost of a bygone era, to occasionally cry out in vain. Pushed into obsolescence by the mobile. *Mobile.* Danny tried to recall either of his parent's mobile numbers, his Lumia having been rendered inoperative after he'd dropped it in the puddle while he was waiting for a taxi the night before. Random strings of digits flashed through his mind, none of them convincing. The future was dead too.

Danny found himself walking back through the bowels of strip-lit shoparama, people rushing to and fro, a swirling consumerist vortex pulling him down towards the drain. *Being pulled through the bowels to the drain,* he summarised. He shuddered at his summary, the gross imagery of it. He glanced inside as he passed the most pristine, white-walled Greggs he'd ever seen, a plethora of pastries sat beneath plasti-glass, staring out at him, taunting him, he and his grubby penny and stomach full of hunger, his cigarette-craving lungs and head full of pain. He ascended a set of stairs, the Disney store to the left of him as he reached their top, then approached a balcony and stared down at the shoppers bumbling about far beneath. *What the fuck am I doing here?* The question stumped him. He didn't even know what he'd meant by it, let alone how to answer it. What had he meant by 'here'? Here in St. David's Shopping Centre? Here in Cardiff? Here on Earth? Here amongst the living?

He was in St. David's Shopping Centre because it was pissing down with rain outside. He was in Cardiff because he was a fucking idiot with ill-thought out ideas who'd somehow wound up penniless and destitute, hundreds of miles from home. And he was on Earth, and alive, because...

More pertinent questions battled past the jaw shocks to wrestle with his consciousness. *Who the fuck were them pair with the hammers?* They'd been looking for him. 'Danny', they'd kept on saying. 'Danny'. But they'd thought him someone else; Joseph Bradfield. The man who'd taken his Lumia. The connection bewildered him.

Danny stared down at the swirling shoppers, his thoughts as distracted and unfocused as their unsynchronised movements. Then it occurred to him, through the fog and fug of pain and misery; *Yeller.* The fucker who's fiver he'd fucked off with on Wednesday. That was it; the only logical answer. That big, burly drug dealer. He should've known better than to cross him. Now he was here, lost and alone, entirely vulnerable, right in the middle of Yeller's city, with Yeller's thugs and spies lurking all around him.

No, he thought, halting the madness. *How the fuck could Yeller've found out where I was?* Easily. All it would've taken would've been one person from Yeller's party to have seen him in Live Lounge, or at the gay club, or at any other point whilst he'd been wandering around Cardiff in the last twenty-four hours. *But would anyone go that fucking mental over a fiver?* A drug dealer might. A drug dealer with a reputation to uphold. If word were to spread that a uni student from Leeds had robbed off with money from right under the nose of the mighty Yeller, the local hoodlums would have a field day. Perhaps the girl had even been in on it. *What were her name?* Claire. *Claire.* It'd been her who'd told him to go downstairs and answer the door, while she remained upstairs in the bedroom. *Jesus* – she must've been part of the plan. *And the Asian girl?* Maybe her too. Then he remembered meeting her, a few days before that, in the Wetherspoons... she'd plied him with drink, asked him a bunch of weird personal questions... *fucking hell!* It was all part of the conspiracy.

Danny trembled with fear, which caused pain to ripple out from his jaw with even greater intensity. The enormity of his mistake was now clear to him. He'd made a powerful enemy, and surely couldn't stay in Cardiff, in Wales, a moment longer. *But how the fuck am I supposed to get out of here?* He'd already exhausted every option. Trains and taxis were a bust. The bank was no help at all. Telephoning family or friends had proved impossible. Taking his mobile to Cash Generator had been counted out even before he'd broken it. He supposed he could put out a plea for assistance on Facebook, but without his Lumia's internet access, he'd require an internet café, which would require money, with which he could just as easily escape on a train or a Megabus. He had to face reality – he was stuck in Cardiff. A hostile city. Enemy ground. He felt his heartbeat quicken; *this is it.* His end had found him. *No,* he argued against himself, *this is a panic attack. Get a grip.* But the heartbeats were accelerating, mounting towards a crescendo...

Danny turned away from the edge, away from the shoppers swarming around on the floor below. He pressed his right hand, hard, against his chest, struggling to feel and count his heartbeat. Failing, he stretched out his arm and pressed the index and middle fingers of his left hand to his right wrist; he supposed it seemed normal, a beat every second or so, *but what's normal?* He noticed a silver-haired elderly gent in a green jacket eyeing him with suspicion, then quickly shifting his gaze away when it became clear

Danny had noticed him. Danny looked beyond the elderly gent in the green jacket and clocked other shoppers doing the same, no doubt because of the wound on his jaw and his odd compulsion to pulse-check, but he couldn't discount the possibility there were spies amongst them. *You're not safe here.* The shopping centre was too open, too crowded, too obvious. He'd entered the consumerist church seeking sanctuary, but had been confronted with the reckoning and realisation of an all-powerful, all-seeing God, an omnipotent overlord, Heaven-bent on vengeance. *Escape. Escape. Escape.* He repeated the word, a mantra, something to focus on, to block out the fear of an imminent heart attack. *Escape. Escape. Escape.* He saw malice in the face of each person who passed him. *Escape.* The whole city was against him. *Escape.* The whole world. *Escape.* He'd entered the consumerist church seeking sanctuary. *Escape.* Sanctuary from the rain. *Escape.* Sanctuary from reckoning. *Escape.* Inside, he'd been confronted by the face of God. *Escape.* All-seeing. *Escape.* All-powerful. *Escape.* A vengeful God. He had angered him, here in his kingdom of Cardiff, and now... *Escape. Escape. Escape. Escape.*

03.12pm

"D'you think we've been fired?" Tom asked.

"I'd say it definitely looks like it."

They'd gone for a swift pint after it'd happened, then a spliff, then they'd come to where they were now, the betting shop across the street from Live Lounge, where Sean had just lost twenty pounds on a video roulette machine, and had slotted another twenty in, and was now playing. Tom watched him, tapping the screen and the buttons below, placing virtual representations of real cash across the board, tapping again, watching the roulette wheel spin, his corner-of-the-screen cash total swelling and receding at random. The funk of weed blanketed Tom's thoughts, keeping them warm, as he looked, mesmerised, at the roulette wheel's rotation and the cash total, ticking upwards and downwards, no logic to its movements. Above the bleeps and the blips of the betting shop's bandits, a song was playing, a song that Tom recognised - 'Dolemite', by The Creeps: *"Hanging around like a stalactite, / feeding off the state like a parasite…"* Tom wondered if it was the album version or the edited version, where the lyrics had been neutered for radio. *"…drinking, and smoking, and chopsing all night, / who the heck do you think I am?"* It was the radio-neutered version. The original said 'who the fuck'.

Tom thought about the lyrics as he watched the video roulette screen. The dole. That's where he'd be on Monday, back down the dole office. Scribbling down two dozen things he'd done to try and find a job as he sat outside the Job Centre on sign-on day. He would do that until the lack of funds started getting to him and the novelty of abundant free time wore off, then he'd find another shitty call centre job. He'd carry on until the new job had thoroughly done his head in, and he'd gone past being able to motivate himself to put in even the bare minimum of effort required. He'd get fired again, which was preferable to quitting, because quitters didn't get dole money. He'd repeat the process ad infinitum. *Ever decreasing circles…*

He wondered if he'd ever break free of the cycle as he watched the roulette wheel spin, Sean's cash total now on a definite downward trajectory, the chorus of The Creeps song repeating to fade out: *"Who do you think I aaaaaaam? / Who do you think I am?"* There had to be something else out there, some remotely enjoyable way of making a living. He'd applied for glamour graduate positions, media jobs and the like, and gotten nowhere. Interning anywhere wasn't really an option, being that it'd disqualify him from collecting the dole, and his parents weren't going to cover his living expenses at his age. *"Who do you think I aaaaaaam? / Who the heck do you think I am?"*

Tom looked away from the video roulette screen, the cash total now down to a dangerously low £7.47. He pulled his iPhone from his pocket and tapped out a message to Steve. *'What u up to tonight man? Fancy a few drinks in town?'.* He slid the phone back into his pocket and watched the roulette screen. The total had tumbled to £4.20 in less than a minute. He continued to watch as some American EDM-pop hit followed The Creeps. By the time it had reached its chorus, the cash total had hit zero. Sean turned away from the screen, a glum expression on his face. Tom offered his condolences for the forty pound that had just been frittered away, before asking, "What do you wanna do now?"

"I don't know mate," Sean said, face miserable, "find another job. Shouldn't be too hard."

"I mean now-now. Fancy another pint somewhere?"

"Nah man, I should probably get back. Try and keep myself from pissing the last of my pay away."

03.47pm

"So they fired you in front of everyone?"

"Yeah."

"That's harsh butt."

"Yeah… what time do you finish?"

"Six."

"Fancy grabbing a pint or something after?"

"Ah, I'm sorry man," Gareth said, seeming genuinely sorry, "but me and Beth are going for dinner with my Mum and Ed tonight."

"No worries," Tom said, failing to hide his disappointment.

"Maybe we can get out and do something tomorrow?"

"Yeah."

"Yeah, give me a text or something."

"Yeah, cool."

Gareth noticed a customer standing near his counter, a lamp in his hand.

"Cool, get in touch tomorrow man," Gareth said, heading in the customer's direction.

Tom turned his back on John Morgan's department store's home decorations department and headed off, through menswear, towards the exit. He pulled his phone from his pocket to check the time – 3.49pm – and saw that Steve had replied to his earlier message: *"Cant tonite soz boss, got a date x'.*

Saturday 1ˢᵗ September

01.29pm

Tom's eyes blinked into consciousness as he saw his mother's face, scowling at him. It took him a few seconds to realise where he was – he was at home, in his bed, with his mother standing in the doorway.

"Are you actually going to get up today?" she asked.

He groaned and shut his eyes.

"What the hell were you even doing last night to get back home so late?"

He tried to remember.

"You woke us up again when you came in as well. What am I gonna do with you?"

He didn't know. *Fuck.* The first stab of memory penetrated his consciousness. *I got fired.* It was obvious from his mother's put-on, half-hearted chastisement that he hadn't told her yet.

"Well I'm going out shopping now anyway. Do you want anything?"

"I'm alright," he mumbled, throat croaky from too many cigarettes.

"You sure? Because it'll be too late if you change your mind later."

"Yeah."

She sighed. "Alright. Well try and get up at some point today."

She closed the door and walked away, leaving him alone to sift through half-formed memories of the night before. He cringed at each half-remembered encounter, blurred faces peering out from the hangover... he felt dry, hollow... needing more sleep, but craving water, knowing food – stodgy, greasy food – could help right the wrong he'd done himself... he began compiling a list, ordering his needs – *a cup of tea; whatever foods in the fridge...* he heard the front door of the house slam shut. His mum had left. He decided to satiate his basest mental need first.

He sat up and placed his feet on the floor. The room was off-balance, the world unsteady. He sighed and mumbled something incomprehensible. He got to his feet and staggered across the room to the chair at his computer desk. He moved the mouse and the PC hummed into life. *Must've switched it on when I got in.* He double-clicked the Firefox icon and, in his hungover funk, accidentally tapped 'Restore Previous Tabs'. He started clicking the little 'X's in the top right-hand corner of the screen, then stopped at the BBC News tab, something wrong, something very wrong… it took several seconds for his brain to register the wrong thing, then several seconds more for the brain to process it, and to translate image into language, to make itself real to itself… *That's me.* He stared at himself, at a picture taken from Facebook, of him standing in the street early-morning after a party back at uni, bottle of High Commissioner whiskey in his hand, gurning for the camera. *Why am I on BBC News?* Then he finally looked away from himself and moved his eyes a few inches across the page to the headline besides the picture: 'Police seek new suspect in Daniel Covell murder'. He looked at the headline, then back at the picture, then back at the headline, then back at the picture, again and again, until some connection between them was irrefutable. Thinking nothing, he clicked the link. In years to come, he would describe the initial reading of that article as being akin to a super-massive K-hole (or, during media interviews, as being 'like a nightmare'). *Tom Atwood… 26… Caerphilly… new CCTV footage has emerged… near the spot where Daniel Covell's body was found…* He may as well have been reading his own obituary.

The next time he realised that reality was still a thing which he was a part of was when he heard the front door open. "Tom," he heard his mum call up the stairs, her voice wavering. There were other sounds around her; boots hitting the hall's wooden flooring; men muttering to one other. *Police.* He scrolled back up through the page, thinking nothing consciously, but something within him propelling the mouse wheel upwards. He stopped when he found it, boots now creaking their way up the stairs towards him: *'…new footage was discovered by Rory Gallagher and Ji Eun Kang, two journalists working for the South Wales Post.'* The boots were almost at the top of the stairs. *So that's how you spell Ji Eun…*

Friday 31st August

The rain still hammered, relentless. Danny was standing in the scant shelter of a staff-only access door behind a Marks & Spencers, staring through the rainfall at the gay bars of Charles Street, the only place that had offered him any kind of comfort in the preceding few fucked-up end-times days. He had no idea what the time was, his Lumia having been reduced to a lifeless black slab. All he knew was hope.

He'd been standing in the doorway's purgatory for an infinitely indeterminable time-length, umbrella-wielding people splashing through the puddles in front of him, when he finally saw a face that he recognised. It took a few seconds of squinting through rainfall to confirm it, but the face with the hood wrapped tight around it was indeed one of the gays he'd befriended, the average blokey sort-of one. Danny run out into the rain to confront him.

"Danny!" Frank said, aghast. "Jesus, what the hell happened to you?"

The Danny Daggers he saw before him was a markedly different Danny Daggers to the one he'd drank and smoke with the night before; his hair had been flattened and darkened by the rain, his face looked drained of colour, his eyes desperate and fiendish, and *what the fuck is going on with his jaw?*

"Someonestryingtokillme," Danny slurred, "pleasehelpme... please..." Danny trailled off, emotion getting the better of him, tears bubbling up under his eyes and disappearing into the streaks of rain pouring down his cheeks.

05.42pm

Tiger Tiger was fucking rammed. Tom had been standing at the bar for minutes, trying to catch a bartender's attention. He finally got it and shouted to her, trying to make himself heard above the din. A second half-price happy-hour pint of Cobra was soon in front of him. He turned his back to the bar to scan the booming mass of bodies all around him, cacophonously chit-chatting, trying to make themselves heard above the music, most in work clothes, guys in shirts with ties removed and top buttons undone gripping half-priced pints, ladies in dresses and blouse/skirt combos that were both work- and going out-out-appropriate gripping glasses of wine or cocktails. Tom took a sip and focused in on the music raging with the chit-chat for volume supremacy; it was that Keysha (or Keha, Keia, however the fuck she spells it) song, the one with Pitbull. *Fuck.* Tom hadn't realised how fucktardedly cheesy the lyrics were until that moment. '*Timmmm-ber*'. The same word a lumberjack yells to alert those around him to the felling of a tree. Used to signify the going down of a happening. Tom took a swig of his pint. *Fuck the music. Pints're half-price.* There was a multitude of women around him, scores of them, but there was no obvious in on any of them. *Too early*, he told himself. *Keep drinking.* He took another swig of his pint. He figured everyone else would've just finished work. He was already a ways ahead of them, a few pints and a spliff into it. The weed had worn off, pints doing their thing, beer buzz coming in. He took another swig of his pint. He wondered if he'd ever wander in here for after-work drinks on a Friday again. *Of course you fucking will,* he scolded himself. *Where else are you gonna end up working other than another fucking call centre in or around town?* He took another swig of his pint. There had to be more than that, surely; the edge of his potential, the edge of his world, had to extend farther than the industrial estate sprawl of the Cardiff call centre circuit. He took another swig of his pint. *You're free of it now,* he reminded himself. *On day release from open prison,* he argued. *With the potential to abscond,* he reasoned back. *Like that Simon what's-his-face feller, the one that done all them stabbings.* He took another swig of his pint. *Six,* he counted. Six call centres he'd worked at. Sky customer service, at Conduit, in Cardiff Gate. That cold-calling life insurance one, in Atlantic Wharf industrial estate. The short-lived stint at the swine flu advice hotline. Britsh Gas, just off the end of St. Mary's Street. Admiral, which was pretty much next door to Tiger Tiger. And Mitchell-Loveridge, from which he'd just been fired. Tom took another swig of his pint. There were plenty more he'd not yet worked at; dozens of them, scores of them. He'd heard the theory; that customers, or 'potential' customers, responded more positively to regional accents, so entry-level call centres had sprouted like acne over Great Britain's nether regions, pock-marking South Wales, the North of England and Scotland. The general public found the accents of these areas agreeable, working-class, friendly, but unauthoritative, so anytime problems escalated or serious issues arose, the customer would be transferred to a call centre in the South-East of England, where someone with a reassuringly superior Thames estuary accent could deal with it for them. Tom took another swig of his pint. *No more call centres,* he resolved. That would be easier said than done; they were the only non-minimum wage job he'd been able to get so much as an interview for since graduating from uni. Tom took another swig of his pint, then placed the empty glass back down upon the bar, and started pushing and excusing his way outside for a cigarette.

Tom then stood on the steps outside Tiger Tiger, at the end of Greyfriar's Road, a little ways down the street from the Hilton. Two girls were standing beside him on the top step, sheltered from the rain still hammering the world beyond. He lit a cigarette and looked up and across the street at the massive grey tower block that housed the Admiral call centre. *Forget call centres,* he told himself. *They'd've been out of mind by now if you were still working in one.* He was right; it was Friday, and Friday night meant not giving a fuck about Monday morning, whether there was a job for him to go or not. He glanced to his left, to the two girls, one white, one black, then shifted his gaze back to the big grey tower block, trying to think of something to say to them. He'd only ever kissed a black girl once, late at night at some indie club back at uni. He'd gotten her phone number, and sent a message the next day, but as was typical in around seventy, perhaps eighty, percent of such cases, she'd never replied to him. He looked back past the Admiral building, up the street towards the Hilton, and saw a huddle of familiar faces moving fast through the rain, hoods pulled up tight over their heads: Bradley, Justin, Harry, Keith... *fuck*. Tom threw his half-smoked cigarette out onto the street and turned his back on them, then sprinted off down Greyfair's Road, through the rain, away from them.

_ _ : _ _ *pm*

"Does it hurt?"

"Likefuck," Danny answered, slumped on the couch in Frank's small studio apartment.

"I've got some paracetamol here somewhere."

Danny gulped, swallowing blood-thickened saliva, before trying to speak again: "Anythingstronger?"

"Stronger?" Frank smiled. "There's some vodka. I might have some ketamine lying around."

Danny groaned. "Please."

Frank rose from the pouffe and looked with pity at his haggard house guest. "Do you not reckon you ought to go to the hospital?"

"No." It was the first time the idea had occurred to Danny. Perhaps it was the right thing to do. *Not now though. Tomorrow.* He was far too comfortable where he was.

"Are you sure? It looks pretty serious."

"Illgotomorrow."

Frank nodded his acceptance. "And you've not got any idea who it was that done this to you?"

"No," Danny admitted. All he had was paranoid internal rambling and a hunch too crazy to vocalise.

Frank took a few short steps to the kitchen area and started clanking around with bottles and glasses.

"Doyouhaveanycigarettes?"

Frank stuck his hand in his jeans pockets for his e-fag, then thought of the nasty blood-smeared abrasion on Danny's jaw and decided against sharing it. "I think there might be some rolling baccy here somewhere."

He returned to Danny and handed him a glass of vodka and Coke. Frank took a sip from his own glass and watched Danny clasp his glass in both hands and bring it to his lips. Frank then walked over to his double bed and pulled a shoebox out from under it.

"Have you seen the news today?"

"No."

"Crazy shit. Three or four people killed around town in separate attacks. I don't know if it's got anything to do with what happened to you."

Danny didn't answer, instead focusing on the restorative buzz of alcohol pricking his brain. Frank returned to the pouffe, placed the shoebox down on the coffee table and opened it. He picked out a near-empty and decidedly old-looking pouch of Drum rolling tobacco, then soon found a stick of filters and some red Rizla to go with it. Frank handed over the materials and continued searching through the box. Danny rested the half-drunk vodka Coke between his legs and concentrated on scraping the dry tobacco from the bottom of the packet and laying it out on a Rizla paper.

"Can you remember much of what happened last night?"

"No."

"You looked like you were on a bit of a mad one. You tried it on with some girl, and when she rejected you, you went up to Myrig and started trying to pull him."

Fuck. The moment Frank said it, a memory of the event returned to Danny.

"Then you disappeared," Frank laughed. "I suppose them YouTube videos of yours have given you a bit of a reputation to live up to, eh?"

Danny lifted the rollie to his lips and, with some difficulty, stuck his tongue out and licked it before rolling it shut. "Haveyougotalighter?"

"No," Frank said, looking into the shoebox, "no, I haven't. You can light it off the stove if you want."

Danny got to his feet, forgetting about the vodka Coke between his legs, and watched as it tumbled to the floor, spilling its contents over the shag-pile carpeting. Danny stared down at the mess, inert, not quite comprehending what had just happened. After a few seconds, he looked up at Frank, who was looking back at him with some concern.

"Fuck," Danny said. "Sorry."

"Don't worry about it," Frank said, rising from the pouffe. "Chuck us a dishcloth from the kitchen, I'll clean it up now."

Danny moved to the kitchen area and threw a dishcloth back across the room to Frank, who fell onto his hands and knees with it and started mopping the spill up.

"Maybe you ought to get some rest," Frank said.

"Imalright," Danny said, clicking the stove into light and carefully bending down towards it, fag clenched between his teeth. He lit the rollie successfully after a couple of puffs and turned the stove off.

"Do you want another drink?"

"Ermm...ifyoudontmind,yeah."

"Bring the stuff over."

Danny returned and placed the Diet Coke and Glen's vodka bottles down on the coffee table. He then slumped back down on the sofa and pulled hard on the fag in his mouth, causing more blood and pain to bubble up and spunk out from the wound in his jaw. Frank poured another vodka Coke and handed it over, then resumed searching through the shoebox.

"Here we go," Frank said a few moments later, holding up a plastic baggie with a little white powder inside. "You sure you can handle this, in your state?"

"Yeah." Danny had never been surer of anything in his life.

09.42pm

Tom was in the back garden of Buffalo Bar holding court. The rain had stopped and the garden was consequently full of smokers, though its wooden benches were sodden from the earlier downpour, forcing all to stand. He'd cornered a couple of fresher girls, already in town, getting acclimatised to the Welsh capital before the following week's enrolment.

"It's not as big as I'd expected," said the girl with pasty-pale skin, black hair pulled back beneath an Alice band, and a deathly dull Midlands accent, "but mind you, the only city I'm really familiar with's Birmingham, and that's pretty massive."

"Yeah," said the big-eyed blonde beside her, Southern English, overly enthusiastic and up for it, sipping on one of her buy-one-get-one-free cocktails every time someone else was speaking, "it all seems very centralised, if that's even a word."

"You can walk everywhere in town," Tom agreed, throwing himself into the role of local expert, "you never need to take a taxi."

"How long've you been here?" the boring Brummy asked.

The dreaded question. Tom had been hoping for a little while longer to overwhelm them with the force of his booze-boosted personality before it came. He had two options: black and white, ying and yang, good and evil; he could tell the truth, tell them that he'd grown up not far from Cardiff, that he was still living in his mum's house a short train ride away from the city, and that he'd graduated a fair few years earlier and done the sum total of fuck all of worth with his life in the years since; or he could lie.

"Two years," Tom lied.

The blonde looked at his face, and scrutinised it for several seconds before speaking: "Did you take a gap year or something?"

"Yeah," Tom said, the lie compounded. "I took a year off to go travelling."

"Yeah?" the blonde said, her stance softening. "Where'd you get to?"

"Thailand," Tom said.

"Cool," the blonde said.

"Did you spend a whole year there?" asked the mundane Midlandser.

"Yeah, well, near enough. I ended up stuck in hospital over there, actually. Some fucking Yank broke my jaw."

"Fuck," the blonde intoned.

"What happened?" asked her boring friend.

Tom spluttered through as much of a story that had happened to his friend Jacob as he could remember, passing it off as his own and keeping the girls entertained enough, until some twat with a west Wales accent and a trendy haircut appeared behind them and slapped the blonde on the arse.

"Oi oi ladies! What's occurring?"

"Scott!" the blonde beamed, turning to face him. "Where've you been?"

"Fuck knows," the twat said, clearly pissed, "where haven't I been?"

"This is Tom," said the Brummy bore.

"S'apnin' Tom, you getting fucked up tonight or wha'?"

"This is our flatmate, Scott," bore began explaining, as Tom tuned out.

"Let's get some fucking shots in mun, I got a thirst what needs quenching!" Scott bellowed, leading the girls up the steps into the bar, leaving Tom behind. He pulled his cigarettes out of his pocket and saw there was only one remaining in the packet. He sparked it up and tossed the empty packet down on one of the rain-sodden benches. *Freshers*. It suddenly dawned on Tom that he must've been at least a half-decade older than them. *And the rest*, he corrected himself. If they were freshers, they were probably eighteen years old, and as he was fast approaching his twenty-seventh birthday, he was probably near enough nine years older than them. *Fucking hell. Almost a decade*. He did the maths – *when you were sixteen, they were seven*. He had a sudden flashback to his own uni days, to him and Sam, pissed up outside Cheapskates, seeing some guy trying it on with two girls. They'd walked right up to him and shouted out 'Wanko!', pretending to know him, saying they'd thought they'd been in the same halls as him, and that everyone had known him as Wanko, and the poor cunt had fallen for it, and tried to remember, as the girls he'd been chatting to lost interest and slipped away. Fucking hilarious it'd been. *Now I'm fucking Wanko*. He pulled hard on the cigarette, and thought about sending Sam a message. Sam had slipped off to Spain a few years prior, and had been teaching English there since. Tom couldn't remember the last time he'd spoken to him. He pulled his iPhone out of his pocket, and then stopped himself. *No. Live in the moment*. He stared down at the phone, at the lock screen, then gave way to some compulsion within himself to share himself with someone, to seek confirmation that he'd not slipped entirely into obscurity. He clicked the icon for WhatsApp and fired a quick message over to Steve: *hows the date going?* Then he put the phone away and concentrated on the cigarette, concentrated on his drunkenness, then forced himself out of his self-imposed isolation, his cigarette nearing its conclusion, and did a quick 360 of the beer garden. In a fast and fluid flow of movement, he'd dropped the cigarette to the floor and walked over to an Asian girl, small, red cocktail in her hand, sitting beside a few others who were engaged in animated conversation without her, on just about the only benches in the beer garden that had been sheltered from the earlier rainstorm.

"*Ni hong go ka wa kari ma ska?*" Tom asked.

The Asian girl looked up at him blankly.

"*Ni hong go ka wa kari ma ska?*" Tom asked again.

"What?"

"I'm sorry," he said, before trying again, more slowly this time: "*Ni hong go ka wa kari ma ska?*"

"What?" she said again, agitated.

"I'm sorry, it's Japanese. I thought you might be…"

"I'm fucking Chinese."

Tom turned away as the Chinese girl turned to the guys and girls beside her, who'd noticed Tom's ill-fated approach, and left his failure to be savaged in a flurry of 'what the fuck's and 'what a dickhead's as he walked towards the door leading inside and to the bar.

_ _ : _ _ *pm*

The kaleidoscope room stopped inverting in on itself and seemed to be levelling off at something approaching pre-ket reality. *This is Danny Daggers,* Danny Daggers told himself, the two not quite one and the same. The music's tempo still seemed off, stretched and warped, Tom Yorke-ish vocals giving Danny something to measure the music's electronic blips and bleeps against, and it was wrong, and he was aware that he wasn't yet perceiving time correctly, and probably wouldn't be again for a while. But he at least knew where he was now, even if his thoughts were still floating above the surface of it, thinking in the third person. At least his thoughts were no longer trapped in the depths of a K-hole, peering up and out at a mangled reality. Danny suddenly became aware that Frank was talking. He reached for a glass of vodka Coke on the coffee table, took a sip, then looked at the sofa seats either side of him, hoping to find the Drum pouch, and also hoping there were enough crumbs of tobacco still inside to form a serviceable rollie.

"That's strong stuff, yeah?" Frank said, aware that his guest was aware again.

"Yeah," Danny mumbled, still looking for the Drum pouch.

"This music's spinning me out," Frank said, getting to his feet within a half-second of saying and consequently realising it. He was soon at the laptop, perched on a bookcase on the other side of the room, as Danny found the Drum pouch and started tearing the thing apart to scrape off all of the small amount of brown crud that remained clinging to inside of the packet. "Any requests?"

"No," Danny said, total concentration going into forcing his fingers into scraping at the tobacco.

"Let's get something a bit more upbeat on," Frank said, replacing the moody electronica with a more upbeat, but still synth-led, sound.

Danny recognised it as the sweet female vocals came in; Chvrches. His mind recoiled at it. *No vocals,* he wanted to shout, but the effort of shouting was beyond him. Instead, he scraped the last few flecks of dried tobacco off the white of the ripped-up Drum pouch's interior, the vocals and music jarring, it all being played at some awkward speed, maybe two-thirds of what it should've been, and the whole thing was just... *wonky.*

Danny licked the rollie shut and then looked about him, at the sofa, then the coffee table, for a lighter. He shut his eyes and grimaced. *The stove.* He'd have to stand up and walk over to it. He gripped the glass from the coffee table and swigged down most of what remained. When he opened his eyes again, Frank was looking straight at him.

"Yknowhorsesvenotimeperception," Danny mumbled.

"What?"

"Horses," Danny said, slower, most of the pain from his jaw lost in the fug he'd laid over himself, "hvenotimeperception."

"Time perception?" Frank repeated.

"Yeah."

"What?"

Danny closed his eyes again. *Fuck's sake.* Why the fuck had he had to say anything? "Horses...," he paused and took a few breaths before continuing, "have... no... timeperception."

Frank stared at him. *What?*

Danny looked at Frank and closed his eyes again. There was no point trying to explain it any further. He had more important tasks to direct his energy towards. Danny opened his eyes and forced himself up into a standing position. With intense concentration placed upon the movement of his limbs, he staggered, step-by-step, to the stove, Frank staring at him all the while, wondering if the ketamine hadn't broken him.

If it weren't for this fucking jaw-ache I'd be able to explain myself, Danny told himself, leaning in to get the fag lit. The comment hadn't been a total non-sequitor; someone had told him once, maybe Stu, at halls, that horses had no time perception. 'You can just keep running them until they drop dead, because the horse has no idea how long it's been running for,' Stu had said, or words to that effect. And ketamine's primary function was as a horse tranquiliser. And one of the most noticeable effects ketamine had on humans was altering their own sense of time perception, thus rendering the Chvrches song that was now playing *un-fucking-listenable.* Danny turned the stove off and hobbled back towards the sofa, intermittent drags upon the slender rollie helping him navigate his course.

"Do you want another drink?" Frank asked.

Danny looked at the little black liquid remaining in his glass. "Alright."

"You know, I was supposed to be meeting Myrig and Megan and Mandeep and them lot again tonight," Frank said, heading to the kitchen area with the glasses as Danny returned to the sofa. "I don't suppose you'd want to join us?"

No. Danny needed a night in, a quiet one, just a couple of vodka Cokes and a few lines of K, with a bed awaiting him at the end of it all, dryness and comfort, shelter from the rain.

"I can lend you some clothes, maybe. Them ones you're wearing are soaked."

Danny touched his jeans and T-shirt with his left hand, his right holding the rollie; they remained pretty damp. He hadn't really noticed. "Cheers."

Danny remained on the sofa, zoning out to the wonky music. Some indeterminate time later, Frank was back in front of him, placing two filled glasses upon the coffee table and tossing a plain navy T-shirt and some standard denim jeans on to the sofa besides Danny. Danny got to his feet as Frank sat down upon the pouffe. Danny grabbed his glass and swigged a good deal of vodka Coke, then placed the drink down and pulled his sodden T-shirt off over his head. He noticed Frank looking at him, then quickly looking down at the floor, as he dropped the T-shirt onto the sofa. Danny's desire to stay in, to not go out, was strong, all-consuming. He unbuckled his belt and let his damp jeans drop to the floor. Frank looked back up, at Danny's slender frame, barely an ounce of fat on him. Danny stepped out of his jeans, wearing only tight black trunks. He grabbed the glass and took another big gulp of vodka Coke, then placed the glass back down and reached for the ketamine baggy. He tipped a little out onto the coffee table, then crushed and carved it into two lines with Frank's provisional driver's license. Danny picked up a rolled-up twenty pound note and hoovered a slim line of K into his left nostril, looking to spread the damage, having delivered the earlier loads to his right. He handed the note to Frank, who leaned forward and snorted his own line. Reality receding, distorting, Danny slowly pulled down his black trunks and stood in front of Frank, completely naked. Frank hesitated for a moment before gently grasping Danny's hips with his hands. Danny placed his hands upon Frank's head, then gently pulled at his hair. Frank pulled Danny towards him and kissed his stomach softly. Danny closed his eyes, his previous conception of reality melting away, a new one emerging.

Saturday 1st September

Tom stumbled down the steps into Bogies, down the spiral staircase to the basement club that once was Barfly, half-remembering a blur of all the nights and all the gigs he'd spent inside, all soon to be erased, the venue earmarked for destruction, to be filled in with cement and replaced with student housing. Each step brought back a memory – snapping the signed Every Time I Die ticket in half with Sian; he and Gareth sitting on the shelf at the side of the dancefloor at the Thrice gig, others hopping up to join them and bringing the shelf crashing down to the floor; that time that Blood Brothers broke their kick drum five minutes into their set and spent the next half an hour improvising semi-acoustically; that crazy heavy double-header of Poison the Well and Dillinger Escape Plan that he'd caught with Steve; back to the Teen Spirit gigs, when Gareth and Steve's bands had taken the stage; and a thousand other bands and moments and memories – Gonzo on Tour, Zane Lowe pissed up as fuck posing for a photo with them; Lostprophets doing the same way back when, before their lead singer had been revealed as the nonce to end all nonces; gig upon gig – Funeral For A Friend, Million Dead, When Reason Sleeps, Dopamine, Cardia, Hondo Maclean, Instruction, Midasuno, The Red October, A Fine Day To Exit – then he entered the room, the music blasting – Blur, *'Girls and Boys'* – and the first thing he saw was a girl, a twenty-something, perhaps pushing thirty, hair dyed blonde, black dress, really into the music; he moved towards her, the song taking over... lyrics about '90s love and paranoia... he was dancing with her, moving with her, and within a minute he was kissing her, holding her, then she pulled her head away, their arms still wrapped around one another, and she smiled at him, a drunken smile, then she leaned her head back in towards him, and whispered something about him coming to her car with her...

* * *

Reality was returning, filling Danny with dread. He could hear the shower in the next room, over the music, still Chvrches, vocals and instrumentation unaligned, reality at odds with itself. He was lying upon the sofa, clad in the dry clothes which Frank had provided for him. He suddenly threw himself up into a seated position. Reality. Reality was dawning on him. His arsehole ached, a dull throb, less severe than that in his jaw, but far more perturbing. *What the fuck...* the first bit of interior monologue he'd been burdened with in some time. He looked at the coffee table, at the little liquid remaining in his glass, and then at Frank's glass, still half-full. Danny downed both glasses in quick succession, then grabbed the twenty pound note that lay rolled-up besides them, as well as the baggie powdered with residual ketamine. *Go. Go now. Escape. Escape. Escape.* Danny stood up. The room was off-balance, off-kilter. *No,* he reminded himself, *that's not the room, that's you.* He listened carefully for a moment, past the mangled music, for the shower, still running. *Escape. Escape. Escape.* Danny staggered uneasily across the room, to the spot by the front door where he'd taken his shoes off. He bent down and touched his Vans, a jolt of dull pain rising through him as he did so. They were sopping wet. Besides them were a typical pair of grubby-white-tipped black Converse, bone dry. Danny pulled one onto his right foot in a hurry, too much of a hurry, for it sent him off-balance entirely, and he tumbled to the floor. He did the laces up as he lay there, then grabbed the other shoe, pulled that on and did the laces up, then pushed himself back to his feet, swayed for a second or two, before turning a Yale lock and pushing the door open, as quietly as possible, then stepping out in a pitch-black hallway and letting the door creak closed behind him. He stood swaying in the darkness for a moment, then became cognisant of faint light rising up from beneath. He descended the stairs, gripping the banister as he staggered downwards, eventually reaching another door, another Yale lock, and then stepped out into the street, glowing orange from the streetlights. *Twenty quid,* he reminded himself. Not a bad result. He started thinking about how far that would get him on the train. *Far enough to get the fuck out of Wales.* Maybe back to Bristol; he'd made friends there – more so than in Cardiff, at least. He looked in both directions, up and down, at another Cardiff street of identical Victorian terraced housing. He had absolutely no idea where he was. At one end of the street, he could see the lights from kebab shops and fried chicken joints. He stumbled towards them, ketamine making his motion a mess. *The rain's stopped.* He carried on towards the lights and started smiling. *Twenty quid and the fucking's rain stopped.*

* * *

Tom woke up in motion, bathed in orange light from the street outside. It took him a few seconds blinking in the orange to realise where he was; laid out on the back seat of her car. He groaned and grunted something, alerting her to his presence. She pulled over. He got out. If he'd said anything to her, or she to him, it was forgotten as she drove away, the sound of her car's engine echoing out in the late-night/early-morning quiet. He blinked through the daze and fog of recently-ended sleep and got a handle on where he was and what had happened. The car hadn't travelled far from the multi-storey car park just off the Hayes that she'd taken him to. He must've passed out on the back seat... *during or after?* He shuddered with shame. He was standing now across the street from the museum, large terraced buildings behind him, most belonging to the university. He took his iPhone from his pocket and pressed the home button; nothing. Dead. No idea what the time was. He looked both ways, from habit more than any risk of any car coming, then crossed the street to the park and the fountains that lay in front of the museum, the park's black iron gates locked up for the night. The sky was still dark, beyond the orange glow of street lights. *Must be 3... 4...* he had no idea what time they'd gone to the car together. And even less idea at what point he'd passed out on the car's back seat. He shuddered again as he walked, every inch of him cringing at the patheticness of it. *At least it isn't raining...*

* * *

Danny was sat on a curb on a small bridge, hovering a few metres over the River Taff, staring across at the Millennium Stadium, its hulking blue-and-red frame illuminated, white arches jutting out of it. He was barely concentrating on the rollie he was constructing. He lifted an ill-formed cigarette to his mouth, slid his box of matches open, struck one and lit it, then threw the used match into the river. He'd spent the best part of a tenner on a 3-in-1 box of Amber Leaf and a little bottle of Glen's vodka, reasoning the remaining tenner would be enough to see him over the border, into Bristol, into his home country, at the least. He took a swig of vodka and grimaced at the taste of it, before carefully screwing the cap back on. *This rollie's well sloppy,* he noticed, seeing in the thing he was smoking a suitable metaphor for a sloppy couple of days in Cardiff. *It's been a fucking experience, anyway.* An experience he could not wait for the end of, but an experience nevertheless. He stared at the stadium, at that symbol of where he was, and wished his phone had been working to take a picture of it. He pulled his Lumia from his pocket, tried once again in vain to turn the damn thing on, then stared at his reflection in its cracked black screen, at the fucked up mess that hammer shot had made of the lower left side of his face. He'd been taking the ket in small bumps, chaining cigs and swigging Glen's for an indeterminate length of time, and had found himself dipping in and out of recollection and reverie, all the episodic randomness of his life until that point, random snatches of childhood and teenage years, all of it loosely connected, barely coherent... *This fucking thing's cursed.* He stared at his cracked reflection. *Cursed.* He supposed it was a kind of mirror, in a way... maybe breaking it had brought seven years bad luck upon him. *Bollocks.* But the thing was fucking useless now. He rose to his feet, still staring at himself in the cracked screen of his Lumia. *None of the worst of this shit would've happened if it hadn't been for this fucking thing.* He'd had enough of it. He held his hand out over the railings, stared at the Millennium Stadium, took a deep drag from his rollie, then opened his hand and let his Lumia fall into the river. The second it'd left his hand he regretted it. *You probably could've got a fair few quid selling it on ebay, however fucked it is.* "Fuckinghell." *Idiot.* Danny took two more quick tokes on his rollie, then tossed the half-finished loosely-wrapped thing over the side into the river, then leant over the railing to peer down into it. The Lumia had hit a rock, and was now lying on top of it, staring up at him, reflecting the orange glow of the late-night/early-morning sky. Without further thought, he climbed the railings, which were about a metre tall at the most. He fumbled over them, getting his right foot caught in them, as his other foot dangled unseemingly over the other side; in a confused fumbling second he was falling, and a second after that he'd hit the stone, and he was lying there, water rushing over him, blood seeping out of his skull...

* * *

Tom stopped on the bridge. The sky had started to brighten. True morning was approaching. In front of him was a 3-in-1 box of Amber Leaf and a bottle of Glen's vodka with the cap off. Tom had been walking in circles, killing time, planning to wind up at Central station to catch the first train to Caerphilly, which he figured would probably be at around 5.30 or 6. The best of his drunkenness had worn off, and he briefly considered taking a swig of the vodka. He quickly discounted the idea, and instead bent down and picked up the Amber Leaf. As he leant forward, he felt some discomfort. He checked quickly around himself, making sure no-one was watching, then stuck his hand down the front of his jeans and pulled off a condom. He flung it over the side of the bridge into the river, shuddering with shame at the sight of it. *What the fuck's wrong with you?* He kicked the bottle of vodka, causing it to smash against the railings. Then he walked away from the bridge, along the riverbank, deciding to wait outside the station.

He let his mind sit idle as he walked and rolled a cigarette with the new-found tobacco, not wanting to dwell on the mess of a night that was now nearing in its end, trying to avoid committing any of it to memory. He heard his footsteps upon the wet ground as he walked, the only sounds other than the low hum of distant traffic in the city beyond. He licked the rollie shut and lit it, then felt a vibration in his pocket. He took a drag and pulled his iPhone out; it had been resurrected from the dead, its battery now a reasonable 38%. He juggled the rollie and the iPhone between his hands as he pulled his earphones from his pocket, untangled them, and stuck them into the headphone jack. He stuck the earphones in his ears and the phone back in his pocket and then let songs wash over him and block out thought as he carried on towards Central station.

He reached the station's exterior in true blue morning light, an M.I.A. song playing. He looked up at the clock embedded in the station's exterior; the little hand was hovering at just-before quarter-past. Quarter-past five. The trains would be running soon enough. Tom walked over to one of the big stone blocks jutting out of the ground outside the station and sat down. Thought re-entered Tom's mind as he wondered how much effort and expense had gone into hauling those stone blocks to the outside of the station, when benches would've probably been far cheaper, and more comfortable. He idled on some loose connection to the mystery of Stone Henge as M.I.A. faded away and mournful piano chords rose up in his headphones with the eerie sound of a crowd arguing layered over the top of them. *You've been fired,* Tom reminded himself. He smiled. *No work Monday.* The void, work's absence; perhaps the chance he'd been waiting for. *You can do anything now.* What it was he would do he had no idea, but the possibility of it filled him with hope and happiness, making him forget all about the mess of a night he'd just staggered through. Tom closed his eyes, the music soothing and entrancing him. The piano chords and the crowd continued. He saw a succession of images, unconnected to thought, sleep coming… then the piano gave way to a crash of strings, mournful vocals following in behind them. Tom took his iPhone from his pocket to find out the source of the melancholic mumbling – Morrissey. The Smiths, 'Last Night I Dreamt Somebody Loved Me'. A drop of water splashed on the centre of the screen. The screen turned black, save for a little wheel of white spinning where the water had landed. The battery had died. *Planned obsolescence.* Tom looked up at the sky. It was starting to rain.

FURTHER INFORMATION

www.haydnwilks.com

Twitter: @haydnwilks

Email: haydnwilks@deadbirdpress.com

Printed in Great Britain
by Amazon.co.uk, Ltd.,
Marston Gate.